KABOOM

Kaboom

PEGGY HOFFMAN

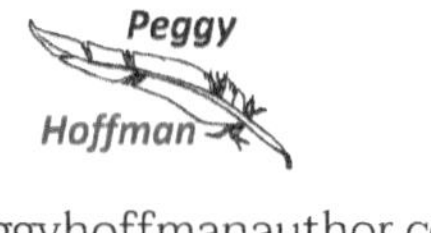

www.peggyhoffmanauthor.com

ALSO BY PEGGY HOFFMAN

Avalon

Chivalrous

For Rick. Always.

Chapter One

He'd heard stories, whispered behind hands in locker rooms, about what to expect the first time a guy had sex, but the reality was immeasurably more awesome than those half-believed smutty tales. Not even ninth-grade sex education class had prepared him, when he and his classmates had tried to mentally block out the image and voice of a teacher describing The Act, as clinically as if he was instructing them how to change a tire. His main memory of that class had been the video of an actual childbirth that had been shown while most of the students refused to look and simply muttered, "Gross!" until it was all over.

The supposedly experienced guys in the locker room talked about things like popping one's cherry – what the heck did that mean? – about which girls in school might or might not be willing to Do It, about packages and pussies, which sounded more as if they were discussing Amazon and the vet's office than lovemaking. But they never talked about love.

It was that omission that bothered Clay the most. When he and Julie finally got up the courage, and found the opportunity, to Do It, it wasn't just sexual intercourse. It wasn't just popping their cherries or doing the nasty or getting laid. It definitely wasn't fucking. It was lovemaking, with a capital L. Those locker room boasters had no clue what they were talking about. Despite the awkwardness, the uncertainty, the fear of getting caught, he absolutely loved her.

They were trembling, literally trembling, the both of them, as they walked up the stairs. "Are you sure your parents aren't coming home tonight?" she asked. "Or your sister?"

"No," he assured her. "They're at my aunt and uncle's place in Milwaukee overnight to meet their new baby. I didn't go because I'm seeing the recruiter tomorrow to sign papers." He hoped his bedroom didn't smell too much like dirty gym socks and sweaty running shoes.

They lay on his bed and, even though they knew they didn't have all night, kissed for a long time. Despite their earlier trembling, she was warm beneath him, even warmer when they got their clothes off. He touched her, and she let him. He kissed her, and she encouraged it, kissed him back, pulled his tongue into her mouth. She tasted sweet and warm and it was a good thing they were laying down, because his knees went so weak, he wouldn't have been able to stand upright. Every inch of her smooth, fair skin was his to caress, and every inch of him was hers to command as she wished. Though there was one part of him that needed no command or instruction. It surged to life like a heat-seeking missile, commanding him to action.

They both giggled a little at the challenge of opening the condom packet without tearing the whole thing to shreds. She tried to help him apply it but he pushed her hand away.

"I'll do it," he insisted, knowing that if she touched him at that moment, this whole erotic adventure would be over way too soon.

It took a moment for them to find their rhythm, how they fit together, how to move. Instinctively he gave himself to her and just as instinctively, she took him in. It was both bliss and pain, ecstasy and oblivion, climax and surrender. He felt her contract around him, and her intake of breath, that momentary stillness before climax, carried him away to shatter inside her, as he heard his voice roar some explosive word that wasn't in the dictionary in her ear, and her own sweet moan accompanied it.

They trembled again afterward, still lying together, slick with perspiration. "Clay," she murmured. "Oh, Clay!"

Just hearing her say his name at that moment, in that breathy whisper, was the most beautiful sound he'd ever heard. He kissed her, gently this time, along her throat, her cheek, her lips. He had no words capable of describing his wonderment at this moment, but closed his eyes and put all of his love and adoration into one simple sigh.

"Julie..."

"Julie," he whispered again, but she didn't answer.

"Who's Julie?" a voice he didn't want to hear asked, and he opened his eyes, not to his bedroom at his parent's home, not to see his girlfriend, but to see the brown and green camouflage of an army sergeant's uniform next to his hospital bed. "Is she someone you'd like us to contact for you?"

He'd woken up. He didn't want to wake up. He wanted to stay in his sweet dream of memory. He didn't want to be here, in a military hospital with a patient liaison leaning over him, offering support and help.

"No," he muttered, turning his face into the pillow so the well-meaning sergeant wouldn't see the tears in his eyes. "There's nobody you need to contact."

Lufthansa Airlines Flight 430, non-stop from Frankfurt, Germany to Chicago O'Hare International Airport, landed exactly on time, and it was the smoothest landing Clay Maslowski had ever experienced.

It was also the most painful.

At five foot ten, Clay was hardly a basketball player, but his knees still bumped against the seat back in front of him at the moment of touchdown, and the pain rippled up and down from that point with an intensity that made him hiss, though he tried to swallow it.

It was completely, utterly unfair that he should continue to feel pain in a limb he no longer possessed. Instead of a left leg, under his khaki slacks was a technological monstrosity of polypropylene and titanium, all thanks to Kaboom.

Maybe he should have tried to get a seat on the other side of the aisle, so that his left leg would be on the aisle side. The Army had booked him a flight home in the Economy cabin. Maybe he should have paid the hefty upgrade fee for a seat in business class. Maybe he should have stayed in Germany.

However, the problem was that his knowledge of the German language was limited to being able to order a beer and find the bathroom. Not to mention that even if he were fluent enough in German to converse with Angela Merkel, he'd be just as helpless and useless there as he was going to be in his hometown. He did know a few words of Spanish however, which he'd studied in high school, choosing it due to a leaf on his family tree.

While most of his ethnic heritage was Polish, there was also a family legend that there had been an ancestor from Spain a few generations back on his mother's side. Most of his relatives were fair-colored northern European types, but the DNA of that half-mythical Spanish blood seemed to have trickled down to Clay and bestowed upon him dark brown hair, dark brown eyes, and skin that would get tan under a hot stare.

It was probably also the source of his delight when he and a couple of his former Army buddies had snagged a few days' leave in Barcelona, before Kaboom. While the other guys had been satisfied with discovering the city's nightlife and tapas bars, Clay had preferred exploring the place more thoroughly. He hadn't been interested in trying to flirt with the local girls or find out how many glasses of sangria it took to get goofy. He'd preferred walking down La Rambla, stopping for a lunch of paella, then continuing to its end at the Christopher Columbus Monument. Taking the elevator to the viewing deck rewarded him with a fine view of the city and the Mediterranean Sea. He'd watched the ferry boats cruising towards Majorca and thought, *next time*. A short bus ride – he'd prided himself on figuring out the public bus rather than the tourist bus – had taken him to the Sagrada Familia, the weird, colorful basilica designed by Gaudi and still under construction though it had broken ground in 1882. He'd earned points with his mother by going into the sanctuary and lighting a candle.

But that was a lifetime ago, before Kaboom had changed everything.

He sat stiffly during the entire nine-hour flight, clutching his cane. There was a pretty girl sitting in the middle seat next to him, traveling with another even prettier girl sitting in the window seat. Early in the flight, they tried to talk to him and even flirt, but he was in no mood. He responded with half answers and non-committal grunts, and finally closed his eyes and pretended to be asleep. But he was very much awake and clearly heard Pretty Middle Seat Girl say, "I don't think he speaks English."

Pretty Window Seat Girl responded, "Maybe he's mentally challenged."

"Too bad," Pretty Middle Seat Girl said. "He's cute."

How wrong they were. He wasn't cute. He was hideous, thanks to Kaboom.

"What's with the cane?" Pretty Window Seat Girl wondered.

"Maybe he twisted his ankle," her friend guessed. "That shouldn't hinder anything."

The girls both giggled, while Clay's throat clenched. If only he had a twisted ankle. What they didn't know was that he didn't have an ankle at all on the left side, nor a calf nor even a knee. They'd be absolutely horrified if he were to hitch up the bottom of his pants leg and reveal the hideous prosthesis beneath it, and that would put an abrupt end to their flirting attempts. Who would ever want to flirt with an AKA – Above the Knee Amputee? No woman with any sense at all, that was for sure. It was even worse than being a BKA – Below the Knee Amputee. What sucked even worse was that there were official acronyms for the condition.

As much as he was pretending to be asleep, he still heard the girls seated in his row rustling and twitching, and then, Pretty Middle Seat Girl touched his arm. He jumped as if he'd been shot, and couldn't help but open his eyes and stare at her. He had to restrain himself from screaming, *don't touch me*!

She was attractive, but she wasn't Julie. Smiling, the girl said, "Sorry to bother you. But we need to ..." She pointed in the direction of the bathroom at the back of the plane, in case he didn't understand English.

They wanted him to get up and let them out. Sure, he'd just hop up and into the aisle for them.

If only it were that simple. Instead, he had to grab the back of the seat in front of him and pull himself up on his right leg, which probably annoyed the person sitting in that seat. Putting weight on his prosthesis, so that he could lurch into the aisle with his good leg, his real leg, hurt like hell, and he doubted he could keep the pain off his face. But he said nothing to the two girls as they easily scrambled out of their seats and headed back to the toilet.

There was no way he was going to go to the effort of sitting down and getting back up again when they returned, no matter how long they took to do their business. He'd already gotten a dirty look from the occupant of the seat in front of him, which was only to be expected, the way he'd jerked on the seat back when he'd been forced to use it as a prop to drag his maimed carcass upright. It was, fortunately, a fairly smooth flight today. A blessing, when crossing the North Atlantic could frequently get bumpy. The last time he'd flown over this part of the globe, on his way to Afghanistan, it had been so turbulent the flight attendants had been instructed to sit down and strap in, right in the middle of serving meals. Today, no such turbulence bothered them, but he still declined the in-flight meal. He'd never thought that airplane food was as bad as its reputation, but he just couldn't eat.

Leaning hard on his cane, he braced his other arm against the overhead bin, as he prayed that nobody else came down the aisle needing to get past. The girls didn't take long, but even for that short time, the gentle vibrations of the plane still sent waves of pain up and down his leg to pierce his brain. He tried futilely to remain absolutely still, and focused his eyes on the No Smoking light in front of him.

The two girls returned and slid easily back into their seats, thanking him for letting them through with smiles and nods, because they weren't sure if he spoke English. He declined to educate them and didn't bother acknowledging their attempts at basic human interaction, as he struggled to get back into his seat. He fell into the seat with an ungraceful plop, especially distressing for a former athlete. To avoid any accidental touching in the cramped space, he waited until both the girls had fastened their seat belts before putting his back on.

Then he closed his eyes and pretended to be asleep again, though he doubted the two girls were fooled.

He had tried to get a seat in the very last row of the plane. It had been bad enough, having to gimp and limp to his seat down the narrow aisle, which was challenging even for the able-bodied. But the closest he'd been able to get was in the third row up from the rear, the aisle seat on the left. The aisle seat on the right would have been preferable, so that his prosthesis would be on the aisle side, but he hadn't been able to procure that one either. Or maybe it would have made no difference. Crippled was crippled, no matter which side of the airplane you were on.

He had been on enough flights to understand the disembarking protocol. You deplaned starting from the front while everyone behind you impatiently waited their turn. Clay would rather die than have two hundred pairs of eyes boring into his back while he climbed awkwardly to his feet, or rather, to his foot. That horrid prosthesis, attached to his horrid stump, wasn't really a part of him.

The official term was residual limb. But let's be honest. It was a stump.

In the past, being military had gotten him priority boarding. But he'd hated the reason for being boarded first today, because now he was disabled. Medically discharged from a promising career in the United States Army, thanks to Kaboom.

When he'd arrived at the Frankfurt airport to board his flight home, he'd been pushed to the gate in a wheelchair by a Red Cross volunteer. If that hadn't been the most humiliating experience ever. With his khaki slacks covering the fake leg – he wasn't calling it "his" – his outward appearance was that of a healthy, able-bodied young man, being rolled through the airport by a five-foot-tall lady whose age appeared to fall somewhere between that of his mother and his grandmother. She'd even had a pass to accompany him through the security checkpoint to the gate, along with some fancy paperwork that got them through with the controlled substances in his backpack.

When they arrived at the gate, Clay insisted on getting to his feet – his foot – and walking, or rather gimping, down the jetway and onto the plane, hating every tap of the cane that accompanied each slow step.

Tap, clump, tap, clump. He was certain every other passenger was looking at him with either pity or annoyance for his slowness, and he hated feeling both. To add insult to injury, the petite, motherly Red Cross lady who'd brought him to the gate hugged him before he could get away, and said, "Good luck, soldier."

Soldier. He wasn't a soldier anymore. There was no place in the Army for a guy with only one leg, a guy who'd gone Kaboom. All he was now was a fucking pathetic freak.

It didn't take any advanced mathematical skills to figure out how many people he was going to annoy. Even a kid could do that math. Two rows behind him, three seats on either side of the aisle, plus the two girls in his row. That added up to fourteen people who were going to have to wait for him to gimp up the aisle before they could get out.

He was in hell, all due to Kaboom.

When the passengers ahead of them were all up and out – and it didn't take nearly as long as Clay had hoped it would – he again had to grab firmly onto the seat back in front of him to pull himself upright, hoping and praying that the girl sitting next to him didn't offer to help. There wasn't room for him to lean forward to facilitate getting up, as he'd been taught in physical therapy. At least the occupant of the seat in front of him was already up getting his bag from the overhead bin, and no longer in a position to be annoyed by Clay's clumsiness.

Even a normal person would be feeling stiff after a nine-hour flight, stuffed into a narrow seat in the Economy cabin. But add in a prosthetic leg that he was still unaccustomed to, and the terrifying hope that his rigid immobility would deflect the train wreck of phantom pain in his non-existent leg, as a result, all of his joints – even the ones he no longer possessed – were stiff and sore.

He stumbled, grabbed his cane before it had a chance to fall out of his reach, and held onto the seat back until he stopped wobbling, trying to ignore the stares of those fourteen people waiting for him.

The overhead bin above his seat was already open, thank goodness, and he was able to drag his backpack out with his free hand. The flight attendant had put it in the bin for him when he'd boarded. But not only did he not want the helpless feeling of that assistance again, even if he did, the flight attendants were all at the front of the plane smiling at the departing passengers and asking them to come see us again.

He had the backpack in his hand, but he couldn't sling his arms through the straps with one hand, and he wasn't steady enough on his pins yet to let go of the cane to use two hands. Having to rely on the cane for balance made him feel like he was one-handed as well as one-legged. If he sat back down to free his hands, he'd be exposed to even more pitying stares from those fourteen people waiting for him to get his ass in gear.

At that sad moment, he heard a breezy, "Let me help you with that, dude," and a smiley teenager from the row behind him grabbed the strap and pushed it up to his shoulder before Clay had a chance to decline. He transferred his cane to his other hand, wobbled a moment, then the young man pushed the other strap into place on his other shoulder for him.

He nodded a quick, embarrassed thanks to the smiley kid, then began the long, painful gimp-clop up to the front of the plane.

By the time he got to the door, and the flight attendant was telling him she hoped Clay would fly with them again soon, he was sweating. As soon as he made it through the airplane door and onto the jetway, he limped over to the right side to allow his fourteen followers to pass by, feeling like he should be apologizing to them as they passed, for delaying their departure.

The smiley teenager who'd helped him with his backpack breezed by, glanced at Clay and said, "Have a nice day," as he trotted quickly away. He was probably in a hurry to get to his girlfriend, Clay guessed.

Clay had had a girlfriend once. Before Kaboom. But not anymore. As soon as he was lucid enough to sit up in bed after waking up in the hospital in Germany, to realize what his future was going to be, he'd asked for the use of a laptop, and sent her an email. A very short message.

"Julie. It's over between us."

Just five words, brutal and stark. It was a surgical strike, a traumatic amputation, just like his leg, and caused by the same IED. But just because he'd broken up with her, didn't stop him from seeing her with his mind's eye every waking moment.

Julie. His Viking Princess. He'd met her on the first day of his senior year of high school when they'd sat next to each other in history class, though for a while he'd been unable to talk to her.

She was beauty personified in Clay's eyes. Tall and fair and blue-eyed, and with a figure that even at seventeen made everyone with a Y chromosome sit up and take notice, and golden, natural to the root blonde hair that no hairdresser could reproduce. When she smiled, it filled her eyes, but he was terrified to talk to her.

It wasn't that he was shy around girls. He wanted to talk to girls and go out with girls and do all the things that horny teenaged boys want to do with girls. His only problem was that he was hampered by a fairly serious case of adolescent acne.

He did everything he thought was right to treat it. He washed his face frequently, limited his intake of greasy foods, tried to avoid touching his skin. Nothing helped. He was getting to the point where he thought he might have to ask his mother to make him an appointment with a dermatologist.

The history class he shared with Julie was right after lunch, so he was able to be in his seat early, in the hopes of having time to talk to her before the bell rang. After a few hesitant days of awkward attempts at conversation, of drawing away in embarrassment due to his unpleasant skin, Julie walked into class and plunked a shopping bag down on his desk.

"What's this?" he asked in surprise.

"It's a skin care regimen," she replied. "Use this according to the directions and it should clear you up real quick."

He looked into the bag with suspicion.

"It's not makeup?" He didn't know whether to be ecstatic that she'd noticed him, or devastated that she'd noticed the state of his skin.

"No silly, it's not makeup. It's cleanser, toner, and lotion. It's very effective. You'll like how it works, I'm sure."

"No thanks. I'm not using your girly stuff."

"Oh for goodness sake," she replied with an eye roll. "It is not girly stuff. It has no perfume. Completely gender-neutral. Use it, then when you get it cleared up, you can ask me out. Of course, you could ask me out today, but I get the feeling you won't."

She was right, but still, he hesitated.

Her blue eyes twinkled at him. "I'll make you a deal. If you use this and don't see an improvement in a week, I'll go to the Homecoming dance with you."

"And if it does work?"

"I'll, let me think, still go to the Homecoming dance with you."

"Why are you doing this for me? Giving me this stuff?"

"Are you kidding? I'm trying to snag the cutest guy in class before anyone else does. Look, my brothers used this on their acne, and now look at them."

"Your brothers?" The type of brothers who might pulverize a guy who lusted after their sister?

"Yeah. Kyle and Zach Peterson. You know who they are, right?"

Clay's jaw dropped in shock. "Your brothers are the Peterson twins?"

The Peterson twins were legends at their high school. They had been seniors the year Clay was a freshman. He was pretty sure that their photos would appear if one were to do a Google search for Norse gods. Every girl at school wanted to date them, and every boy wanted to be like them. Lowly undeserving freshmen such as Clay could only worship from afar.

Though everyone in the Peterson family was blond, blue-eyed, and attractive, Kyle and Zach weren't identical twins, and that only doubled their legendary status. They were both athletes, but in different sports. Kyle was the homecoming king their senior year, and Zach was the prom king. The girls they had dated were the envy of every female in town. Zach had been the class valedictorian and Kyle had been the salutatorian. Or maybe Kyle had been the valedictorian. They'd both gotten perfect scores on their SAT tests. Zach received a full-ride scholarship to Northwestern, both undergrad and medical school, and was now a resident at Evanston Hospital. Kyle had also been heavily recruited, chose Notre Dame, and currently practiced law at a fancy downtown office. It was anticipated he'd be the youngest person to make partner in his firm's history.

And Julie, his Viking Princess, was their baby sister.

And they had suffered with acne, just like Clay? Just like real human beings? If this product had been part of making them what they'd been, Clay couldn't use it fast enough. While he washed with the cleanser and applied the toner, he fantasized about kissing the blonde beauty who'd given them to him.

His mother did insist that Clay reimburse Julie for the cost of the skin products, and by the time the Homecoming dance came around, his skin had improved enough to feel confident in taking Julie to the event. By Christmas, he was completely clear and miracle of miracles, Julie kept telling him how handsome he was.

She even had her own pet nickname for him. Cowboy.

It wasn't that there was anything even remotely cowboy-like in his nature. He didn't own a pair of cowboy boots, or a cowboy hat. He didn't listen to country music. He had nothing against country music; he just happened to prefer classic rock. He'd never ridden a horse, never been to Texas, and the closest he'd ever gotten to a cow was the meat department at the grocery store.

It was his name. Clay was short for Clayton, a name his mother had chosen after hearing it in some movie or television show she'd been a fan of. Apparently at his baptism, the priest had balked because Clayton wasn't a saint's name, and hadn't bought his mother's claim that it was a variation of Charles. But his middle name of John got the ceremony rolling.

The first day he'd met Julie, she'd giggled a little and said, "Clay? That's such a cowboy name."

And from that moment on, he was her Cowboy, and she was his Viking Princess.

O'Hare is the third largest airport in the United States, both by volume of passengers and in physical size. It's as big as its own city. Clay had, in the past, before Kaboom, joked that getting through the place was like landing in Milwaukee and walking the rest of the way to Chicago. He wasn't joking about it today. His gait was no longer a carefree bounce, but a slow, lopsided progression. He walked like an old woman rather than a young man who used to run like the wind.

It was a long, painful clop-limp from the jetway through the terminal to Passport Control. There was even an escalator to navigate. Clay waited until everyone else had passed him before hesitantly stepping on. At least at the top the thing just sort of slid him off onto the tile of the upper level without him having to navigate anything.

By the time he approached the Passport Control kiosks, he was in agony. Would this day of pain never end? His fingerprint images, his damn DNA, were being embedded into the metal handle of the cane. At least he'd had the forethought to put his passport in his pocket, so he wouldn't have to take off his backpack to dig it out. But even after scanning it in the self-serve reader, he still had to continue to the DHS counter, and there was a long serpentine arrangement of ribbon and post barriers, meant to manage long lines of arriving passengers. If it had been full of people, it would have looked like a line for a ride at Disneyland, and would have taken him an hour to navigate. His parents were supposed to be waiting on the outside of the Customs area to pick him up, and he'd already kept them waiting quite a while. However, his limping slowness proved to work to his benefit at the moment. All the other passengers had gone through by now. He was literally the last person there. There was a DHS guard there whose job it was to guide passengers to the passport scanning kiosks, but now that there was for the moment, nobody to shepherd through, she looked at Clay with his cane and his face pinched with pain, and stepped in front of him.

"Here," she said. "No need for you to go through the whole line when there's nobody ahead of you. Just go straight through." She unhooked a ribbon barrier from its post and waved him through the opening, then scooted ahead of him with a quick step that Clay darkly envied to unhook several more of the ribbon barriers, giving him a straight path through.

"Thanks," he muttered, trying to muster up an expression of gratitude as he limped towards the nearest DHS station.

"No problem," the lady replied brightly, glancing at his cane. "Hope you feel better soon."

Clay knew, in his rational brain, that her words were merely a blithe, generic phrase, most likely expressed to lots of impaired people passing through here. But he couldn't help but silently whine, in his new, cynical state of mind, *yeah right, like that's ever going to happen.*

Get well soon. Feel better soon. He'd been hearing that a lot since Kaboom. But he wasn't sick. He was crippled. He didn't have a common cold that would go away with a few days of rest and some over the counter products. Even pneumonia was curable. What Clay suffered from was permanent and incurable.

By now he was not only sweating, but in serious, throbbing pain as well. The handle of his cane was becoming permanently fused to his hand as he handed the Passport Control officer his passport. Damn, he had left his Army ID card inside his passport, and after stamping it, the officer said to him, "Welcome home, soldier. Thank you for your service."

Clay muttered a brief thanks as he slipped his passport back into his pocket, but inside, he was despairing.

I'm not a soldier. I used to be one. I used to serve my country. I used to have something to contribute. But now – I'm an incomplete man with no purpose or future. My world has gone Kaboom.

Once he cleared Passport Control, the next challenge was going to be getting his bag from the baggage carousel. Would he be able to lift it off the conveyor with one hand while maintaining his balance with the cane? Maybe the smiley kid who'd helped him retrieve his backpack would be there to grab it for him. No, Clay was sure he'd already sprinted off to his girlfriend's arms.

Clay would be neither sprinting, nor be in a girlfriend's arms, ever again.

"Clay!" He heard a familiar voice call his name. There were very few people around him, because nobody else from his flight was so slow and limping. What were the chances of another person with his name being in the vicinity? Maybe he was hearing things. But it sure sounded like his father's voice calling his name.

"Clay! Over here!" He followed the sound and saw what appeared to be his father a few feet away, waving at him and calling his name. Surely his eyes were deceiving him.

But no, it wasn't his imagination. It really was his father, in the flesh, crossing the few feet of space between them to surround him in a paternal hug. He almost melted to the floor with amazement and emotion. It had been so many months since he had felt the human touch of family, and he certainly hadn't expected to see his dad here, in the sterile area of the airport, well before the exit where passengers were usually met.

Dad still used Old Spice. It was an inherently paternal fragrance, associated with home, familiarity, security. He kept repeating, "Clay, Clay my boy," and Clay almost lost it right there in a puddle of heartbreak. "It's OK, Clay," Dad insisted. "It's OK."

When Clay was twelve, his parents took him and his sister Brooke to Six Flags. Clay had barely made the minimum height requirement for the Goliath roller coaster, so he and his dad had gotten on while his mother and Brooke waited, Brooke fuming that she wasn't tall enough to ride with them. By coincidence, they were in the very first car. As they chugged slowly up the incline towards the apex of the track, Clay suddenly regretted that he'd been tall enough for this ride, and was filled with childish terror. His dad had seen his fear, patted his hand, and said, "It's OK, Clay. It's going to be OK."

Although realistically they both knew there was absolutely nothing his dad could have done should that roller coaster car careen off the rails and crash to the ground, but still, if Dad said it was going to be OK, then it was going to be OK.

Now, today, with his dad's arms around him, Clay was, just for a moment, transformed back into that scared twelve-year-old boy on his first roller coaster, being told by his dad that it was going to be OK.

When he'd been at basic training, there had been a phrase, a mantra, that he and his buddies had repeated over and over, to get through the rough parts.

Suck it up like a vacuum cleaner.

Every recruit in their platoon was surprised that the drill instructors had any voice left after the first two days. Somehow, they always did. When those drill sergeants had been screaming at them nonstop, when the recruits thought they couldn't possibly perform one more pushup or run one more yard, when they felt they would never satisfactorily learn the proper cleaning, assembling and disassembling of an M16A2 assault rifle, or stuff one more fact into their brains about the illustrious history of the United States Army, they would catch each other's eyes and silently mouth, "Suck it up like a vacuum cleaner."

You will not cry.

Just because this was his dad, just because his had been the first voice from home he'd heard on the phone after Kaboom, just because his life was never going to be the same again –

You will not cry.

Suck it up like a vacuum cleaner.

You. Will. Not. Cry.

Clay had coded on the medevac transport plane on the way from Afghanistan to Landstuhl hospital in Germany, which was a fancy doctor-speak way of saying his heart stopped. Probably due to wishful thinking. They'd jump-started him, so he'd been told, just like on TV, with paddles on his chest and someone yelling, "Clear!", sending three thousand volts of electricity to invade his faltering heart, inspiring the reluctant ticker to come back to life, or at least to a facsimile of it.

He must have regained consciousness for just a moment, because he recalled a brief glance of the ceiling above him, a hand patting his, and a voice saying, "Hang in there, Corporal. It's going to be OK."

That voice had sounded disturbingly like his father's did at this moment.

"Dad, how did you get in here?" he croaked, willing the sniveling tone out of his voice. "They don't let non-passengers back here."

His dad released him from his embrace, and Clay had to steady himself with his cane to remain standing.

"Well," Dad said, with emotion in his own voice, "I called a guy at the Army and reminded them that my son was a Purple Heart recipient. The Army called the TSA, the TSA called the airline, and I got a return call saying they would be happy to give me a pass to meet you at Customs, and to thank you for your service. I think there may have been a phone call made to the Department of Homeland Security in there too."

"You didn't have to go to that trouble," Clay said, but Dad wasn't having it.

"You have luggage?" Dad asked abruptly, and Clay nodded. "Let's go grab it. Your mother and Brooke are waiting for us."

By the time they got to the baggage carousel, Clay's black duffel bag was the only luggage left to be claimed, riding a lonely jaunt around the rotating belt. As they walked there, Clay could tell his dad was keeping his stride deliberately slow-paced, to keep pace with Clay's arduous limp, trying to hide curious glances towards his legs. Clay was grateful that they didn't encounter one of those electric carts that transported handicapped people around the airport. As exhausted as he was, as much pain as he was in, it still would have been beyond humiliating to have been carted around like that, almost as humiliating as it had been to be pushed in a wheelchair by that petite, elderly Red Cross lady.

When they got to the carousel, Dad stepped forward and grabbed the bag quickly, sparing Clay the embarrassment of attempting to extract it.

Finally, finally, they approached the exit doors. It felt as if hours had passed since that plane had touched down. He couldn't wait to get this whole ordeal over, but he still had to face his mother and sister on the other side of that door. And then, please God, he could get home, crawl into bed, and forget he existed.

As much as he'd missed his mom and Brooke, as much as he wanted to see them again, he still almost wished they wouldn't be there.

How could he face them? How could he bear to see their eyes, filled with sympathy and curiosity? Searching for the son and brother they'd said goodbye to, facing their realization that the old Clay didn't exist anymore, and in his place was a feeble imitation of the man he'd once been. They'd be expecting to see a real man, but they were going to be sorely disappointed because all they were getting was a medically discharged cripple. He wouldn't be surprised if they turned and ran away in horror.

Dad stepped back a little so Clay could go through the door first. He wished his dad would precede him so he wouldn't have to wait and watch Clay's limping. But at least the final door was the kind that opened automatically with some kind of sensor, like the doors at the grocery store, so he didn't have to try to negotiate that. When it opened, he couldn't see his mother or Brooke at first, because there was a big group of people standing there, apparently waiting for another passenger. The person they were waiting to greet must have been pretty important because several in the group carried American flags and a hand-painted sign saying, "Welcome Home".

But – oh God no – that was Brooke, his sister, holding that Welcome Home sign, and it had his name on it. He recognized an aunt, an uncle, a cousin or two, a couple of his parent's neighbors, and several childhood friends in the welcoming group.

No, this couldn't be. They were there as if to welcome home some kind of hero. They shouldn't be here, because he was no hero, and certainly not deserving of this exuberant welcoming committee. It would have been too much even if he'd been coming home on a normal leave, as he'd planned to months from now. They were treating him like some kind of celebrity.

Go away, he wanted to shriek. Go find some real hero to greet with your signs and flags. I don't deserve it.

The group surged forward at the sight of him, and if he'd been able to, he would have turned and run. Horror washed over him, and he wanted to disappear. It was bad enough his family had to see him like this. To have his other relatives and acquaintances there as well, seeing him with his cane and knowing what was, and wasn't, under his slacks, was beyond humiliating. His mother got to him first, hugging him fiercely, and he was filled with embarrassment.

It wasn't because his mother was hugging him in public, but for the reason he was here in the first place. He should have been arriving here months later, while on official leave, with honor.

He endured the hugs and welcomes and back pats from the rest of the group with silent resignation, focusing on not slipping and falling from the contact. He would die of embarrassment if he lost his precarious balance and fell on the floor. What if his prosthesis made a loud, artificial ping of titanium hitting the floor? What if it came loose?

They all probably thought he was an ungrateful jerk, with his lack of acknowledgment or appreciation. It was a barrier, to try, unsuccessfully, to ignore the truth of his situation.

When finally everyone had greeted him, welcomed him home, hugged and kissed and patted him, they let him and his parents get out the door. His dad's car waited at the curb, being minded by his Uncle Craig, who was defending it from being ticketed by an airport police officer, while Uncle Craig pointed at the handicapped tag hanging from the rear-view mirror.

A handicapped placard. For the cripple, Clay. This was worse than hell.

The airport cop relented when he saw Clay's cane and limp, and the depressing group of well-wishers all disbursed to their own vehicles as the Maslowski family got into their car and pulled away.

They made him sit in the front passenger seat while Brooke and his mother sat in the back. His dad dropped Clay's luggage in the trunk before getting into the driver's seat and starting the car.

It was the same car they'd used to drive him to the airport before he'd left for his deployment to Afghanistan. The same scent of recent cleaning, the same tiny ding on the rear fender from a runaway shopping cart, the same St. Christopher medal hanging on a chain from the rear-view mirror.

His last journey in this car seemed like a lifetime ago.

Clay used to own a car. It hadn't been fancy, in fact it bordered on junky. But it had gotten him from Point A to Point B, and it had been his. He'd sold it without regret before leaving for basic training, and put the proceeds into a savings account to save up for an engagement ring for Julie. He wouldn't need those funds now.

He hadn't been sitting in the front seat the day of Kaboom. He'd been in the back, behind the driver, Sergeant Lopez. The left tires had run over the IED and the explosion had lifted the Humvee ten feet in the air. His last conscious feeling before waking up in the hospital in Germany had been a taste of death and dirt in his mouth.

"God!" He heard the word moaned softly, desperately, and realized it had come from him. His father's hands jerked a bit on the steering wheel in surprise, and his mother leaned forward from behind him to lay a hand on his shoulder.

"Clay, are you alright?"

"Yeah, Mom," he muttered, embarrassed. His mind had skittered away from the peaceful suburban landscape to Afghanistan, the land of the hundred-pound IED. What a head case he'd become. His mother believed him when he said he was OK, and sat back in her seat, removing her hand from his shoulder.

He kind of wished she'd left her hand there. It helped remind him where he really was, and where he wasn't anymore.

Not only was he a head case, he'd become a total baby too, needing his mommy's hand on him to get through something as mundane as a drive in the family car.

He swiveled his head, looking out each side window, to the front and back windows too, scanning for threats. But all he saw was Wheeling, the suburb he'd grown up in. Walmart and Starbucks, churches, banks and houses, a strip mall where his mother said a Kmart store had once stood, back in the olden days.

Maybe he could get a job as a Walmart door greeter.

No, that wouldn't work. Clay was fairly sure that the store management would require their greeters to smile at the customers entering the store. He hadn't smiled since Kaboom, and was sure he would never be able to smile again.

He wasn't even qualified to work at Starbucks. Everyone from Julie to his platoon mates had told him his coffee-making skills were appalling, and Julie should know. She was a professional chef. She'd gone to culinary school at Kendall College downtown and was now a chef at Morton's Steakhouse in Schaumburg.

When they passed St. Joseph the Worker Catholic Church, he had to avert his eyes. Once he had hoped to marry Julie in that church. But that wasn't going to happen now. Like everything else, that dream had exploded with Kaboom.

Julie, it's over between us. The words were carved into his heart and the wounds were still open, painful and bleeding.

When they finally pulled into their driveway, he was glad he had stayed at Landstuhl until his prosthesis had been fitted. He'd rather spend the rest of his life at that military hospital in Germany than have to see a wheelchair ramp leading up to his parent's front door.

Someone on their street must have been having a party, because there were cars parked in front of their house and across the street. When they pulled into the driveway, his mother managed to hop out of the seat behind him and opened his door. His face flamed red because his mother had to see that he had to physically grab his left thigh with his hands in order to swing his leg out of the car door. The titanium was less than obedient.

Dad parked the car in the driveway but he opened the garage door with the clicker. Of course, with bicycles and other assorted items in the garage, it would be difficult for him to open the door wide enough to exit, what with his prosthesis, his cane, his limp, his damn disability. Even with the door swung open to its max, it was awkward, almost as difficult as getting up from the airplane seat. Everyone else was out well before he dragged his pathetic carcass upright.

Dad opened the trunk with his clicker.

"Brooke, take Clay's bags up to his room," he instructed. Brooke pulled his duffel and backpack out without complaint and carried them in the kitchen door.

Great. Another highlight of his inability to take care of himself. His little sister had to wrangle his luggage because he couldn't do it himself.

He tried to follow his sister into the house, but, surprisingly, his mom stood in front of the door, and indicated the other door, which led into the back yard.

"Come on," Dad said, opening that door. Clay just wanted to go to bed. He'd already had his prosthesis on longer today than he should have. His stump was begging for relief, and he was not in the least interested in going into their back yard. But getting into the house would, apparently, necessitate pushing his mother bodily away from the kitchen door, something he wouldn't do even if he could. With great reluctance, he followed his dad into the back yard.

Chapter Two

Clay had walked into a nightmare. All the relatives and friends, and then some, who'd been at the airport with their depressing signs and flags were there in his parent's back yard, as if this were some sort of celebration. The signs and flags were still there, planted in the ground like a shrine. The aroma of charcoal lighter fluid and hot dogs filled his nose.

A party? Were they serious? What were they celebrating?

"Welcome home, sweetie," his mom said, pressing a brief maternal kiss to his cheek.

"Mom, no," he protested, unable to articulate how horrified he was to see all these people, looking at him as if he was some sort of hero.

Go away, he wanted to yell, but of course he didn't. *This isn't a celebration. This is a tragedy, an abomination.* God, they were smiling at him, patting his back again, offering him a beer, a soda, a water.

He didn't want to be here. It was too crowded, too insecure. His heart started to pound as he looked for an avenue of escape. It was horrible. *Horrible.* How could they host a damn party, as if his homecoming were some sort of joyous occasion?

Their backyard picnic table was covered with a cheerful red and white checked table cloth and paper plates, condiments and napkins. Two grills were set up for preparing food. His Uncle Stan, Uncle Craig's brother, paused in his inspection of the coals to wave at him with a spatula and offer a cheery, "Hey there, Clay!"

He wanted to vanish, just sink into the earth beneath his feet and cease to exist. But no such luck. He found himself looking around in search of a way to disappear. His dad assumed differently.

"Here, Clay," he said, pulling up a lawn chair in the shade of the patio. Clay had no choice now but to sit there, with friends and relatives coming around trying to talk to him, acting as if they were glad to see him, as if he were a normal person. But it wasn't normal. Nothing was normal. He wasn't normal, and he wasn't supposed to be here. He hated every moment of it.

Uncle Stan was now loading up the grill, cooking up hamburgers, hot dogs and kielbasa. Their family didn't bother with generic kielbasa from the local grocery store. His dad regularly went to a Polish butcher in the city and got the good, authentic stuff. Normally Clay would have been first in line for one of the kielbasa sausages he could smell, but today, he wasn't tempted. There was even a cake, from a bakery, with the words "Welcome Home, Clay" written in frosting. How depressing was that?

They sat him in that lawn chair in the shade, like it was a seat of honor, though he'd never felt less honorable in his life. Someone pressed an open bottle of beer into his hand. He held it, but didn't drink any. Not only did he not want it, but he'd been told that alcohol inhibited the efficacy of painkillers, and he couldn't risk that.

Another advantage to holding the beer bottle was he could use it as a defense. It kept people from trying to give him other things, a soda, a water. His Aunt Jeanette came over.

"Would you like me to go in and put on some coffee for you?" she asked, smiling at him as if he was a little kid.

"No thanks, Auntie." He indicated the warming beer bottle in his hand as if to say, *I've got what I want to drink.*

If Clay were the type of person who liked being waited on, he could easily have had six or eight plates of food, a dozen beverages, half a dozen pieces of cake. But he wasn't able to even think about eating. His stomach was threatening mutiny. If he'd tried to take a bite of cake, he'd most likely choke. It was probably delicious. It was probably red velvet, his favorite. But even so much as one bite would stick in his throat.

Cake was for celebrations. It was for weddings and graduations and baby showers. Clay had never felt less like celebrating in his entire life. One bite, one crumb, of that cake would asphyxiate him. Since Kaboom, food had held no appeal. In fact, it downright turned him off.

So he sat, in a lawn chair in the shade, refusing the well-meant offers of his parent's guests, assorted relatives, neighbors and friends, defending himself with that un-drunk bottle of beer.

When Clay was fifteen, his grandfather died. It was the first time he had ever attended a funeral. It unnerved him completely to see adults, including his parents, crying. After the funeral Mass, everyone was invited to his aunt's house for lunch.

There was food. So much food. Clay had never seen so much food set out at one time in one place before. It was more than Thanksgiving, more than Christmas. There had been a cake that day too, though without frosting words printed on it. The atmosphere then had been disturbingly celebratory as well, almost like today.

Clay stood back against the wall, stiff and itchy in the new suit his parents had insisted on buying him the day before, because the suit he had worn for his confirmation was too small now. He wanted to yell then as he wanted to yell today, *why are we having a party? This is nothing to celebrate.* His grandmother sat in a chair across the room while everybody fussed over her, but it was obvious to Clay that she hated it just as much as he hated the fussing going on around him right now.

In the three days since his grandfather's death, his grandmother seemed to have shrunk, and she had not been a robust woman to begin with. Was Grandma remembering what Clay did about his late grandfather? Grandpa had always, since Clay could remember, carried a roll of Lifesavers candies in his shirt pocket. All of the grandkids – Clay, his sister, their cousins - always somehow managed to come up with a scratchy throat whenever they saw him, a condition that could be soothed only by a Lifesaver from the roll in Grandpa's pocket. Even his aunt's dog learned to beg for them.

Who was going to distribute those candies now?

His aunt approached his grandmother's chair with a plate of food. "You have to eat something, Mommy," she said as she pressed the plate of food into Grandma's hands. It was completely weird to hear someone address his elderly grandmother as Mommy. Grandma took the plate but made no promises to eat it, although the food appeared to be delicious. As Clay watched, unnoticed, grandma just pushed things around on her plate, cut them up and made it appear as if she had actually eaten some of it. A dinner roll slid off the plate and onto the floor, to be snarfed up by his aunt's dog so quickly nobody else noticed. Grandma would be able to take credit for eating at least that much.

He felt that he ought to go over and say something to her. As the oldest grandchild, perhaps it was his responsibility to comfort her. He went and found a chair and pulled it up next to where his grandmother sat. She looked at him, smiled and handed him the plate of food, saying, "Could you take care of this for me, please, *kochanie?*"

He wasn't sure if she wanted him to dispose of it, or eat it.

"Sure, *babcia*," he replied, using one of the few Polish words he knew. The other was the endearment his grandmother had called him, *kochanie*. It meant, roughly, sweetie.

This whole death thing was really confusing. It seemed like they were all being punished for something. Whatever sin they'd committed had resulted in the removal from their lives of a beloved husband, father, grandfather. He couldn't imagine anything his sweet little grandmother could have done to deserve such a punishment.

The priest at the funeral Mass had said his grandfather had ascended to heaven, and made it sound like heaven was a pretty cool place, a reward of some sort. But apparently the cost of that reward was eternal exile from the decedent's family, friends and home. How wonderful could heaven be to warrant such a separation? How much of a reward was it if everyone was crying about it?

The priest had also said, ashes to ashes, dust to dust. So which was it? Was Grandpa up in some faraway heaven, enjoying himself, being rewarded for his virtuous life by playing golf every day and eating foods that weren't good for him without consequence? Or had his death rendered him into a pile of ashes and dust? These were things that Clay wondered, but didn't dare ask.

But it was the after-funeral party that confused him the most, more so than the tears, the somber church service, the itchy suit and constricting necktie. It was still too much of a celebratory vibe for Clay to take in.

He was glad to see his grandmother was not here at this other gloomy get-together today. Not long after his grandfather's death, Grandma had succumbed to dementia and now resided in an assisted living facility where she could have professional, around-the-clock care. He was very grateful his parents had not brought her here today to see the wreck that her *kochanie* had become.

Even his three friends Ren, Doug and Jeremy were there in his backyard, at this dreadful party. The Posse. That was what the four of them had called themselves as kids, and their parents sometimes still used that term to refer to the group of them. Clay wasn't the only one whose name had been chosen from a medium of entertainment. His friend Ren, who lived across the street, had literally been named after Kevin Bacon's character in Footloose. However, despite years of dance lessons and wishful thinking on his mother's part, this Ren couldn't dance to save his life. They'd played together as kids, gone to high school together, run track together. After graduation, they'd gone their separate ways, but they'd kept in touch.

Clay hadn't been in contact with any of them since Kaboom.

They pulled up lawn chairs near him but he barely said hello and refused to look any of the three of them in the eye. But he didn't miss the looks of, *what's up with that*, that they exchanged among themselves.

"Hey, Clay," Doug said. "How's it hanging?"

Clay just shrugged.

Jeremy stepped up next. "So, um, we heard that you ..." He trailed off, unsure how to phrase it. Clay gave him the briefest glance that dared, *Go ahead. Say it. You lost your leg.* But Jeremy apparently wasn't brave enough, and he just blushed and didn't say what he'd heard.

Ren tried next. "Wow man, it really sucks."

You think?

Doug stepped back into the fray. "We've been emailing you for months, dude. What's with the silent treatment? That's not cool."

Like Clay cared if he was being cool or not.

"Why didn't you call us when you, um, when you were in the hospital?"

For the same reasons he didn't call anyone, the same reason he broke up with Julie, refused to let his parents come to Germany. He didn't want to see or hear their pity and horror at his situation. He didn't want to see it or hear it today either.

Jeremy put in, "So your mom told us you were awarded a Purple Heart."

Like he cared about the stupid Purple Heart either.

"Can we see it?"

"No."

"Aw, come on," Ren wheedled.

The anger erupted out of him from a place that hadn't existed before Kaboom.

"I said no. Fucking no!"

His outburst drew eyes, some curious, some irritated, including those of his mother, who gave him a scolding glance that clearly admonished, *potty mouth.*

He looked away from her disapproval, hating himself.

He just couldn't be proud of that Purple Heart, despite the fact that it had been presented to him by a general. What had he done to earn a medal? Nothing. It remained buried at the bottom of his backpack with his dog tags. It was, after all, the award they gave to guys who were in the wrong place at the wrong time. Somehow people seemed in awe of it, as if he'd done something special, something worthy of a medal, an award. But he hadn't achieved anything. He'd only lost everything.

"Geez, Clay," Doug protested, "you don't need to get your panties in a bunch. You want to go to the Dam Inn later for a beer? Catch up on old times?"

They'd gone to the Dam Inn, an old Wheeling watering hole that had been in business since the time of the Model T, frequently once they'd all turned twenty-one. The last time he'd been home on leave, just before deploying to Afghanistan, the Posse had taken him there for a farewell party and gotten him drunk on Chicago Handshakes, a variation of a boilermaker comprised of a shot of Jeppson's Malört paired with a glass of Old Style beer. They hadn't been able to correctly pronounce the name of the liquor even before drinking it, and afterward their attempts to do so dissolved into drunken giggles. Their inebriation had been facilitated by the bartender, a red-headed goddess with a soft spot for military guys and who slipped them a few on the house, before pouring the four of them into a cab, since they had neglected to assign a designated driver. It had been a good time and a touching send-off from his bud-dies, despite the pounding headaches and queasy stomachs they'd stoically endured the next day. Now, he wasn't inter-ested.

"It's Sunday," Jeremy reminded them. "The Dam Inn is closed. How about the PS Pub, Clay? I think they're having karaoke tonight."

"No." He didn't add, thank you, and after his response to their last request, they declined to push the issue. It wasn't long before they left.

He hated the way he'd yelled at his good friends, hated the looks of confusion and anger on their faces that had shown when they glanced back at him as they walked away. Obviously they were all hurt and more than a little pissed off at his terse refusal to talk or to join them for a beer, and at his vague lack of enthusiasm when they reminded him to stay in touch. They'd probably go out for a beer without him and have a bet-ter time without his grouchy ass ruining their fun anyway.

Part of him wanted to call them back and apologize, take them up on their offer. But more than that, he was relieved that they left him alone. They were his best friends, but now he was a stranger. A freak. He didn't know what to say to them and they didn't know what to say to him.

It was just a miserable, humiliating, embarrassing, not-cool experience. And he still had to try to be tough. He didn't want anyone to think he was a wimp.

He'd been a nice guy, a happy guy, before Kaboom. A guy with manners and pride and a purpose. He'd loved playing practical jokes on his buddies and had come close to wetting himself with laughter when one of his platoon mates sat on a whoopee cushion that Clay had snuck into his bunk.

And yet all of those attributes had been destroyed by that IED. The actual explosion had lasted mere seconds, but its effects were infinite.

The Posse had barely left him alone, when to his utter dismay, he saw another familiar face. Oh God, he couldn't believe the person who was approaching him now. It was Coach Swanson, his high school track coach.

"Hi Clay, how are you?" Coach asked with an outstretched hand. Clay squelched an urge to refuse to shake hands, but he didn't put much effort into it either.

Coach Swanson had always treated his athletes fairly. Yes, he'd yelled at them when they could have done better, but he also didn't hesitate to offer praise when they did well. He was a guy they could talk to, sometimes even about issues having nothing to do with the track team. He respected the boys on his team and as a result they respected him too. Clay could be honest with Coach.

"Absolutely, positively, one hundred percent crappy. But, thanks for asking, Coach."

"I ran into your mother in the grocery store the other day," Coach explained. "She told me about you," Coach cast a sympathetic glance at Clay's legs, probably wondering which one was flesh and which one was fake. "She told me you were coming home today and invited me to come say hello."

The polite thing would be for him to thank Coach for coming, for expressing concern, for appearing to care about what had happened to Clay. But any good manners he had possessed in the past had disappeared in Kaboom. Though he wasn't quite as rude to his former coach as he had been to his childhood friends, and refrained from swearing, still he barely acknowledged the man's attempts at friendliness.

But Coach Swanson persisted. "Do you have plans for the summer?" he asked.

No, he had no plans, not for this summer, not for his life. But no way in hell was he going to let Coach know what a nothing he was now, though it was probably obvious. The man was no dummy. Clay just shrugged and let Coach interpret it as he chose.

"You know, we have a summer track camp at school over the summer vacation."

Yes, Clay knew all about summer track camp. He'd attended it. Back when he'd been able to run.

"My assistant coach had to bail on me – a family emergency of some kind." Why was Coach telling him this? Did he enjoy pouring salt into Clay's wounds? "I had an alternate lined up, a kid who's about to graduate, but then he found out his family is taking him to Europe so he's out too. Imagine, he'd rather climb the steps of the Eiffel Tower than supervise a dozen teenage kids. So I was wondering if you might be willing to come over a couple of days a week for a few hours and help put the JV squad through their paces, the week after next when school is out."

Shock rippled through Clay. Did Coach Swanson not know? Did he think Clay had left the Army voluntarily? When his mother had seen him in the grocery store, surely she had told him the whole tragic story. If he'd been whole he would have jumped – literally – at the opportunity. But in all stark, hideous reality, how could he be expected to help coach runners, when he couldn't run himself? How could he even look at them? It would break his heart, if it wasn't broken already.

It was on the tip of his tongue to rudely refuse, the way he'd refused his friends' offers. But something kept him from uttering the discourtesies to Coach. He just clenched his teeth and said, "I don't think so."

"You wouldn't have to do anything strenuous," Coach assured him. "Just tell the younger kids what they're doing wrong."

Anything strenuous? He couldn't even do anything non-strenuous.

"Think about it, Clay," Coach persisted. "You were one of my best guys, and I don't mean just as a runner."

Coach had surely gotten Clay mixed up with someone else. Did he not recall Clay's smart-ass mouth, his jokes and pranks? He'd thought the only reason you couldn't see the gray hair Clay had given him was because Coach Swanson had blond hair and the grays subtly blended in.

It was funny how people only remembered the good things about you when you almost die.

"I know you have a lot on your mind right now." Coach was, apparently, not put off by Clay's lack of enthusiasm. "Give me a call if you change your mind." He handed Clay a card with his phone number on it and Clay took it and put it in his pocket, surprising himself. Then Coach mercifully left him alone and went over to talk to Clay's dad. Dad handed Coach a can of soda. The two men were probably comparing notes on what an ass Clay was being.

They'd better get used to it. That was his new reality. Could he possibly sneak away from this morbid party? Probably not. He couldn't sneak anywhere. He could barely move.

His peripheral vision perceived someone watching him. Not another one! Were people taking numbers, like at the grocery store deli counter, for their turn to talk to him? Instead of asking for sliced pastrami or fancy cheese, they were annoying him with requests to talk, to do things, to be alive. This day was getting more and more hellacious by the minute. He wished everyone would just go away.

But no such luck. A little girl he didn't recognize was standing there. She looked to be about five or six and had a wild mop of dark curls over startling green eyes. The girl walked right up to him, way too close for Clay's comfort, into his personal space – a place he didn't want anyone to transgress.

Were they bringing in random kids off the street now, to stare at the crippled freak as if he was a new exhibit at the Lincoln Park Zoo?

"Hi," she said, but without smiling. "Are you Clay?"

Normally, Clay liked kids, in small quantities. Today, putting up with one, especially a kid with her stern direct gaze, was something he had no interest in enduring. He didn't bother answering her, in fact, ignored the girl completely.

"Hey!" she said sharply, louder. "I'm talking to you."

"Well stop it."

The kid frowned at him. "You're rude."

"Go away."

But the kid refused to go away. "How come your heart is purple?" she asked. "Hearts are supposed to be red, not purple."

"My heart ain't purple," he retorted. It was non-existent. Maybe his poor grammar was a bad influence on the nosy kid, but right now, he didn't care.

"Well Stephanie says you have a purple heart."

Whoever Stephanie was, she should learn to be more specific when talking to children. "The Purple Heart is a medal," he admitted. "Not the heart in your body." His real heart was a cold dead mass of congealed goo.

The annoying kid kept talking to him. "And she said you have an artificial leg. Can I see it?"

His shock at her bold request got him to look at her, and he narrowed his eyes and tried to look scary.

"No," he said simply.

"But I want to see it," she insisted, as if she was requesting to see some ordinary thing like a hat or a shoe.

"You talk too much. Go away."

"No," the kid said quickly. "You're not the boss of me."

"You're a pain in the ass, kid. Scram."

"You can't say that. It's a bad word."

"I can say whatever I want," he snapped. "You're not the boss of me either. And I say, scram."

Great. He was so far gone he was arguing like a five-year-old, with a five-year-old. But he couldn't help himself.

Before he could prevent it, she leaned against his leg – no, his prosthesis. God, what if the kid noticed that what she was leaning against wasn't a living limb, but a fake thing made of metal and plastic? She'd probably end up emotionally scarred for life.

"Get away! Don't touch me!" he barked, and the kid jumped away as if she'd been burned, giving him a death glare. But at least it prevented her from continuing her painful requests to see his Purple Heart and his prosthetic leg.

"Miranda, there you are." Yet another well-meaning guest approached him and placed an affectionate hand on the annoying kid's shoulder. It was his cousin Stephanie. Was she babysitting for the girl? Or had she simply brought another kid to gawk at the invalid?

"Hi, Clay," Stephanie said, smiling at him. She was just a couple of years older than him. They had played together as kids, hung out together at family gatherings, Thanksgiving, Christmas. If she hadn't been his cousin, he might have had a bit of a crush on her, before he met Julie.

"He's rude," the little girl said, looking up at Stephanie. Who was this kid? She didn't resemble any family member Clay could recall. "Why is he such a meanie?"

Clay shot the kid a dirty look. He felt angry and at the same time, guilty. How dare she call him a meanie? OK, so maybe he had spoken rudely to her, but under the circumstances, wasn't he entitled?

He was tempted to proclaim his innocence, to say he was not a meanie, but really, what was the point? He turned his head and looked away from both the kid and his cousin.

"This is my cousin, Clay," he heard Stephanie say to the girl. Miranda.

"Clay is a big fat rude meanie," the kid said. "I only wanted to make friends and he yelled at me."

"Well he has a lot on his mind," Stephanie said.

He heard a sound from the kid that sounded like, "Hmmph!"

"Miranda, sweetie," his cousin went on, "why don't you go over to David." She pointed out her husband, who was over by the grill, putting mustard on a hot dog. "He'll help you get something to eat."

"OK," the girl agreed. "Bye, Meanie!" she said to Clay, then trotted off to David, his cousin-in-law, who greeted her with an affectionate ruffle of her curly hair and took her to the table where food had been laid out. Now she was probably telling David what a big meanie his wife's cousin was. Who was this kid anyway?

"I'm sorry if Miranda bothered you," Stephanie said.

Clay just shrugged.

"So," she went on, "How are you, Clay?"

He refused to look at her. "Oh, I'm just groovy," he muttered, letting extreme sarcasm fill his voice. Surely his cousin Stephanie, along with everyone else here at this awful party, knew about his missing leg.

"I'm sorry," she said. "This must have been an awful experience for you."

Awful didn't begin to describe it. Fortunately Stephanie didn't try to ask for details. Now if she'd only go away.

"You're probably wondering who Miranda is."

Clay was curious about the kid but wasn't about to let his cousin know that.

"She's a foster child. She's staying with David and me."

Stephanie sat down on one of the lawn chairs recently occupied by his now-departed friends, apparently planning to stay and chat awhile. "It's like this. David and I found out we can't have kids of our own. I'll spare you the medical details. But it's just not going to happen."

Even in his morose state, that was a shocker to hear. All through their childhoods, every time he'd seen Stephanie, all she'd ever talked about was being a mom someday. If anyone was meant to have their own children, it was Stephanie and David Nowack. What a shitload of bad luck for her.

He chanced a quick sympathetic look towards her but lowered his eyes before she noticed.

"That sucks," he muttered.

"Yeah, so we've decided to become foster parents instead. Miranda has been with us for about a month now. Her parents were killed in a car accident caused by a drunk driver. She was stuck in the car with their bodies for three hours until they got her out. She's so brave, it just breaks my heart." Stephanie glanced over towards her husband and the little girl for a moment, and Clay thought he saw moisture gather in his cousin's eye. She hadn't looked teary when telling him about her and David's infertility issues, though that had to have been the worst thing she'd ever had to experience. But looking towards the tragic little girl they were fostering seemed to produce even more emotion. "Sometimes she wakes up screaming, the poor thing."

Clay didn't wake up screaming. He had Vicodin to take care of that.

"Even though we've only had her for a short time, we love her. We'd like to adopt her if we can."

Somehow Clay knew he should be expressing sympathy to his cousin for the unfortunate turn her life had taken, but he couldn't. An adopted kid in place of a biological kid didn't, in his mind, come close to the despair of a prosthetic limb in place of a flesh and bone leg.

Finally Stephanie gave up trying to be sociable with him, and stood to leave. He tried not to flinch away from her sympathetic pat on his shoulder.

"You take care, cuz, I'll talk to you later." She left him and he watched her join her husband and the kid across the yard.

Unbidden, he recalled her in their childhood, how all she'd talked about whenever he saw her was babies, children, how many boys, how many girls, potential names. She and David had been married almost three years and it occurred to him that he didn't remember them talking about babies at all since then. They'd probably been going through hideous fertility tests this whole time.

So what. He had more important things to worry about than his cousin's reproductive issues, like how he might be able to escape this dreadful party full of people who seemed to be crazy enough to admire him. Or maybe he was the crazy one. His mental health was still up for debate.

The next-door neighbors even brought their dog, a cute mutt that previously Clay had enjoyed playing with and had even snuck treats to when its people weren't looking. The dog came over, sat down and looked at Clay expectantly, head cocked, one ear bent. Did it want a treat, a head scratch, a ball to be thrown for him to fetch? He wasn't going to provide any of those, but the stupid canine, whose name Clay had forgotten, didn't get the hint.

That dog was the only living creature that Clay finally looked directly in the eye. When Fido or Rover or whatever its name was looked at him, Clay let it see his unshuttered eyes without trying to hide the physical or emotional pain he felt. The dog wouldn't care.

They say that animals can see things humans can't. Spot or whatever its name was looked back at Clay's eyes, and the dog saw things there that Clay wouldn't allow any of the humans around him to see. The pooch quickly back-peddled on all four feet, gave a startled, frightened yelp, and ran off in search of his mommy, apparently losing his desire for an unauthorized treat. Even dogs thought he was a freak.

Finally people started leaving, realizing that their supposed guest of honor was not going to be in any way sociable. Part of him was glad to see them go, while another part wanted their company. But mostly it was a relief not to have to talk to people or have them talk to him or look at him or feel sorry for him or be revolted by him. He planted his cane on the cement patio under his chair and pulled himself up to escape into the house, feeling wrung-out and exhausted. His stump was sore and begging for him to remove the prosthesis, and he wanted to fall into his bed and sleep forever. He left it to his parents to say goodbye to all those friends and relatives they'd invited to this ghastly gathering, and tried to ignore the flags and celebratory signs still planted in the grass of their back yard.

There was just one obstacle between him and that bed. Or rather, thirteen of them.

Stairs.

Stairs that in the past he had bounded up three at a time. Stairs that, in his childhood, he had slid down using a flattened cardboard box as a sled. He'd gotten into a lot of trouble with his mother for that stunt. The stairs had never been an obstacle before. Now they might as well be Mount Everest.

His parents had offered to set up a bed for him in the small den off the living room, but he had turned the offer down. If he was going to be stuck living in his parent's house like a college drop-out, he was at least going to sleep in his own bed, not on a cot in his father's den.

He was supposed to be able to climb the steps without holding the handrail. He'd practiced it in rehab. But this was the real world. He was tired, in pain, mentally and emotionally depleted. He needed that handrail like a lifeline.

He had to swing his leg a bit to get the prosthesis up each step. The artificial knee didn't bend exactly like the real one. He was careful to raise his fake leg high enough, with an exaggerated knee bend, so as not to catch his fake toes on the edge of the step. He'd done so in physical therapy a couple of times and the results were undignified to say the least. The whole process was a chore, learned painfully in the hospital. Lead with the real leg, remember to place the prosthetic foot next to the flesh and blood foot before attempting the next step. One hand holding the handrail, the other gripping the cane. In the hospital, the therapists had actually touched his stump while manipulating it with exercises intended to increase his range of motion, which they told him was even more important than strength. How did they not immediately barf from the disgustingness? They made him to practice in front of a mirror, and he hated that.

Was it really only thirteen steps? It felt like a hundred. Halfway up he had to stop, exhausted and sweating, starting to regret his stubborn pride at refusing the offer to set up a bed for him downstairs. It was however, more than just pride. The downstairs bathroom was only a half bath, with no shower, and he really needed a shower. He could smell himself, and it wasn't a good smell. After crossing seven time zones between Frankfurt and Chicago, he couldn't remember the last time soap had touched him. After a brief rest, he continued his awkward, painful struggle up the remaining steps.

His bedroom had barely changed since he'd left for basic training, almost four years ago. A shelf his dad had put up held his track trophies, next to a poster of Usain Bolt. The furniture hadn't changed nor the paint color nor the brown and white striped window curtains. The room was the same; the man occupying it, not so much.

There was one addition, not of Clay's doing. A pair of crutches were propped against the side of the bed. Obviously his parents had followed the instructions of the doctors they'd spoken to at Landstuhl before he'd returned home. He hated them. Not his parents, nor the doctors. He hated the crutches, and the fact that he sometimes had to use them.

A part of him wanted to grab those running trophies off the shelf and smash them into smithereens, rip that poster down and tear it to shreds. He wanted, was oh so tempted, to scream and cry like a crazy man. But he desisted, afraid that his parents or sister might hear him.

It would be easy to just fall onto the bed, but he really needed that shower. Not only did he smell like a goat, but he'd already had the prosthesis on for much longer than he was supposed to. He wasn't even supposed to wear it every day, but rather alternate some days with leaving it off and using crutches.

That wasn't going to happen, no matter how much it hurt.

He sat on the edge of the bed and undid his slacks, lifting his rear to pull them down and off. Then he eased the socket off and let the prosthesis fall to the floor, trying to ride through the wave of pain that the movement cost him as he removed the tight-fitting shrinker sock that covered his stump.

No, not remove. He'd been informed that putting on and removing the prosthetic limb was called donning and doffing. It sounded like Santa's disabled reindeer.

The residual limb was still red and angry-looking and scarred. His knee had only been partially destroyed, but there wasn't enough left to repair or even replace, and the surgeons had removed the knee remnants. They'd had the nerve to tell him that was a good thing, because it left enough skin to cover the stump. It was hideous, it was ugly, it was disgusting. And why on God's green earth did the scar holding the skin flaps together at the bottom of his stump have to look like a smile? He hated having to even see the horrible thing.

He'd listened to all the scientific terminology such as transfemoral and ablation, and hated that he was expected to understand and accept it. To him, it was still a torn-apart stump attached to a fake, pretend hunk of artificial material.

They told him he was lucky. Lucky! Ha, that was rich. His traumatic amputation, concussion and a slight hearing loss had been his only injuries. As if that wasn't enough. Or too much. But he'd had very little shrapnel or debris in the wound, and had so far avoided the bone infections suffered by many IED victims.

In truth, the prosthesis was lighter than he'd expected such a thing to be, yet bore his weight surprisingly well. He should have appreciated the quality and technological advancement that had gone into its creation, but somehow he just couldn't. He pulled off his shirt, his briefs and the sock on his right foot, and tossed the prosthesis and shrinker sock on his bed

There was one good thing – if anything about his situation could be called good. He had a bathrobe hanging in his closet that was way too big for him. His sister Brooke had given it to him for Christmas last year, but had accidentally chosen a robe from the Big and Tall department. She'd liked the color, a deep rich shade of blue, and had neglected to check the size. At the time, he'd thought the huge thing was amusing, so he'd kept it rather than exchanging it for one more suitable to his lean, compact frame. When he put it on, he had to practically wrap the sash around him twice, but the most important thing was that it fell to below his knees, or rather his knee, covering his stump. He still had to use the hated crutches to get out the door, now that the prosthesis was off. He pulled down the hem of the robe to make sure it concealed the unsightliness of his stump.

Like that would fool anyone.

It was only three steps to the bathroom. He prayed it was unoccupied. His parents would use the master bathroom accessed through their bedroom. That left only Brooke as a possible user, and he was pretty sure she was still downstairs in the back yard, giggling with her friends.

He used to run the four hundred meter in fifty seconds. Now it took him two full minutes to travel twenty feet.

All hope of making it into the bathroom without having to endure any human interaction was dashed when his father appeared from seemingly nowhere.

"Clay, do you need any help?" His dad's face was full of concern. He appeared to have acquired a few gray hairs at his temple since Clay had seen him last, but maybe they were just a lighter shade of blond. Because Clay was the only brunette in a family of blondes, Brooke sometimes called him Cuckoo. She'd started using the nickname after learning in a fifth-grade science class that the cuckoo bird would sneak its eggs into the nests of other birds so that the other bird parents were forced to feed it even though it obviously didn't belong to them.

"No, I've got it," he muttered, flushing with embarrassment at his dad seeing him on crutches, with only one leg protruding from beneath that too-large bathrobe. He hadn't been the blushing type of guy before. He hated this feeling of vulnerability, there in the hall where anyone might see him. He should have left the prothesis on and taken it off in the bathroom.

Dad put a hand on his arm. "Seriously, Clay, if you need any help with – things..."

"I don't need your help!" he barked. "I can do it myself!"

Immediately he felt contrite, snapping at his father like that. Just because he had hair on his chest now didn't give him the right to snarl at his father like a snotty teenager.

"Dad, I'm sorry." But Dad didn't look like Clay's outburst had angered him. He just looked sad.

"Do you know what the most helpless feeling in the world is?" Dad asked.

Yeah, Clay had a pretty good idea about that. Helpless was being pushed through a public airport in a wheelchair. It was needing to be helped with something as simple as putting his backpack on his back. It was having his baby sister wrangle his luggage. Helpless was dragging his carcass up a simple flight of stairs.

His dad leaned against the wall next to the bathroom door as if he were tired. "The most helpless feeling in the world is when you get a call from the Army, and they use the words, wounded, your son, and critical condition all in the same conversation. Your mother cried so hard I thought she was going to be sick. She cried more than she did over Amelia."

Amelia was the baby sister who had been born and died on the same day, back when Clay was nine and Brooke barely three. He knew that his parents had experienced some fertility issues, which was why there were more than six years in age between him and Brooke. Amelia had been an unexpected but joyous surprise, but some last-minute complications had resulted in her living only a few hours, and his parents had been devastated. Clay had never even seen her. She was like a phantom sister to him. It was hard to grieve over a baby sister he'd never seen. He had grieved more for his parent's anguish over the loss.

His parents had come home from the hospital and almost never mentioned Amelia's brief existence. He realized later that it was just too painful for them. There had been a funeral, but his parents and grandparents had been the only mourners present. Clay and Brooke had been deemed too young to attend.

There was a photo, taken by a nurse at the hospital while his mother was still under the anesthesia following the emergency C-section, that his parents had finally shown him, for some reason, on the day of his confirmation, perhaps feeling that on that day, similar to a Jewish boy's bar mitzvah, that he was now a man. A tiny pale infant, eyes closed, with a small tuft of dark hair on her head. Other than the fact that his mother had cried on a regular basis for a long time reminded Clay that Amelia had ever existed at all.

He needed to get out of this hallway and into the privacy of the bathroom. He hated having anyone, even his father, see him on crutches, and they chafed his armpits.

"Too much too soon?" Dad guessed, waving a hand towards the back yard that encompassed the welcoming committee and party.

Clay could only nod, his throat thick. "Yeah, kinda," he managed to choke out.

"I'm sorry, Clay. I'm so sorry. This was all my fault." His father's eyes were – no they couldn't be – wet with tears.

No, no. This couldn't be happening. This was his father, Dad, his rock. Dads didn't cry or even get misty-eyed.

"I should never have suggested you talk to that Army recruiter," Dad admitted. "But you seemed so lost after you graduated from high school. I know college wasn't the right path for you, but those jobs you had for that first year seemed so petty. I knew you had more in you than that, it just needed an avenue to make itself felt. I thought with your athleticism and your strength, that the military might be a good fit. I'm so sorry, Clay. If I'd known it was going to end up like this, I never would have suggested looking into it."

"Dad, you couldn't know," he protested. "Nobody could. And nobody forced me to enlist. I mean, yeah, you suggested talking to the recruiter, but I made the final decision. I know if I had decided not to enlist, you wouldn't have pushed it."

Now he felt doubly like shit, for somehow making his father feel that he was to blame for the loss of Clay's leg. He shouldn't have come home, shouldn't have imposed himself on them. All he'd done was make them cry and feel guilty. He should have stayed in Germany, or gone – where? Somewhere where his family didn't have to look at him with pity, guilt and revulsion.

Dad wiped his eyes. "I'm surprised we didn't see Julie here today," he said. "You told her you were coming home today, didn't you?"

"No, Dad. Julie and I broke up." Saying those words hurt like hell.

His dad looked sincerely shocked. "You never said anything. What happened? I thought you two were going to –" He stopped, seeing the look of heartbreak on Clay's face as he imagined his father finishing his thought.

I thought you two were going to get engaged.

"Are you saying she broke up with you? While you were deployed? I find that so hard to believe. Your Julie – I really didn't think she was the kind of girl to give up on a guy while he was deployed. I thought Julie was stronger than that. I can't believe she would dump you because of your injury."

Injury. That sounded so inconsequential. Like a sprained ankle that he would recover from.

That was just the problem. Julie wouldn't have broken up with him because of his amputation. She would have stuck with him through good and bad until he dragged her down into the black abyss that was his life now, and he loved her too much to let her do that. Dad just didn't get it.

"It wasn't like that, Dad. She didn't break up with me."

"I'm so shocked," his dad replied. "What could that lovely young lady do to make you want to break up with her?"

She didn't do anything. He really didn't want to have to enunciate, to his father or to anyone else, that he'd cruelly dumped Julie, the love of his life, because he couldn't bear the thought of her spending her life with a cripple, stuck with him due to pity and obligation.

"Do you mind, Dad? I really don't want to talk about it."

Dad put a hand on Clay's shoulder. "All right, son, if that's how you feel. But if you do need any help, you know your mother and I are always here for you. You know we wanted to come to Germany when you were airlifted there. I practically had to tie Brooke to her bed to keep her from stealing my credit card and dashing off to the airport to hop on the next flight to Frankfurt. I'm sure I saw her Googling the German translation for, where do I get the train to Landstuhl."

Clay had been driven the eighty miles from Landstuhl Regional Medical Center to the airport in Frankfurt in a van owned and operated by the Red Cross. The scenery between the hospital and the airport was allegedly beautiful, but he hadn't paid attention to any of it.

"That would have cost you guys a fortune," he told his dad, but his voice was weak.

"It didn't matter. We just wanted to see you."

"I know, Dad, and I'm sorry I made you stay away. But I just couldn't handle you guys seeing me in the hospital."

Clay had insisted that his family not travel to see him. He'd used the excuse that he didn't want them to bear the burden of the cost of the trip, but in reality, it had been because he couldn't bear for them to see him in a hospital bed with a flattened blanket on one side. Sometimes he thought, if he didn't peek under that blanket, he could pretend the leg was still there. Nope. No amount of denial or wishful thinking was going to change his reality. The first time he'd seen the amputated limb, looking like it had been chopped off with an ax and beaten with a bat, a pain had ignited there and traveled to his brain like a bullet, until he had to restrain himself from screaming with both his mental and physical anguish.

He'd hated being forced to walk around the ward on crutches, having everyone look at him, with his stump showing. The first time he'd put weight on the prosthesis had hurt like hell. It made him want to give up then and there.

To have his parents and sister see him like that – he would have dissolved into a pathetic puddle of gelatinous sorrow. It would have killed him to see the revulsion that was sure to cross their faces as he struggled on the parallel bars he'd been forced to lean on while learning to walk with the prosthesis. Those bars looked very much like gymnastic parallel bars, but neither Clay nor any of the other patients were throwing a gymnastic routine on them. He'd hung on them, an arm draped over each bar, struggling to move his legs in a walking motion like a real live boy. Even his good leg, the one made of flesh and bone, had hesitated to perform. He'd rather die than have his family see him like that. While at Landstuhl, he'd spoken to them only by phone, declining to even use Skype. He spent most of the phone calls struggling not to cry.

He didn't want visitors. No doubt they meant well, but he was in no mood for tea and cakes with a dollop of pity on the side. He'd felt alone and scared, but he still told them to say home.

His parents had been called from the field hospital in Afghanistan but he hadn't been able to talk to them then, due to being unconscious for two days, by which time he was at Landstuhl. They had all put on a brave face – or rather, a brave voice – during their conversations, but Clay was perfectly aware that it was all an act, at least on his part, and he was pretty sure his parents knew it too.

They'd been upset and hurt when he finagled it to stay in Germany rather than transferring to Walter Reed, where they could have easily visited him, and when he insisted they not come to see him at Landstuhl.

"I'm sorry I made you stay away," he told his father. "But I wanted to wait until I could walk on my own."

It would have devastated him beyond endurance for them to see him in that hospital bed, in the wheelchair, standing on crutches with an empty pants leg pinned up so it didn't flap around. And yet here he stood with his father, on crutches with the left side of his oversized bathrobe obviously empty for all to see.

His two Army comrades had called him, but he hadn't taken their calls. He was afraid they'd want to talk about Sergeant Lopez, who had been in the seat in front of Clay, driving the Humvee at the time of Kaboom. Lopez had died in that seat.

He should be grateful to be alive, but somehow he wasn't. He knew it was selfish, but he couldn't help but think that maybe Lopez had been the lucky one. For him, there was no pain, no rehab, no learning how to live disabled. There was only resting in peace.

Clay had earned the respect of his platoon mates because he shot at Expert level, and despite not being the tallest guy in the group, outran pretty much everyone. They wouldn't respect him if they could see him now. So he didn't call or text or email or Skype any of them.

It was bad enough for his family and childhood friends to see him now with the cane, knowing what was under his pants leg to necessitate its use. They could cover it with a flesh-colored stocking, put on a shoe and a sock that might fool some people for a minute, but it was still a fake leg.

He could have requested to be sent back to the States sooner, to do his rehab at Walter Reed. But he had practically begged to stay at Landstuhl until his prosthesis was fitted, so that none of them would see him in recovery or rehab. Maybe his stubborn pride was stupid and immature, but he had no control over his emotions anymore, and having his parents or

Brooke or worst of all, Julie, see him like that would have killed him.

A convenient backlog at Walter Reed had allowed him to stay and do his rehab at LRMC. He'd gotten so agitated at the prospect of his parents and sister showing up, to see him incomplete, that his LNCO – the Liaison Non-Commissioned Officer, a sergeant who coordinated his care - had reluctantly suggested that his family not travel to Germany just yet. That temporary delay had morphed into a continuous delay until finally they had resigned themselves to waiting until Clay was ready to come home, a journey he delayed as long as he could get away with. Somehow, stupidly, he'd thought if they didn't see him until he was upright on his own two feet, or in reality his own one foot, that they could all pretend that nothing had changed.

He was an idiot. Everything had changed. He scarcely thought of himself as a man anymore, not a proper man, but only the partial thing he had become.

His father so obviously wanted to help him, do anything he could. There was one thing.

"Dad, could you get me a bottle of water?" He'd forgotten to bring one upstairs with him, and there was no way he was going to make the trek down to the kitchen and back up, especially now that he'd removed his prosthesis. He'd rather die of dehydration.

"Sure!" Dad's eagerness at being able to do something helpful for him was painful to see. "I'll leave it in your room for you, OK?"

Clay nodded, mustered an ungracious thanks to his dad, slipped into the bathroom as his dad trotted easily down the stairs to fetch the water, and made sure to lock the bathroom door firmly behind him.

He had grown up in this house, so he knew it would take a full minute for the shower water to heat up to a comfortable temperature, so he just stuck his hand in behind the shower curtain and turned the knob.

He looked at the toilet. God, even using that was going to be a project. Finally he sighed, turned around, sat down, tucked it in, and peed like a girl. Even that movement was painful. Was this how the rest of his life was going to be, having to plan every maneuver, every common task, as if it were the opening ceremony of the Olympics?

He'd figured out how to get into the tub one-legged. He sat on the edge of the tub, swiveled and lifted his right leg into the tub, pushing open the shower curtain to get in. It was a good thing the shower had a curtain rather than a sliding glass door. He wouldn't be able to sit and pivot on the sharp frame edge of a shower door.

When he pushed the shower curtain back, his heart plummeted. They had installed a grab bar. A fucking metal bar for a cripple to hold onto. To make it even worse, there was a shower seat in the tub like a ninety-year-old would use.

Brooke used this bathroom too. Her toothbrush was propped in a plastic glass next to her lumpy toothpaste tube. She squeezed from the top. Her girly stuff crowded out his things in the medicine cabinet. The last time he'd been home on leave, he'd had to put his deodorant on the edge of the sink because her cosmetics took up all the rest of the space. She surely had to have seen the modifications to the bathroom to accommodate his disability. His complete and utter mortification almost made him cry. Surely his humiliation had been complete when Brooke had been the one to wrangle his luggage. Now he might as well have burned his man card to ash.

He had always been the big brother, she his baby sister. He'd wanted to be her hero, the guy who protected her from bullies and watched over her, though he'd tried to feign disinterest because looking after a little sister wasn't considered cool. But he'd always taken his responsibilities as a big brother very seriously. He would be willing to kill or die to keep her safe. Her security had been one of his reasons for putting his name onto that enlistment contract.

Now, he couldn't protect her from anything. He couldn't even bathe himself without special accommodation. It killed him that he actually used that grab bar and that shower seat.

At least he could shave and brush his teeth without too much problem. He leaned his hips against the sink and was able to use both hands, but he didn't let the crutches get far. He'd need them to get back to his room.

He should have recognized the face in the mirror as his. Physically it was the same face as before. But he wasn't the same person as last time he'd been in this house, looking into this mirror. It was a different, not him Clay looking back at him, a person he barely recognized, with dark circles under his eyes and frown lines on his forehead. A definite downgrade from who he'd been before. It was a person he didn't like at all, but a person he was stuck with, thanks to Kaboom. He was powerless. Useless. Lost.

Back in the safety of his room, he dropped onto his bed, feeling exhausted. It was the bed upon which he'd had sex for the first time. And the second time. And the last time. Which had been the same time as the second time. He'd driven almost to the Wisconsin border to buy the condoms, not so much that he feared detection, but more that if any of his friends saw him, they'd laugh their heads off at him for being such a late bloomer.

Thinking about Julie only added to his pain, like stabbing a knife into his heart. He'd loved her, his Viking Princess, since high school. They'd both been so nervous, and yet eager and frankly, horny at the same time. And yet, thanks to Kaboom, she was no longer a part of his life in any way, shape or form. Even when he closed his eyes, he could see the concise email he'd sent her imprinted on the insides of his eyelids.

Julie, it's over between us. No explanation, no reason, no apology. He hadn't even included his name at the end. She could tell it was from him from the email address. He wondered what she'd thought, how she'd felt, upon reading it. Whatever her reaction, it had to be less awful than how she'd react were she to see him now. When his parents had called him in the hospital in Germany, they had offered to contact Julie, to tell her what had happened to him. He'd refused the offer, panicked, and insisted they not call her. "I'll take care of it," he'd promised them, not revealing that he had already sent her that cruel, brief email breaking off their relationship. He would literally die if he heard her voice, her tears, her sympathy, on the phone. His parents apparently believed him when he said he'd contact Julie and didn't mention the subject again.

He massaged the stump and checked it for skin issues, the way he'd been taught in the hospital, before applying a clean shrinker sock. He'd been reluctant to watch when they measured his stump – residual limb – in preparation for creating the prosthesis, but had no choice but to pay attention to the proper application of the shrinker socks he would wear under the cuff for about the next year.

It had to be tight, smooth and tapered or the limb would get torn up. They had made him practice it, doing it over and over until it was the right tightness to ensure a proper fit for his prosthesis, and as much as he loathed the whole process, he was good at applying the sock.

He was going to be like this forever, and he hated it. Each time he realized it, it was like being struck by lightning, over and over. Kaboom kept happening in his mind, unwilling to let him forget. The prosthesis wasn't like a cast that would be sawed off at a later date. His condition was frustratingly permanent.

Why did they insist on using those stupid technical terms? Edema. Residual limb. Why couldn't they just say it like it was?

Edema sounded like an exotic tropical disease. It was swelling. And residual limb? Who were they kidding? It was a stump.

He picked up the prosthesis, pulled off the sock and shoe from the artificial foot, and stared at it for a long time. There had been a freckle on the top of his left big toe, when he'd had a left big toe, a left foot, a left leg. It was gone now, along with the rest of the limb. Stupid of him to mourn the loss of something as small as a freckle. But that bit of pigmentation had been a part of him that wasn't there anymore. Instead of a real left foot, his prosthesis bore a vaguely foot-shaped metal appendage with mere hints of toe separations.

There was a window next to his bed, that looked out over the front yard. He restrained himself from using the prosthesis to break the glass and throw it out like a javelin. Instead, he dropped it on the floor next to his bed and lay back with an arm over his eyes.

That was when his brain started to do the one thing he wanted least to do – think – as he began imagining conversations he didn't want to have.

"Hey Clay, I heard you took the fight to the enemy," the voice in his head said.

"Hey Clay, I heard you were sent to Afghanistan."

"Hey Clay, I heard you got blown up." Why would it not shut up?

"Hey Clay, I heard your leg got blown off like a Fourth of July firecracker."

"Hey Clay, I heard you're a useless cripple now."

He ground the heels of his hands against his eyeballs until he felt they'd pop out of their sockets, but it didn't quiet those imaginary conversations.

"Hey Clay, I heard you got your buddy killed."

He gulped back a sound that was part sob, part scream, dug into the bottom of his backpack for the bottle of pills lying on top of the flat presentation box containing his Purple Heart, and read the instructions on the label.

Take one by mouth as needed, not to exceed four pills per day.

Four pills? What would happen if he took six of them at once, or eight or ten or the whole bottle? It was almost full. The prescription had been refilled just yesterday.

It would be so easy. A handful of pills. One bottle of water. A few seconds and they could be down his throat.

Would death come instantly, like the sudden slamming of a door? Or would he slowly drift off into a sweet oblivious sleep of release, his brain synapses shutting down one by one?

What would his parents think when they found him? Or, please God no, what if Brooke was the first person to come across him, stiff with rigor mortis, with that little orange pill canister laying empty on the floor next to his bed? Would she scream? Would he be able to hear it from Purgatory? Would they cry over him, or had they cried over him enough already?

Clay opened the bottle – foolishly they had given him a non-childproof cap – and poured the white capsules into his hand. There were probably thirty of them. He rolled them back and forth in his palm, both tempted and repulsed by the forgetfulness they could bring him, and stared at them for a really long time.

His pain would end, but his family's pain would be just beginning. His father already felt guilty, somehow responsible for what had happened to Clay. Dad would blame himself even more if he realized that he had been an unwitting accomplice to an awful deed, having provided the bottle of water to aid in the ingestion of those narcotics.

He tried to breathe, to think, to focus. Do it. Take the coward's way out. Don't do it. Be a man. Make a decision. His hand holding those powerful little pills was sweaty.

It was either a really stupid, or a really courageous decision. But he poured the pills back into the container, leaving only one in his hand, and set the pill bottle onto the nightstand to pick up the bottle of water his father had left there for him. He popped that one, safe pill into his mouth. It stuck a little in his throat even though he washed it down with a huge slug of water.

Come on, you little chemical wonder. Work your magic.

After setting the water bottle back on the nightstand, he returned the cap to the pill bottle and re-buried it into his backpack, next to the hated Purple Heart box, where he wouldn't have to see it or think about it or be tempted by it at least until morning. For good measure he tossed the backpack to the bottom of his bed and nudged it onto the floor with his foot, so that he would be unable to reach it without crawling out of bed.

He thought about his mother, his father, Brooke, Julie. *I love you*, he said silently to each of them, and that was what had inspired him to pour those painkillers back into the bottle.

It didn't take long for the medication to travel through his bloodstream to produce numbness, and that was exactly what he wanted. The Vicodin prevented him from waking up screaming, but it didn't stop him from dreaming.

It sucked that he had dreams about being normal and two-legged, doing normal stuff like running and swimming, climbing stairs, doing his job, all without a limp or a cane. And it sucked even more that he remembered those dreams.

Clay loved swimming. If he'd had time for two sports in high school, he would have been on the swim team too. But now he was certain that if he got into a pool, he'd only be able to twirl around in circles, like a boat with only one oar.

The dreams he had would give Freud the creeps. He didn't know which ones were worse – the dreams about Julie, who he couldn't have, the dreams about running, which he couldn't do anymore, or the dreams about his Army basic training classes on learning to disassemble, clean and re-assemble his weapon.

The group of them reciting, "This is my weapon, this is my gun. One is for shooting; the other is for fun." The drill instructors got really mad at any recruit who made the mistake of referring to his weapon as a gun. The DI's yelled – because it was apparently physically impossible for them to speak like normal people – that their gun resided between their legs. Their M16A2 was a weapon. The recruits in their turn were always surprised that the DIs didn't all blow out their vocal cords by day two.

As horrible as that dream was, at least tonight he didn't dream about Kaboom.

Chapter Three

Clay woke up in the morning to the sound of tapping on his door and his mother's voice calling his name. So she would have been the one to find him, if he'd done the stupid, easy thing last night. Mom, though usually cool, calm and collected, could scream really loud when startled or frightened. How loud would she scream in trauma if she'd had to see him lying here dead? He didn't even want to imagine it.

"Clay? Are you decent?" she asked through the door.

Decent? No, he wasn't decent. He'd never be decent again in his life. But his mother most likely meant, was his body covered sufficiently for her to come into his room. He was wearing a tee shirt and boxers, and the blanket covered his leg and stump. His prosthesis was still on the floor next to his bed, and while he wished he'd thought to have covered it up, maybe his mom would ignore it.

He struggled to pull himself to a sitting position. It was difficult with only one heel to push against the mattress. The phantom pain he'd experienced yesterday on the airplane assaulted his non-existent leg again, as if to taunt him as he struggled to drag himself up by his thigh muscles, and he bit his teeth against the foul language he knew his mother disapproved of.

She had some kind of mysterious mom-power that enabled her to open the door while carrying a tray at the same time.

"I brought you some breakfast," she said unnecessarily as she set the tray on his lap. "Now, don't go expecting this every day, sweetie."

"Mom, you didn't have to bring me breakfast in bed. You shouldn't have."

Although he sincerely appreciated her kindness, and the food looked and smelled delicious, it kind of made him feel even more invalid-like to have his mother bringing him food on a tray, carrying it upstairs to his room.

"Well, it is my day off," she reminded him. His mom was a hairstylist with her own salon in nearby Prospect Heights. Mondays were her slow days so she usually took that day off and worked on Saturday.

"Your dad had meetings today and had to go to the office, but he'll be home tomorrow. Brooke might be able to stay home from school a day or two but this close to the end of the school year, she also needs to be thinking about final exams coming up soon."

His father was the president of a janitorial services company with its offices in downtown Chicago. They cleaned half the office space in the Loop.

This was awful. His family was coordinating days off so somebody would always be around to supervise the helpless member of the family. Himself.

"You guys don't have to stay home with me," he said. "I'll be fine." That last statement was a total lie because he wasn't fine and would never be fine again. Did his mother have any inkling of his temptation over a bottle of pain pills last night? Did she think he needed around-the-clock supervision?

"Here, your dad and I got this for you." His mom set the tray on his lap, tactfully ignoring both the prosthesis on the floor and the lack of lumpiness under his blanket, and handed him the bag that had been hanging from her wrist.

There was a box inside the bag, small but heavy. "What's this?" he asked.

"Open it," Mom said with a smile.

When he followed her instruction, he discovered it was a smartphone. In fact, it was the latest, greatest, most expensive smartphone he knew of. He'd had a phone, an older model ready for an upgrade, before he'd left for basic training, but he'd sold that too and put what little he'd gotten for it into the Ring Fund.

"Thank you, Mom," he said, touched. This expensive phone was way more than he'd expected. "You didn't have to do that."

Mom ignored his protest. "We've already entered all our numbers into the contacts and the home phone too."

While Clay's parents were pretty current with modern technology, they still maintained a landline phone in the house, but there wasn't an extension for it in Clay's room. Which was probably why they'd gotten him this phone, so he'd have some contact with the outside world rather than hiding here forever like a leper. Little did they know, that was exactly his plan.

"Brooke says you can sync it so that you have access to your music."

His music. God. His music.

Musically, Clay had been born in the wrong generation. His friends all thought he was demented, to be as obsessed as he was about classic rock. He'd never let anyone's opinion sway him. They told him it was stupid to prefer music that had mostly been created before he was born. He ignored them. As far as Clay was concerned, no decent music had been written since 1990. Except for Adele, of course. He'd always had a continual soundtrack running in his head, with songs from Bon Jovi, Hall and Oates, Journey and others constantly popping into his brain. But the music had been silenced since Kaboom.

His friends had made fun of him for his musical passion, but when they went to the karaoke bar, he ruled. They stopped teasing and they listened, because he could sing. He was the karaoke king.

He had neither sung nor listed to a note since Kaboom.

"For goodness sake, Clay, it's like a vampire cave in here," his mom complained. She crossed to the window, pushed open the curtains, and let in copious amounts of bright, cruel sunshine. She even opened the window, and he could hear sounds coming in. Birds chirping, a car driving by, the swish of breeze in the trees. All the normal sounds of suburban living.

He hated those sounds.

Mom walked out of the room, and he thought she'd left him to his misery, but she was back in two minutes with a laundry basket, and to his horror, reached down and unzipped the duffel bag that Brooke had carried upstairs and set next to the wall.

"I should have just told Brooke to leave this in the laundry room," she said.

"Wait!" he yelped. "I'll do that. You don't need to unpack for me."

"It's OK, Clay," Mom soothed. "I'm sure you want your stuff washed before it gets stinky. I don't mind throwing it in."

"No," he pleaded. Jeez, the way he was trying to prevent his mom from unpacking for him, she probably thought he had porn in his bag. But he hated the thought of her going through his stuff, asking questions. "I'll unpack it." He couldn't help but let a childish wheedling tone creep into his voice.

"OK, sweetie," his mom finally relented. "I'll leave the laundry basket and come back for it later when you've unpacked."

She left the laundry basket on the floor, came over and sat next to him on the bed. He tried to discreetly scoot away so that she wouldn't accidentally brush against his stump, even though it was hidden beneath the blanket. It wasn't because it might cause him pain to have it bumped, but because he was certain it would gross his mother out to have contact with it.

She put her arms around his shoulders and gave him a tight hug, like she had yesterday at the airport.

"Oh, Clay, my poor little boy. I'm so sorry about all of this. I'm so sorry about what has happened to you. I wish I could make it all go away."

He sat stiffly, refusing to return her hug, even though he really wanted to. There was a time when a hug from his mother could fix anything that was wrong in his life. Too bad it didn't work that way anymore. He just sat there like a rock, not responding, using all his strength to keep from crying.

When she released him, she looked at the tray of breakfast she'd brought him.

"Clay, you've hardly eaten anything."

Of course he hadn't eaten. A nibble of toast and a sip of coffee had been the limit of his tolerance. "Sorry, Mom," he mumbled. "It was nice of you to make this, but I'm just not hungry."

She picked up the tray and looked sadly at the wasted breakfast. "You need to keep up your strength," she admonished.

Why, he wondered. For what purpose did he need to keep up his strength?

When he didn't answer, she mercifully left and took the tray with her, but with a quizzical look that wondered what normal young man would object so strenuously to having someone else take care of his dirty laundry for him.

When she was gone, he used his cane to hook the handle of his duffel bag and pull it towards him. The first thing on top that he pulled out was the hefty envelope stuffed with his discharge papers and medical records. Its solid weight just confirmed that all that he was now was a discharged former soldier and a medical case, and those two sad conditions generated a lot of paperwork. He tossed the package on the floor and it slid across the carpet to stop in front of his dresser. When he got out of bed – if he got out of bed – he'd bury it in a drawer.

It wasn't his fear of revolting his mother with any stinky, dirty laundry that made him refuse to allow her to unpack for him. It was the fear of her wanting to look at those files he'd been sent home with, of having her read the pitiful documents that separated him from the Army. Fear of having to see her pain and disgust if she were to read the details of his amputation, his surgery, his prognosis, his pitiful mental state.

It took some painful leaning and stretching, but he was able to retrieve his bottle of pain pills from his backpack and take another one. The one from last night had long since worn off. Hopefully it would be safe to leave them in the drawer of the nightstand next to his bed. He briefly considered giving the bottle to his mother and asking her to dispense them for him. But that would only reinforce her belief that he had to be supervised, taken care of, prevented him from hurting himself, and then he would never, ever have another moment's privacy in his entire life. It would be worse than basic training where they literally had to go to the bathroom in a public men's room with no private stalls even for the most personal needs. He could regulate his medication himself.

With his mother gone, he scooted across the bed to reach the window she'd opened, and closed the curtains with a firm swish, symbolically defeating that normal happy sun.

He hated the sunshine. It was way too normal and happy. He preferred the vampire cave analogy his mother had used. Dark and depressing. That suited him way more than sunshiny and bright. He lay back and wondered what he was going to do for the rest of the day. Or the rest of his life. If he wasn't even qualified to be a Walmart door greeter, what else was left?

He hoped and prayed that his mother would leave him alone while he pulled the dirty clothes out of the duffel and tossed them in the direction of the laundry basket she'd left on the floor. He dragged himself out of his bed with the hated crutches only long enough to shove the partially unpacked duffel bag into his closet, and to bury the package of paper-work in his dresser drawer under some clean clothes, where hopefully it would stay hidden forever so that he could forget it existed.

He was safely back in the security of his bed when he heard his mother's footsteps outside the door, and he quickly laid down and pretended to be asleep. It had worked at deflecting the girls sitting in his row on the airplane. She came in and he could sense her looking at him, but he still lay there trying to fool her into thinking he didn't know she was there. Finally he heard her sigh and heard the plastic creak of the laundry basket as she took it out of the room. He ought to thank her for doing his laundry, when he'd done it himself for years, but then she'd know he was awake and she might want to talk to him. So he kept up his pretense of being comatose, which he was sure didn't fool her for a second.

Don't push him if he's not ready. The doctors and his LNCO had talked to his family on the phone before he returned home, and he was aware of what they'd been told. *Don't push him to tell you about what happened. Don't push him about his plans for the future, or even for tomorrow. Give him time to process, to grieve, to heal. Wait for him to be ready to talk.*

His parents were in for an infinitely long wait.

It was amazing how exhausting it was to lay around doing nothing. By midafternoon the morning sunshine had been re-placed with clouds, dark clouds called reality, and it started to rain.

He scooted over to the edge of the bed to close the window and for a few minutes sat watching the rainfall. It was like his soul – dripping, chilly and wet. He used to like running in the rain. Some of his track teammates had whined about the rain is if they would melt if they got wet. Not Clay. He'd enjoyed the feel of cool raindrops on his skin, the splashing sound of his shoes when he crossed a puddle, the screeches of the guys he shook water on. Now all he'd be able to do in the rain would be to sit in one of those puddles and splash around until he was a filthy mess, as he'd done when he was six years old. His mother had scolded him then for getting his clothes all dirty and making more laundry for her. He doubted she'd complain now.

The lack of structure paralyzed him. After four years of being told when to wake up, when to eat, when to work and how to train, he now found the alleged "freedom" from those restraints impossible to process. He'd been part of a squad, part of a platoon, part of a company, battalion, brigade and division. Now he was alone. Now he was just a civilian.

He missed the structure, the sense of purpose, the satisfaction of being part of something bigger than himself. He missed his cammies. He missed his army comrades, despite having dissed them since Kaboom.

The inactivity gave him way too much time to think.

He lay in his bed all day, barely squeezing up the energy to hobble across the hall to the bathroom. He was just settling in for nap number three when he heard his mother's voice floating up from the bottom of the stairs.

"Clay! Time for dinner."

As soon as the words entered his consciousness, he could smell pork chops. His mouth watered and he almost got up to jump down the stairs to the dining room, until his ambulatory-challenged status crashed upon him.

"Not hungry, Mom," he yelled back, not even certain if his words, which were a lie, carried all the way down.

After a minute of silence, Mom's voice sounded again.

"Clay! Dinner!"

He didn't respond. Hadn't she heard him the first time? He was trying to ignore his belly, which was reminding him, *food*, when Mom opened his door with a determined crack.

"Clayton John Maslowski!"

He barely had a chance to yank the blanket over his pathetic remains.

"Did I ask you if you wanted to join us for dinner? I did not. I'm *telling* you, get dressed and come eat!"

There were two people in the world he didn't dare disobey. A drill sergeant who barked the order to drop and give him twenty, and his mother when she used his full name.

"Fine!" he grunted. "Just give me a sec, OK?"

"All right," she agreed. "But don't make me come back here and drag you down."

It took him so long to attach the prosthesis, pull on a tee shirt and some sweat pants, which slid easier over the prosthesis than slacks or jeans, and hobble carefully down the stairs, that he was afraid she would resort to coming back and dragging him down, but he managed to present himself at the dining room table before Mom's patience wore out.

They were all seated at the table waiting for him. His mother had rearranged the dining room chairs, because the one left for him to use had arms. He reached behind himself to grasp it for stability as he sat, stepping back with his fake leg to unlock the titanium knee. His parents and sister stared at him. His dad took hold of his arm to help, but Clay didn't say thank you.

Mom made them say grace holding hands, as she always had. In addition to thanking God for the food they were about to eat, she also thanked Him for Clay's safe return. Clay himself wasn't so grateful.

It was so normal, so homey, so familiar. His mother saying grace, then giving his father the stink eye when he tried to put too much gravy on his potatoes. Dad twitched a bit but obediently surrendered the gravy ladle and passed the dish to Brooke. Brooke, in turn, took the minimum amount of green beans she could get away with. Sitting there in their dining room, seeing his family only from the waist up, almost made him forget, just for a second, about the stump lurking beneath the table. But that feeling of normalcy was quickly dissipated whenever he moved.

He could tell they were curious, wanted to know everything, but were afraid to ask, and he was afraid to tell them. Instead they just talked about trivial things. Or more accurately, his parents and Brooke talked. Clay just pushed food around on his plate and hoped they were fooled into thinking he was eating. The meal that had smelled so good a few minutes ago had lost its appeal now that it sat in front of him.

It was almost possible, here with his family, to forget about his pain and anxiety, to feel almost normal, listening to Brooke talk about school, his mom and dad talking about work. But he still picked at his food without enthusiasm, until his mother admonished him for not eating when she'd made what she'd always thought was his favorite. He hoped she wouldn't give him a direct order to eat the way they'd done in the hospital. While Clay's mom was the sweetest, most loving person he could think of, there were times when she could put a basic training drill instructor to shame.

She wasn't wrong. The food she had prepared was one of his favorite meals, but he had gotten into the habit of disinterest in food since Kaboom, and it was a hard habit to break.

He heard a sound – it wasn't supposed to be there. His mother and Brooke were talking, making it hard for him to identify the noise. Something inane, Brooke mentioning something that had happened at school. But that sound...

"Shush!" he snapped, holding up one fist in a "stop" gesture. If only he'd thought to employ the "stop and shut up" gesture a few minutes, or seconds, before Kaboom. The three of them stared at him.

"What is it, Clay?" his mother asked.

"What's that?" He turned an ear towards the window. What was that sound? *It wasn't supposed to be there.*

"That is Dean O'Reilly's muffler," his dad said. "It's been roaring for a week. If he doesn't get that fixed, he's going to wake up every baby in the neighborhood."

"No, it's – shh, let me listen!" Clay insisted, feeling panic sweep through him. But his dad was right. It was just the neighbor's loud car. It wasn't an incoming RPG or gunfire or even the engine of a Humvee. Just a car on an ordinary suburban street, and he had made his family stop their dinner and stare at him as if he were insane. Smart one, Clay.

He was pale and sweaty. "It's just a loud car," Brooke said. "Jeez, Clay, get a grip."

"May I be excused," he mumbled in his mother's direction, as if he were a pouty twelve-year-old.

"But Clay, you've hardly eaten anything." His food rearranging hadn't fooled her this evening any more than it did when she'd brought him breakfast. He looked down at that meal, something he'd wolfed down a few months ago. Now it made him feel sick.

Mom made no further protest as he leaned forward in his chair, pressing his fake toes against the floor and using his butt muscles to press back, making sure his fake knee was locked and his legs were together, as he got up and limped out of the dining room.

Out of the corner of his eye he caught the movement of his dad starting to get up also. Mom put a hand on Dad's arm, shook her head slightly, and said, "Give him time, Lloyd."

No. Don't give him time. Or consideration or sympathy or help or love. He didn't deserve them.

In the living room, out of his family's view, he had to stop and, as Brooke put it, get a grip. He hurt all over, both inside and out. He wanted to be numbed into a protective cocoon that would shelter him from the world. Numbness was what he craved. He hated feeling. Feeling hurt. He wanted to not feel, to not care, to stay numb.

But numbness eluded him. He still felt, both physically and emotionally. Right now he felt weak, and sat down on the nearest seat, the bench of the piano upon which he and Brooke had both taken lessons in their childhood. If he opened the lid of the bench, would he find the Greatest Hits of the 80's for Piano still there? There were photos on top of the piano, familiar family pictures that had been there for years. Brooke's First Communion, his high school graduation. The photo the Army had taken of him on his first day of basic training, standing stiff and proud in his first uniform.

He reached up and picked up one of those photos, staring at it as if he'd never seen it before, though it had sat in this spot for almost five years. It was a photo his mother had taken and had printed, of him and Julie the evening of their senior prom, him wearing a rented tux, white with a blue cummerbund to match Julie's dress. His jaw had dropped and his mouth gone dry when he'd first seen her in it, with its low neckline and thigh-high side slit. He'd been almost afraid to take her to the dance, for fear that every other guy there would try to steal her away from him.

In the photo, the two of them were smiling in a way they hadn't since that night. He looked so happy in that photo; he almost didn't recognize himself.

Suddenly, he wanted to sweep all those photos off the piano top, knock them to the floor. Smash that glass in the frames under his feet until the shards made him bleed. Those weren't photos of him, the person he was now. They depicted a man who didn't exist anymore.

But even if he did that, stomped on the shards of broken glass, he would bleed only from one foot. Titanium didn't bleed.

Maybe the frame slipped out of his hands. Maybe he threw it on the floor. He couldn't tell, but the next thing he knew, the glass was shattered at his feet, the frame broken. He fought back the tears that threatened to erupt from his throat.

The noise of the breaking glass brought his mother running in from the kitchen.

"Clay, are you OK?" she gasped.

"Yeah, Mom. I dropped the picture frame. I'm sorry."

"Don't worry, sweetie. I'll sweep it up. You didn't cut yourself, did you?"

He shook his head miserably, wondering if he'd feel it if he were to pick up one of those shards of glass and squeeze it in his fist.

He ought to offer to clean up his own mess, but he was too fucking disabled to wield the broom and dustpan. All he could do was apologize again.

He had to get away from those photos, those pictures of the former, disappeared person he'd once been. If he didn't, the rest of them would end up broken on the floor too. His mother was saying something and he had to force himself to listen. To hear her.

"I'll get a new frame for this tomorrow, and we'll put it back, good as new."

Nothing was ever going to be as good as new. Once, when he'd been eight or nine, he'd broken an antique cup and saucer his mother had proudly displayed. He'd been horsing round like he knew he wasn't supposed to indoors, and the cup had been knocked to the floor, shattering into way too many tiny shards to even consider gluing it back together. His mom had cried, after she'd yelled at him for his carelessness. That cup and saucer were one of the few mementos his mother had of her grandmother, who had managed to bring it with her when she'd fled Poland as a young girl, one step ahead of the Cossacks, according to family legend.

He'd felt so bad about the cup's destruction that he'd begged his grandfather to take him to the Wheeling Sale Barn to search for a replacement. He'd been dragged there once with his parents and had been bored senseless while they browsed the antique stalls. Despite his grandfather's warning that he would never find an exact replica of the shattered cup, still he'd taken Clay to the antique mall, where Clay had bought, with his allowance, birthday money and a loan from Grandpa, another dainty china teacup to give to his mother. Mom had thanked him sweetly, kissed him and called him a darling, and put the new cup in the same place where the one he'd broken had formally resided, anchored down with museum putty. But they all knew it wasn't a real replacement for the cherished family heirloom. It wasn't as good as new. Nothing ever was.

"No!" He spoke more sharply than he ought to his mother. None of this was her fault and she didn't deserve snot from him.

But still...

"Please. Just put it away." He turned his head away from the photograph his mom had retrieved from the wreckage of the frame and glass. Mom looked for a moment as if she was about to argue the point, but thankfully desisted.

"I'm going to go to bed. I'm sorry about the mess." He flapped a useless hand toward the broken glass and frame, and avoided looking at the happy smiling faces visible in the photo in his mother's hand.

He turned towards the stairs, hoping the effort of sweeping the mess up and, hopefully, hiding the prom photo in a drawer, would occupy his mother enough to prevent her from seeing him drag himself up the stairs.

But Julie and that stranger in the white tuxedo were still smiling.

"Clay, sweetie," his mother's voice came from behind him.

Clay had in fact suffered a slight hearing loss in his left ear as a result of Kaboom, but he still heard his mother calling to him. She was probably going to say something about how sorry she was about what had happened to him. How much she wished there was something she could do to help him. But there was of course no way of getting over this, nothing she or his father or anyone else could do to make a difference, and thanks to his new rude persona, he pretended he hadn't heard her, limped away and dragged himself up the stairs. Hiding away in his room was way more important than anything else right now.

Again he had to rest and catch his breath even before he got to the top of the stairs, sweating as if he'd done a full workout. There was a sound floating up, not the scary sound of a car muffler that he'd stupidly thought was some sort of danger. He cocked his right ear – his better ear – towards the sound, though he couldn't see anything from this spot other than the stairs he'd just climbed.

It was his mother. She was crying. He was certain her tears weren't over the picture frame he had broken. She was crying about him. Even though he'd been told they'd cried over him, hearing it made it all too real. What kind of shitty guy makes his mother cry? He heard his father come into the room, and could picture Dad putting a comforting arm around Mom's shoulder as she sobbed, "Oh, Lloyd!"

He hiked painfully up the remaining few steps, got into his room, and took his nightly pain pill to block out the sound of his mother crying.

That was about all the human interaction he could endure for today.

Chapter Four

Clay woke up the next morning with a raging hard-on.

"Down, boy," he said to the tent pole under his sheet, though it was heartening to know that even though he didn't have a left knee, the middle knee still functioned. Not that it mattered, now that he'd broken up with Julie. All that blood flow and nothing to use it on.

He'd dreamed about Julie almost nightly the whole time he'd been gone, including his time in the hospital. Since the day he'd left for basic training, he'd been determined, focused on being faithful, despite the temptations. Waking up with morning wood had been a familiar situation, with only one method of relieving the pressure, though he hated doing it.

But no matter how raging his hard-on was, he absolutely, positively was not going to jerk off here in his parent's home, in his childhood bed.

Instead, he tried to conjure up any mood-killing scenario he could imagine. But not even imagining being naked outside in January was any help, and that was saying a lot, considering the bitterness of a Chicago winter. But then he thought about Kaboom, the mental and emotional equivalent of a cold shower, and the hard-on deflating mission was accomplished.

Each day, somebody was at home - Mom or Dad or Brooke. Missing work or school to check up on him. His surly attitude and lack of interest in anything kept them from bothering him too much, but there was always someone nearby, wanting to help. His mother returned his laundry, clean and folded, but left the basket with him and let him put it away himself. She probably still thought he had porn stashed in his room somewhere. He didn't, but he also didn't enlighten her about it. One day she made him vacate his room long enough to change the sheets on his bed. Another task he'd done himself for years, but couldn't do anymore, when at basic training he'd made his bunk tight enough for the DI to bounce a quarter off it. The recruits who failed to make up their bunk tight enough to repel that quarter had their bunks stripped and they had to keep trying until they got it right.

Nobody even tried to bounce any coins off his bed now.

Each evening, they made him join the family for dinner. He showed up at the dinner table when called, because he'd learned that when it came to his mother's insistence on it, resistance was futile. He still couldn't eat much, so each evening he got scolded for it. Afterward, they always wanted to do something together, as a family. He always declined, even when his mother invited him to play cards with her and Dad while Brooke was upstairs, possibly doing homework, but more likely playing Minecraft.

"No thanks." By now they should be used to him refusing to join in on anything.

"Aw, Clay," his mother cajoled. "Give me the chance to make up for the way you trounced me at Texas Holdem the last time you were home on leave."

He enjoyed that game, or at least he had, before Kaboom. But he wasn't home on leave now. He was nowhere.

"Watch a movie then?" Dad suggested.

"I don't think so."

The next evening, his dad asked if he'd like to watch the Cubs game with him. He declined again, even though that was one of the things he'd missed the most while being gone on deployment. He'd been at infantry training at Fort Benning in

Georgia when the Cubs won the World Series, and he and his dad had celebrated the event over the phone.

As if he would ever again find enjoyment watching athletics of any kind. He couldn't even play ping pong, and he hated chess, which he knew Brooke was itching to teach him.

He knew what they were doing. Not leaving him alone. Making sure somebody was there to supervise the cripple, take care of him like an invalid, protect him from himself in case he decided to do something stupid to relieve the pain of his shattered body, his shattered soul.

He'd be lying to himself if he said he hadn't thought about it, in the first few weeks after Kaboom. His deterrent had been the knowledge of the pain and grief it would heap upon his family. Suicide, the chaplain in Germany had told him, doesn't end pain. It just transfers it to someone else.

Clay woke up the next morning with a plan.

I'll go out for a run.

He flipped the covers off, intending to grab a pair of shorts and run a few miles before breakfast.

Then he hit the floor with a thud. The pain shot up his legs, through his back, and into his head. He had completely forgotten, just for one idiotic moment, about his amputation. The four-letter word that exploded from his mouth was one that his mother would never tolerate. She didn't allow swearing in her presence, but it was a bad habit he'd picked up in the Army.

But if ever a situation called for an expletive, this was it. He'd been taught how to fall during rehab, because falling was inevitable, in a manner so as to minimize pain and damage, but this fall didn't happen the way he'd been taught. His world was pain. He was surprised he hadn't broken an arm or wrist.

They couldn't see him like this, not his mother or father or anyone else, on the floor, writhing in pain and as helpless as a turtle on its back. Luckily the house was quiet that morning and nobody came running to his room. Had they all finally left him alone? He tried to scoot his body back next to the bed, and the effort of it brought tears to his eyes. Suddenly the bed looked ten feet tall. How was he going to get back up on it? There was no way in hell he was going to remain on the floor for someone else to have to help up. Was his stump bleeding? No, he didn't see any blood on the shrinker sock. That was good, at least. How could he have been so stupid as to forget about this, the most traumatic thing he had ever experienced?

He sat there for a while, hissing with pain. Only the fear that someone might come in and see him there on the floor gave him the strength to grab the side of the bed and pull himself up. It took as much grunting and effort and pain as his entire nine weeks of Army basic training. Basic had been the most difficult thing he had ever done in his life up until that point, but it was the easiest thing he ever did in the Army.

When he dragged the stump up and onto the bed, the living hell of pain rolled over him again. He grabbed his bottle of pain pills out of the drawer and swallowed one without even needing water to get it down, and willed himself into an oblivious, Vicodin-induced sleep.

The only trouble with sleeping was the dreams. The dream of running, the dream of being a track star.

His feet were in the starting blocks, his fingertips touching the white painted starting line on the rubber surface of the track. The Oval of Pain it was sometimes called, but Clay knew the pain would be justified when he crossed the finish line.

The starting gun fired, and he took off, sprinting ahead of the other runners, finding his stride, setting the pace, kicking up dust for his rivals to eat. It was the 3200 meter, the longest running event, and by the first bend, the other runners were no longer in his peripheral vision. It was just him, digging deep, barely feeling his feet touching the ground, soaring around the track. When he crossed the finish line, Julie was there waiting to hug him. He went into her arms and kissed her, and she didn't seem to mind one bit that he was sweating, even though she was wearing her prom dress. Which would have been weird, but since this was a dream, it seemed normal.

After a minute of passionate kissing however, he realized he was no longer wearing his running shorts and singlet. He was wearing his army combat uniform, and when he looked down in surprise, his left boot disappeared, just melted away like an ice cream cone left out in the sun. Then his left leg flew off from his body, flying up into the air to disappear in a puff of smoke. Before he could react, his right leg flew off too, as if chasing after its partner. The blood gushed out from the stumps, staining the beautiful blue silk of Julie's gown into a purple sheath of disgustingness.

The intense pain he felt wasn't from his limbs. It was a knife being stabbed into his heart, and he screamed.

Julie's arms were still around him, holding him up now that his legs were gone, but when his arms flew off, she screamed herself and stepped away from him so that his torso and head fell to the ground and rolled away to fall into a black yawning hole that somehow, dreamlike, opened up at the edge of the running track. He could see other people in the distance, indistinct, too far away to help him.

For some reason, seemingly impossible for a torso with no arms or legs, his face remained above ground level, so that he could see Julie running away from him, screaming and crying. Somehow he could tell that tears were streaming down her face even though she was running away. Just as his clothing had morphed from running togs to his ACU, Julie's elegant prom gown and delicate shoes had magically been replaced with his track clothes and shoes. The better for her to run away from him in.

And then he fell down completely into the cold dark abyss of nothing, with a scent of damp earth and leaf mold in his nose, never landing on anything, just falling, endlessly, with Julie's horrified screams echoing in his ears. He called out, "Julie, come back!" but it was useless, and the stabbing pain in his heart spread throughout his body, even to his traitorously absent arms and legs.

But even when she disappeared, he could still smell his blood on her.

"You should call her."

The voice speaking to him wasn't part of his dream, and he opened his eyes, blinking and confused.

Brooke stood in his doorway, smirking at him. Clay flushed, embarrassed to have his sister observe him thrashing and moaning. At least he hadn't thrown off his blanket, and his stump was still covered.

"What are you doing here?" he snapped. "Why aren't you at school?"

"It's Saturday, Cuckoo," she replied, throwing back his grouchy, snappish tone.

Saturday. He'd ignored simple things like the day of the week since being home.

"Dad and I are going to the hardware store, then we're going to get some lunch and take it to Mom at her shop. Do you want to come with?"

What, leave the security of his bedroom? No way.

"No," he replied rudely. "I'm busy."

"Busy doing what? Laying around doing nothing?"

Laying around doing nothing was his life now.

"You should call Julie if you want her back so bad," she said.

No. He didn't dare call Julie, ever.

"Ren was here to see you," Brooke added.

"Ren Sauter?"

"How many guys named Ren do you know?" Brooke asked, with a hint of snottiness in her voice that she'd probably learned from him. "Of course, Ren Sauter. Dad told him to come back later because you were sleeping. Personally I think he should have sent Ren up here to yank your lazy butt out of bed."

"I'll be sleeping if he comes back." After the way he'd treated his friends the day he'd come home, he was surprised any of them wanted to have anything further to do with him. Ren had always been the most forgiving one of the group. But Clay still couldn't bear to have to talk to any of them.

Brooke raised her eyebrows at him. "How do you know?"

He didn't answer that, just said, "Go away. Close the door." He also ignored her suggestion that he call Julie.

"Jeez, Clay, you've turned into such an unsociable hermit since you've been home."

"Yeah, well you try losing a leg and see how sociable you are. Now get out and don't let the door hit you on the ass when you leave."

But she didn't leave, despite his surliness.

"I'd think in your situation you'd want your friends around you," she insisted.

"What do you know?" he barked. "You have no fucking idea what I want."

Even though he refused to look her in the eye, he could sense her twitch at hearing his profanity. In their childhood she would have snitched on him to their mother for it.

"Why are you acting this way? What has happened to you?"

Stupid question. Kaboom had happened to him.

"They're your friends," she went on. "They only want to see you."

See him. Talk to him. They'd ask him about it. About Kaboom. Maybe they'd want to see his prosthesis. No, he couldn't handle that, couldn't handle how they'd see what a deformed freak and complete head case he'd become.

He couldn't chance it. Yes, they had been his friends, just like his Army comrades whose calls and emails he had ignored. He didn't know what to say to any of them, and he was afraid to hear what they might have to say to him.

"I don't have friends anymore," he replied. "If they come back, I'm not home. Tell them I'm dead."

"Oh that will make them happy," Brooke snorted.

"I don't fucking care if they're happy! Get out of my room."

"You mean your hermit cell."

He had to get rid of her before he cried. He thought perhaps his swearing would chase her away, but apparently his kid sister was made of sterner stuff than he realized.

She took a hesitant step into his room, her face filled with sympathy and consideration. He couldn't stand seeing those expressions directed towards him.

"Clay." Another step towards him, across the threshold of his bedroom door, and he could see all those feelings on her face – pity, concern, empathy, caring – all of the things he hated seeing.

"Do you want to talk about it?" she asked.

Oh God, not her too. It was bad enough being forced to sit in the office of a professional shrink with a Ph.D. Now he was expected to talk about it with his teenage sister? He'd rather lose his other leg.

He felt so brittle, so sharply fragile that it would take no more than a hard smack for him to shatter into a thousand pointy pieces, as if he was made out of thin, cheap glass.

"No, I don't want to fucking talk about it!" Anger burst out of him.

"I'm trying to help," she protested. "You don't have to swear at me."

"Get out!" he bellowed, feeling his face heat up with anxiety. "I don't want to talk to any of you. Just leave me alone."

If this exchange had happened when he and Brooke were kids, her next words would have been a loud, piercing, "Mom! Clay's being mean to me!" and it was true he was being mean and snotty and every other rude term there was. That was his new reality. But today she snapped, "You know Clay, I'm really, really sorry about what happened to you, but that doesn't give you the right to be a complete and utter jerk." Then she obliged him by leaving, but slammed the door hard as she did so.

A lot she knew. What had happened to him gave him every right to be a complete and utter jerk.

Once, a long time ago, before Kaboom, he'd been laying on his bed flipping through Sports Illustrated – strictly for the articles and not because it was the swimsuit edition – and he'd heard the most ungodly screaming emanate from Brooke's bedroom next door. He'd dashed through the door expecting to rescue her from an ax murderer at the very least, to discover her quivering and pointing.

"Get it out, get it out!" she'd begged.

"It" turned out to be an innocent little spider, quivering worse than Brooke as it hung from its silk thread. He'd hated killing the tiny thing, but he would have hated it even more if his sister died on the spot from a massive stroke. But he did toss a teasing, "Scaredy-cat!" at her as he left the room with the spider in a piece of tissue, because Brooke insisted that even deceased, she didn't want it in the trash can in her room.

If she found a spider in her room now, she wouldn't beg for his help, even if he could dash next door. Because he was a complete and utter jerk. The spider would die of old age before he could get to it anyway, if it didn't die laughing first.

It was an altogether shitty day. He lay in his bed listening to the hum of the air conditioner while his father and Brooke left on their errands without him. Lord only knew what she'd said to Dad about his insolent mood. Fortunately their father didn't come up to give him a hard time about his rudeness to his sister. Dad usually left that kind of discipline to their mother anyway. Later, he heard the car pull into the driveway, and a few minutes after that he heard the lawnmower start up. Peeking out his window, he watched his dad push the machine across the yard.

Lawn mowing had been Clay's job, until he'd left for basic training. He'd done it when he'd been home on leave too, or cleared snow from the driveway, depending on the season.

Another simple task he couldn't do anymore. While others were being productive, he couldn't even find the willpower or strength to extract himself from bed. His rude outbreak to his sister had been the most energetic thing he'd done all week.

The front door slammed and a moment later feet pounded up the stairs. Brooke and a couple of her friends chattered and laughed as they passed his door on their way to her room.

He could hear them jabbering through the wall. It annoyed him. They were so depressingly happy and frivolous and normal. At least they didn't try to talk to him or come gawk at him. He was considering knocking on the wall in an effort to shut them up, when the whole giggling gaggle of them burst out of Brooke's room, back down the hall and down the stairs, without so much as a word in Clay's direction. He was both relieved and annoyed at the way they ignored him. They slammed out the back door and he was again left listening to the calm hum of the air conditioner that his parents had turned on yesterday when the weather got hot. Brooke was probably telling her friends what a huge jerk her brother was.

He felt like shit for being so rude to his sister. He hadn't missed the look of hurt that had shown on her face for just a moment, before the anger. He hated being such a rude jerk to her, but he couldn't help himself anymore. It was as if his soul was possessed by a demon.

He was a runner. Or at least, he used to be. It was what he did, who he was. Since childhood, his favorite feelings had been the wind across his face, the feel of his feet on the track, the euphoria of beating the competition as he crossed the finish line. He ran for fun, he ran to compete, he ran to air out his soul. It made him feel alive.

And now? He was stuck in his bed in a world of pain and incompletion, knowing he'd never run again.

Chapter Five

He showed up at the dinner table at the appropriate time, only to save himself being summoned there by his mother, but still didn't eat as much as she would have liked. He was just about to make his escape back to his room when Mom said to him, "We'll be leaving for church at nine tomorrow morning, so be ready."

"I don't think I'll go to Mass, Mom," he replied. What would be the point? He already knew he was going to hell, and for a lot of reasons. For swearing. For being a wimpy-ass crybaby. For being a total snot to the little sister he actually loved fiercely. For hurting Julie. For hating himself, the world and everything in it.

Father Cross, the priest who had presided at his confirmation and who, he presumed, was still in residence at St. Joseph's, would be shocked if he were to realize how much hate, despair and self-loathing resided in Clay's heart.

The boys in his confirmation class, in their sixth-grade rudeness, had joked about the appropriateness of a Catholic priest being named Cross, while the girls had sighed at the romantic notion of, as they put it, a really cute guy giving up everything, including sex, to serve God. Clay and his friends, who were completely clueless about both religious vocation and the psyches of twelve-year-old girls, had merely pretended to understand both.

He might as well have told his mother he had plans to commit murder.

"Oh yes, you are going to church, young man. It is not an option. Nine a.m. Be ready."

Jeez, he was twenty-three years old, not twelve. But if he was going to live in his parent's home, he should expect to abide by their wishes.

To be perfectly honest, he hadn't minded going to Mass in the past. It was true he hadn't been quite as diligent about it since leaving home for the Army as he'd led his mother to believe, but he hadn't ever tried to slither out of it when home on leave. He'd spent most of his time in church fantasizing about watching Julie walk up that aisle in a long white gown.

But now – he was sure the place was going to be way too peopley for his liking.

"OK, Mom," he gave in as he limped towards the stairs. His dad gave him a look of sympathy.

"Nice try, kid," Dad said in a low voice. Brooke said nothing, because she wasn't speaking to him.

If he was going to have to go to church, he'd have to plan which part of the sanctuary would be the best place for him to sit. Like planning the opening ceremony of the Olympics.

His first impulse was to request to sit in the rear, near the door. Easy in, easy out. Minimum exposure to the other worshippers. But that meant he'd have to traverse the entire length up the aisle to take communion, and everyone there would see him. People who'd known him since childhood, when he was normal. That would be awful.

If he requested to sit up front, he'd have to limp all the way up there upon arrival, and down the aisle again at the end of the service, exposed to the stares of the other parishioners already seated. It was the reverse of getting off the airplane – at the end of the service the people at the front left first, passing everyone on their way to the exit. Equally as bad.

The lesser evil would be to choose a pew in the center, equidistant from the front and rear.

His genuflection when they arrived at the centrally located pew was shallow to say the least, but at least he didn't fall on his face in front of everyone. When he sat down he could slide across the pew on his butt so that his parents and Brooke could get in. For the first time since the day he arrived home, he wore real clothes. Sweat pants and tee shirts had sufficed otherwise.

When it came time to stand for the procession, he pressed his right foot – his real foot – hard against the floor, grabbed the back of the pew in front of him, and muscled himself upright. It was distressing how difficult that was and how much it hurt to do. Fortunately the wooden pew back he held onto wasn't wobbly like an airplane seat, so he didn't annoy the person sitting in the row in front of them.

He tried to keep his mind blank during Mass, blocking out everything, the prayers, the homily, the priest. If he allowed himself to think or listen, he'd end up crying and asking God what he'd done to deserve this and was this really all part of some grand plan. It wouldn't go well. Though he did pray a little bit at one point. He prayed he didn't get a bone infection, which afflicted many amputees, and which would necessitate having the stump opened up to be cleaned out.

At the Eucharistic prayer, when the congregation began to kneel, he started to panic. What if he got down and couldn't get back up again? He must have made a sound of distress, because he felt a gentle hand on his arm and looked up to see his dad giving him the, *it's OK* look and just the tiniest head shake to indicate that he didn't have to kneel completely. Jesus would understand.

He leaned forward and just angled his right leg in the direction of the kneeler, and hoped that would be considered to be sufficient. Standing at the end of the prayer was a little easier this time. Maybe he was getting used to the physical challenges of the service. But he couldn't help but glance at the crucifix on the wall behind the altar. Despite His suffering and death, at least Jesus still had two legs.

Making his way up to the front for communion was just as awful as he'd feared it would be. He just looked straight forward, trying to ignore the worshippers he passed, not even acknowledging people he knew. Maybe they thought he was deep in prayer. To be truthful, he was deep in terror.

They were looking at him, staring at him, because he was limping, because he used a cane. Despite knowing that Father Cross would bring communion to those people who were physically unable to approach the altar, something in his youthful pride made him decline that option, despite the pain and stares he endured.

When he got to the altar, he realized he was going to have to take the communion wafer by mouth rather than in his hands as he'd usually done. Leaning on his cane gave him the free use of only one hand, and it would be disrespectful to risk allowing the Host to be dropped on the floor. He watched his parents ahead of him. They had always preferred the traditional method themselves, so he mimicked them when it was his turn. Brooke gave him a brief, curious glance, and Father Cross stopped briefly, laid a hand on Clay's arm, smiled and said quietly, "Bless you, Clayton."

Surprisingly he found himself choking up at the simple, kind words. What kind of pansy-ass wimp had he turned into?

He couldn't even manage to sneak away from greeting the priest at the door after Mass. Father Cross smiled warmly and gripped Clay's hand with both of his.

"It's so nice to see you," he said, as if this were a social occasion. He was surprised his parents hadn't invited Father to that fiasco of a party the day he'd come home. "Please call me anytime if you'd like to talk."

Though Clay had been taught from birth to respect priests and nuns, he still couldn't squelch a silent, sarcastic, *yeah right*. Talking to a priest was worse than having to talk to a shrink.

When they got home, he was able to plead a headache – which was true – and they let him slink up to his room and even gave him an evening off from joining the family at dinner. When he got to the top of the stairs, something made him look back down toward the bottom. Brooke stood there staring up at him. Had she watched his entire slow, awkward climb? Did she look kind of – sympathetic? No, he must be misreading her expression. She thought he was a complete and utter jerk.

As soon as she saw him looking back at her, she turned and flounced away without a word.

Chapter Six

Mom knocked on his door in the morning but didn't try to bring him breakfast. Good. He hated for her to waste food he barely ate.

"Clay," she said, "I'm sorry but I'm going to have to go into the shop today. One of my girls is off sick and we're booked solid. Will you be all right alone today? Your father has already left for work and Brooke's already left for school."

"Yes, Mom," he assured her. Finally they were leaving him to his own devices. The constant supervision was irritating. He'd proven to himself that he could be trusted alone that first night when he refrained from ingesting his entire bottle of pain pills. The refill had come in the mail on Saturday and his mother had given it to him without hesitation. "Go ahead," he assured her. "I'll be fine."

"OK, you have a nice day, sweetie," she stepped in and gave him a maternal kiss on the forehead. "You should get outside some," she suggested. "You're pale."

When she left, he thought, *maybe I will get outside for a little while.* He had survived leaving the house for church yesterday, though he hadn't enjoyed the experience. Maybe there was life outside his bedroom. Being a weekday, most of the neighbors, and his former friends, would all be at work or school. The chances of random people stopping by to try to see him were low.

He pulled on a tee shirt and attached his prosthesis. Somehow, despite the warmth of the day, the prosthesis still felt cold when he slid it on, and he winced at the ensuing pain. He put on a pair of shorts, then sweatpants over them. It didn't matter how hot the weather got; he was not leaving his fake leg exposed to anyone's view. Not even his own.

When he got to the bottom of the stairs, he was surprised at the loneliness of the empty house. Hadn't he been trying to avoid everyone since the moment he arrived home? He'd been craving privacy. How could it be that he now found himself missing some companionship?

The coffee pot in the kitchen was still warm and he poured himself a cup and drank it. In the hall closet he found two rough blankets, nubby souvenirs from a long-ago Mexican vacation, and draped them over his shoulder to carry them as he made his slow, careful progress out the back door.

He hesitated for a moment on the grass. Did he really want to do this? Venture out into the outdoors, away from the safety of his bedroom? Their back yard was fenced in and relatively private, but he was still cautious. Realistically though, it was doubtful the neighbors on either side or in the house behind them were looking. He dropped the blankets on the ground and spread one out with his cane, maneuvering himself with some difficulty to the ground to sit on it, but kept the second blanket covering him from the waist down. He wiggled out of his sweat pants, then undid the prosthesis and slid it off. It didn't matter how hot it was or how private the yard was, he was not going to allow his stump to be exposed to view. The running shorts he wore under the sweat pants didn't come near to covering it.

He had to admit, the sunlight, warmth and breeze felt good, as he lay down on his back, sandwiched between the two blankets, and pulled his fancy new phone out of his pocket. He'd figured out how to sync it for access to his favorite music, but he still hadn't listened to a single song, not since before Ka-boom. He put in the earbuds that had come with the phone, navigated to his music, turned up the volume, and lost himself with people who couldn't see that he was a cripple. The ear-buds blocked out cars and lawnmowers and kids yelling, all the normal sounds that now bothered him.

The music flowed into his brain, into his soul, consuming him with a fierce familiarity. The music became him, and he became the music. He was the singer, the guitarist, the drum-mer, the song's subject in all his pain or jubilation.

It had been so long, too long, since he had felt this belong-ing.

Steven had just finished his tryst in an elevator, and Jon was now living on a prayer. Next up, Freddie would be confessing to his mama that he'd killed a man.

He felt something touch his side, a small nudge, startling him out of his musical oblivion and back to reality. His eyes had been closed, lost in the music. When he opened them, an angel stood above him.

Julie.

It was Julie, her blonde hair lit to glowing by the sun's light behind her. The blue eyes that were his heart looked down at him with a combination of love, and really pissed off.

She had nudged him with her foot. He yanked the earbuds out and sat up. The movement made him realize he was wear-ing shorts and his prosthesis was off, but thank God he still had the blanket over him.

It wasn't her, couldn't be her. It was his imagination. His fucked-up brain was torturing him again, taunting him with the one thing he wanted most in the world, but couldn't have. He didn't dare look her in the eyes. If he did, she'd disappear, like every other dream he'd had before.

He was speechless under her gaze, both in surprise, and stu-pefaction. He'd expected to endure the rest of his life without ever seeing her again. He wasn't even sure yet if she was real, or a figment of his imagination, until she spoke.

"Why did I have to find out about this from Jody Salazar?"

Stupidly, he asked, "Who's Jody Salazar?"

"She lives across the street from me. You remember her, the girl with the teeth."

Oh, yeah, he remembered Jody now. She had a serious, obvious overbite that made her look like a female Freddie Mercury. Clay had in the past wondered if she could sing like a female Freddie.

"Her little brother is in Brooke's geometry class. Apparently the whole class found out about what happened to you when she broke down crying in class. Thirty high school juniors were told, but not me. What's up with that?"

The village of Wheeling might have a population of over 38,000, but it still had that small-town, gossip-passing network, with the everybody into everybody else's business vibe of a tiny hamlet.

She sat down on the blanket next to him. Right. Next. To. Him. Her knee touched his leg – his right leg, thankfully, and he could feel her presence, sense her essence, in a way no other human being had ever done. God, he loved her but God, he couldn't let her see him like this.

He turned away from her. On one hand, he wanted to bury his face in her lap and scream out all of his despair and hatred and fears. On the other hand, he wanted to erect a wall of ice around himself to keep her away.

She put a hand on his arm. Just that small touched warmed him up all over. "Talk to me, Clay."

He couldn't talk to her. He was speechless. More so than when he'd been a constrained teenager with acne, more than the first time they'd made love.

He kept silent, kept his face averted. He was supposed to be the strong one, had been strong. But now, what could he say to her? To anyone? That he was going to be fine? That would be the world's biggest lie. What he really wanted to do was to scream, *Why me?*

Julie put her hands on his shoulders. He tried not to feel her fingers on him. But he was only wearing a tee shirt, not a suit of armor.

Her breath against his ear, her lips near his neck, made his heart do flip flops in his chest. Did she know what her touch did to him?

"Tell me, Cowboy."

That silly nickname, the little secret pet name that only Julie called him, melted his heart. But he still didn't want to tell her about it, couldn't make himself say the words. He just said, "No." It was difficult even producing that one word, and it came out in a childish whisper.

"Yes," she insisted.

"You don't want to hear it."

"Oh yes I do. If it happened to you, I want to know. You used to tell me everything."

She kissed the side of his neck, then turned his shoulder so he faced her, and he reluctantly raised his gaze to her face. He couldn't resist Julie when she kissed him, when she touched him.

What she saw in his eyes must have been truly awful, must have truly frightened her, because she twitched away from him for a moment and an expression of combined horror and grief filled her face. Then with a gasp of emotion, her arms were around his neck.

"My God, Cowboy, what happened to you?"

What had happened to him was the reason he'd sent her that cruel breakup email after Kaboom. Kaboom had happened. He'd wanted to call her, wanted to hear her voice, wanted to respond to the emails he was certain she had sent after he'd broken it off with her. His fingers had hovered over the appropriate keys on that borrowed laptop in the hospital a hundred times, until he'd finally closed it and never looked at his email again since that day. If he'd contacted her, she'd think they had a future together. She'd stick with him out of pity and obligation, despite the fact that he was a mere shell of a person. Clay loved Julie too much to let her do that.

She knew him so well, knew what he was vulnerable to. Julie was both his weakness and his strength. He could not resist her. Had never been able to. Not in high school when she'd given him products to cure his acne, and not now when she wanted him to tell her about the worst thing that had ever happened to him. He couldn't avoid showing her his unshuttered eyes, was unable to use the half-shut, not meeting the eyes directly look he'd been using since Kaboom.

"You can tell me, Cowboy, you know that," she insisted, her direct blue-eyed gaze captivating him. "You can tell me anything and I'll still love you."

No, she wouldn't still love him. She couldn't, if she was smart.

But then, if he told her, she'd be so horrified, that perhaps it would convince her that it was in her best interests to leave him to his misery. He shifted a bit away from her, pulling up his right leg and putting his face against his knee. His only knee. Maybe he could say the words, but he couldn't do it while looking at her face, at those lips he wanted only to kiss, those eyes that owned his soul.

This was Julie, the girl, the woman, who had held his heart in her hands since they'd been seventeen, and still did, despite his crude attempt to break up with her. He owed it to her to tell her what had happened.

"We were riding in a Humvee." He heard her sigh – a sound of satisfaction that encouraged him.

"Go on." He wasn't sure if she said the words audibly, or if his heart merely heard them telepathically.

"We didn't have one of the fancy new MRAP vehicles with the blast deflecting armor that day. They're trying to phase the Humvees out but we still had a bunch left. They'd given us training on how to spot stuff like land mines or IEDs. Looking for small things out of place, like a stack of rocks or dead goats, or a spot where it looked like the dirt had been disturbed recently. Or if there were groups of people hanging out along the side of the road as if they were waiting for something to happen. Our motto was, stay alert, stay alive. But this one, we missed."

His throat felt dry as he spoke, for multiple reasons. One was that it was the most he had actually spoken aloud since he'd arrived back in the States. His voice was unaccustomed to use, other than his few angry outbursts and minimal, miniature conversations. Another was that it put the memories back into his head, playing in his brain like watching a horror movie he couldn't tear his eyes away from even though he knew how bad it was going to get. He kept his forehead pressed to his knee, his lips almost touching the rough blanket. But not even that position impeded his awareness of Julie sitting next to him, listening to his tale of tragedy.

"Why were you even out there, riding around in a truck?" she asked. "Why weren't you,"

He sensed a movement of her hand, as if to indicate an imaginary location of security.

"The irony of it is, we were escorting a delivery of medical supplies to a local village. In exchange, they were supposed to give us some leads on the locations of Taliban terrorists."

To his amazement, he was actually enunciating the words, telling Julie about the events of that awful, life-changing day. He hadn't said these words aloud to any other human since that moment. But somehow, now that he'd started the story, he needed to finish it.

"It was a cold morning. Really cold. But we somehow managed to joke about it, making up stupid ways to describe how cold it was. The comparisons were getting dirtier and dirtier as we drove, and we were laughing."

"You mean like, colder than a witch's tit?" she suggested. "My brothers say that every winter."

"That was like kid's stuff compared to some of the things those guys made up. We all had our heads on swivels of course, but still, I just remember laughing, and then, all of a sudden, *kaboom!*"

The word ejected out of his mouth, not loudly but with an emotional intensity that hurt his throat and his heart.

"I'd always wanted to ride in a helicopter. I got a ride that day in a Lakota – on a stretcher, but I don't remember it. The next thing I knew I was waking up in the hospital in Germany, with a chaplain sitting next to me waiting to explain why I was on a ventilator and why the blanket on my left side was flat.

"Two of the other guys had broken bones, bruises, nothing permanent. They're recovered and back in the unit now. The fourth guy, Sergeant Lopez-" He paused, remembering the hole that had been torn in his heart when they'd told him about Sergeant Lopez. "He got sliced by a piece of shrapnel in his carotid artery, and bled out before the medics even got there. He's buried at Arlington. I didn't get to go to his funeral."

He hadn't laughed since that day.

Suddenly her arms were around his neck, her lips soft against his skin, the heady scent of her skin and the light perfume she always wore filling his senses. He had dreamed, fantasized about her scent every day since they'd been apart. It was a subtle, light scent. You had to be close to her to inhale it.

And inhale it he did, drawing it into his sensory receptors, so that he'd have something to live on, a small spark of memory to sustain him for the rest of his life when she left him.

"Oh, Cowboy, my Cowboy," she said, with a catch in her voice.

That was all it took.

He cried.

It wasn't the pretty, classy crying like you'd see in a soap opera, with a glistening tear rolling down a cheek. No, this was a full-on ugly cry, complete with a river of tears, runny nose and gulping, gasping sobs. His ribs ached from the crying.

It wasn't the first time he'd cried since Kaboom, but it was the first time anyone else had seen it or heard it or felt it. He held onto Julie real tight, as if he didn't know she was going to leave him. This was exactly why he had told his family not to come to Germany, why he had told Julie nothing at all about what had happened to him.

His crying gave him a headache, a pounding headache. He could feel the pulse beating in his temple. Thud, thud. It pounded like the drumline of a high school marching band. The lump in his throat hurt, as if he'd swallowed a golf ball.

Even before he was done, he turned away from her, wiping his face with his hands, trying to compose himself. He could hear Julie sniffling too.

"Go home, Julie," he said harshly, hating himself as he heard her gasp. But he still managed to choke out more cruel words. "Just go away."

He wouldn't look at her. He'd break down again if he did.

"No," she insisted, her own voice catching. "I'm not going anywhere until you tell me why you broke up with me. You sent me that horrible email, with no explanation, then not another word from you. I sent you so many emails trying to ask you why, and you never answered me. I love you, Cowboy. I thought you loved me too. Why did you do it? Tell me."

He couldn't look anywhere but at her feet. Her two whole, complete feet at the ends of two complete, normal legs.

"Do you know how many guys asked me out while you were gone? I carried a laminated photo of us in my pocket at all times to show them that I had a boyfriend." She pulled a photo out of her pocket and showed him, but he couldn't look at it, a photo of the two of them from before Kaboom.

"I can't be your man anymore, Julie."

With horror, he saw her gaze leap to his crotch.

"Oh, my God!" she gasped. "Oh God, Clay, I didn't know! I thought it was just your leg-" She was looking at his crotch as if taking his words completely literally.

Just his leg? How could she say *just his leg*, as if that wasn't bad enough?

But that part of him, where she was staring in horror, still worked just great. He realized that each morning when he woke up throbbing for her. Maybe it worked a little too well, considering it was probably never going to see action again.

"No," he said miserably. "Not like that."

"Then like what? I deserve to know, Clay. I gave you my virginity."

"I gave you mine too," he said quickly.

"I didn't think that mattered so much to guys."

"It did to me."

"Unless -" He could hear the hesitation in her voice. "Unless, there's someone else? All this time you've been gone – did you meet someone else? There were women in your army unit, weren't there? What about that time you went to Spain on leave?"

Shock rippled through him in a palpable wave. Not only had he never, ever, been with another woman, biblically speaking, he'd barely even spoken to any. With the female soldiers in his unit, it was all business and politeness.

The closest he'd come to female interaction had been at Landstuhl hospital in Germany. A couple of the nurses had pretended to flirt with him, in an attempt to cajole him into eating. He had resisted both the flirting and the meals.

Finally, the nurses had quit the pretend flirting. He was soon confronted by a very real doctor who had threatened him with medical nourishment. The doctor had been a captain, who did not suffer fools like Clay lightly. Even though Clay was already aware that his career in the Army was over, he still recognized a direct order when he heard one. The thought of having a tube inserted through his nose, down his esophagus and into his stomach horrified him enough to make him man up and eat his dinner the way it was intended to be eaten, at least while the doctors and nurses were still observing.

The only other people to ever see him naked had been the doctors and nurses who'd stabilized him before loading him onto the medevac flight to Germany. That definitely did not qualify as a date, especially since he didn't remember any of them.

"Someone else!" he screeched. "God no! I've never so much as looked at another girl. They don't exist. Not since that first day of school when you sat next to me."

Julie smiled a little at the memory. "Mr. Oldenkamp's history class. I was so lucky that seat was vacant. You were the hottest guy I ever saw."

"I had zits," he reminded her.

"I know, but I could see the handsomeness under them. And in here -" she placed a hand on his chest, and underneath her palm, his heart flipped. "I could tell you had a beautiful soul too. The exterior package – that's just an extra added bonus."

"You make it sound like I'm some sort of prize catch."

"You are."

That was a big honking negative. "I'm not the same person I was back then."

"Of course you're a different person. Everyone changes as they grow up. I'm not the same person I was in high school either."

"But this is different. You don't really want to be stuck with a cripple. You could do so much better."

"Don't you tell me what I do or do not want, Clay Maslowski. If you think something as minor as losing your leg is going to get rid of me, you are absolutely wrong."

She'd always worn the same perfume, a light flowery scent that he loved. It turned him on. It was Julie. There were probably lots of other women in the world wearing the same brand, but it wouldn't smell the same as it did on Julie. He imagined her applying it in the hollow of her throat, between her breasts. Aw, God, he was getting hard at the thought of it. He didn't want her to go away. He wanted her to stay there, holding him, forever. He drew in a deeper, fuller breath, filling his lungs with her, and knew he could happily drown in the scent.

But he needed her to leave. "Julie," he started to say, but she interrupted him.

"Do you remember my cousin Josh?" she asked, seemingly out of the blue.

"Yeah, I remember him. Smart guy. Knows more about computers than they know about themselves."

"He's pretty close to legally blind without his glasses. They're as thick as the bottom of a soda bottle. His wife has to color code the bottles in their shower so he doesn't try to wash his hair with her peach scented body wash. It doesn't mean he can't live his life or have a relationship."

"That's not even close to the same thing. Being nearsighted is nothing like the traumatic amputation of a limb. He at least still has his eyes, even if he does need to wear glasses."

He tried really hard, but failed, to avoid looking in the direction of the elephant in the room, his former left leg, which though even discreetly covered with the blanket was still obviously not there. The titanium foot of the prosthesis protruded from under the blanket at an obscene angle that made it obvious it wasn't attached to him.

Julie followed his gaze. "Oh my God. You broke up with me because you lost your leg? You ass!"

"Lost my leg?" His insides felt fizzy as if he was a soda can being shaken. "I didn't lose it. You lose your car keys. I lost my favorite Matchbox car in the grocery store when I was five. I didn't *lose* my leg. It's not misplaced somewhere. It was blown off. Shredded into bits of bone and tissue mixed into the dirt. They never even found my boot."

Julie's brief irritation melted away. "God, Clay, I'm so sorry. But why didn't you tell me, call me when you regained consciousness? I couldn't imagine why you sent me that email, why you thought you should break it off. I want nothing more than to be with you."

"I didn't want you there. I didn't want you to come. Not you or my parents or Brooke."

"Why wouldn't you want us to be with you? People who love you and care about you?" Her voice was starting to tremble too, as if she might cry as well.

Don't cry, Julie, his mind said. *I'll dissolve into nothing if you cry too.*

She audibly gulped back her emotion. "If it were me I would want you and my family by my side, no matter what condition I was in. The only thing I'd have a problem with would be having to see your casket."

"Well I'm not you. You're too good for your own good. I didn't want you to see me, OK? I didn't want anyone to see me there, like that. I still don't want it. So go home and forget about me."

She didn't leave as he'd requested, just sat there next to him.

"Look, Julie, I love you but you need to get as far away from me as you can, as fast as you can, because if you stay around I'll only drag you down, and you deserve a better life than that."

She looked at him as if he'd slapped her. Now he felt even worse. He'd hurt her, when his intention had been to help her.

"Do you remember the first time I told you I loved you?" she asked. "The first time I said it out loud?"

Of course he remembered. How could he ever forget the first night they'd made love? It was the day he told her he had decided to enlist in the Army. He and his dad had talked to the recruiter together, but when he decided, he told her first.

"If you recall, I didn't put any conditions on it. I didn't say, I'll love you unless something bad happens to you. I just said, I love you, without qualifying it."

The memory thumped his brain like a hammer. About two seconds before losing their virginities, he'd cupped her face in his hands and whispered, "Are you sure, Julie?"

She'd put her arms around him, pulled him close and whispered, "I'm sure, Cowboy. I love you."

And about two seconds after the loss of virginity, he'd whispered back, or maybe it was a moan, "I love you, too."

"That's still true," Julie continued. "I meant it. I still love you and I hope you still love me."

It was easy, perhaps, instinctive for some, to declare love during the act of sex, but in their case, the love had endured even afterward.

"You didn't know back then that I was going to turn into a hideous freak."

"You are not a freak and you are not hideous."

"I don't want to talk about it anymore. Please just go away." He hated saying the cruel words, but they were necessary. Julie just sat back and gave him the exact same stink-eye look his mother gave his father over the gravy ladle. Had the two of them gotten together and practiced it?

She moved quickly. Before he could stop her, she grabbed his new phone lying next to him and looked at the screen.

"Is this yours?"

"Yes," he admitted. "My parents gave it to me."

"Wow. I wanted one of these but I couldn't afford it. I had to get the lower model." She turned away from him and started tapping on the device's keys.

"What do you think you're doing? Give that back."

"I'm sending myself a text so I have your phone number."

"Don't do that."

"Too late. It's done." She replaced the phone where it had been, and a moment later her phone beeped from her purse.

"I am going to leave now but not because you tell me to. I have to go to work."

He should have realized that, seeing the way she was dressed, in what he thought of as her chef uniform – crisp black and white striped slacks and a white tee shirt, over which she would don a white double-breasted tunic and long, wide apron when she got to the restaurant.

"I've been promoted to sauté chef. You'd know that, if you read your emails."

He couldn't look at her. As much as he felt she should go away and forget about him, he still couldn't bear to see her walk away from him. Quickly, before he could protest, she grabbed his shoulders and kissed him, briefly but intensely. He tried not to respond but it was impossible not to, and for a moment he allowed himself to get lost in the pleasure of it.

All too soon, she pulled away and jumped to her feet.

"I'm so glad you're alive," she told him. "I'll be seeing you soon. You can count on that, Cowboy."

And then she was gone, the scent of her perfume and the memory of her lips on his floating behind her, and he was both relieved, and devastated at the same time.

After a few minutes he pushed off the blanket that had covered his lower half and quickly, before anyone else showed up, reattached the prosthesis and pulled the sweat pants over his shorts. It took him four tries to get to his feet. What had he been thinking, coming out here and laying in the grass as if he could just hop up and down at will? Seeing Julie again drained him and he ached all over, both physically and emotionally. He needed to get back inside so he could limp up the stairs to his room and take a pain pill.

Maybe there was life outside his bedroom, but he wasn't a fan.

Chapter Seven

Julie showed up the next day with a cake. Not a premade cake from the grocery store bakery department. Not a cake made from a boxed mix. Julie never cooked from a mix. She brought a made from scratch, award-winning level confection. Clay knew without asking that even the frosting was made from scratch. But just like the cake his mother had served the day he'd arrived home, he couldn't eat any.

He didn't see her when she brought it. She'd been on her way to work again and he really had been asleep, dulled by his pain medication. He knew that she worked long shifts, especially as one of the junior members of the staff. Brooke had accepted the cake Julie dropped off and put it on the dining room table. His sister had been giving him the silent treatment since he'd rudely rebuffed her attempt to talk to him, and he really couldn't blame her. At dinner he noticed his parents looking at the two of them ignoring each other, but fortunately they refrained from asking questions.

Cell phone protocol dictates that one does not answer an unknown phone number. So when a local, but unfamiliar, number rang on Clay's fancy new phone, he didn't answer it. If the caller really wanted to talk to him, they would leave a voicemail message, which he might or might not listen to.

Later, out of sheer curiosity, he listened to the voicemail the caller had left.

"Hello, Clay, my name is Nathan Jacoby. I was given your phone number by Julie Peterson. I'm a retired Staff Sergeant, and a volunteer with the Wounded Warrior Project. Julie told me you were having some difficulty adjusting to civilian life as an amputee."

Was this guy for real? Difficulty didn't even begin to describe it. And how dare Julie talk about him and his disability to a stranger, behind his back? He forced himself to listen to the rest of the message.

"I thought maybe we could get together and talk about some of the issues you're experiencing. There's a Starbucks on Dundee Road next to the Inland Bank. Are you familiar with it? If you're free on Tuesday at sixteen hundred I'd love to meet up and talk."

Of course Clay was familiar with that Starbucks. He'd been there. He had lived in this town all his life. But as to whether he was going to go there and talk to some stranger, when he couldn't even talk to his own family or friends, that was another story altogether.

"You can call or text me at this number," the call concluded. "I look forward to meeting you."

The guy could look forward all he wanted, but Clay seriously doubted he'd find it in him to actually meet with him.

He didn't want to meet up with this guy, some healthy, able-bodied soldier, even if he was retired, who apparently thought he could do something to help Clay. Like sitting together over coffee with a stranger was going to magically make his leg grow back. He'd scream if he had to listen to one more well-meaning person who had no idea what he was feeling or had been through telling him that his life wasn't over, that there were still possibilities for him. What a crock.

Why then did he send the guy a text agreeing to meet him? He should ignore the message or decline the invitation. But maybe this other former soldier needed to be told in person that he was wasting his time with Clay Maslowski.

He told himself he was going to blow the guy off even as he downloaded the Uber app onto his fancy new phone. Only a residual vestige of Army pride to honor his commitment got him out the door before his parents got home from work. He didn't bother telling Brooke, who was in her room playing a video game, where he was going. She still wasn't talking to him.

He made a point of being at the curb before the driver got there, to spare the person the sight, and himself the embarrassment and effort, of maneuvering down the driveway.

When he walked, or rather limped, into the coffee shop, his heart was hammering in his chest, and he was already desperate to go home. Yes, it was irrational, but he was on the verge of a panic attack. Or maybe he was having a heart attack. He felt cold, as if he'd been pierced by a sliver of ice, despite the fact that it was about 85 degrees outside.

As soon as he entered the door, which had been held open for him by another customer who gave a curious glance at his cane, a tall, dark-haired, slightly older guy immediately strode towards him, with a loping, confident gait. Clay had walked like that once, before Kaboom.

"You must be Clay," he said.

That should be obvious. He was the only crippled person present. "What's left of him," he replied, hating how sullen he sounded.

The man extended a hand and shook Clay's with a firm grip. "Nathan Jacoby. It's nice to meet you. Can I get you an over-priced coffee?"

"No," Clay replied. When had he become such a rude little shit? "Thanks," he added, reluctantly.

He didn't want to be here. There were normal people here, staring at him and his cane. Traffic sounds from outside and the voices of the coffee shop staff calling out customers' names. It was all too threatening. Despite the ice-piercing sensation in his chest, still his hand on his cane was sweating.

"Come on," his new friend offered. He had sharp blue eyes that looked like he wouldn't take any nonsense from a maggot like Clay. "What?"

Clay shrugged. "Whatever. What you're having."

"Great. I hope you like pumpkin spice."

Clay loved pumpkin spice, but still couldn't muster up enthusiasm

"It's barely June," he protested. "You can't get a pumpkin spice latte this time of year."

"Ha," Sergeant Jacoby said with a smile. "Just watch me. I have a special arrangement with the barista. Wait here, I'll be right back." He indicated the vacant table next to him and Clay sat down, glad to be off his feet – his foot.

As Jacoby waited at the counter for their over-priced coffee, Clay looked around. What the hell was he doing here, with all these normal happy people? He didn't belong here. He didn't know how to be around people anymore. He needed to go home. He needed a pain pill.

Sure enough, despite the season, the guy returned five minutes later with two steaming cups emitting the sweet fragrances of pumpkin and exotic spices. Though he wouldn't admit it out loud, Clay was impressed. Not even the Starbucks at Fort Benning would make a pumpkin spice latte before September.

He held the warm cup in his hand and let the familiar scent of the flavors waft through him.

"So how are you doing?" retired Staff Sergeant Jacoby asked.

Why did everyone in the world ask how he was doing? It should be perfectly obvious. Rather than giving this guy the straight scoop on just how crappy he was doing, Clay just shrugged.

But the warmth of the paper coffee cup was somehow comforting in his hand. Jacoby let Clay's rudeness slide as he took a sip from his own cup.

"I know that this is a difficult and stressful adjustment for you," he said.

You think? Jacoby didn't know the half of it.

"What I would like to do is to offer you a support mechanism to help smooth out that adjustment."

"You're wasting your time," Clay retorted. "There's no point."

"I disagree. There's definitely a point, Corporal."

"Don't call me Corporal."

"Why not? That was your rank, wasn't it?"

How did this guy know all these things about him?

Julie. He'd spoken to Julie and she'd told him the whole pathetic story. Not good.

"It was my rank. Emphasis on the *was*. I'm not a corporal or anything else anymore. I've been medically discharged."

"All right," the guy said agreeably. "May I call you Clay?"

Clay just shrugged. The sergeant could call him Poindexter for all he cared.

"I gotta go." The old Clay would have picked up his coffee cup – surprisingly he had drunk it all – wiped up any residual drips, and deposited the cup and napkin into the appropriate trash receptacle. But the old Clay had gone Kaboom, and the new Clay just got up and left his detritus on the table. He hobbled to his feet, but Jacoby got up too and gathered up their coffee cups.

"Where are you parked?" he asked.

"I'm not. I don't have a car."

"Then how did you get here today?"

Releasing the one word was like having a tooth pulled. "Uber."

"Not driving yet?"

His one-word reply was sullen, brief and offered no details.

"No." The unspoken words hung between them, like the news scroll at the bottom of a TV screen. *Not driving yet, since you lost your leg.*

"Do you have someone to help you get around? Someone who takes you to your doctor's appointments and so on?"

Yes, he had someone. Several someones. His parents had reminded him multiple times that they would gladly chauffeur him, or allow him the use of one of their cars. Even Brooke would be able to drive him places. She had gotten her driver's license while he was in the hospital and had called him to tell him about it, with excitement bubbling in her voice, despite having gotten up at some ungodly early hour to call him with the news, due to the seven-hour time difference. Normally he would have been proud and happy for her, and full of advice. But he'd barely responded to her happy news and clearly heard the disappointment in her voice at his lack of congratulations. Most likely Julie would also be willing to help him with transportation, but he wasn't going to ask.

He wasn't going to request any of them to drive him anywhere. He didn't want to see the pity in their eyes as they did so, and he was too uncertain to try and drive himself with his prosthesis. He was supposed to be following up with doctors and counselors at the V.A. hospital, but he had no intentions of doing so.

He pushed open the door and Jacoby reached out to steady it, still talking.

"You know, we have volunteers who will gladly transport you to your doctor's appointments. I'll drive you myself once the school year ends. When you're ready to start, I could go with you and help you get used to it. Are you free on Saturday?"

Sure he was free on Saturday. He had no life. He tried to be indifferent, but still he was curious. What did Jacoby mean by, when the school year ends? He was too old to even be a college student.

"I'm busy," he said pulling out his phone to book another Uber car to take him home. Hopefully he could get one set up before this do-gooder offered to give him a ride. "Thanks for the coffee," he said, not really feeling grateful, but hoping that Jacoby would get the dismissive hint, as he tapped the Uber icon on his phone.

Where to, the screen asked. There was no option for "nowhere" so he was forced to choose "Home".

"You're welcome," Jacoby replied. "Let's get together again when you have more time to talk."

Had Clay's eagerness to leave fooled this guy into thinking he was actually busy, actually had a life? Highly unlikely. He didn't look at all stupid.

For once, luck was with Clay. His ride showed up quickly enough to forestall Jacoby from offering him transportation, and he got into the vehicle as quickly as his disabled status allowed him.

"I'll call you," Jacoby assured him, but Clay didn't respond as the Uber car pulled away.

As luck would have it his mother pulled into the driveway just as Clay was making his awkward exit from the car, and she smiled and waved at him cheerfully.

"Hi there, sweetie. Where were you?"

It was just normal Mom curiosity but he still wished she wouldn't have asked.

"Went out for coffee," was all he admitted.

"That's great!" Mom enthused, as if he'd invented penicillin or something. "Did you meet up with your friends?"

He used his newly acquired non-committal grunt to avoid answering. He didn't want to have to tell his mother he'd been having coffee with another former soldier who wanted him to Talk About It. She'd only encourage it.

Mom opened her trunk and pulled out two bags of groceries. Clay knew he should get them for her and carry them into the house, but he couldn't. By the time he even limped up to the door, she had already gone inside, set down the bags and was holding the door open for him.

For some reason she didn't object when he said he didn't want any dinner. Maybe she saw the despair in his eyes. He was going to have to work on that.

As he lay on his bed for another lonely, boring, unproductive evening while his family ate dinner without him, and probably talking behind his back about what a complete and utter jerk he was, he started to feel bad.

What was wrong with him? Dumb question. He knew perfectly well what was wrong with him. He was an amputee with a prosthesis and a cane. But why did he have to be such a jerk, such a rude little toad, to everyone who cared about him? Was it helping anything or anyone to treat people as if he were a bear with a thorn stuck in its paw? No, it wasn't, but he didn't know how to stop.

Or was his new negative attitude going to drive them all away from him? He wanted to be left alone, to brood in lonely silence, didn't he? So maybe continuing to be a snot of a guy was the best course of action.

Chapter Eight

R etired Staff Sergeant Nathan Jacoby was a giant pain in Clay's ass.

The man made a complete pest of himself, calling, leaving voice mails, sending text messages asking to set up another meeting. He sent links to seemingly dozens of websites he thought Clay might find helpful - veteran's service organizations, resume writing articles, support groups for amputees, employment agencies. What good would that do? He wasn't qualified for anything, not even a Walmart door greeter.

There was a monumental, daunting amount of confusing digital paperwork for him to wade through. The VA, insurance, the Transition Assistance Program, disability and unemployment benefits. "I can help you fill out the forms and obtain your verification of military experience and training documents," Jacoby offered via text message. That offer almost came close to breaking down Clay's resistance.

Why was the guy wasting his time with a lost cause like Clay?

There was a cliché about enlisting in the army, straight off a recruiting ad. Go in a boy, come out a man. Yes, it was the corniest of clichés, but it had been true. Clay had been pretty much a boy when he'd headed off to Fort Benning, despite having been nineteen. The challenges and discipline of basic training, the teamwork of the infantry, and deployment to Afghanistan had all been a part of his transition from boy to man. But compared to war, basic training had been the weakest thing ever.

Until Kaboom. What Clay hadn't been told was that getting oneself blown apart destroyed all that hard-won maturity. That one horrible moment, when his career and life had shattered in the debris of an IED blast, had regressed him emotionally back into an angry, selfish twelve-year-old.

Like a twelve-year-old, he wanted to ignore the communications, or reply with a terse, *leave me alone*. But his rudeness at the coffee shop hadn't deterred Staff Sergeant Nathan Jacoby then and he doubted it would do so now.

Not only did the retired staff sergeant contact him several times a day, but so did Julie.

He wanted to accept the call, hear her voice. He wanted her to come hold him again, the way she had the other day when he'd broken down and cried in her arms. But he couldn't allow it, despite how much he wanted, needed, to see her, touch her, inhale her scent into his soul. Sending a text was safer. He wrote his text in all capital letters, the digital equivalent of yelling.

"Why did you give my number to that guy? You had no right to go behind my back and tell some stranger about me."

"But Clay, you need some help," she texted back. Even though it was digital words on a screen, he could still discern the caring and compassion she foolishly still felt towards him. He didn't send a response, but she texted again.

"If you won't talk to me, talk to him. I think he can help you. He seemed to understand your situation."

She was wrong about that. Nobody could understand his situation. He didn't understand it himself. He wanted to talk to Julie. He wanted to bury his face between her breasts and whisper every guilty, painful, sordid, life-changing detail rattling around in his soul. Too bad he couldn't do that. He didn't deserve that sort of comfort.

He was staring at the phone, contemplating whether or not to reply, when a third message from Julie appeared on the screen.

"I love you."

"Well you shouldn't," he texted back, then set the phone to silent.

He took his evening Vicodin, then while waiting for it to take effect, thought, maybe it wouldn't kill him to talk to this Jacoby guy again. But did the staff sergeant have any idea what Clay was feeling? How could he? Their only common bond was service in the Army. Maybe this guy was serving as a volunteer with wounded warriors merely to assuage his guilt over coming out of it in one piece, when Clay and others like him hadn't.

Some nasty little reasonable voice in his head suggested, you'll never know what Sergeant Jacoby's motives are until you find out. And you aren't going to find out laying around in bed.

Though he'd managed to skip family dinner tonight, still his mother stopped and tapped on his door later. After making sure he was covered, he reluctantly invited her in.

"This was in your pocket when I washed your clothes," she said, handing him a small white card, the card his former track coach had given him at that horrible homecoming party, when he'd made the improbable offer of Clay helping him out at summer track camp. He wished his mother wasn't so diligent at checking pockets when she did laundry. It was a habit she'd gotten into when Brooke, at age four, had left a red crayon in her pocket that wasn't detected until they all ended up with pink underwear after it melted in the washing machine. But he had no alternative now but to take the card and thank his mother for bringing it to him. He was tempted to toss it in his trash, but something made him look at the words printed on it.

Brent G. Swanson, Head Track Coach, Wheeling High School

There were two phone numbers listed, one for his office, the other for his cell phone. It was 9:00 p.m. Clay could take the coward's way out, call the office number and be assured of getting a voice mail, and tell him thanks but no thanks, he wouldn't be able to help with summer track camp. But Coach had put up with Clay and his shenanigans for four years, as well as countless other impudent high school kids. If that didn't require the patience of a saint, Clay didn't know what did. Maybe he deserved the courtesy of a personal call. Or, maybe getting a work-related call at 9:00 p.m. would annoy Coach enough to tell Clay to get lost.

It took him several minutes to man up and get up the courage to press the numbers on his fancy new cell phone. Maybe Coach wouldn't answer if he didn't recognize the number, and Clay would still get the easy way out in the form of a voice mail.

He was either lucky, or unlucky, because Coach answered with a brief, serious, no-nonsense reply of, "Swanson."

"Uh, Coach? It's Clay. Clay Maslowski," He found himself stuttering a bit as he said his name, like a wimp. Maybe Coach had forgotten who he was, or put him out of his mind after Clay's lack of enthusiasm when he'd made the request for assistance.

But weirdly, Coach responded with what sounded like glee.

"Clay! I'm so glad you called. It's good to hear your voice. We're going to start with some drills Monday morning. Can you be at the track at about 8:00 a.m.? If you could spend a little time with the younger boys, the junior varsity squad, that would be so great. A couple of them have older brothers who ran with you so they'll know you."

Damn. Coach just assumed Clay was calling to accept the task, as if he had something to contribute. No, he had to tell him he couldn't do it, both physically and emotionally. He'd have to dredge up rudeness on a scale that he'd used towards his sister the other day. But he hated what a jerk he'd been to Brooke, and he didn't want to be the same kind of jerk to his former coach, a man he'd always liked and respected.

"Actually," he started to say, and he could practically feel Coach Swanson's anticipation through the phone. Would he be upset if Clay turned him down? He'd probably want to know why, but Clay just couldn't make himself enunciate the words he'd have to say.

I can't coach runners. I can't run or jump anymore. I can barely walk and I couldn't stand to be around athletes who can do all those things.

"Listen," Coach went on, "I know you won't be able to run yourself. Your mother did tell me about your, uh, situation when I saw her before you came home."

Situation. That was a nice euphemism. It sounded way less sucky than amputee, cripple, useless husk.

"But I wouldn't expect you to run with them. You can do more good by watching them and telling them how to set up, how to stride, how not to get hurt. I'm sure you remember what we talked about back when you were on the team. It's as much a mental exercise as a physical one."

Clay hesitated. He really wanted to help out his former coach. Before leaving for basic training, and when home on leave, he'd attended high school track meets several times and had enjoyed talking to him about the current team members. But now, it was all different and he couldn't do it.

"So what do you say, Clay? Monday morning?" Coach waited for him to answer, like a relay runner anticipating the baton to be passed into his hand.

"No, I can't," Clay said. Except that the words didn't come out of his mouth like that. His brain said no, but somehow, his mouth said, "Sure, Coach. I'll see you Monday."

"That's outstanding!" From the enthusiasm in Coach's voice, you'd think Clay had given him a gift. "We'll see you then."

You are a first-class idiot, Clay thought after he disconnected the call and lay back on his bed. Why in the world did he agree to this? He could have let Coach down and refused to help. This was surely the most masochistic thing he had ever done or thought of. He still had a few days before he was expected at the high school. He'd call Coach back before then and tell him that he couldn't make it.

He got another text from Jacoby. "What are you doing Sunday morning? I have a guest pass to my gym burning a hole in my pocket."

The gym? Oh hell no. Clay was seriously never planning to set foot in a gym again. Fortunately, he had a convenient excuse, provided by his mother.

"Sunday is no good for me," he texted back. "Gotta go to church."

At least he was spared the humiliation of having to limp into a barbershop to get his hair trimmed. There were advantages to having a mother who was a hairdresser. In the months he was in the hospital, they hadn't been diligent about reminding him to keep his hair within military regulation length. There had been more important things to take care of at the time, like saving his life and teaching him to walk on a prosthesis.

He hadn't really minded the scalp-grazing buzz cut, except when he remembered Julie putting her hands in his hair. Since that wasn't ever going to happen again, Sunday after Mass he asked his mother to give him a haircut in the kitchen.

It was a normal occurrence. His mother had always cut his hair and his dad's, and even Brooke's, at home. Though today she only trimmed it a little, leaving enough to curve along his ear and collar.

"You don't need to keep it in an Army buzz cut anymore," she said, as if his reason for no longer being in the Army was somehow by his choice. "You look so cute when you can get a little length to it."

For the first time since Kaboom, he rolled his eyes. Lord, his life was over now. When your mother said you were cute, that was the kiss of death.

At dinner Sunday night, he spoke up voluntarily, surprising them all a little. Apparently, they'd gotten used to him not talking.

"Mom, can I ask you a favor?" He was, surprisingly, nervous about the request he was about to make.

"Tomorrow morning, could you drive me over to the high school? I told Coach Swanson I'd meet him there." He didn't specify that he was being asked to help coach the track team. That would be outside the realm of believability. He still couldn't believe he'd agreed to it.

"Of course, sweetie," his mom agreed immediately. "I'd be glad to."

"I have a better idea," Dad said. "Why don't you drop me off at the train station in the morning, and you can just use my car? There's no point in having it sit in the parking lot all day if you can use it. Just don't use up all my gas and pick me up at six."

Clay hadn't been behind the wheel of a motor vehicle since before Kaboom. Driving with only one usable leg seemed like an impossible thing. His dad got up and pulled a spare set of car keys off the hook just inside the kitchen door. They were the keys Clay had used when he'd driven his mom's and dad's cars in the past. It would be more convenient than using Uber, but still, he was afraid to drive, for more than one reason.

"Um, thanks, Dad, but I'm not ..." his voice trailed off, unwilling to admit his fears in front of his family. He couldn't make himself say the words out loud, "I'm not ready to drive yet. I don't know if I'll ever be ready."

Dad looked a bit hurt at Clay's refusal, but put down the set of keys he'd been offering. Mom gave Dad one of her, *don't push it* looks and repeated, "I'll be glad to give you a lift. Be sure and take your phone so you can call me if you need a ride home."

Now he felt like a child, needing to call on Mommy for transportation, but it was less bad than trying to drive himself and probably failing miserably.

Chapter Nine

What was he doing here, he asked himself as his mother dropped him off at the end of the school's north driveway, and he limped down the path past the tennis courts to where the running track made a stretched-out oval around the football field. The gate was open, the track teams and Coach Swanson were already there. Surely this was the worst mistake he'd ever made in his life. He was actually going to hang out at his former high school, at the track where he'd run sprints just a few years ago.

Why had Coach Swanson invited him here? Hadn't he noticed that his former athlete was a cripple now?

To add insult to injury, there was a chair – it looked like one stolen from a classroom – with a manila file folder taped to the back and his name written on it with a black marker, so that everyone there knew that he, the fake assistant coach, had been brought here merely by the pity of the real coach.

The worst part was that it not only had his name written there, in Coach Swanson's bold handwriting. It read, "Coach Maslowski". What a piece of fiction.

There were legs everywhere. White legs, brown legs, black legs. Two per person, all made of natural flesh and bone and muscle, all wearing shorts, because they had nothing to hide. Legs that would bleed if you stuck a pin into one. If he were to stick a pin into his left leg, its only result would be a slight ping of titanium.

At Landstuhl, they had to wear shorts to rehab and to physical therapy, so that the therapists could see the prostheses and assure they were properly fitted. Most of the patients had no problem with that directive, allowing their hardware to be on display like a shiny new toy. Not Clay. As soon as he could, he covered it up with a pair of sweatpants, the same pair he was wearing today, despite the fact that that the forecast was for a high of 85 degrees.

Clay had learned, in some long-ago high school class, that the sense of smell evokes memories more profoundly than the other senses. Whoever had figured that out had been really smart.

The aromas of sunblock, macadam, grass, chalk and sweaty running shoes transported him back to his high school days, when he had run on this track, when he had two legs, when he won, when he was a star. Their scents filled him.

And anticipation. Yes, anticipation had its own strong, palpable aroma, stronger than any of the other more physical elements. He'd felt that sense, that smell, of anticipation, that spike of adrenaline, when his feet had been in the starting blocks, back in the day. Waiting for the blare of the starting gun, assessing the other runners, focusing his attention and power towards the finish line. It made the five toes he still had tingle in anticipation with an itch to settle into the mark position.

What are you doing here, Maslowski?

The kids were standing around, looking at him, waiting for instructions.

There was a fairly substantial group present, between those planning on running cross country in the fall, indoor track in the winter, and track and field in the spring. He recognized a few as the younger brothers of guys he'd known in high school. A couple of them wandered over to the starting blocks on the track and set their feet against them as if they planned to start a race then and there.

"Not yet," he called out by reflex. "Warm up first."

Obediently the kids came back and stood in front of him with a respectful, "OK, Coach."

Coach. They called him Coach, as if he were for real. He glanced over at Coach Swanson across the field with the varsity runners, supervising as they stretched out, sitting on the grass and pulling on their toes with an outstretched leg.

He had committed to this; had told Coach he would help these kids. Now, he had to put his money where his mouth was. He couldn't run or even warm up with them, physically, but then, Coach Swanson wasn't doing so either.

"Stretches first," he instructed. "You don't want to end your season before it starts with pulled muscles. Everybody, put your ass on the grass."

"OK, Coach. Sure, Coach."

They kept calling him Coach. He could get used to this.

They followed his instructions, though a couple of kids had trouble reaching their feet with their hands. He leaned forward in his chair to watch.

"You guys are doing weight training in your off time, right?" he asked, and most of the boys nodded. "Good. You all need to enroll in a yoga class too."

Noses wrinkled. "Seriously, Coach? Yoga is for girls."

"No," Clay countered. "Yoga is for core strength and flexibility. You don't have to worry about the meditation part if that's not your thing. But you will do better if you get some yoga training on your own time. It will increase your chances of making the varsity team."

Most of the kids still looked doubtful, but one of the boys, a familiar-looking redhead, was nodding in agreement.

"My older brother was on the team. Remember him, Coach?" He looked at Clay with something like worship in his eyes. "Ryan Hamilton."

Clay remembered Ryan. He'd been a sophomore when Clay was a senior, the only sophomore to make the varsity team since Clay had. "Ryan went to yoga classes when he was running," the younger Hamilton boy said. "Our dad made fun of him for it but he went anyway."

"Plus," Clay put in, "you'll be in a room full of girls wearing tight pants. Gotta love that, right? Who knows, you might end up with a date."

The boys, none of them older than fifteen, got all pink-cheeked and giggly at the prospect. One of them closed his eyes, put his hands in a lotus position, and intoned "Ohm," but stopped when Clay snapped, "Shut it!"

The kid complied with a contrite, "Sorry, Coach."

"Did you go to yoga when you were running?" another one asked.

"Sure did," he admitted, though he declined to reveal that he had never dated nor even talked to any of those girls in tight yoga pants. Not until he met Julie.

"Ok, now that you're stretched, slow jog once around. Jog, not sprint, and no starting blocks yet. We'll get you guys fit into them in a little bit."

While the kids jogged, Clay allowed himself to relax for a moment. Maybe he could do this, instructing them, telling them what to do and not do, without having to participate himself.

When he was satisfied the kids were warmed up and stretched out sufficiently, he allowed four of them to place their feet into the starting blocks, to get the feel of them.

"Remember," he said, recalling what he had learned at their age. "Running is the most natural thing humans ever do. We've been doing it since the dinosaurs walked the earth."

One hand tentatively lifted in a, *can I say something* gesture.

"Uh, Coach, not to be argumentative, but the dinosaurs were extinct before humans evolved."

Clay was ready for that statement. "Or, maybe they sucked at the hundred-yard dash, and the dinosaurs caught them all and ate them."

The kids all laughed, as Clay remembered laughing when Coach Swanson had said the same thing.

Maybe he could do this. He was in the open air, which was good. He could see in all directions, no dark mysteries around him to spring out and yell, *Boo*. Maybe he was safe here.

He had four boys line up on the track, with a knee at the starting line to use their lower leg as a measurement, then had them position the front starting block next to the base of their foot. "Put the second block one foot back from the front one," he instructed. "You may adjust this positioning later as it suits you, but this will give you a good starting point." The four boys set their feet in the blocks after positioning them according to Clay's instructions.

"Now, for the mark position, put the knee of your rear leg on the ground with your hands touching the track at shoulder width, and your weight on your fingertips. Shift forward just a bit, with your head down. Keep your body in a straight line, and relax! Don't twist, don't bob your head. You're not at a rock concert. Try not to tighten up. It will only slow you down."

Across the track, Coach Swanson, the real coach, working with the varsity runners, fired a starting gun.

Bang! The simple small pop magnified in Clay's brain into the dangerous crack of a terrorist's sniper rifle.

"Take cover!" he shrieked, throwing himself from the chair and reaching for the nearest kid in the line of fire.

But there was no gunfire, no eye-stinging dust or smell of gunpowder, nothing blowing up or exploding. There was only himself, lying on the grass next to the stupid classroom chair, with a dozen teenagers standing around him looking as if an alien had just dropped out of the sky.

"Coach, you OK?" a voice asked with concern.

"Coach, do you need help? Maybe we should get Coach Swanson."

"Maybe we should call 911. I think he had a stroke."

Hands were touching him, pulling him upright. He couldn't get enough air.

"Don't touch me!"

He didn't realize how severely he'd barked the command until he observed the expressions of hurt and confusion on the kids who were just trying to help him.

"Don't call Coach. Don't call 911. I'm fine."

No, he wasn't fine. Who was he kidding? *I have to get out of here.*

"I'm OK," he muttered. He was a liar. He was far from OK. "I just need some water."

A water bottle was pressed into his hand as he pulled himself into a sitting position. God, had his prosthesis come detached, or had his sweatpants hiked up to reveal it? Dizziness swept over him and for a moment he felt like he might pass out. He wanted to hide in the smallest, darkest corner he could find.

"What happened, Coach?" He wasn't sure which kids were speaking because he was too embarrassed to look higher than their shoes. Those poor deluded kids, thinking he was a coach.

"You don't look so good." One of the boys was edging away. Maybe he thought Clay had something contagious. Maybe he was going to run and fetch Coach Swanson, the real coach. Because a lunatic like Clay had no business trying to guide a group of fifteen-year-olds.

Unfortunately, Coach Swanson noticed him on the ground with his runners standing around rather than running, and came trotting over, the starting gun still in his hand.

"What's going on?" he asked.

"Dunno, Coach. When you shot off the starter, Coach fell on the ground and yelled out. I think he thought someone was shooting a real gun."

"Aw, shit." The kids all looked shocked at Coach uttering an expletive in their presence. "I didn't think of that." He tossed the starting pistol on the grass. "Leave it there!" he snapped when one of the kids moved as if to pick it up.

Coach knelt down next to him. "Clay, I'm sorry, I didn't realize that might bother you."

I have to get out of here.

"What's wrong with him?" one of the kids asked.

Everything.

"He's having a PTSD episode," Coach Swanson said.

He might as well have said Clay was spewing out the Ebola virus, the way the kids looked at him in horror and started backing away.

Five minutes ago these kids had been calling him Coach, with admiration in their eyes and respect in their voices. Now they looked as if they were afraid of him, at the realization of what a fraud their alleged fake imposter of a so-called Coach he really was. To them, people with PTSD were crazy and should be locked up with the rest of the loonies. They shouldn't be allowed to be around impressionable teenagers. What if some of them were considering a career in the military? He'd scare them away from it completely, between his blown-off leg and his insanity. The recruiters would hate him.

His pulse was thundering. If he was a racehorse, they'd probably consider putting him down. Coach Swanson looked up at the boys.

"Practice is over for today. Go home."

They stood around, glancing at Coach in confusion, while Clay sat there panting like a mentally challenged dog. He tried to open the bottle of water one of the kids had given him but his hands were too sweaty to twist the cap.

"Go on. Go tell the other guys too." He waved a hand over to where the varsity runners were waiting. "Tell them we're done for today."

"But Coach," a couple of voices protested. "We just started."

"Go on. We'll start again tomorrow." With reluctance and confusion filling their faces, the boys started edging away, pulling phones out of their gym bags to call for rides.

I have to get out of here.

Though Clay had no direct memory of the Humvee exploding around him and his squad, the terror and blinding pain of it still inserted itself into his brain, threatening to rob him of his rationality. He closed his eyes, squeezing them tight against the shape of darkness engulfing him.

"I'll help you get to your car," Coach Swanson said. "I'm really sorry, Clay, I didn't realize the sound of the starter pistol would be an issue, I should have thought of that ahead of time."

He had no car. He couldn't drive. He wasn't part of this team, and it was a fantasy for him to think so. Running was freedom. Amputation was slavery.

"I didn't drive here," he admitted, opening his eyes, but keeping his gaze on the ground so he wouldn't have to see the looks of pity and disgust on the faces of the track team kids.

"Oh, then in that case, I'll give you a ride home. We'll try this again tomorrow."

Tomorrow? No, he could never come back here and face them.

"No, Coach, you don't have to," he protested. Having Coach Swanson drive him home was worse than having his mother drive him. He'd be returning the defective merchandise, the neurotic basket case who fell to pieces at the sound of a simple starter pistol. Maybe after everybody was gone he'd get another Uber.

His left leg burned with pain from thigh to toe and damn that was so unfair, that he still had to endure pain in a limb he didn't have. Phantom pain, the doctors had called it. It freaked him out every time it happened. The pain was unpredictable and changeable, sometimes burning, sometimes stabbing, sometimes twisting. They'd told him it was psychosomatic, which meant it was in his messed-up brain, because of course titanium didn't feel pain. What the doctors couldn't tell him was how long the phantom pain was going to last.

He wished everyone would just go away and leave him to his misery. But Coach Swanson insisted on helping him get up so he could sit back in the chair, the one with the folder bearing the words "Coach Maslowski" taped to the back. The kids were obeying the instructions to go home, gathering up their things and moving off towards the school driveway.

A feminine voice pierced his foggy brain. "Hi there, Mr. Swanson. Hi, Clay. Is everything OK?"

That voice. It was Julie. She was standing there a few feet away, looking too sexy for words in denim shorts and a cute yellow shirt. Some of the varsity runners were giving her the eye. If he'd been able-bodied Clay would have dashed over and told those creeps to put their eyeballs back in their heads.

Coach was shaking her hand. "Hello there, Julie. If you came to watch practice, I'm afraid we're quitting early today."

So Coach Swanson remembered Julie. Not surprising. She had attended every one of his track meets their senior year, both at home and away. Even in the rain. Even driving the fifteen miles all the way down to Schaumburg.

"I came to see Clay," she said.

Clay couldn't look at her. What was she doing here? Hadn't he told her there was no hope for them anymore?

Her hand was on his shoulder. "Are you OK?" she asked. He closed his eyes for a moment, both loving and hating the feel of her touch, but glanced up just enough to see Coach Swanson step away and give her a, *we need to talk*, glance and the two of them turned away from him, though he could see Coach Swanson glance back at him as he spoke to Julie in a voice too low for Clay to hear. He did, after all, have a slight hearing loss.

Great. They were talking about him. Coach was most likely telling Julie what an insane idiot her boyfriend was.

No, not boyfriend. Ex-boyfriend. He'd taken care of that relationship months ago, shortly after Kaboom. The two of them – Coach Swanson and Julie - came back to where he was sitting, still trying to uncap that stupid bottle of water, and Coach said, "I'll leave you in Julie's capable hands. Can we try this again tomorrow? I promise we'll only use a whistle, not starter guns."

Clay started to say, wanted to say, *no I can't*, but Julie spoke up on his behalf before he could get the words out. "Sure, Mr. Swanson." And the coach, damn him, just nodded agreeably, said, "Thanks, see you tomorrow," and scooped up the starter pistol off the ground before loping off across the football field. Most of the kids had left already while Clay had been there having his panic attack.

He was left there with Julie, who he wanted, needed more than anyone or anything ever in his life, but who he wished would go away too.

No, he didn't want that, even though it would still be for the best. But rather than leaving him there she knelt in front of him and took his hands.

"Cowboy? Are you alright?"

He wished he could lie to her and tell her that yes, he was all right, but he couldn't. He shook his head.

"Hearing the starter gun upset you," she said. It wasn't a question. Obviously Coach had told her about his flashback attack. "Did it remind you of things that happened in Afghanistan? Shooting?"

He still couldn't talk, just nodded, and gave up trying to open the water bottle. He dropped it on the ground, no he threw it, fully expecting the thing to split open and spill out. But it didn't, and Julie calmly picked it up, pulled up the edge of her shirt to wipe the cap, opened it and handed it to him. He hadn't been able to open it; his hands had been too shaky. But he gulped half the water down, because his throat had gone dry at the tiny glimpse of Julie's stomach that he'd seen when she used her shirt to wipe the bottle cap.

He remembered her fair skin, when they'd been in bed together, pale and beautiful next to his tan flesh, back before Kaboom. It had been almost a year ago but he hadn't forgotten kissing that very spot. His memories could feel his fingers and lips caressing, as they undressed and explored each other. He shouldn't be recalling that time of bliss. It only hurt him because he knew it was over, but how do you instruct your brain not to remember the best thing that ever happened to you?

"Come on," she encouraged. "My car is parked just over here." She stood up but her hands were still holding his, and he let himself curl his fingers around hers, wishing they could stay like that forever.

"What are you doing here?" he muttered, keeping his butt on the chair. He wasn't ready to try to stand up yet.

"I went to your house to see you, and your mother told me you were here helping your old track coach."

"That was a stupid thing for me to do," he muttered.

"Mr. Swanson felt really bad about the starter pistol," she said. "That's why he sent everyone home. He was embarrassed that he'd been so insensitive."

Embarrassed? *Coach* had been embarrassed? How could he have been? He wasn't the one diving for cover on a running track because he'd thought they were being attacked, when there was in reality no threat at all.

PTSD episode, Coach had said. It was the first time the term had been applied to him since he'd left the hospital. It was like anxiety on fire. It sucked. It blew. He wondered if that fancy new phone his parents had bought him had access to an online thesaurus so he could look up more synonyms for sucked the big hairy meatball.

"You and Coach were talking about me behind my back." His accusation was the whine of a spoiled brat, and he hated himself for it.

"Well then, talk to me to my face." How was it possible for a person to want something, and to not want that same thing, with equal ferocity? He couldn't look her in the eyes. Look what had happened last time he did that. He'd ended up bawling like a baby. She had a way of looking at him as if he was the only significant person in sight, and she still did so now.

Julie sighed. "I told Mr. Swanson I'd see that you come back tomorrow."

"I'm not coming back here. I can't," he said. "And it's Coach, not Mr. Swanson."

"Actually he told me I could call him Brent."

The surprise of that momentarily pulled him a bit out of his post-panic fog. "Coach said you could call him by his first name?"

Clay would never, ever in a million years, even consider addressing Coach Swanson as anything other than Coach, even if he was an adult now. Allegedly an adult, that is. Since the moment of Kaboom, his adulthood had hung by a thin, fragile thread.

Julie let go of his hands and picked up his cane where it lay on the ground next to his chair. Handing it to him, she said, "Come on, let's go. I don't have to be at work until five so I'm all yours until four."

All his? No, she wasn't all his. Surely she must remember that email he'd sent her right after Kaboom. But she was holding his arm, helping him to stand up, steadying him as she guided him towards her car parked in the lot, and he let her because he was too weak to resist her. He allowed her to put him into the passenger seat of her car. When she got in the driver's seat, she turned towards him.

"You were wrong," she said. "It's not over between us. I won't let it be."

"But, Julie," he started to protest.

She interrupted him. "I know you said that in your email. But I'm not accepting it. You were traumatized at the time and under the influence of strong painkillers."

It was true he had been on some pretty massive doses of medications then, but he'd still been lucid enough to know what was right where Julie was concerned, even if the right thing killed him inside.

"So!" she said brightly, as if this were some normal summer day and they were off to amuse themselves. "What do you want to do?"

It wasn't a matter of what he wanted to do, but what he needed to do.

"I need to go home."

Julie shook her head as she pulled out of the parking lot and onto Elmhurst Road. "It's only nine-thirty. We have almost all day. Have you had breakfast? Let's go get -"

He cut her off. "No! I need to go home!"

This whole getting out, doing normal stuff, acting like he had a reason for being, had been a huge mistake and he needed to get back to the safety of his lonely bedroom and take a pain pill. It only hurt him to see Julie pretending that they were still a couple.

She looked hurt. "Don't you want to spend time with me, Clay?"

Of course, he wanted to spend time with her. He wanted to spend forever with her. But it didn't matter what he wanted now. Better for her to think of him as a rude jerk, like his sister did, than to have to experience the pity and disgust that she would surely feel if she spent much time around him. Better not to know how she'd be dragged down by obligation if he selfishly hung around her. He'd be like a rock on a chain around her neck, a big heavy rock, dragging her down to drown in his nothingness.

He looked out the window so he wouldn't have to see the same expressions of hurt and confusion he'd seen the day she'd found him in his back yard. He couldn't lie and say no, he didn't want to spend time with her, but he couldn't tell her the truth either. His silence hung between them like an invisible but solid barricade.

After a moment he heard her sigh. "If that's really what you want, I'll take you home. Your mother told me to not push it and to give you time."

Great. Not only was she discussing him with Coach, but with his mother too. And with that sergeant she'd contacted. This wasn't how a non-existent relationship was supposed to be.

Mercifully she had him in his parent's driveway in a few minutes, but put her hand on his arm, capturing him before he could get out of the car.

"What time should I pick you up in the morning to go back to the school?"

She had to be kidding. "I'm not going back there, ever. Don't pick me up."

"Why not? Brent said he wouldn't use the starter pistol if it bothered you."

"It doesn't matter. I can't face them again."

"I don't see why not. Having PTSD is nothing to be ashamed of. If you want, I'll stay there with you."

He couldn't let her do that, as much as he would like to. She worked long, late hours at the restaurant, and the last thing she needed was to get up early after a grueling shift to babysit for him. Besides, he didn't like the way some of those senior boys looked at her. Not that he had any right to be jealous.

"No, I said I'm not going back. I'll send Coach a text telling him not to expect me."

Her hand was still on his arm and he looked at her fingers. Just five slender feminine fingers, yet they held him in place more than anything ever could.

"I don't think I told you how absolutely sorry I am about your leg," she said. "I know it's the most horrible thing that could possibly happen to a person. But I'm not giving up on you, Cowboy. Don't think you can get rid of me that easily. I want to help you get through this so we can be together again. Did you meet with that guy from the Wounded Warrior Project?"

"Yes," he admitted.

"Good. I hope you keep meeting with him. He seemed really nice when I talked to him, and I think he'll be a big help for you. I want to help you too if you'll let me."

"Julie." He didn't know what else to say. Or at least he couldn't get the words he wanted to say out of his mouth. Maybe the best thing would be for him to just get out of the car now before he cried again. But the next thing he knew, they were embracing. He didn't know if he leaned towards her or if she leaned towards him, but their arms were around each other, they were as close as they could be in the bucket seats of her car. His head was on her shoulder, and her head was on his shoulder. It felt so right, so comfortable, so wonderful, and he never wanted it to end. He didn't cry and she didn't kiss him, but it was still everything.

"You don't need to be afraid anymore, Cowboy," Julie said against his skin.

Afraid? He wasn't afraid. He was many things, but not afraid. He was depressed, traumatized, hopeless, but he was not afraid.

Or, maybe he was. Afraid of being seen, being gawked at, being judged. Afraid of unexpected noises and unfamiliar places.

He had no right to be here like this, in her arms, feeling the arousal he always did whenever he saw her or touched her or thought about her. She wasn't his anymore. They had broken up months ago. Or so he thought.

When they finally separated, he was surprised to be able to look at her without falling apart or terrifying her with his haunted eyes. She kissed his cheek, just a brief peck, and said, "Let me know if you change your mind about the track team. Brent could use your help."

He could only nod, his speechlessness now due to the magic of her touch rather than to his trauma. Although his heart wanted him to stay there with her forever, he knew he had to leave her before she either assumed they were a couple again, or encouraged him to go back to the school.

Nothing like a PTSD episode to set a romantic mood.

He grasped his cane and opened the door, but before he tried to get out of the car, he reminded her, "It's not Brent. It's *Coach*."

"Coach to you, Brent to me," she said with a smile and a little giggle. "But I'm not sure if I can do that, I mean call a teacher from high school by their first name, even though we've graduated. It's too weird. Are you sure you don't want me to come back in the morning to pick you up?"

"Don't pick me up. I told you I'm not going back."

"I don't mind," she persisted. "You know I'm here for you. Whatever you need."

"What time did you get home from work last night?" he asked, though he was pretty sure he knew the answer.

She looked a bit surprised at his changing the subject, but went along. "Well, by the time we closed, cleaned up, and prepped for tonight, I left at about one a.m."

Julie still lived at home with her parents. She hadn't gotten her own place when she started working because she'd been saving up her money for the life that she and Clay had been implicitly planning together. By the time she drove home to Wheeling, it was probably after two before she could go to bed. He knew that at her restaurant, the bulk of the drudgery chores went to the junior staff members such as her. Then she'd been up to come to his house and to the high school in the morning. For what? To see him? That wasn't fair to her.

"You weren't there all alone?" he asked, his throat constricting with fear at the thought of her walking out to her car alone at that late hour, in the dark, parked at the far end of the parking lot to keep the closer spots open for customers.

"No, we have a security guard who comes in when the restaurant closes and makes sure everyone gets to their cars safely when they leave."

He felt an irrational jealousy towards that unknown security guard who had the privilege of walking Julie to her car in the early morning darkness. Maybe he had held her door open for her. Maybe he had asked her out.

He shouldn't be jealous. She wasn't his woman anymore, even if she did come to see him and express her concern at his idiotic lunacy.

It might have been rude, but he got out and limped up to his front door without saying goodbye or looking back, even when he heard the swish of her window opening.

"See you soon!" she called out, and by reflex he turned and looked back to see her waving cheerily, just as if this was a normal day and he was a normal person. He didn't respond, because he was basically an asshole. Even he didn't want to spend time with himself. How could anyone else want to do so? It just reinforced his belief that Julie was too good for her own good, and he didn't deserve her.

His mother heard him come in and smiled at him as if he deserved it.

"How was your track coach?" she asked. "Did Julie find you? Was that her in the driveway? Why didn't you invite her in? I wanted to thank her for the lovely cake she brought over."

The truthful answers to those questions were, Traumatizing, Yes, Yes, and, Because it would break my heart, but he couldn't say any of those to his mother. And he hadn't eaten any of the cake Julie had brought to them. His parents and Brooke had enjoyed it, but the confection conjured up too many memories of being with her. He just mumbled some excuse and limped up to his room.

It was way too soon for him to take another pain pill. He was supposed to wait four hours in between, and it had barely been two. But he needed one bad, and he took the pill with him to the bathroom. He'd forgotten the half-drunk bottle of water someone had given him back at the high school track, had left it on the ground. He was a litterbug as well as an insane freak.

He lay on his bed with his arm over his eyes trying without success not to think about the morning's events.

Coach said his reaction to the sound of the starter gun was an *issue*. It was way more than an issue. Coach still wanted Clay to come back and continue to help with the track team, despite his panic attack. Coach had told Julie to call him by his first name. He hadn't extended that offer to Clay. But then why should he? Julie gave up on much-needed sleep after a long, tough work shift to come see him, to try to help him. She'd wanted to spend time with him but he had rudely rebuffed her instead, afraid to take that kind of emotional risk. Afraid to take a chance.

He grabbed his phone and sent a text to Coach Swanson saying he wouldn't be able to help him at track camp anymore.

His simple "Sorry' was a weak ending to the message, when he should be apologizing profusely for his behavior and bad influence on those poor kids.

Face it, Clay, he thought as the effects of the Vicodin kicked in. *Your life sucks.*

Chapter Ten

He got a text from Jacoby that very night, and wondered if Julie had called him to tell him about his coaching debacle. Apparently he had agreed to meet with the guy at Starbucks again and Jacoby wanted to confirm a day and time. Clay didn't recall any such agreement but the way his mind was messed up now, he may very well have done so without realizing it.

Somehow he found himself again taking an Uber to meet with Staff Sergeant Jacoby, who was already there with two pumpkin spice lattes on the table when Clay arrived. Why could he not say no? He purposely set the meeting for Wednesday when his parents would be at work. He didn't tell Brooke where he was going, not that it would matter. Now that she was done with her junior year of high school and free for the summer, she stayed up late and slept in late in the morning. He hadn't seen her when he left the house, but that wasn't the issue. They hadn't spoken a word to each other since his rude outburst at her last week. Surprisingly, Jacoby had no problem agreeing to meet him at ten a.m. Didn't he have a job to go to? Or was his life's work devoted to putting Clay on a spot he didn't want to be on?

He knew if he asked Julie, she would pick him up and take him to this meeting. But then she'd probably end up talking to Sergeant Jacoby about Clay as she had with Coach Swanson. Jacoby would probably invite her to call him by his first name too. Clay could probably get away with calling the guy Nathan rather than Jacoby or Sergeant, but his Army habits prevailed.

"Are you going to your physical therapy?" Jacoby asked as they sipped their pumpkin spice lattes.

Clay shrugged, which Jacoby correctly interpreted as a negative. "And why not?"

He shrugged again, trying to look uncaring, but his blush gave him away.

"Let me guess." Jacoby lifted his hand and started counting off on his fingers. "You don't think it will do any good. You think it's a pointless bunch of hokum. You're too proud to admit you need help. You think your life is over so why bother. You can't drive yet – either because you haven't tried or you're still on pain meds. Which is it?"

Clay refused to answer and just stared at the stupid cup of coffee Jacoby had bought him. Jacoby gave him a moment to answer, an opportunity he refused to take. Another effect of Kaboom. He couldn't talk about it or how he felt, when before that he'd been an open, talkative guy. The staff sergeant was probably going to tell him that his body would adjust to the prosthesis and that after a while he'd forget it was even there. Easy to say for someone with two legs. Clay was aware of this amputation and prosthesis every waking moment.

Jacoby hit the nail on the head. "It's all of the above, isn't it?"

Of course all of those reasons applied. As far as Clay was concerned, those were all the reasons he needed.

"Do you have plans for your future?" That was the million-dollar question, the one that neither his mother, father or Julie had dared to ask. But Staff Sergeant Jacoby, he asked.

Oh Clay had plans all right. Big plans. Important plans. He was going to spend the rest of his life living like a hermit in his parents' home, sleeping in his childhood bedroom, living on disability and pain pills and feeling sorry for himself.

That was a great plan for life, wasn't it?

His future and his plans for it had vanished, as surely as if it had been blown away by a bomb. In fact, that was exactly what had happened.

He'd had a crazy plan in his head, before Kaboom, to attend Ranger School. Clay's battle buddy from basic training, Noah Gadsden, had been deployed to Afghanistan with him and the both of them had aspired to become Rangers. They had been training and practicing the physical requirements, the proper assembly of the M60 rifle, and planning to attend Army Jump School to become airborne qualified. The CIB – Combat Infantry Badge – he would have earned after completing his deployment would be an advantage as well. Noah had been with them in the Humvee on the day of Kaboom but his injuries had been minor, so Clay had been told. Even though they'd been friends for almost four years, he hadn't been in touch with the guy since that day, so he didn't know if Noah had gotten into Ranger School without Clay.

He was getting tired of just shrugging in response to questions. Maybe if he answered them with words, the sergeant would quit asking.

"Maybe. I'm thinking about it."

Jacoby seemed satisfied with the vague answer and didn't press for details.

"Tell me what things make you happy."

That was an easy one. "Right now, nothing."

"OK, then what made you happy before you lost your leg?"

"Julie. But I screwed things up with her. My sister, but she's not talking to me. Music."

"You still have music, don't you? You didn't suffer permanent hearing loss in the explosion?"

"A little, on the left."

He sort of still had his music. He could listen to it, but singing – he wasn't sure if he'd ever be able to do that again.

"Why is your sister not speaking to you?"

"I said some rude things to her. In fact, I was a total jerk."

"There is an easy fix to that."

Yeah right. Easy for him to say. Jacoby wasn't the one who had broken up with his girlfriend, pissed off his sister, and made his parents cry.

"You just go to her, look pitiful, say – what's your sister's name?"

"Brooke."

"OK, you say, Brooke, I was a total jerk and I apologize for saying rude things to you. Please forgive me. If you can squeeze out a tear it will help immensely."

Looking pitiful and squeezing out a tear wouldn't be hard at all.

"Now with your lovely Julie, it might be more difficult to make amends. Flowers may have to be involved."

"How do you know she's lovely?" he asked, with undeserved jealousy.

"She sent me a photo of you two, so I would recognize you when we met. See?"

He held up his phone and Clay found himself looking at a photo of himself and Julie taken just before he'd left for his deployment, him standing proud in his uniform, Julie smiling just as proudly as she held onto his arm. It was a digital version of the same photo Julie foolishly carried in her pocket to show to other guys who asked her out.

The sergeant would probably be displeased if Clay were to grab away his phone and smash it on the floor so he wouldn't have to look at that smiling photo. It was just as bad as the pictures in his parent's living room. But the Army had taught him to respect those who outranked him, and the respect was still embedded in him despite his medical discharge, so he let the guy keep his phone and didn't even ask him to delete the photo.

He found, despite himself, that he was starting to like this guy. Jacoby exuded an aura of contentment with his life, a sentiment that had eluded Clay since the moment of Kaboom.

"No, I can never make things right with her. I have no right to. She deserves better." That was why he'd sent Julie away every time he saw her. It was the right thing to do, wasn't it?

"Did you deserve her before you lost your leg?"

"I thought so."

"Then you still deserve her now. You're the same person you were before and I'm sure she will understand that."

It was so easy for Jacoby to say. Just apologize. Offer flowers. Those were far too simplistic fixes to his messed-up relationships, as if those casual suggestions could fix the unfixable.

"I can't have Julie back because I love her," he said.

Jacoby arched an eyebrow. "Care to explain that one?"

"Isn't love supposed to be caring more about the other person than yourself?" Clay asked. "That's why we can't be together. I love her too much to put her through that."

"I think I know a thing or two about being in love," Jacoby replied. "Another part is respecting the other person enough to believe in them."

When Clay offered neither argument nor agreement, Jacoby asked, "Have you talked to a counselor?"

"More than I ever want to again." The shrinks had been on him like white on rice from the moment he'd woken up after his surgery.

What did the psychiatrists know about what he had been through? They had been in combat themselves, they'd said, but hadn't lost so much as a fingernail, not to mention a limb. They wanted him to talk about it and to get it all out. Like that would help. Talking about it would just expose his already-obvious weakness, that vulnerable soft underbelly that the Man Code demanded be protected at all costs. He talked just enough to get through the session, then rolled back to his room and crawled inside himself. The counselors were probably writing in their case notes, *loser.*

Those stupid shrinks, telling him to think about all the good things he should look forward to. What did they know, with their fancy PhDs mounted in a frame on an office wall? They all had two normal, attached legs. How could they possibly understand what he was feeling, experiencing, just because they had gone to school long enough to put the title Doctor in front of their names? They were just feeding him shit and calling it sugar.

Jacoby wasn't done with his interrogation.

"How are your parents doing?"

Why should he ask about people he didn't know?

"I guess they're OK. They tiptoe around things. Offer to help. Act all optimistic."

They wanted the old Clay back but they weren't going to get him, because the old Clay didn't exist anymore.

"I know it may be difficult to talk to family," Jacoby said, "even though they support you endlessly. But they might not understand what you're going through. For some guys, it's more comfortable talking with other veterans, because we've been there."

"What's the point?" Clay retorted, hating how whiny he sounded.

"It's about self-respect and pride," Jacoby retorted back. Two things Clay no longer had, thanks to Kaboom. "Getting help is not an admission of failure, you know. It's an admission of caring. When did sitting around feeling sorry for yourself ever get you anywhere?"

"You sound like a shrink." Clay's observation was not meant as a compliment. "What do you do in civilian life?" What could the guy do that gave him the freedom of sitting in a coffee shop at ten a.m. on a weekday? If he was another shrink, Clay doubted he'd be back for another meeting, even if the guy did buy him coffee.

"After the Army, I took advantage of my military educational benefits and finished my degree, and got my master's. Now I teach history at Fremd High School."

He was a Fremdie? Even though it had been almost five years since Clay had graduated from high school, his loathing for Wheeling's rivals still flowed through his veins. He'd left the Fremdies in the dust at their last track meet, back in the day. Because back then, he could.

"What is it you want out of life?" Jacoby asked.

What he wanted out of life was the impossible. He wanted the ability to time travel, to about ten minutes before Kaboom, and to have ESP so that he could tell Sergeant Lopez to hit the brakes.

"It's not a matter of what I want. Not anymore. You know what I did in high school?"

"Did your homework, stayed out of trouble, respected your teachers?"

"I may have missed an assignment once in a while, but I did most of it. I'll admit I smarted off to a teacher once or twice but nothing too egregious."

"You must have come away with something if you kept the word egregious in your vocabulary."

"I was on the track team. A runner. Pretty ironic, isn't it? I was pretty good if I do say so myself. Set a record or two at my high school. At Basic Training, I actually looked forward to the daily runs, even with the thirty pounds of gear. I almost always came in first, and I won the running award in my class at Basic for the two-mile run. The other guys were getting shin splints because they weren't used to running that much, but not me. I loved the obstacle course and the runs."

He'd loved the endorphins, the runner's high – a free and legal rush with no side effects other than sweat.

"Now I can barely walk."

"That will improve with practice," Jacoby assured him, but Clay had his doubts. "Let's go back to your high school escapades. I want to hear about the most egregious thing you ever did."

Clay found himself almost smiling at the memory. Almost.

"One time I snuck a frog into school and put it in a teacher's desk drawer. But I made an error in judgment when I chose which teacher's desk to put the frog in. It was Mrs. Anderson, the biology teacher. She opened the drawer and the whole class heard little Kermit there say, ribbit. We expected her to scream or faint or something. But she just smiled, picked the thing up and said, aren't you just a handsome little thing. I think that frog fell in love with her. She took it home and kept it as a pet."

Jacoby chuckled. "I once had a student put a snake in my desk drawer. Just one of those harmless little garter snakes you can get down by the Des Plaines River. I didn't scream or faint either. You've got to be a little tough to be a teacher, you know. I picked it up and held it in front of the class and asked, whose little brother is this? You never saw twenty-seven kids get quiet and stiff so fast in your life. The bell rang and I said, nobody moves until someone claims this. The kids started to get antsy – they needed to move on to their next class, lunch, band practice. Finally the culprit stood up and claimed it. I tossed it at him and told him to make sure it got returned somewhere safe. Safe for the snake, that is. The guy screamed like a five-year-old when I threw that snake at him. He was the biggest kid in the class too, and kind of a bully."

"I get what you're doing," Clay grunted. "You're trying to get me to think about other shit so I forget about my leg. Well it's not going to work."

"It did for a minute."

Jacoby had obviously studied Psychology of Cripples 101 at the same time he'd gotten his teaching degree. He'd hit the nail on the head again.

Some mornings when Clay first woke up, he forgot for just a second about his amputation. But the feeling of normalcy was fleeting to say the least, and dissipated as soon as he moved, and especially since the day he'd fallen.

"You've come a long way," Jacoby said. "Right after your accident -"

"It was not an accident," Clay snapped. "This happened on purpose, by terrorists who wanted to kill Americans."

"OK. I'll rephrase. After you lost your leg, you were flat on your back at first, right?"

That was right. Especially after sending Julie that brutal breakup email. He'd closed the laptop, laid back and stared at the ceiling for a long time, trying not to cry. Trying not to scream or howl or curse.

"It's a process. You were on your back, then in a wheelchair, then on crutches. Even after you were fitted with the prosthesis you had to use a walker for a while. Now you've progressed to the cane. There's no reason not to expect to walk without it eventually, even to run again someday."

Sergeant Jacoby had sure done his research on the progress of a cripple.

"I hate seeing people staring at me. When I came home from Germany I had to go to the gate in a wheelchair and everyone we passed had to stare at me. I hated it. I wanted to just disappear and never be seen again. Even walking, the way I limp and use a cane, they still stare."

"People will stare. It's human nature. They can't help it, and they don't mean to be rude. It can be overwhelming at first. But trying to hide away from it won't make it stop. Just look back at them. Look them in the eye, like any other normal person.

Give them a look that says, so what if I'm on crutches or use a cane or even a wheelchair. That doesn't make me a freak."

Jacoby was wrong. The need for those accessories did make Clay a freak.

"Let me ask you this," Jacoby went on. "Who in your life has rejected you due to your amputation?"

"What do you mean?"

"Who has shut you out, shunned you, broken off a relationship with you, due to your losing your leg? Your parents, your family, your girlfriend, your friends? Who among them has said, get away from me, I don't want to be seen with you? Come on, name me one person who has abandoned you due to your situation."

He had to admit, nobody had treated him like that. Everyone had tried to keep or renew the relationships he'd had before Kaboom, even his former track coach. His cousin Stephanie's foster child had only walked away from him because he'd been rude, not because he was an amputee.

"Well, none of them," he was forced to admit. "But that's because they haven't seen it. If they did, it would all be different."

"How do you know? Who has seen your leg, your prosthesis, and how did they react?"

Nobody. Nobody had seen him but himself, and medical professionals. The closest anyone had come had been the day his father had come upon him in the hallway on crutches, wearing that oversized bathrobe. He'd been a lot more careful since then.

"They'd be grossed out if they saw it. I don't even want to see it."

"You can't say that for certainty unless you put your money where your mouth is. People can't help being curious. It's human nature. There's no point in hiding it away as if it were something to be ashamed of."

Jacoby could make all the claims he wanted, but until he'd walked a mile on Clay's prosthesis, he didn't have a clue what he was talking about.

"If it were someone else who had suffered such an injury – a family member, a friend, an Army comrade, would you call them a freak and push them out of your life?"

No. He'd never do that to anybody he cared about.

"Then, Corporal Maslowski, you should have faith that your family and friends, and especially the woman you love, would do the same. But when you're all grouchy and won't talk to them, they don't know what to do. It's not their fault."

Clay had been more than grouchy, since Kaboom. He'd been downright surly. Did Jacoby call him Corporal just to rub salt in his wounds?

"Even going to Mass is a huge chore that I have to plan in advance," he grumbled, partly because it bothered him and partly to change the subject.

"Well, I'm Jewish so I wouldn't know about that," Jacoby said.

"There's no way my parents, especially my mother, would let me stay home."

"Do your parents know how depressed you are?"

"Crippled, depressed – what's the difference?"

"The difference is, one's physical, the other is emotional. And I really don't like the term crippled. It sounds way too limiting."

"That pretty much sums up my life. Limited."

"Now, that attitude comes from being depressed. And you have it in you to improve both of those situations."

"Sometimes I wish ..." Clay's throat filled up and got tight, rendering him unable to vocalize the thought, because what he sometimes wished was an awful, horrible thing.

A hand covered his, not in a sexual way, just in a comforting way. He looked up into Jacoby's sympathetic eyes.

"Sometimes you wish you'd been the one who'd bled out," Jacoby guessed. "Maybe you wish you were the one to be buried at Arlington, and that your parents were the ones with a flag in a nice wood case, with your posthumous Purple Heart attached, displayed in the living room, where they'll see it every day and cry over you?"

"I don't want that, the grieving part for my family. They've cried more than enough over this as it is. But, Jesus, I ..." He paused for a moment to compose himself, and Jacoby removed his hand from Clay's to steeple his fingers under his chin, listening.

"Did it ever occur to you that maybe they think you're worth crying over?"

No, that thought had never occurred to Clay. It wasn't true anyway, was it?

"I was even so stupid as to take up my high school coach's offer to help him with summer track camp. You know what happened? He shot off a starter pistol and I..." He was too embarrassed to tell Jacoby how he'd fallen on the ground, expecting incoming gunfire. "Coach said I was having a PTSD episode."

"That's nothing to be ashamed of."

Jacoby was wrong. Clay had been utterly mortified at the sight of those kids standing around staring at him

"So you had a PTSD episode? I'm not surprised. I'm not terribly fond of things that go boom myself."

Perhaps, but Jacoby hadn't experienced Kaboom like Clay had.

"I went into complete, full-on idiot mode. Those kids were looking at me like I was crazy."

"Did you explain your situation to them?"

"Of course not. They'd never understand."

"Why not? They're high school students. They're supposed to be learning things. That's the whole point of being in school, to learn things."

"What would they learn? That their supposed assistant coach was a fraud, a cripple and a lunatic?"

"No, they could learn that a brave man made a great sacrifice and that the experience can have adverse effects on him afterward."

Adverse effects. Another weak description of how Kaboom had made him a monster.

"I don't think this was in their curriculum."

"What did your coach do when this happened?" Jacoby asked.

"He canceled practice for the day and sent all the kids home."

Jacoby winced as if he felt pain. "Wrong thing to do in my opinion," he declared. "He should have kept them there, should have had you talk to them so that they could understand what happened and why. A large part of overcoming PTSD is simply talking about the experience, getting it out into the open so other people can understand what you've gone through."

Those kids could have stuck around until they were a hundred, but Clay sure as hell wasn't going to explain anything to them. Let them Google "PTSD episode" for themselves. He didn't want to have to see the expressions on their faces when they did. He'd rather gouge his eyes out.

"Your coach – I'm sure he's a great guy – but he had a teachable moment there and he missed it."

A teachable moment?

"Maybe I should call over to Wheeling High School and talk to him."

Oh great. That was just what Clay needed. Two high school teachers getting together to discuss him and his disability. It would be like parent-teacher conferences all over again. No, it would be worse.

"What happened after that?"

"Julie showed up. She wanted to spend time with me, go out to eat. Talk."

"Did you?"

"No. I made her take me home." He declined to give Jacoby specifics, embarrassed at how rude he'd been. He was starting to think he'd made the wrong decision that morning.

Jacoby looked disbelieving. "You passed on the opportunity to spend time with that lovely young lady, to do what? Sit alone and brood?"

When put like that, it sounded kind of stupid.

"Did the counselors in Germany suggest you write a journal?"

Clay rolled his eyes. "Maybe." Stupid suggestion.

"You should try it. It doesn't have to be a professional book. Nobody else even has to see it. But it might help to record your thoughts, feelings, memories."

How could he write that shit down when his thoughts were a mess, his feelings were black, and his memories were things he'd been trying to suppress?

"You need to try it," Jacoby persisted as they left the coffee shop. "If I let you off the hook you'll just lay around in bed all day (that was right) and that's not good."

Chapter Eleven

Just to prove Sergeant Jacoby wrong, Clay did not lay around in bed all day. He showed up at the dinner table without being summoned and he really did try to eat a little more.

"I'll help you with the dishes," he said later, as his sister stood up and picked up her plate from the table.

Three voices fell silent and three pairs of eyes stared at him as if he'd sprouted horns. He had never, ever voluntarily offered to help with the dishes before. His parents continued to stare at him as he grabbed his cane and dragged himself to his feet.

"I need to talk to Brooke." He looked down at his plate of half-eaten dinner, afraid to see rejection in his sister's eyes.

Clay's mother looked at his face, turned to his father, and said, "Lloyd, we need to go check the oil in my car."

"But, Gail," his dad protested, "Remember, I just had the oil changed last week. We don't need to check it again."

"Yes, we do," Mom insisted. "Now."

Again Dad started to protest the unnecessary desire to check the oil until Mom said, "Lloyd!" in a sharp voice that made both Clay and Brooke stare at their parents. "Oil. Car. Now." The words weren't loud, but had a definite, obedience-demanding aura of Mom-steel in them, as she gave her husband a look that apparently communicated things without words in a way that only people married thirty years could do.

"Oh, yeah, right, we need to check the oil in your car now," Dad said, almost as if hypnotized, and within seconds they were out the door, leaving Clay and Brooke to talk in private.

Clay could only take one plate at a time, so Brooke had everything cleared in the time it took him to get two plates from the dining room table to the kitchen counter next to the sink.

"I'll rinse," he offered.

"Good idea," Brooke said. "You have no idea how to load a dishwasher."

He was glad at least that she spoke to him, though she ignored him as she loaded dishes, her shoulder as cold as February.

"Brooke," he pleaded. He held onto the plate she was about to take from his hand until she looked at him. His parents had decamped the house because his mother knew, telepathically, that Clay wanted to talk to his sister privately, to set things right. He didn't want to blow his chance. "I'm sorry about how I talked to you the other day. You're right, I was a jerk and I had no right to be, and I apologize."

She stared at him for a moment, his contriteness apparently confusing her.

"Who are you," she asked, "and what have you done with the real Clay?"

"He doesn't exist anymore," Clay said, which was true. His mind and soul were battered and overwhelmed.

She was still for a moment, then she set down the plate, turned and hugged him so fiercely it almost knocked him over. Suddenly he was her big brother again, the big brother who had protected her from bullies, comforted her when she was sad, fixed the flat tire on her bike.

In his heart, he felt a part of himself that had been broken, reconnect and heal itself.

"I'm sorry I called you a jerk." Her voice was sniffly against his shoulder.

"It's OK." He leaned against the counter for stability and patted her back a little, though in reality, it was Brooke who comforted him more than anything. "You were just trying to help, but I was too stupid and angry and I'm sorry I took it out on you like that."

Brooke gulped and sniffed against his shoulder.

"Don't cry, Brooke," he said. "Don't you dare."

"Don't you tell me what to do, Cuckoo. I'll cry if I damn well need to cry. Maybe I'm tired of being the strong one in the family."

"You, the strong one?"

"Yes. Mom and Dad were a wreck after we got that call about you. I can't remember how many wet tissues I had to pick up off the floor. Especially after you told them to stay home."

"I'm sorry. I didn't mean to hurt you guys worse. I was just too chicken shit to let you come and see me."

Brooke drew back and wiped her eyes as Clay steadied himself with his cane. "God, it was horrible seeing mom and dad crying after we heard about what happened," she said. "Daddy was the worst. He cried more over what happened to you than Mom did over Amelia."

If his mother had cried over him more than she had over Amelia, and his dad cried more than his mother, that had to have been pretty horrifying for Brooke to see.

They had all cried over him when he left for basic training, when he'd been assigned to infantry training at Fort Benning, when he'd left for deployment. But it had been different then. They'd been proud of him, of what he was doing, of the man he was becoming. Now they shed only tears of grief rather than pride, and it was all his fault.

"Why you, Clay?" she asked. "Why did it have to be you?"

"Do you think I haven't asked myself that, every minute since it happened? Or at least, every minute since two days after it happened."

"What happened those first two days?"

"I was in a coma." Brooke nodded, remembering. "But every minute since then I've asked and wondered and raged at God – why me? Why not the guy next to me or anybody else in the world?"

Brooke picked up a plate from the counter as if to put it in the dishwasher, then set it back down and looked at him.

"Dad and I were at the mall one day, about a week before you came home," she said. "He was picking up a gift they were having engraved for one of his guys at work who's retiring. Anyway, on the way to the store we walked past the Army recruiting office."

Clay remembered that place. How he'd been both nervous, and excited, sitting at the recruiter's desk, signing the papers that would commit himself to his Commander in Chief for four years. He had been just about to email that recruiter to tell him he planned to re-enlist for another four years, when Kaboom had happened.

"I stopped to look at the poster in the window." She blushed a little. "The guy they used must have been a model rather than a real soldier because he was hot, not a cuckoo like you." Brooke called him by the nickname Cuckoo because his dark coloring stuck out against his blond parents and sister. But the term cuckoo was also sometimes used as a slang term for crazy and in that it was certainly accurate as it applied to Clay.

His sister thought guys in ads were hot? Clay felt sick to his stomach. It seemed like just yesterday she was into kitty cats and unicorns.

"Dad saw me looking at it, and he must have thought I was going to go in there and sign up myself because he grabbed my arm and literally pulled me away, and said, *no*. Don't you even think about it.

"But I've been thinking about it a lot, ever since we got that phone call from the Army. I'm considering enlisting too after high school. There was a sergeant from the hospital in Germany who called us all the time to update us on how you were doing and when you would come home. He was really helpful and nice and comforting when we talked to him. I talked to him a couple of times when Mom and Dad weren't home when he called, and he told me a lot about what he does there."

Clay remembered that sergeant. The official job title was LNCO – Liaison Non-Commissioned Officer. He had escorted Clay's gurney when he'd arrived at Landstuhl in a medically-induced coma, and had coordinated everything he'd needed outside his actual medical treatment. That liaison had communicated with Clay's family more than Clay had himself, made sure he got to all his physical therapy sessions, supervised his first attempts at walking with crutches, explained everything Clay needed to know while he was there. He'd dealt with Clay's bad attitude, lack of cooperation and general despair with calm compassion, and had brought a chaplain to his hospital room more than once when Clay was at his lowest emotional point of depression. He really should have been more appreciative of all that the liaisons had done for him and his family.

"I want to do something like that," Brooke was saying. "I want to be a patient liaison and help guys like you who've been wounded."

"Mom and Dad won't like that," Clay warned.

"I know," she admitted. "I haven't said anything to them about it yet. Don't tell them I'm considering it, OK?"

He nodded, his emotions thickening at the thought of his baby sister making plans like that, to follow him into the Army, to try and help others who had experienced what Clay had.

"Clay, I'm sorry about what I said to you when I was eight."

He had no idea what she was apologizing for. The two of them had been exchanging good-natured insults since Brooke had begun to talk.

"I'm sorry I said you were adopted. I was only mad at you for something. I don't even remember why. But I didn't mean it."

"That's OK, Brooke. Jeez, you were eight years old. But you know, after that I asked Mom why I was the only one in the family with dark hair and eyes. She told me I looked just like the pictures of her grandfather, so, meh."

He stuck his tongue out at his sister and she laughed.

"All I wanted was my big brother back," she said. "But instead I got this guy who looked like him, but wasn't him."

"I'm afraid the big brother you used to have doesn't exist anymore," he admitted.

Brooke shook her head. "No, I refuse to believe that. My big brother Clay is still in there. You just need to let him out."

"I wish I could believe that. You're stuck with me. Can I be your big brother?"

"Yes, please. Are you done rinsing?" She put the final dishes in the machine, and Clay handed her the detergent. When she'd added it and closed the door, she started it up and while they listened to the warm, homely whirr of water, she said, "I'll forgive you for talking mean to me if you forgive me for calling you a jerk."

"You got it, sis."

"But I still haven't forgiven you for that stunt you pulled when I went out on my first date."

For the first time since Kaboom, he chuckled.

The last time he'd been home on leave, before Kaboom, Brooke had introduced him to a boy, a date with whom she was attending a school dance. His baby sister going on a *date*. Shit.

When he heard the date was coming to pick her up at their house, Clay donned his uniform and put the fucking fear of God into the kid, demanding to inspect his driver's license and proof of insurance, grilling him as to where they were going and at what time he would have Brooke home, as well as demanding assurances that the boy's intentions towards his sister were completely and utterly honorable and that drinking anything stronger than fruit punch was not going to happen. He was only sorry that he didn't have a weapon with him at the time that he could casually caress during the conversation.

To his credit, the date had held up to the intimidating interrogation remarkably well and didn't even wet his pants, while Brooke stood there red-faced with embarrassment and fury, which he was sure he was going to hear about later. But, hey, that's what big brothers were supposed to do, right?

Their parents had wisely remained in the kitchen, where they sat drinking coffee and trying to keep their laughter low enough so that Brooke and Clay didn't hear. After Brooke and her date had left, his dad had busted a gut and said to Clay, "You reminded me of your grandpa the day I had my first date with your mother."

To which his mother had replied, with her own laughter, "Oh, he wasn't that bad."

Clay for his part had been totally weirded out at the concept of his parents ever being teenagers going out on a date.

Chapter Twelve

Now that it was summer and Brooke was out of school, Clay never knew whether she would be at home during the day or not. But what he did not expect was to limp down the stairs, hobble into the kitchen, and see Julie sitting at their kitchen table drinking a soda, just as if she belonged there.

He was stunned speechless. Julie however, was prepared.

"Hi there, Cowboy. Do you want to go see a movie?"

When he found his voice, he croaked, "How did you get in here?"

"Through the door, of course. I knocked, Brooke answered, and here I am."

A half-consumed bowl of corn flakes on the table indicated Brooke's recent breakfast, or, seeing that it was almost noon, perhaps it was her lunch. She had left the milk on the table. Clay picked up the carton and opened the fridge to put it away, and asked, "Where is Brooke?"

"She went upstairs. Why? Do you need her to protect you from me?"

If anyone needed protection, it was Julie. Protection from him and his depression. Her being around him could only be unhealthy for her. He might infect her with his broken mental state.

"I mean," he amended, "why are you here?"

"I told you, I'd like to go to a movie with you. Or if you'd rather, we could stay here and talk. Or go for a drive. Anything as long as we spend time together. Since your sister is home, I don't think it would be a good idea for us to go upstairs to your bedroom." She wiggled her eyebrows at him suggestively, and at the thought of it, he immediately got hard.

"Julie, I told you,"

"I know what you told me. But you didn't mean it. You're still my guy and I'm still your girl."

"But we can't be."

"Why not? Because you lost your leg? Do you think that means I don't still love you?"

"It means you shouldn't."

"That's just stupid. Let's go to a movie. It will have to be a matinee because I still have to work tonight."

He tried to think of a reason to say no, but in his heart, he wanted nothing more than to spend time with her.

"I've missed you so much and now that you're back, I don't want to be away from you anymore."

"I missed you like crazy the whole time I was gone, too," he admitted. "But -"

She refused to allow him to repeat the reasons why they shouldn't, couldn't, be together anymore.

"I miss your smile, Cowboy. Smile for me."

Because it was Julie who asked, and because he loved her, he tried his best to create a smile. He moved his facial muscles and she winced.

"That's not a smile. That's a scowl. Let me see some teeth."

He showed her teeth, and she winced again.

"That's kind of terrifying. I see we're going to have to work on that one."

Having her close to him, right there in his parent's kitchen, ought to have filled him with hope. He wanted to do anything she asked. But he couldn't and she ought to understand that. He especially couldn't go to a movie theater. It was too dark, too crowded, too uncertain. Once they turned down the lights, he wouldn't be able to see every threat that might be coming at him.

"I don't think I can go to a movie," he was forced to admit. "I don't know if I can handle it."

"I'll hold your hand," Julie promised. "We can sit in the back row and make out like we used to."

Surprisingly he found the notion of Julie holding his hand in a dark scary movie theater to be just the thing he needed to feel safe. As for the making out, that possibility filled his brain with all sorts of unlikely outcomes, things he should not be thinking about because they truly were not a couple again. He had broken up with her, remember? But Julie didn't seem to believe it. He knew he shouldn't agree to go to a movie with her. She would only come out of it thinking he had changed his mind about the breakup. But he couldn't help himself and against his will found himself agreeing to the idea, getting into her car with her, driving away from his house.

At the theater they looked at the options listed. "What would you like to see?" she asked.

An action thriller? In the past that had been his favorite genre and Julie had even enjoyed them too. But no, it would be loud with the sounds of guns and crashes and explosions. The poster advertising it even depicted a fireball, which he couldn't bear to so much as look at. After his experience hearing the starter gun at the high school track, he was sure he would die at the sights and sounds in that action movie, even if it did star Jason Statham.

He passed by the option of a horror film. Neither he nor Julie had ever cared for them, mainly because the victims were always so stupid, and they got tired of yelling at the screen, "Don't go into the basement, dummies!"

They chose a comedy. There was less chance in a comedy film of loud noises and explosions, of guns and bombs and things that would send him into a panic attack. Julie did however insist that they sit in the very last row and he agreed, despite having to limp slowly up the theater's steps to get there. Having that wall at his back would be safer.

When the lights went down for the previews, his body clenched and went into high alert. Julie sensed it and squeezed his hand. She must have been baking, because she smelled like cinnamon. He loved the smell of cinnamon. Discreetly, trying not to be obvious so Julie wouldn't notice and consider him a perv, he inhaled her scent, breathing in the subtle cinnamon fragrance, letting it fill his soul.

"It's OK, Cowboy," she murmured. "I'm here."

As promised, she held his hand during the entire film.

This was unbelievable. He was sitting in a movie theater, with Julie, holding hands. They had done this so many times in the past.

But that was just it. The past. Today was the here and now, and it was all different. They were sitting there watching a movie, holding hands, but they were not on a date, were not a couple. They couldn't be. He was still a cripple, and she was still too good for her own good.

They didn't make out the way they used to do when they were together, but he had a feeling she wouldn't object if he tried it. But having her hold his hand, being close enough to her to hear her laugh at the funny parts and sigh romantically when the couple in the movie ended up in love, was almost as wonderful. He didn't have a panic attack or a PTSD episode, but by the end of the film he was still exhausted from the effort of trying to remain strong.

After the movie he agreed to get lunch with her. He knew he shouldn't, that the more time they spent together would only hurt the both of them, but he was helpless to resist. She looked at him with those gorgeous blue eyes, smiled at him with a mouth he wanted to kiss more than he wanted to breathe, and he couldn't say no.

They ate at Eggsperience, just around the corner from the Starbucks shop where he'd been meeting with Staff Sergeant Jacoby. It was late enough in the afternoon that the place was quiet, which he was glad of. He insisted on sitting with his back to the wall again so he could scan for threats. Julie gave him a small glance of concern but didn't argue with him or comment about it. As his mother did, she chided him for not finishing his food, and she insisted on paying the bill, just as she had purchased the movie tickets, because she had invited him to go out today.

"You can pay next time, Cowboy," she said, just as if there was going to be a next time. Just as if there was going to be a *them*. He really shouldn't be encouraging her about them becoming a couple again. He needed to make her understand it wasn't going to happen. But he couldn't force himself to say words he didn't want to say, couldn't make himself repeat the reasons why. She seemed to think that the loss of his leg wasn't a hindrance, and he hated to have to remind her that it was all the hindrance in the world.

When she took him home before leaving to go to work, she kissed him briefly and said, "This was fun, Cowboy. I'll see you soon."

As he stood in the driveway watching her leave, he felt, as he had the other day with Brooke in the kitchen, a part of his shattered heart seemed to heal a bit, reconnect to normalcy, even as he limped into the house and went to his room to remove his prosthesis.

Apparently Clay had become Jacoby's special project. He kept texting. Let's have coffee. Let's practice driving. Do you need a ride to the high school? Have you thought about writing that journal?

Yeah, right. He regretted telling Jacoby about his pitiful attempt to be an assistant coach for the summer camp. Damn the fact that Jacoby was a teacher and had the summer off, with seemingly nothing better to do with his time than to nag at Clay.

Then again, maybe he should let Jacoby give him a ride to Wheeling High School. As a Fremdie, he might spontaneously combust when setting foot on its property.

But no, he was still afraid to return to summer track camp. He sent Coach Swanson a text telling him he wouldn't be able to come back, and Coach had replied that it was too bad, that he was sorry, and if Clay should change his mind he was always welcome at the track practices in any capacity.

His father had a computer in his den and when Clay requested permission to use it after dinner that evening, dad agreed gladly. Clay sat down in front of it, opened a word processing document, then sat staring at the blank screen. The cursor blinked and blinked, taunting him. He stared at it for twenty minutes but it didn't go away. A million words flowed through his brain, through his soul, a million feelings, impressions, fears, emotions. But none of them obliged him by flowing through to his fingers laying on the keyboard.

He couldn't do this. It was stupid. Why write down anything about himself? Nobody would want to read it, unless they had serious masochistic tendencies. Jacoby was just being a teacher, handing out homework assignments. But Clay wasn't in his class, didn't attend his school, wasn't obligated to complete this assignment just because Staff Sergeant Jacoby told him to.

But he hadn't told him to do it. He hadn't ordered him, the way Captain Doctor Dennison had ordered him to nourish himself in the hospital. He'd suggested it, and appeared to have faith that Clay could do it and that it would help him. Ha. What did Jacoby know about what might help Clay? He wasn't the one who'd been blown up by an IED. Nobody could know what it felt like to be blown up, unless they had been blown up themselves.

Clay finally typed two words, and just those seven letters exhausted him.

It sucks.

Perversely he printed out the pathetic page. He'd take it to show Jacoby, wave it in his face to show him what a stupid idea this had been.

Weirdly, when he limped into the coffee shop holding that page, Jacoby smiled a huge grin, the piercing blue eyes lighting up with laughter.

"That's outstanding! Next time try four words. Maybe someday I'll let you read mine."

His next entry was four words. *It sucks big time.* After that, the floodgates opened, and multitudes of words flowed from him, until he felt guilty for hogging his dad's computer. Maybe he should get one of his own. The sheer volume of what he wrote astonished him, but he was never going to let anyone else read it. Not because his spelling was atrocious. There were wavy red lines under half his words. Spellcheck would fix that. Not because he was uncertain where to place commas or semi-colons, so he just left them out. It was because he found himself writing down his innermost grief, sorrow, guilt, despair, vulnerability, documenting his pain, both the physical and the emotional. He put a password on the document so nobody else could open it. For a moment, around page twenty, he wondered why he was doing this, other than because Jacoby had suggested it. Nobody else was ever going to read it, not even Jacoby. Clay couldn't even bear to read it himself. But now, he couldn't seem to stop pounding his hurt onto that keyboard. The words *hate, pain, despair, uselessness,* flew from his fingers like sparks. He documented his depression, lack of purpose, anger towards his situation in life. How he felt as if he'd been tossed into a lake with a rock tied around his neck, sinking down to the very bottom of cold, dark water. The hollow-ness of his soul, as if God had shoved a vacuum cleaner up his ass and sucked everything out.

And what happened when one was at the very bottom of something? Where could one go from there? There was only one direction possible. Up.

There was something liberating about putting these words on paper, or onto a hard drive as it were, that amazingly drained away some small piece of his despair. Why had the shrink in Germany not forced him to do this? He probably had suggested it, but Clay was too busy trying to block out the world to hear it.

When he found himself exhausted from the work, he considered a title. Something more meaningful than just the default Doc1. It took only a moment for the title to inspire itself, and he renamed the document, "Kaboom and All That Comes After." Then he moved it onto a flash drive, but before he signed off of his father's computer, he went online and ordered himself a laptop.

Chapter Thirteen

"My little sister told me she's considering enlisting in the Army," Clay told Jacoby the next time they met. It was becoming a regular thing for them, he realized, meeting twice a week to drink premature pumpkin spice lattes and to talk about things, mostly Clay's problems. It was starting to feel almost – normal.

"What do your parents think of that idea?"

"She hasn't told them. God. They will shit kittens."

In the way of Murphy's Law, a sweet grandmotherly woman walked by right next to their table at that precise moment, and paused to give Clay a scolding glance.

"A nice-looking young man like you shouldn't be using language like that in public," she said, then proceeded to a nearby table where a teenage girl sat. Clay heard the girl say, "Guess what, Grandma! Starbucks has a secret menu and they can make you butterbeer if you ask!"

Jacoby laughed outright. "I think she likes you." He nodded at the grandmother. "Are you into cougars, Clay?"

At Clay's shocked look, he amended, "Oh, yeah, you already have a girlfriend."

"No, I don't," Clay snapped.

"Are you sure?"

"We broke up."

"Really? When did that happen?"

"Right after this happened." He swept a hand subtly towards his left leg.

"Did you both break up, or did you just break up with her? Because I spoke directly to the lovely young Julie, and she clearly referred to you as her boyfriend. Not ex-boyfriend, not former boyfriend. She just said her boyfriend was having trouble adjusting to civilian life as an amputee."

"What the fuck difference does it make?" It killed him a little to have to think about Julie and their non-relationship.

"Watch it, Clay," Jacoby warned. "Your cougar might come over here and slap your face."

"Hmmph!" was the only response Clay could manage.

Jacoby leaned towards Clay and asked, in a lower voice, "How about sex?"

Despite his utter shock, Clay somehow managed to dredge up enough of a sense of humor to choke out, "No offense, Staff Sergeant, but I'm straight."

Jacoby laughed loud enough that all the other customers, including Clay's cougar and her granddaughter, looked at them with smiles, and Jacoby slapped him on the shoulder.

"So am I," he said. "I wasn't offering. I was asking about you and your girlfriend. I know it can be a little awkward at first, but you'll get the logistics of it figured out pretty quick. As for me, I'm married to the most beautiful woman in the world."

That couldn't be true, because Jacoby wasn't married to Julie. But he let the guy have his opinion.

"We have three gorgeous children. The third one was born after."

"After what?"

Jacoby looked at him with disbelief and repeated, "After." He reached down and lifted the left leg of his slacks a few inches to reveal a titanium ankle just like Clay's protruding from his shoe.

A thunderbolt of inconceivability slapped at Clay's brain. *No.* It was impossible. He had seen the man walk, stride, drive. No cane, no limp, no hesitation. No gritting of teeth, no grimace of pain, no appearance of having to plan every movement like the opening ceremony of the Olympics. The man projected an image of happiness, of normalcy. How could that be? He stared with complete and utter shock at the familiar sight of titanium that Jacoby casually revealed.

"Oh my God." He could barely speak. "I had no idea. You?" He couldn't enunciate any more words.

Jacoby let his pants leg slip back into place, exhibiting absolutely no embarrassment at revealing his prosthesis in public. Clay could never do such a thing.

"I guess I should have told you when we first met. I just assumed you knew I had an AKA also. I'd still be in the Army otherwise. That's why I wanted to mentor you. We have a lot in common. No one can tell you what it feels like to be blown up except someone who has been blown up."

"But you don't even use a cane. How do you do that?"

"Practice. Physical therapy. Thoughts of being there for the people you love. More training. To quote Churchill, blood sweat and tears. I do still have a cane, just in case, and a pair of crutches too. I use them around the house when the prosthesis bothers me and I just want to take it off."

Clay's head was ringing with shock and his mind completely boggled. Never in a million years would he have guessed that Staff Sergeant Jacoby was an amputee also. He seemed so normal, not only physically, but emotionally as well. Why wasn't he an emotional wreck like Clay? How could he be so calm, so purposeful, with a career and a family and all that normal stuff? Was it really possible?

Kaboom!

The world exploded and Clay found himself thrown from his seat to the Humvee's floor and his head bounced off something and his leg hit something, and damn that hurt.

Someone was screaming and someone was crying, but there was too much dust permeating the air to see who it was. It seemed like half of the earth in Afghanistan was flying around them, dispersed by the IED.

Lopez – damn, Lopez was bleeding from the neck and gurgling helplessly as the blood spurted out like a fountain around a piece of shrapnel embedded in his throat.

But no. Wait. Back up a step.

He hadn't heard the screams or seen Lopez bleed out. He'd been knocked unconscious immediately, the most convenient concussion ever. He hadn't seen the spurting blood nor had he heard Lopez's last words, which had been desperate pleas to anyone within earshot to tell his wife that he loved her. He hadn't seen the life fading from Lopez's eyes nor had he felt the guys from bravo squad in the truck behind them pulling him out and screaming for a medic, for an evac chopper. There was no memory of the trauma in a tent known as the field hospital at their base. He'd been unconscious for two more days and had even missed the oh so lovely ten-hour medical transport flight to Ramstein Air Base in Germany, courtesy of the United States Air Force, and the three-mile ride via AmBus to Landstuhl Regional Medical Center.

He hadn't been able to attend Lopez's funeral because he'd been in surgery that day. He'd only been told about those things afterward.

The chaplain was there now, sitting next to him, putting an arm around his shoulders, trying to help him sit up, calling through the post-Kaboom ringing in his ears.

"Clay! You OK, man? Did you hit your head?"

He gasped, and it wasn't Army Chaplain Father Saniti there with him, but rather Staff Sergeant Nathan Jacoby trying to get his sorry ass up off the floor.

Where was he? How had Jacoby gotten to Germany? He hadn't even met the guy until he'd returned stateside. *Think, Clay!* Stateside. He wasn't in Germany anymore nor was he in Afghanistan. He was on the floor of a Starbucks shop in Wheeling, Illinois, cowering under a table like a dog afraid of thunder.

It took a moment for Jacoby's features to come into focus. "I thought you were a priest," Clay said stupidly.

"A Catholic priest?" Jacoby laughed. "Don't tell my rabbi that. He'll have a conniption."

Clay's right leg was wet. Was he going to lose that too, or had he pissed himself? He could feel liquid warmth seeping through his slacks but didn't dare look. "I think I'm bleeding."

"That's coffee." A definite fragrance of pumpkin spice was wafting from the wet fabric of his slacks.

He needed a minute to get his eyes back into focus and to try to breathe his heart rate down to a level that reduced his risk of an immediate, fatal stroke. This was worse than the starter gun at the track field.

The grandmother and her granddaughter were staring at him in horror. She definitely wouldn't want to be his cougar now. But it was the granddaughter gaping at him as if he were a wild animal escaped from the zoo that cut his heart into a million pieces and made him want to run away and hide. But he couldn't run anywhere anymore. A damn unfair situation for a former track star.

This was why he should have stayed home.

"What happened?" he asked, as, with help from Sergeant Jacoby, he finally got back up into the chair. Jacoby handed him some napkins and Clay dabbed futilely at the spilled coffee.

"One of the employees dropped a metal coffee carafe on the floor. I think he's being scolded by his boss now because it'll have to be washed again."

Just when he thought he'd progressed to a feeling of safety, of something almost resembling normalcy, a supposedly harmless incident like a dropped coffee pot sent him off the deep end again. This whole getting out into the world again thing had been a really bad idea.

"Is this how it's always going to be, going into panic mode every time I hear a loud noise?" He tried to ask the question clinically but it was impossible to keep the despair out of his voice.

Stupid question. How could Jacoby possibly know something like that?

"Uncertain," the man answered. "It's different for everyone."

That was an acceptably vague answer. But the guy had done his research.

"It's possible you may have continual issues with unexpected loud noises. For the most part, the shock and panic tend to diminish with time. But then, some veterans can't ever watch a fireworks display again, or stay calm during a thunderstorm, for the rest of their lives. Only time will tell for you."

Oh, God, thunderstorms. He glanced with fear out the window. The sun was shining and there were only a few puffy white clouds dotting the sky. But this was summer in Illinois. That could change in an hour. Thunderstorms were inevitable. Would he be able to withstand a thunderstorm without falling to pieces? Hearing the sound of a metal coffee carafe falling on the floor had nearly killed him. What was he supposed to do on the Fourth of July? Instead of attending the fireworks display at Heritage Park with his family, he was going to have to endure the evening with earbuds in his ears, the volume of his music cranked up, and a pillow over his head.

"Don't you dare say to me that time heals all wounds," Clay insisted. "A million years of wishful thinking isn't going to make my leg, or yours, grow back. If you try to feed me that cliché, I'll -"

"You'll what? Smack me? Get up and walk away?"

Clay looked at him sharply. He knew Jacoby had said that because he knew that getting up and walking away would be difficult.

"I'm not talking about the physical wounds, Clay. Other than to assure you that you will learn to live with it more easily as time passes. But the emotional wounds -"

Clay interrupted, "A million years isn't going to heal that either."

Before Jacoby could answer, Clay insisted, "I need to go home."

"Not yet," Jacoby insisted. "You need to learn to deal with these unexpected sounds and loud noises. Running home every time something startles you is not going to help."

An employee approached their table with a mop. "Sorry, man," the kid said. "Didn't mean to scare you." He mopped up the spilled coffee on the floor, picked up the cup and lid that Clay had knocked over, and offered, "Would you like a fresh one? On me."

"No, thanks," Clay muttered, too embarrassed to look the kid in the eye.

"OK," the kid agreed amiably, as if having customers fall on the floor in a psychotic fit was an everyday occurrence here.

Jacoby continued, "For most, the effect diminishes over time. I think it will be like that for you too. I'd be willing to bet that next year at this time, they could drop a whole case of coffee pots right next to your ear and you'll barely flinch."

"I hope so." Clay hoped he never again had to see a kid like that young girl staring at him like he was some sort of alien. And not a cute friendly alien like E.T. More like the alien that bursts out of a poor bastard's chest while everyone else screams and pukes.

"How do you manage it?" he asked Jacoby. "Especially being a teacher? You're so, I dunno, so well-adjusted."

"I wasn't always. I spent a lot of time, those first weeks after it happened, lying in that hospital bed, asking God, why me? Why do I have to live like this? Why couldn't I have been the hero under a plaque at Arlington? They said I was lucky I survived at all. Some luck. You're not the only one to have those thoughts, those wishes. Survivor's guilt can be a terrible, powerful thing.

"But if not you, if not me, it would have been someone else suffering, some other family grieving. It came to me, after a period of selfishness, that despite what had happened to me, I still had a lot to live for, people who loved me and would prefer that I remain alive no matter how. My wife, my kids, my mother. If I'd died my mother would have dug me up just to yell at me for it. You have no idea of the guilt trip a Jewish mother can lay on a guy. I didn't want to have to go through that by wishing I'd died. I'd gotten it once already when Renee and I got engaged. You can't imagine the heap of guilt a Jewish mother lays on her only son when he marries a shiksa."

"A what?" Clay was confused. "What country is your wife from?"

"She's from Minnesota. She moved to Chicago to escape the brutal northern winters, ha ha. A shiksa is a woman who's not Jewish, the nightmare of every Jewish mother."

"Your mother didn't like your wife?" Clay was pretty sure his mother loved Julie, sometimes, he thought, as much or more than she loved him.

"Oh, my mother likes Renee a lot. Her only objection was that she isn't Jewish. Or at least she wasn't. She converted so we could get married under a huppah."

"A what?" Clay asked again.

"So we could have a Jewish wedding. Both our families were definitely not happy about it. That first Christmas and first Hanukkah were pretty awkward. But the moment our first child was born, everything was forgiven. Both sides forgot about any objections. It's amazing, the healing power of a grandchild.

"As for being a teacher, every school year, a few days after the semester starts, I show up at school wearing cargo shorts so everyone can see my leg. It comes as a shock a lot of times, I have to say. I explain how it happened, answer any questions. I take the prosthesis off and let the kids touch it if they want, and I tell them that I was incredibly honored to have served and even if I'd known this was going to happen, I'd do it all again in a heartbeat."

Clay shuddered. He couldn't bear for anyone to see his prosthesis, to know that one of his legs was manufactured rather than organic. He hadn't allowed anyone to see it, not his family, not Julie. Especially not Julie. And to take the thing off, detach it from his stump in front of witnesses? Clay had thought he was a brave man, before Kaboom, but he doubted he would ever possess the courage to remove his titanium monstrosity where anybody could see it.

"Do they ask about the Purple Heart?"

"Yes. I bring it with me and show it to them if they ask to see it. I've even had female students say they think my prosthetic leg is sexy."

Sexy? Clay couldn't think of anything less sexy than his prosthesis.

Around them, the coffee shop relapsed back into its normal rhythm, as if he hadn't had a panic attack here just a few minutes earlier. The grandmother and her granddaughter had stopped staring at Clay, finished their drinks and left. Now that he was back in his chair, didn't appear to require medical intervention, and was carrying on a coherent conversation, the world around him seemed to return to normal.

"My goal, Clay," Jacoby went on, "is to offer you hope, and to try to convince you that it's real. I don't have to give you back your dignity and pride. You never lost them. They're just in the background, waiting for you to acknowledge them."

"My dignity is so far in the background it may never come out again." He glanced towards the floor he had recently been sitting on, having his second PTSD episode this week.

"I thought the same thing once," Jacoby admitted. "But my wife convinced me that it would get better, and she was right."

Clay could have had that. With the clarity and insight that comes to a Monday morning quarterback, he realized, he could have had that with Julie. What if, instead of pushing her away with that cruel unexplained email, he had called her and said, *I've been wounded, I need you*? She would have been at his side as soon as a plane could get her there. She probably could have talked the Air Force into flying her directly to Ramstein Air Base, only three miles from Landstuhl Regional Medical Center. It would have had her at his side much sooner than traveling the eighty miles from Frankfurt, the nearest commercial airport. How would he have felt, both physically and emotionally, with her there, caring and loving him and telling him it was going to be all right? And he could have believed her. She would have made cakes, from scratch, for the entire staff at the hospital. She would have become best buddies with his LNCO. She would have pushed his sorry ass into the psychiatrist's office and would have made him talk, and would have made him listen.

"Renee came to Landstuhl right away," Jacoby said. "She told me every ten minutes that she loved me and that we would be fine, and I had to believe her."

"I wouldn't let anyone come see me in the hospital."

"Why not?" Jacoby asked. "You know there are lots of people who donate their airline miles so that family members can fly out there."

"I was afraid I'd cry. And I broke up with Julie in an email."

"If you think I didn't cry, you're wrong," Jacoby assured him. "The moment my wife walked into my hospital room, I became a total snotty waterfall. It was ugly. But she didn't mind."

Julie hadn't seemed to mind either, that day he'd allowed himself to cry in her presence, in her arms. In fact, she seemed to be glad to be able to offer him comfort, and he realized now, he'd been glad to finally be able to let it out. He was beginning to think he'd made the wrong decisions regarding his time at Landstuhl. Would his parents, his sister, his Julie, have been a comfort to him if he'd allowed them to visit? Would they continue to feel the same way about him if they were aware of all the gory details of his condition? Somehow he couldn't quite believe so. But for the first time, he allowed Jacoby to drive him home rather than insisting on using Uber. The guy drove a blue minivan, complete with back seats filled with all the typical suburban family gear of sports equipment, assorted jackets and shoes, even what appeared to be computer parts.

Jacoby drove just as normally as any two-legged man, and Clay was jealous.

"It helps that we lost our left legs rather than the right," he said, smiling as if they were in some sort of club. "Easier to drive with the right foot. Sometimes if we're on a long drive I take the thing off and throw it in the back seat. But I have to remind the kids it's not a toy for them to bonk each other with."

How could he make jokes about this, Clay wondered incredulously as they pulled into his driveway. But then, Jacoby's acceptance and good humor had practically made him forget about the psychotic episode he'd had in the coffee shop.

Surprisingly, Jacoby got out of his van instead of just letting Clay out. "I'd like to come in and meet your family, if you don't mind," he said, just as if they were a normal set of acquaintances. "I'm sure most parents want to make sure that the people their kids are hanging out with are of good character, and not taking him to a strip bar or anything."

"I've never been to a strip bar!" Clay said defensively. He'd resisted any such invitations from his comrades while in the Army, feeling it would be unfair to Julie for him to look at other women undressing.

"I have," Jacoby admitted. "Once. For my bachelor party. I found it to be more sad than titillating. I felt rather sorry for those young ladies who felt they had no other options in their lives."

It was Saturday afternoon. Both his parent's cars were in the driveway. There was no good reason why he could resist the idea of bringing Jacoby into his home to meet his family.

Retired Staff Sergeant Nathan Jacoby charmed his parents from the first hello. Within moments it was as if they'd known each other for years. But after a few minutes of coffee and polite conversation around their kitchen table, Jacoby turned to Clay and said, "This is the part where you need to go in the other room so we can talk about you behind your back."

"You what? No. You can't."

Was he kidding? Sending Clay out of the room in his own house as if he were a misbehaving child? Who did he think he was? First Coach Swanson and Julie, and now Sergeant Jacoby and his parents, talking about him behind his back. Was he going to blab about the incident with the dropped coffee pot at Starbucks? About his despair at how difficult his life had become? Was he going to tell them that Clay was depressed and in need of psychiatric care?

He might just have to rethink their entire friendship.

Jacoby made a little shooing motion, and his parents didn't do anything to prevent it. Not even when he stood up and took a hesitant, limping step towards the door, expecting them to say he didn't really have to leave the room. Not even a muttered, "What the fuck" got him off the hook. For once, his mother just ignored the expletive and waited for him to leave.

He limped out into the living room, where he made sure to bang his cane against the wall just to show his annoyance with the whole situation, and flopped down on the sofa, picking up the TV remote and turning up the volume of whatever appeared on the screen to a level that would have annoyed them if they'd been in the room.

After a few minutes the three of them walked out of the kitchen.

"It was lovely to meet you," his mother was saying, as both his parents shook Jacoby's hand at the door.

"What was so important you had to send me away to discuss?" Clay demanded, hating the petulant way his voice came out. He sounded like a first-grader being denied participation in a playground game, but he couldn't help it.

Jacoby smiled at him. "Just a little friendly conversation," was all he would divulge, then turned to his mother. "I'll ask Renee to email you those recipes," he said, then nodded a goodbye to Clay and left.

Food? They'd been talking about food and recipes? Why did they need to send him out of the room for that? Because he didn't eat enough to satisfy his parents and Julie?

A month ago, he would have told himself he didn't care what anyone said about him, behind his back or to his face. He would have dragged his carcass up the stairs and hidden out in his room, his feelings dulled by Vicodin. Somehow, though, today, he found himself caring, enough to be irritated. Was that emotional progress on his part?

"What was he saying about me?" he demanded of his mother. Maybe the guy didn't want to state to Clay's face that he was a rude little shit for making everyone cry over him. But he hadn't hesitated to be brutally honest up to this point, from the moment Clay had met him.

To his surprise, his mother sat down next to him and hugged him, then kissed his cheek. "You know your father and I love you, don't you, Clay?"

"Well, yeah." He'd never doubted that. They were his parents. They were obligated by the bond of blood to love him, whether he deserved it or not.

"What we discussed was, well, private," Mom said. "I'm afraid I can't tell you about it right now. Don't be upset with Nathan for discussing your situation with us. He only wants to help, as we do. I know that you and he discuss a lot of things that you don't repeat to us, and I wouldn't expect you to. But if it helps you, then that's all that matters."

She had a point. Clay didn't tell her much, if any of the things that Sergeant Jacoby said to him.

Despite his mother's reassurance, a lingering feeling that he was beyond help and that it was all a waste of time still sat over him like a dark cloud. "It's, well, it's completely mean of you guys to be discussing me with other people like that," he complained.

"Don't talk to your mother like that," his father warned.

"It's OK, Lloyd," his mother said with an upraised hand. "I know it may seem mean to you, Clay, but it's done with love, with your best interests at heart."

He still wasn't certain how this type of secret discussion between Jacoby and his parents was helping in any way, but there was no arguing with his mother, so for now, he let it drop.

Chapter Fourteen

"Clay, are you sure you won't come with us?" his mother asked.

"No thanks, Mom."

"But it's the Fourth of July. Don't you want to see the fireworks? You weren't here for it last year."

Last Fourth of July he'd watched fireworks at Fort Benning, while prepping for deployment. He and his comrades had ooh'd and aah'd at all the appropriate moments, and had enthusiastically sung The Star-Spangled Banner at the conclusion. But that was before Kaboom. Now even the thought of random booms and explosive lights terrified him, even if in his mind he realized there wasn't any threat. In his logical mind, he knew the fireworks would be going off a mile away. They'd be set off by professionals, purely for their entertainment value. Nothing would be aimed at him or anyone else. Nobody would be in danger. Not him or his parents or Brooke or Julie.

Would he be able to process the fact that the booms and flashes shortly to ensue were innocent celebrations? Or would he go bat-shit crazy at the first loud sound, as he had at the track field, or even worse, the other day at Starbucks at the mere sound of a coffee pot clattering to the floor? Though he had enjoyed fireworks displays before Kaboom, he couldn't chance how he might react to them now. He was just grateful that Julie was at work and wouldn't be there to see him if he lost it. He didn't want his parents or Brooke to see it either.

His rational brain tried to convince him that it would be OK. But his irrational, screwed-up, anxiety-ridden cesspool of a psyche dominated him at the moment and he found himself quietly terrified at the possibility of hearing or seeing them. His hands were getting sweatier and his heart tripping faster every moment as dusk approached. Clay had seen, heard and felt enough fireworks to last him the rest of his life and beyond. There was no way on God's green earth he was going to subject himself to them voluntarily. He couldn't allow his family to witness his potential breakdown.

"We could stay home if you don't want to go out," Dad offered. "We can watch the fireworks from Washington DC on TV. Then we won't have to fight for parking at Heritage Park."

"No!" Clay tried to keep the panic out of his voice. They were all going to think he was an anti-social jerk, but there was no way that viewing and hearing fireworks, either in person or on TV, was going to work out without him panicking or screaming or falling on the floor.

Brook had been watching the entire conversation in silence but now stood up with a knowing look on her face.

"I'd rather go to the fireworks here," she suggested. "If Clay wants to stay home we shouldn't nag him to come. Let him stay. I'm pretty sure he's potty trained."

She gave him a teasing wink, but he could see compassion in her face as well, and he appreciated it.

There was a twelve-pack of beer in the refrigerator with his name on it, and he intended to drink as much of it as he could, starting as soon as his dad's car pulled out of the driveway. Thanks to online shopping, he had a brand-new Bluetooth-enabled Beats headset that hopefully, with his music volume cranked up to twelve, would help that beer block out the sight and sound and feeling of the soon-to-be exploding fireworks.

His parents seemed to dither endlessly before finally agreeing to go and leave him to his own devices, and finally headed out the door. Before joining them, Brooke stopped and touched his arm, looking at him with concern.

"Are you going to be OK?" she asked.

His first inclination was to lie and say yes, he'd be fine. But he had a feeling Brooke would see right through that misdirection.

"Not really," he admitted, surprising himself that he'd allowed her to see his vulnerability. "But I think I'll survive. Maybe."

He was deathly afraid his admission would make his sister change her mind and insist on staying home to take care of him, but instead, she just squeezed his hand. "Don't be afraid to call or text me if you need anything. Is Julie coming over? Is that why you want to be left home alone?"

"No, Julie is working tonight."

Brooke patted his shoulder as if she was an old hand at comforting people in distress. "OK. We'll see you later."

When they finally left he sat down and pulled out his new headphones to test their sound blocking capacity. He was just about to get that beer out of the fridge and take it up to his room, the better to cover his head with a pillow, when the doorbell rang.

Had his parents changed their minds and come back home? But they wouldn't ring the doorbell. They'd come in from the garage after pulling the car in. It was too late in the evening for it to be a salesman or a delivery.

To his surprise, Nathan Jacoby stood on his front porch. Clay stared at him in confusion, seriously hoping he wasn't intending to invite Clay to accompany him and his family to the fireworks display. He looked past Jacoby's shoulder at his van parked in front of the house, but it didn't appear that the rest of the family waited for them.

"May I come in?" Nathan finally asked, and Clay remembered his manners and invited the guy in.

"What are you doing here?" he asked. "Why aren't you going to watch fireworks with your family?"

Jacoby chuckled. "You don't think I'd make you suffer through this evening alone, did you? Besides, I never go to watch the fireworks. Renee and the kids are used to going without me."

With a flash of insight, he realized that Sergeant Jacoby was here at his home for protection from the fireworks just like Clay was. He was just better at hiding the things that bothered him. He had said that he wasn't particularly fond of things that went boom, but Clay had dismissed those words at the time as being merely something he'd said to make Clay feel better. But obviously there had been more truth to them than Clay had realized.

"Do you want a beer?" he offered as the two of them sat on the sofa.

"Thanks, but I'm driving. I wouldn't say no to a soda though."

"Good. More for me." Clay ripped the top of the case of beer apart enough to retrieve a can and pop it open, taking a healthy swig before he pulled himself to his feet and retrieved a can of soda for his guest. As the other man opened his own can, he glanced at Clay, already starting his second beer.

"I don't know how much of a drinker you usually are," Jacoby said. "But keep in mind that the loss of your leg will affect your tolerance." He gestured towards Clay wiping a beer drip from his lip with his hand. "You have that much less body mass to absorb the alcohol so you probably won't be able to process it like before."

Like before. As in, like before Kaboom. If that wasn't what one might call a vicious circle. It was the loss of his leg that made him purposely want to get intoxicated tonight rather than celebrate his nation's founding, and the fact that he lost that leg was going to facilitate that effort faster than if he was whole. But if he was whole, he wouldn't be here sitting in his living room guzzling down his own case of liquid forgetfulness. He'd be happily enjoying the rocket's red glare.

A headache was already forming and he'd barely started drinking.

"What is that thing?" he asked, looking at the device in Jacoby's hands.

"It's a Discman." Jacoby sounded a bit defensive. "It plays CDs. I use it to drown out the sounds of explosions."

"CDs?" Seriously?" Clay scoffed. Those things belonged in an antique store. Why didn't Jacoby just stream his music like a normal person? "Have we time-traveled to the caveman days?" he asked his friend. "What are you listening to?"

"It's The Magic Flute."

"Never heard of them," Clay said.

"It's not a them," Jacoby said with dignity. "It's an opera. It's Mozart. Would you like to listen to it? Might do you good to get a little culture."

Opera? Mozart? No way.

"No thanks." He struggled not to laugh at the guy. "I've got plenty of culture right here." He patted his phone briefly and enabled the Bluetooth connection with the headset to stream his culture – Classic Rock. "And it's cordless." He snorted at the cord Jacoby had connecting his headset, which at least was a Bose, to his old-fashioned disc player. Talk about old school!

His companion just shrugged good-naturedly as he started his own fireworks-blocking music. "To each his own."

Two hours later, there were two empty soda cans and nine dead beer cans covering the coffee table in front of them. The volume at which he'd been playing his music made Clay's ears ring when he dared to turn it off and remove his headset, but at least it had prevented any sounds or even thoughts of fireworks for the duration. Apparently Jacoby's magic flute had done the same for him because he smiled as he removed his headset.

"Whew," the older man said. "I'm glad that's over."

"You mean your opera?" Clay teased.

"No, the..." He made a gesture of flinging his fingers apart that Clay recognized as a sign for explosion. "Thanks for letting me hang out with you tonight, Clay. It helps to have company, someone who understands the situation."

He stood up to leave, but when Clay stood up too, the room tilted and swirled around him as if he were in the center of a Tilt-a-Whirl at the county fair.

"Whoa!" he muttered as he grabbed for the couch's armrest. It wasn't his amputation making him unsteady right now. It was the copious amounts of beer he'd consumed while listening to Foreigner and Poison. He'd managed a trip to the bathroom earlier without too much trouble, but that had been four beers ago.

"You're drunk, Clay," Jacoby informed him needlessly. "Go to bed. I'll see myself out."

Clay looked at the door for a minute after he heard his guest's van start up and drive away, touched, despite his inebriation, at the realization that the other man had revealed that he too had anxieties about loud noises sometimes. It wasn't just Clay.

He stuck another can of beer into his pocket and made his way even more crookedly up the stairs than he usually did, feeling wobbly and bleary as he lurched into the bathroom and peed gallons. He didn't even want to think about what he was going to feel like in the morning. All that mattered was that he had made it through the evening without an *episode*, and hopefully would be in his bed in some form or another before his family got home, so they wouldn't see him drunk and stupid.

He sat on his bed and struggled to get his pants and prosthesis off with hands that didn't quite cooperate like they normally did. "For fush sake," he muttered. He couldn't even swear coherently tonight, because his tongue felt like a great big fuzzy caterpillar. Well duh. He was trying to pull his pants off over his shoes. Maybe he should have taken the shoes off first.

Leaning over to do that made the blood rush to his head and he almost passed out. Finally he had shoes, pants and prosthesis removed and dumped in a heap on the floor, not even bothering to remove his shirt. He did however remember to get his bottle of pills out of the drawer and somehow managed to get one out without spilling them all on the floor. Maybe the alcohol was going to cancel out the effect of the Vicodin, but he was taking no chances, as he retrieved that last can of beer he'd smuggled up to his room and popped it open, downing the pill and half the contents in one gulp. His fingers lost their ability to grip the can and it fell on top of his crumpled clothes. What he hadn't drunk spilled out to fill the air with a stale beery fragrance.

Then he passed out on the bed. Or he sort of passed out. Somehow, despite being passed out, he still heard his family's footsteps coming up the stairs and their voices speaking near his door. Maybe he should have killed off the last two beers he hadn't been able to finish downstairs. He didn't want to have to explain the mess of beer cans he'd left behind and his current difficulty in talking and performing normal coordinated actions like undressing himself.

"Look at him," he heard Brooke's voice from his doorway. "Asleep like a baby."

"I'm not surprised." That was his father's voice. "Judging by all the beer cans downstairs, I'd say more like unconscious."

"Should I go in there and give him a poke to make sure he's alive?" Brooke asked. Somehow, even as drunk as he was, Clay could sense Brooke about to take a step towards him. Proof of life was provided at that moment as an unavoidable belch overtook him.

"It smells like a brewery in here," his mother complained. Then, mercifully he heard her close his door just as he lost consciousness, grateful at having survived the fireworks for this year, thanks in no small measure to Nathan Jacoby's company.

Usually Sergeant Jacoby contacted Clay by text message, like normal people, but the next day, he called him. Thankfully he waited until the afternoon when Clay had a chance to recover from his hangover, with the help of his pain pills for the headache and some dry crackers for the queasy stomach. Someone had kindly cleared away his treasure trove of empty beer cans downstairs in the morning while he'd been sleeping it off. It was probably Brooke, since his parents were both at work.

"There's a get-together tomorrow that you need to attend," Nathan said. "I'll pick you up at thirteen hundred."

He sounded so authoritative that Clay responded, "Yes, Sergeant," out of pure habit.

Brooke happened to be home the following day when Jacoby arrived to pick Clay up, and walked out to the blue minivan with him, politely adjusting her gait to match with Clay's limp.

"This is my sister, Brooke," Clay introduced her as Jacoby shook her hand and said he was glad to meet her. As Jacoby walked around to the driver's side of the vehicle, Brooke whispered, "Your friend is cute."

Clay shook a finger at her nose. "He's also married, with three kids, and old enough to be your father."

She swiped away his upraised finger. "Oh, lighten up, Cuckoo," she replied as she flounced into the house.

As they drove east on Dundee Road, Clay looked at his friend's profile, wondering if what he'd said to Brooke was true. Jacoby did have one or two strands of gray hair among the black, but given what Clay knew he had experienced, a little premature gray should be expected. He was surprised that since Kaboom, his own hair hadn't gone as completely gray as Professor Dumbledore.

"Sergeant," he said, but before he could complete his sentence, Jacoby said, "You know Clay, you can call me Nathan. We're not in the Army anymore."

"OK, Nathan. Can I ask you a personal question?"

"Sure. In fact, I welcome it. It indicates you're taking an interest in the world again."

Clay hesitated a moment, then asked, "Are you old enough to be my father?"

Nathan chuckled. "Well, not technically. I'm forty. In order to be the father of someone your age, I'd have to have fathered a kid at age seventeen. Can I tell you a secret? My wife and I were both twenty-three when we got married and we were both, um..." He uncharacteristically blushed, and kept his eyes firmly on the road.

"Are you telling me you were a virgin when you got married?"

Jacoby nodded sheepishly.

Holding out for marriage? Until age twenty-three? How downright medieval. And here Clay had thought he had been a late bloomer!

"Wow," was all Clay could say. "Do you normally go around telling people that?"

"No. Just my closest friends. Let's just say, once we figured out what we were doing, we made up for lost time."

Clay was doing math in his head. Brooke was six years younger than him.

"So, technically speaking, you'd be old enough to be my sister's father."

"Why? Did she say I was cute?"

Clay goggled in amazement while Nathan laughed. "Us Jacoby men, we're handsome devils," he joked.

Nathan made a left turn up Waukegan Road and they headed into Deerfield. Wherever he was taking Clay, it looked to be in a very nice neighborhood. A few minutes later they pulled up in front of a large Tudor style house with a lush green lawn in front that Clay was certain was maintained by professional gardeners.

"Are you moving to this house?" he asked.

Nathan grinned. "I wish. An Army buddy of mine lives here. A bunch of us get together every few months to swap lies and compare scars."

Clay had no plans to compare scars with anyone.

The only problem with riding in Nathan's vehicle was that it was a little taller than a regular car. He had to carefully lean out and make sure his real leg was firmly balanced on the ground before his prosthesis. Nathan hopped out and was waiting for Clay to walk up to the front door before Clay even got his door closed. How did he do that? Clay was beginning to think he had imagined Nathan revealing that he was also an amputee. Maybe it was all part of the episode he'd had in the Starbucks shop.

The door was answered by a petite dark-haired lady with a big smile and an affectionate hug for her guest.

"Nathan!" she exclaimed. "It is so nice to see you. Who's your friend?"

"This is Clay Maslowski. He's a newbie."

A newbie?

"Clay, I'd like you to meet Beverly Mikkelson, the most patient woman in the world."

The lady stepped forward and hugged Clay too, and somehow the contact didn't seem to upset him like it usually did. Apparently any friend of Nathan Jacoby's was a friend of hers.

"Hm!" their hostess scoffed at Nathan. "Ross says the same thing about Renee. Come on in. Everybody is in the back yard."

She led them into the house, across a tiled foyer and into a spacious kitchen where two pitchers of lemonade and a plate of cookies sat on the counter. Mrs. Mikkelson picked up the cookie tray and headed towards the back door, calling over her shoulder, "Be dears and bring the lemonade, will you?"

Nathan picked up one of the pitchers and followed their hostess towards the back door, but Clay just stared at the other one. It was full and heavy. Could he carry it one-handed without sloshing it all over the place? Nathan had no problems, but then, evidently the guy was Superman or something. He was reaching for the door handle when he turned around and noticed Clay standing there in uncertainty.

"Do this, Clay," he said, holding the pitcher in his hand against his stomach. "It'll be more secure that way. I have to tell you, Beverly doesn't cut any slack for us around here, so buck up and do your best. If you spill that, she will expect you to clean it up."

The prospect of having to clean up lemonade from this pristine kitchen floor almost made Clay turn and limp back to the safety of Jacoby's van. But not wanting to embarrass his friend, he picked up the pitcher, utilizing arm muscles that had been neglected the past few months, and, as Jacoby showed him, braced the pitcher against his belly as he limped toward the door, his cane clicking on the tile that he prayed wouldn't be dirtied by his inadequacy. Nathan opened the door for him, because Mrs. Mikkelson was already outside.

He did almost drop the pitcher of lemonade on the back porch, but not due to weakness or the awkwardness of carrying it in one hand while he had his cane in the other. It was due to surprise.

A dozen or so guys were hanging around, sitting in lawn chairs or on the grass, talking, showing each other photos, going over to the picnic table on the patio where snacks were laid out, just like any other normal get-together of a group of friends. A couple of kids, apparently the offspring of the family hosting this gathering, were swimming and splashing in a sparkling pool. A burst of laughter punctuated by a few colorful metaphors rang out, and one of the group turned, saw Clay and Nathan, and strode over to greet them.

Each and every one of those guys was an amputee. The man striding over to greet them, Ross Mikkelson, the owner of this lovely home and husband to Beverly, was an AKA like Clay and Nathan, except that he was missing a right leg rather than left. Clay could tell this because the man was wearing cargo shorts with his prosthesis clearly visible, and he walked just like Jacoby did – no cane, no limp, no pain. Clay and Nathan were the only ones there not wearing shorts. A couple of the other guests were BKA's, and Clay couldn't help but stare at one tall guy who had lost both legs at the knee. He at least walked with canes, one in each hand, but he still smiled and laughed and waved Jacoby over as he sat in a lawn chair.

Clay set the pitcher of lemonade on the table before he dropped it in shock. "This is what you mean about swapping lies and comparing scars?" he asked in disbelief. All of these men looked so happily accepting, so well adjusted, so normal, as if parts of their bodies hadn't been replaced by titanium and polypropylene.

His mind reeled at the unreality of it all. He had to have fallen down a rabbit hole into some sort of alternative universe. Surely the Mad Hatter would show up at any moment and set up a tea party.

"Welcome to the prosthetic club. I wanted you to meet these guys," Nathan said, indicating the other guests, "so you could see that, while losing your leg was of course horrible and life-changing, it still doesn't have to be the end of your world. With practice and physical therapy you can walk without a cane, drive, go to school or a job. The prosthesis doesn't have to define you. Ross here, he's an attorney. That guy," he indicated the tall double amputee, "he's an architect. Hi, there, Seth," he called out, waving back at him, "we'll be with you in a minute."

Nathan pointed out a third man, playing with a dog, trying to command it to sit when the pup obviously just wanted to climb up into his lap and cuddle. He was a BKA on the right, and his prosthesis was off, lying on the grass next to him. "That's Eduardo. He has the most important job of anyone here. He's a FedEx delivery driver."

"He's the most important guy here because he brings me my Amazon packages," their hostess said as she breezed by them and walked over to the pool, where she reminded the kids splashing there about sunscreen.

Clay's brain still swirled in amazement, as he tried to remember the names and occupations being thrown at him. He desperately hoped there wasn't going to be a quiz at the end of the day. He stood rooted to the spot where he stood on the patio, as incapable of participating as he had been in his parent's back yard the day he'd arrived home from Germany. But instead of allowing him to sit and brood, Nathan nudged his arm and urged him to mingle.

"None of these guys bite," he said teasingly. "Come and be sociable."

Being sociable had been Clay's biggest challenge since Kaboom.

Their hostess handed Clay and Nathan glasses of lemonade.

"Nothing stronger today," she said. "It's way too early, and most of these guys are driving."

Clay couldn't help but glance at Seth, who had not one but two prostheses showing beneath the hem of his tan cargo shorts. Was he driving? Clay hadn't even considered attempting it yet. He tried to remember the license plates on the cars that had been parked on the street, but couldn't recall which if any bore handicapped plates or placards.

How could they all act so normal and even happy? Why were they not all consumed in desolation by their disabilities, their lack of completeness? Did they not realize their worlds had gone Kaboom?

While he stood there pondering this impossibility, the double amputee – Seth, Jacoby had called him- grabbed his canes and rose to his feet. Even missing both his legs, he seemed to accomplish it with more ease than Clay did. How was he not smashed into shreds by the burden of his reality? How did the man get out of bed in the morning – both physically and emotionally – without the weight of pain crushing him? How did he refrain from swallowing his entire bottle of pain pills at one time, as Clay had once been tempted to do?

"I have an announcement!" he called out, and everyone fell silent. "Tammy is pregnant!" He held up a hand to forestall the congratulations that began to erupt. "There's more. It's twins!"

Nathan and all the other guys surged towards the father-to-be with congratulatory handshakes and back slaps. It reminded Clay a little bit of the surge of well-wishers at the airport the day he'd arrived home, except that in this case, the object of the affection was smiling as if he were the happiest person alive, rather than sulking and frowning as Clay had.

"You realize you're not going to get a good night's sleep for the next eighteen years?" Ross Mikkelson was advising, while Clay's brain reeled and cavorted as he tried to grapple with the happiness, the normalcy of all of this.

"I don't understand," Clay muttered. "Are these guys for real?" He took a gulp of the glass of lemonade their hostess had given him, his throat a bit dry due to shock.

"They're not a figment of your imagination," Nathan replied.

"But they're so -" He was suddenly unable to summon normal English words from his brain to his mouth.

"So normal?" Nathan suggested helpfully. "Accepting? Alive and thriving?"

"All of those." All the things Clay wasn't.

"Each one of these men, as well as myself, as well as you ought to, have come to realize that while their lives are irrevocably altered, that life does go on, and that they have things to live for despite what they, and we, have lost. Coming close to dying has made us appreciate life so much more than we did before. You know, what doesn't kill you, makes you stronger."

What hadn't killed Clay hadn't made him stronger. If anything it had turned him into a whiny little nothing, a complete opposite of the man he'd been before Kaboom. He looked around at this group of other men who had experienced their own Kabooms, and heard no whining, no self-pity, no withdrawal from the world. They were making the best of it, even achieving happiness, if the look on the face of the man who'd just announced his impending fatherhood to twins was anything to go by.

Nathan's voice penetrated his cogitation. "You're not alone in this, Clay. Or at least you don't have to be." He nudged an encouraging hand on Clay's elbow, persuading him to join the group.

He stepped forward, hoping he didn't stumble on the lawn, and the group of amputees welcomed him, offered him a chair, and more importantly, their experiences.

Most of them were like Clay and Nathan, military veterans who had suffered amputation in battle. One had lost his leg in a motorcycle accident, another to cancer. Eduardo the FedEx driver had been born with a deformed foot and had his lower leg amputated as a child to facilitate a prosthesis. They willingly shared their experiences, without self-pity, and asked Clay about his.

He hesitated. He hated talking about Kaboom and its gory details, though he had described the event to Julie. It made him feel like a freak and a monster. But not a single member of this group seemed to feel that way about themselves. Had Clay perhaps been making his situation worse by hiding away and refusing the company of his friends, his army buddies, his family, the woman he loved?

Almost against his will, he found himself responding to the request to talk, though he hesitated and stuttered as he did so. Nobody flinched in disgust or seemed unwilling to hear what he said. They all nodded encouragingly, with understanding. They got it. As Nathan had, they assured him that it was a process, this path to readjustment after Kaboom, that it wasn't something that cured itself in a week or a month, but that at a point in the process, acceptance would evolve and life could, should, and would, be lived. How he lived it was his choice to make. He could do it the hard way, crying and moaning and hiding, or he could do it the mature adult way, learning to thrive and seek happiness.

He was quiet on the drive back to Wheeling, and when Nathan dropped him off in his driveway, still didn't know what to say about the afternoon's revelations. The sergeant didn't push it, seeming to realize that Clay was processing all that had been thrown at him in the past few hours.

"I'll talk to you soon," was all he said, as Clay got out of the van.

Surely it had to be Clay's imagination, but somehow it did seem like walking was just a tiny bit easier this afternoon than it had been this time yesterday.

Chapter Fifteen

Julie called him, bubbling with happiness. "I'm off work on Saturday. Do you know how long it's been since I've had a Saturday night off work? I can't even remember. Let's go out somewhere fun, Cowboy!"

How could he say no to the joy in her voice? Even though they were still broken up, still not a couple anymore, he couldn't resist Julie's enticement. He just hoped they could go someplace small and dim where people wouldn't look at him.

When she came to pick him up, his parents and Brooke were just as happy to see her as they'd been back when he and Julie were a couple, before Kaboom.

"Yay for you," Brooke said to Julie. "You got him out of those dumb sweatpants." Clay was wearing the khaki slacks he'd worn the day he'd returned from Germany. Jeans were just a little too stiff to wear with his prosthesis.

But they didn't go to someplace small and dim. Julie drove with purpose out to Long Grove, to a popular, busy, lively restaurant with a karaoke bar. She had even made them a reservation on the assumption he would agree to come.

Why had she brought him here, to a place he'd enjoyed before Kaboom, when he'd been a whole, happy person? He suffered through wannabe karaoke singers who thought they could do Whitney Houston or Adele or Prince, and was just about to ask Julie if they could please leave now, when she turned to him and requested, "Sing a song for me, Cowboy."

"No." The response was reflexive, a knee-jerk reaction.

"You have such a beautiful voice," she cajoled. "I've missed hearing you sing. Remember the last time we were here, just before you left for the Army?"

She wasn't going to give up on getting him up there in front of a bar full of people who were probably eager to gawk at the cripple. Despite his continued resistance, she requested, "Sing *Faithfully* for me again."

The Journey song was one of his and Julie's favorites. He'd sung that song here for her, just before leaving for Basic Training. Afterward she'd run her hands through his hair, mourning the fact that in forty-eight hours it would be buzz cut by an Army barber. Then they'd gone to his house, to his room, to his bed. His parents and Brooke had conveniently gone out of town overnight.

"No, I can't."

"Yes, you can," she insisted. "I remember when you wrote to me from basic training. You said the drill instructors told you and the other recruits that the word *can't* was to be cut from your vocabulary. There is no *can't*, Cowboy. You can."

Clay had had a reputation as a great singer even back in high school. He could have had the lead in the school musical his senior year. They did West Side Story. The choir director had begged him to audition, although auditioning would have been a mere formality. The role of Tony would have been his for the taking. But the rehearsals would have conflicted with his track meets, so he'd declined. Instead, the lead had been sung by Dominic Fortunato, whose voice had cracked embarrassingly on the high notes.

"In fact I already signed you up for it." She nodded her head towards where the karaoke equipment was set up, towards the bar manager who was looking at his list. The man looked around with a "who's next?" expression on his face and, horror of horrors, Julie waved and pointed right at Clay.

"You *what*?" How could she do this to him? He was stuck with it now. He couldn't refuse without embarrassing Julie.

"Don't worry, you'll be great," she encouraged, urging him to his feet with a hand on his elbow. With more reluctance than if he were stepping into a lion's den with a steak on a string around his neck, he gripped his cane and rose stiffly to his feet, feeling that his prosthesis had to be glowing through the fabric of his slacks.

Everybody was looking at him. He couldn't do this. He just couldn't. His heart pounded as it leaped up into his throat, and he felt a tiny bead of sweat trickle down his spine.

He had lost his leg. Did that mean he'd lost his voice too?

Why was he so nervous? He'd done this hundreds of times before, willingly, successfully. Had Kaboom torn that part of his life away, along with his leg? The bar manager handed him the microphone with an encouraging smile, and he almost dropped it on the floor. His hands had gone slick with nervous sweat and he gave an apprehensive glance at the audience looking at him expectantly as the manager stepped away and left him alone in front of them all.

It was too crowded, too uncertain. He had to get out of here. He saw the bar manager reach towards the laptop, about to press that key that would start his music.

The music started; the lyrics appeared on the monitor. Sweat beaded along his hairline, and his mouth went dry.

They were all looking at him. The freak. The cripple.

No. His physical disability had nothing to do with the stares of the audience. Sure, they'd seen him with his cane, limping. But only Julie was aware of his true condition. Everyone else was looking at him because they'd expected him to sing, and he was standing there silent.

You're a total wimpy-ass coward, something in his brain said. *You've faced down the Taliban in Afghanistan, and yet now you're paralyzed in front of twenty ordinary people in a karaoke bar.*

He turned to the bar manager manning the karaoke equipment.

"I'm sorry, sir," he apologized. The guy smiled at hearing Clay address him as Sir. "Could we start over?"

The man nodded and killed the music.

"First time singing karaoke?" he asked.

"No, I've done it before," Clay replied. "Just not -" He couldn't say, *just not since my world went Kaboom and I lost my joy of everything.* He simply muttered, "just not for a while."

He still wasn't sure he could do this, but he looked at Julie and she smiled at him and he saw her mouth the words *I love you* just as the bar manager started the music again. As soon as the first piano notes started to fill the air, he knew. He could do this. He could sing this because he was the karaoke king and yes, he did still have a voice.

He opened his mouth, and he sang.

The words scrolled across on the monitor, but he barely looked at them. He knew this song, and it knew him. He could sing this song with his eyes closed, and for part of it, he did.

As soon as that first smooth line passed his lips he knew he had the attention of everybody there. People fell silent and listened, even strangers. Usually during karaoke singing, people tended to go about whatever they were doing, coming, going, ordering food or drinks, perhaps wincing if the singer was off-key or screechy, but for the most part only paying attention if they knew the performer. But not when Clay sang. Before Kaboom, when he sang, they stopped what they were doing and listened. Tonight, despite Kaboom, they still listened. They didn't care if one of his legs was made of titanium and polypropylene.

He had eyes only for Julie while he sang, but he was aware of everyone else watching and listening.

He closed his eyes briefly during the drum riff at the end of the first verse, letting the song flow through him.

By the time the song was half through, several of the people listening had activated the flashlight app on their phones and were waving it back and forth the way people used to wave cigarette lighters at concerts in the eighties. He had them in the palm of his hand as he had in the past, before Kaboom. When he hit the high notes he could feel the palpable gasp from his audience. He held the final note for a full nine seconds. Most amateur singers couldn't do that. Some professional singers couldn't do it either.

There was a moment of stunned silence when the song ended, not even the sound of a glass clinking or a bottle being opened, and then the entire bar erupted in applause. Julie stood up, put two fingers in her mouth, and emitted a whistle that was probably heard by every dog in northern Illinois. Unbelievably, she actually turned to the people sitting at the next table, complete strangers, and said, "That's my boyfriend!" The bar manager came running up and shook Clay's hand, while Clay wobbled and swayed and leaned on his cane for stability.

"Man, that was awesome!" the manager said, as Clay panted with exertion. He had done this. He'd sung again. He hadn't lost his voice. Hope fluttered in his heart. He wanted to go to Julie, to hold her close, but the bar manager was still talking to him.

"Hey, listen, I have a friend who's the manager of a Journey tribute band and I know they're looking for a new singer. Would you be willing to let your hair grow long, maybe grow a mustache?"

For a brief time, before Kaboom, before enlisting in the Army, Clay had considered pursuing a career as a professional singer. What a dumb idea that had been. He had barely survived standing up in front of twenty people.

"Thanks," he muttered. "But, I don't think so."

"Are you sure?" the guy persisted. "At least consider it. I have never heard a voice like yours, and I've heard lots of people singing here."

"I know I can sing," Clay said. "But I can't perform."

"Well, when your leg heals," the guy said.

If only. "I'm afraid that's not going to happen." He turned away from the people still applauding and pulled up his pants leg slightly, just enough to let the manager see a few inches of his prosthesis.

"Oh." The one-syllable said volumes.

Had he just revealed his prosthesis, his disability, his lack of wholeness, to a stranger? And it hadn't even killed him.

"Do you mind if I ask what happened?" The guy's face was full of sympathy, empathy, but no revulsion, which surprised Clay. He'd expected the guy to back away, recoil from the sight of metal where there should be flesh.

His voice low, Clay just said, "Afghanistan."

"Shit." It was an expletive of sympathy. "Well, I sure hope you come back here and sing again. In fact, your tab is on me." He nodded over to where Julie sat at their table, beaming at him. "That your girl?"

His girl? Was Julie his girl? She sure looked like it, with pride shining from her eyes, and God, he wished it could be so. He was seriously starting to question his decision to break off their relationship. The bar manager took his hesitation as an affirmative. "You're a lucky guy, dude." He gave Clay a brief back slap. "Come back and sing for us again, would you?"

Clay nodded, his heart filled with mixed emotions, and made his way back to where Julie waited, bouncing with excitement.

"I knew you could do it!" she enthused. "That was so fabulous, my Cowboy."

"I didn't think I could do it at first," he admitted.

"Of course you could," she said, hugging him. Then she put one hand on the side of his face, a gesture of affection that made him glow inside, and murmured, "Let's go home, Cowboy. My parents are away for the weekend."

Home? *Home*? Was she inviting him to her house, to be alone while her parents were gone? This was the scenario he had dreamed of, fantasized about, every moment since he'd deployed to Afghanistan. But now, it was different. He was different, his life was different. So different that he'd had to break up with Julie, the love of his life.

But he wasn't a saint. He'd thought Kaboom had turned him into a cold robot devoid of feelings, but he'd been utterly wrong to think that. He was only a man, a man in love, and there was no way he could or would decline her invitation.

Chapter Sixteen

It was a dream, not real. It had to be. This couldn't be actually happening. He was with his Julie, going into her parent's empty house, slipping into her bedroom in the dark, closing the door. She put her arms around his neck and kissed him, and he no longer cared that he'd broken up with her. They were on the bed and their clothes were starting to melt away when the reality crashed in on him.

He was an amputee. An AKA – Above the Knee Amputee, with two artificial joints to maneuver rather than one. It was much more traumatic than a mere BKA – Below the Knee Amputee. He shouldn't be here, didn't deserve to be here, no matter how much he wanted to. The contest between the desire and the reality tore him apart.

Couldn't he just for once stop being this neurotic basket case, and just be Julie's lover?

His shirt and hers were off, her bra disappeared, and the feeling of her breasts pressed against his chest was driving him wild. All his feelings for her came rushing to the surface – love and lust and a tremendous desire for comfort. His desire for her touch was like a hunger living in his skin. The sudden heat was incredible, a furnace blast of sexual fire unlike anything he'd ever felt before. But the reality revealed itself when Julie hooked her fingers into the waistband of his slacks. A moment later they hit the floor.

And there it was, in all its hideous titanium glory. His prosthesis, that repulsive monstrosity that nobody this side of Germany had ever seen, exposed now to Julie's view, on display for her disgust and rejection. He burned with humiliation that she should see him, the real him, the new and damaged him, his stump and prosthesis revealed in all their scarred deficiency and shiny metallic grotesqueness, and felt himself scoot away from her on the bed.

Time slowed and stretched out as he waited for her to turn away in revulsion.

But Julie did no such thing. She gazed into his eyes, then her hands slipped down to his stump, to the socket of the prosthesis. "Would you be more comfortable with this off?" she asked, as casually as if she were referring to a hat or a sock.

Yes, he would be more comfortable with it off, generally speaking, but then it would be even worse, his stump would be completely visible, no hiding, no covering. He couldn't speak, barely found the wherewithal to nod a tiny bit.

"Show me how." The words were soft, caring, and amazingly erotic.

Don't freak out, don't freak out, his brain was reminding him. He wasn't sure if he was mentally willing the words into Julie's psyche, or his own, but he was pretty sure that freaking out was imminent now that his prosthesis was revealed. He couldn't quite believe he was doing this, but he put his hand on hers and showed her how to press her fingers under the cuff and ease it away from the shrinker sock. The prosthesis was nudged away and fell on the floor with a slight metallic ping.

It was a bit scary to have his prosthesis out of his reach, even though he hated the thing. Maybe because without it he was helpless. One-legged. A freak. He was a freak when he had it on, but he was even more of a freak without it.

"I'm sorry, Julie. You shouldn't have to see this."

"I think I deserve to see it."

"Nobody deserves to see something so gross." And she hadn't even seen the end of the stump under the shrinker sock, the part with the scars.

"It's not gross," Julie insisted. "How can you say that?"

The answer was obvious. "Because it's true."

"Nope, you're wrong," she insisted.

"I hate that thing." There was no need for him to specify what he meant by *that thing*. They both knew he was referring to the great big pink elephant in the room. His prosthesis.

She looked surprised. "Why should you hate it? It's a miracle of modern technology. It enables you to walk."

"How can you think of it as a good thing?"

"Because the alternative would be to not have you here at all and I couldn't live with that."

He wanted to argue the point further, but he couldn't. Julie was kissing him.

"I don't want to hurt you," she said. That was not a problem. There was nothing involving her fingers on him that could ever hurt him. "What about this?" She touched the fabric of the shrinker sock covering his residual limb.

"Leave it," he told her, and then another reality engulfed him.

"Shit," he muttered, his face getting red and hot as he looked away. "I don't have – I wasn't expecting -" He broke off in hideous embarrassment.

"You mean you don't have a condom?" she asked. "Don't worry, I have some." And suddenly, somehow, a foil packet was in his hand. "Not that it matters, Cowboy. I'm on the pill, and I've never, ever been with anyone other than you."

"Me either," he assured her, but still he tore open the wrapper, sat next to her and rolled the condom on.

She lay back and reached for him, urging him on top of her, her hands running along his sides and hips. God, she was positioning them, aligning their bodies, and he had only one knee with which to guide himself. He wobbled and fell prone, trying not to squish her or let his stump touch her. Despair engulfed him.

"I can't do this, Julie, I just can't."

Quick as a snake, her hand was between his legs, groping him, and he almost lost it right then and there in her hand.

"I have evidence here that says otherwise," she declared.

Arousal wasn't the problem. He was so hard he was afraid it was going to break off. The problem was more an issue of logistics. Three limbs entangled where there should be four.

"Lay back," she instructed, and the take-charge tone of her voice turned him on even more.

Julie pulled a pillow from the head of the bed and tucked it under his stump. "Is that more comfortable?" she asked. How did she know to do that?

"I hope you haven't been talking to Jacoby about this."

"No," she said. "Some things I can figure out for myself."

She draped a leg over his waist and slid over him, forcing him to lay flat on the bed with her on top. It was dim, almost dark in the room – he was glad she hadn't wanted the lights on – and with less sight than normal, he let his other senses kick in. The scent of her, her sweet personal fragrance, and the soft touch of her warm, eager skin filled his soul. She leaned forward to kiss him, and his body reacted instantaneously and intensely. A sound that was almost a growl breathed from him, as he fisted his hands in her hair and felt the soft strands caress his knuckles.

"Is this OK?" she murmured against his mouth.

OK didn't begin to describe it. This was heaven. They had never done it like this before, with her on top, but at this moment, it was his favorite thing ever in life. The weight of her on top of him, the way her soft curves fit his body, were pure joy. She rose up, but before he could protest at the slight movement away from him, she came back down with him inside her.

Oh God. Jesus, Mary and Joseph. If he died at this moment, he'd die a happy, satisfied man. She was a part of him; he was in her, they were one complete entity, and he never wanted it to end. His hands moved up to cup her breasts, those perfect, round breasts that his fingers had been longing to caress for almost a year. At his touch he heard her make a sound almost identical to his groaning growl. It amazed him that she was as turned on as he was, and he would never, ever forget the look of fervor on her face, not if he lived to be a hundred.

Maybe they did it for hours, her moving on him, him pumping inside her, or maybe it was only a minute until she gasped, and clenched around him as the sound and feel of her orgasm took him over the edge also, and he surged up with a moaning cry of completion, then pulled her down on top of him to kiss her as he came, to hold onto her and his sanity at the same time.

They were both sweaty when they came back down to reality and disposed of the condom. Then she laid her head on his shoulder with a possessive sigh of contentment.

Right now, he wasn't worried about strange noises or things coming at him. Maybe he was just too spent to pander to his anxieties at the moment. He had always, since the day he and Julie had been apart, remembered and relived every moment of their lovemaking. The tentative, awkward first time, the slightly more confident second time, while he'd been home on leave just before his deployment. But it wasn't only the actual intercourse that he'd remembered and fantasized about. It was also the little touches that had made him smile and sigh, until Kaboom.

The way she brushed her fingers along his temple. When she kissed the corner of his mouth and he could tell from the touch of her lips that she was smiling.

"Why are you crying, Cowboy?"

"I'm not crying," he lied.

She was right though. He was crying, though not sobbing as he had before. But tears were leaking slowly from his eyes, as if someone had stuck a pin into a bottle of water.

"I never thought I'd be here again, with you like this."

"Well it's your own fault."

"Yeah, I got my leg blown off on purpose just to annoy you."

He'd never been the type of man to resort to snotty sarcasm, before Kaboom. But now, it was as if that IED had destroyed his sense of humor, his personality, his soul, as well as his left leg.

"I'm sorry," he said quickly. "I'm a jerk. I've really ruined the mood, haven't I?"

"I'm so happy to have you back, I don't care. I think you have every right to be upset."

He was more than upset. He was depressed, destroyed, useless. How could she still love him like this, when he was so changed, both physically and emotionally? He surely didn't deserve her.

"But, Julie." He was glad for the dark, not only to hide his leg, but also his face. "I'm not a man anymore."

"You're my man, and you were certainly manly a few minutes ago. Do you think it's your left leg that makes you a man? For a smart guy, you can be pretty clueless sometimes."

Yeah, ever since Kaboom, he'd become a complete idiot.

She gave him a little thump on the chest. "It's what's in here that makes you a man."

"I'm not sure I have it there either."

"Do you still love me?"

"Of course I do. I always have. I'll never stop." The words flowed from him, easily, naturally, in a way he hadn't thought possible since Kaboom had happened.

"Then that's all that matters."

She traced a line with one finger along his collarbone, up his neck, which tickled, and around his ear before laying her head back on his shoulder and her arm possessively across his chest.

"What's a Lakota?" she asked, as she cuddled against him and teased at his chest hairs. He wasn't exactly Harry the hairy ape, but he had enough for her to get her fingers into and that was all that mattered.

"Huh?"

"When you told me about the day of your explosion, you said you rode in a stretcher on a Lakota. Is that a kind of helicopter?"

"Yes. All the Army's helicopters are named after Native American tribes or chiefs, like Comanche and Blackhawk and Apache. They named the medical evacuation helicopter Lakota because the Lakota were known as a peaceful and non-aggressive people, and the Lakota helicopter is non-arms-bearing."

Julie kissed his shoulder. "I love it when you talk Army," she murmured. "So in a way, the Lakota saved your life. I should write a thank you letter to their tribal chief."

She pressed her face against his neck. "You smell good, Cowboy."

"I do? What do I smell like? A cowboy?"

"Do you mind that I still call you that? Is it a dumb nickname? Too childish?"

"No, I love that you call me that."

"You smell like – a satisfied man."

At the moment, that was exactly what he was.

It was pleasant, erotic, downright fun to be able to lay here with Julie and enjoy simple pillow talk. Their previous private times together had been hurried and nervous, terrified that his parents or Brooke would come home earlier than expected. Although he had always suspected that his parents had contrived to be away both those times, so that he and Julie could be together before he'd left for Basic, and later for Afghanistan.

"You've got more here than I remember." Julie ran soft fingers across the sprinkle of dark hairs on his chest.

"Yeah, and each and every one of them is inventoried."

"Was that a joke? Finally! Maybe we should list them on a spreadsheet, and give them names. Harry, Larry, Jerry. This one is José. Or maybe we should start at the beginning of the alphabet." She touched one of the not-yet-named hairs. "He's Adam."

"No!" he said quickly, trying not to bark, as she twitched and moved her hand away from his chest hairs. "Not Adam!" The sweet joking moment soured and he turned away from her. Adam had been the first name of his sergeant who had died in Kaboom. He struggled not to think of that, here and now with Julie.

She accepted his shortness with calm. "What's wrong, Cowboy?"

"Nothing," he lied. The last thing he wanted to do right now was talk, or think, about Sergeant Lopez's death, so he changed the subject. "When did you start taking the pill?"

"While you were deployed. I wanted to surprise you when you got back. Instead, you surprised me."

She was beyond kind to refer to his cruel email breaking up with her without explanation, followed by months of silence, as *surprised*.

"You're thin, Cowboy," she said, running a hand over his ribs. It was true, his already lean runner's body had lost twenty pounds since Kaboom, only half of which was due to the loss of his leg. It was a hell of a way to lose weight, not that he'd ever needed to. He'd put on some healthy weight and muscle in basic training, losing his last vestiges of boyhood scrawniness. But since Kaboom, he'd been disinclined to maintain the military physique. Until this moment, he hadn't cared. But Julie was touching him, noticing him, loving him.

Maybe he'd take Nathan Jacoby up on his offer to work out with him.

Her hand that had been noticing his ribs now tightened across his torso, holding him close as she lay her head on his shoulder with a contented little sigh.

"Sleep, Cowboy," she murmured, and he obeyed her.

For the first night since Kaboom, he slept without having to take his pain meds. Also for the first time, he woke up in Julie's bed, with her cuddled up beside him. Julie fit against him like a long-lost puzzle piece, her hand on his chest, her head on his shoulder, blond hair tousled, the soft warmth of her breasts touching his skin.

He wanted to touch her hair, feel those fine, silky strands between his fingers, but he was afraid to move, on the chance that this was merely an illusion that could so easily dissolve into mist.

However, nothing dissolved or disappeared when Julie's eyes opened into his. But now, in the cool light of morning, with his stump as clearly visible as the proverbial pink elephant in the room, it was all different. She was just going to leave him anyway. Why prolong the torture? He turned his face up towards the ceiling.

"This can't happen again, Julie."

"Of course it can." she countered, sitting up and smoothing a hand over her tousled hair. It was unusual to see her disheveled. She was always so smooth, so put together. Seeing her in this early-morning state was so - intimate. "It's not like this is the Middle Ages. We're consenting adults and we've been going together for almost six years. I know people who've been married and had kids in that amount of time."

If that didn't cut his heart into a million tiny pieces. It had been what he'd hoped for, before Kaboom.

"And it's not like it's something we haven't done before," she continued. "Except for the me on top part. I really liked that."

Clay liked it too. But he couldn't allow her to be stuck with a cripple.

The love he saw shining from her eyes almost made him cry. He felt like dirt, for letting her believe they had some sort of future together, as if he were a whole and normal and viable person. He wanted to tell her that she could do so much better, deserved so much better, but he couldn't make the words come out of his mouth.

"You don't think I believed that lame attempt you made to break up with me, do you? You were under the effects of morphine and not thinking straight."

Yes, he had been on morphine and maybe things had been a bit fuzzy, but how could he have done anything differently? Last night had just been pity for the cripple.

Screw pity. His life had turned to shit, but he still didn't want anyone's pity.

"You lured me here into your bed under false pretenses." He'd been seduced by the music.

Why for the love of God was he saying these unpleasant things to her, when he should be telling her how beautiful she was, how sexy she was, how wonderfully, awesomely mind-blowing last night had been, that he loved her?

"No, I didn't lure you. I invited you here because I love you and I want you."

"No, you don't. You can't."

"Don't you tell me what I do or don't want."

"You may think you love me and want me but you're wrong, because I'm not me anymore, I'm not the same person I used to be."

Kaboom had changed everything. Changed his body, his mind, his emotions, his psyche.

"Of course not. Nobody is the same person they were in high school."

"No, not that. I'm still not me. Not anymore. Not since…"

"Since you lost your leg?" She said that so casually, as if it weren't the worst thing in the world. "Do you think that matters to me?"

"It should. I'm a hideous freak now. How can you stand to be even near it?"

"I have no problem with it. I slept next to it all night. It lay against me during the night, because I wanted to be close to you. It didn't bite me or cause a rash or ooze any hideous scum."

"It's still disgusting."

"You're wrong. It's a part of you and as that it will never be disgusting. Let me see it without this wrapper."

"No. And it's called a shrinker sock."

"Why?"

"The stump will continue to shrink a little until it forms into its permanent state. In about a year I'll have to be fitted for a new prosthesis."

Not even his parents or sister had been allowed to view his stump, not even with the wrapping on. Even if he could bear for Julie to see the thing naked, he didn't have a clean shrinker sock with him to put on, and he needed it under the prosthesis.

"Does it hurt?" she asked with concern, and he nodded.

"When does it hurt?"

"When I put the prosthesis on. When I take it off. When I'm tired. When I want to sleep. When anything bumps against it. Whenever I remember what it was like to have two legs. When I remember - running."

At the catch in his voice that he couldn't quite conceal, Julie pulled his head down, onto her shoulder, and stroked his hair, and that made things not hurt so much.

"Have you heard of phantom pain?" he found himself asking.

"No," she said. "But it sounds unpleasant."

"I feel pain in my leg sometimes, the leg that isn't there anymore. That's the worst part. It's bad enough to feel real pain, where you can say, this hurts or that aches, but when you feel pain in a place that doesn't exist anymore, that sucks big time. My leg isn't there, the nerves are cut, but it still hurts. It makes me feel – crazy."

Crazy. That was what he was, and he had just admitted it to Julie, whose regard he craved more than anyone else's in the world. She was surely aware he meant crazy in its most literal sense, insane, demented, in need of serious psychiatric help that he refused to accept. And yet that didn't seem to bother her.

"You're not crazy, Cowboy," Julie insisted. "You're a brave warrior, no matter what you may want to think. I think it just may take a little while for you to feel like yourself again."

A brave warrior? Maybe he'd been one before Kaboom, but now? He wasn't so sure.

"But, being with you eases my pain way more than Vicodin ever could," he admitted. "I know that sounds corny, but it's true."

She asked questions, about Kaboom, about his leg, his residual limb, his treatment and therapy in the hospital. Not prying, voyeuristic, morbid curiosity questions. Intelligent, caring questions, the way she'd asked in the past about his army uniforms and insignias. She made him feel wanted. She didn't avoid looking at his scars or his stump.

And amazingly, he found himself answering her questions, telling her what she wanted to know, without refusing or crying or freezing up with unbearable, constricting pain. The only thing he left out, and was glad she didn't know to ask about, was the death of Sergeant Lopez.

"Cowboy," she said with a sigh, "You are so brave and strong. You're amazing."

"But I'm not strong," he protested. "I used to be a strong man. I'm not anymore."

"Yes you are. You're a strong man who just happened to lose a leg. You just have to dig down a little and get a little stronger. I know you can do it. You're the bravest person I've ever known. You enlisted in the Army and didn't complain once when you were deployed to Afghanistan."

In truth, Clay had been excited more than fearful about his deployment to Afghanistan. He'd been proud to do his duty, serve his country, make a difference. Now all that pride and excitement had been blown to smithereens, into the choking dust of an Afghan roadway.

"All I do is cry, or feel like crying."

"Crying doesn't make you weak. It just makes you human."

"I barely feel human anymore."

"I know this was the most horrible, awful, hurtful thing a person could ever experience, but it doesn't change who you are or how I feel about you, or how you feel about me."

"It did change how I feel about you. It's made me love you even more. I didn't think such a thing was possible, but it is."

He automatically warmed up internally at the sensation of being close to her. He wished he could offer her the universe just to see her smile. He wanted to make her the happiest woman who ever lived. But he doubted he could.

Julie sat up and smiled at him, and the sight of her breasts and rosy pink nipples hypnotized him. "If I'd known when you were coming home, I would have gone to the airport that day and brought you straight here to jump your bones."

That certainly would have been more fun than that ghastly party his parents had hosted. He had a sudden mental image of Julie showing up at the airport that day, edging around the group of relatives and friends to say, "Sorry, Mr. and Mrs.

Maslowski. I know you have a party planned, but I need to take Clay to my house and jump his bones right now."

His parents and Brooke would have shit kittens. Just like his mom and dad were going to do when they found out about Brooke's career plans including the Army.

"What are you feeling, Cowboy?" she asked, obviously reading his expression.

"Worried," he admitted.

"What are you worried about?"

"About everything. Worried if I'll ever feel normal again. Worried if I can provide for us or even for myself. What kind of career can I have? I can't even be a Walmart door greeter."

"We can find a way. Maybe you shouldn't spend so much time obsessing over what you think you can't do, and focus more on what you can do."

"What can I do?"

"You can love me."

Loving Julie was easy, always had been. But living a real life, not so much.

Julie kept saying things like, "I love you, this was wonderful, I'm so happy we finally got to actually sleep together."

With a bolt of horror, he realized she was cuddling up on his left side, right against his stump, her hip touching it. Horrified, he tried to pull away.

"Don't get up just yet," she murmured, her fingers capturing him with a touch.

His torso and leg stiffened like a board, trying not to let his leg stump make further contact with her, until she sat up and looked at him with teasing in her eyes.

"Do you need to get up and pee?" she asked.

Of course as soon as she said it, he needed to do just that, really bad. But he was stuck. Without his prosthesis attached, he couldn't go anywhere unless he had crutches. If he tried to hop one-legged, he'd fall on his face. Plus he was still naked.

His first instinct was to request that Julie leave and give him privacy. But this was her home, her room, her bed. He couldn't kick her out. But he did pull the blanket over himself and try to discreetly roll away from her.

God, he needed to pee.

Maybe he could attach the prosthetic under the blanket so that Julie couldn't see it. Maybe she wouldn't notice his blind fumbling. Maybe he could blindly get his briefs and slacks on to cover the titanium monstrosity. His cane was on the floor somewhere – maybe he could retrieve it and hobble across the hall to the bathroom and she would be oblivious to his disability.

And maybe pigs would fly, and Steve Perry would return to Journey.

Julie put her arm around his shoulder and a hand under his chin, forcing him to look her in the eyes, those blue eyes that owned his soul. Would he frighten her again with the dark despair his own eyes held?

Apparently not.

"Listen to me, my Cowboy," she said. "You've lost your leg. That's a fact and we all know it. I know it's the most horrible, traumatic, awful thing you've ever experienced, but it is nothing to be ashamed of. You are not a freak or ugly or anything like that. You are still my Cowboy, you're still Clayton Maslowski, and I still love you. And I'm not giving up on you. Let me ask you. If our situations were reversed, if something like this happened to me, would you be revolted and reject me?"

Of course not. Never in a million years could Julie do anything or be anything that could kill his love for her. He shook his head.

"What do you do at your house? Do you put your leg on every time you go to the bathroom?"

His leg. She called the titanium monstrosity *your leg* as if it were some normal thing.

"Sometimes. If nobody is around, I use crutches."

"Why only when nobody is around? Surely it's OK for your folks or Brooke to see you using them."

It had been bad enough for his dad to see him on crutches, even with his oversized bathrobe on. He didn't want a repeat of that experience.

"I don't want them to see me like that. I don't want anyone to see me like that," he admitted.

"I seriously don't think it will be an issue if they did."

Stubbornly, he refused to argue the point with her.

"Give me credit, Cowboy, and believe me when I say it's OK. Have I ever lied to you?"

He was mesmerized under her gaze and the truth and strength he saw in her eyes, as he simply replied, "No."

"Good. Now, let me help you to the bathroom."

She grabbed a silky yellow bathrobe that had been lying across the foot of the bed and slipped into it. Even though it covered her breasts and hips almost to the knees, it was still quite the most erotic garment he had ever seen, knowing what beauty was just underneath that thin yellow fabric. He found his briefs on the floor and pulled them on.

She pulled him up onto his foot and put her arm around his shoulder next to him. "Remember when we did the three-legged race at the church picnic?"

They had won that race. Now they wouldn't need to tie two of their legs together. They truly had only three legs between them.

"I'll be your crutch. You can lean on me, just like that song."

Lean on me, when you're not strong.

"I'll hurt you. I don't want to knock you over." His stump pressed against her leg, against that silky yellow robe, but she just accepted that as normal, as if it wasn't grotesque at all.

"You won't hurt me," she assured him. "We can do this."

Having her near, holding on to him, being his crutch and his strength, held an unbelievable sensation of possibility, as he put his arm around her shoulder.

It was extremely awkward, but still somehow erotic, as he leaned on her like a crutch, and they hopped and wobbled precariously as she guided him out her bedroom door, into the hall, and down the few steps to the bathroom. She even opened the door and said, "I'll be here when you're done."

He loved her, a hundred times more now than before, even though he'd thought that he'd loved her completely before. But he still wasn't ready to let her see him pee, no matter what condition he was in, so he closed the door.

He had, finally, mastered the fine art of urinating while standing up on his one leg. Lean against the wall above the toilet with one hand, use the other to aim the gun. The technique tended to make his memory recall the chant he'd learned in basic training.

"This is my rifle." (They'd point to their rifles.) "This is my gun." (The male recruits grabbed their crotches.) "One is for shooting." (Point to the rifle again.) "One is for fun." (Another crotch grab, while half the female recruits blushed and giggled and the other half acted like one of the boys.) A recruit who made the mistake of referring to their weapon as a *gun* would have to repeat the chant at the top of his or her lungs while running through the barracks holding their rifle above their head. Fortunately Clay had never been so careless as to deserve that punishment.

When he looked in the mirror over the sink this morning, it was like looking at a whole different person. He remembered looking at himself the day he'd come home from Germany, and the face he'd seen that day had been so utterly different from the face looking back at him today that he'd barely recognized it as him. This morning, the face he saw in Julie's bathroom mirror was not nearly as haggard, not quite as hollow-eyed, didn't bear the lost and despairing visage it had before. This morning he didn't look at all like he'd terrify another person who looked into his eyes.

That's what the love of a good woman will do for you.

The words flowed into his brain as if God had spoken to him. Julie still loved him. Despite his missing leg, despite his scars, despite his cruelty towards her, sending her that short but brutal email, despite his permanent bad mood and depression. What he had done to deserve such compassion, he had no idea. He'd been an idiot all this time, pushing her away. If only he could stop being such an idiot.

The door was close enough to the sink that he could reach it while holding onto the counter for balance. As she'd promised, she was waiting for him when he opened the door and they repeated the three-legged journey back to her room.

"That worked out well," she declared brightly as they halfway fell back onto the bed.

On a shelf in her room sat a large, purple plush dog with silly googly eyes and a fluffy tail. Clay had won that dog for Julie at the Lake County Fair last year, before Kaboom. It was really unfair, with the advantage he'd had as an expert marksman. The clown face he'd shot water at hadn't stood a chance.

"Why aren't you mad at me?" he asked. "Why aren't you slapping my face and telling me what a cold-hearted jerk I was?"

"I could never slap your face, Cowboy. Touch it, yes." She ran a soft finger along his jaw. "Kiss it, definitely." She kissed him tenderly on the cheek and murmured, "Bristly. But I'd never slap you or yell at you. Because I love you."

"I'm sorry." No apology had ever been more heartfelt than the one he offered now. "I'm sorry I sent you that mean email and didn't contact you after, after – you know."

"Apology accepted," she said calmly, and part of his anxiety and grief slid away from him. "Do you know why I love you, Cowboy?" She ran a hand along his forehead, brushing it with her fingers, then placed it on his chest, over his heart.

"I have no idea," he confessed.

"Your strength. You're so strong, yet gentle and sweet at the same time. It takes a special man to be both."

"And here I thought you wanted me for my handsome face and hot body."

Oops! Big mistake. He had just referred to his body, as if it were something acceptable and normal. He'd joked about it. That was new. But damn it, she made him feel so normal and worthy.

"Well yeah, that too," she replied. "I'm so lucky."

She was in bed with a one-legged freak, and she thought she was lucky? She was the one who was both strong and gentle, far more so than he was.

"I knew we would get back together, be together again," she went on. "Remember when I came over that first day, when you were laying on the blanket in your back yard?"

That day he'd cried in her arms.

"Even though you told me to leave, you said you loved me. I've held that in my heart every moment since then. Hearing you say that, I knew we would be together again."

"I always have loved you and I'll never stop." His love for her knew no bounds, no boundaries.

She put a hand on either side of his face.

"I so love doing this," she said. "Touching you. Looking into your eyes. Your beautiful eyes. But they are still so sad."

He tried to brighten his eyes a little, and she smiled at him. "I want you to feel safe with me, Cowboy. Safe from fear and unhappiness. But maybe that's too much to ask though. I'm just a chef."

"You're more than that. You're my Viking princess. If you stick with me, I know I can do better."

"I know," she replied with a smile. "Come on, get dressed. I'll make us breakfast." She kissed him quickly, then left the room, instinctively giving him privacy to attach his prosthesis.

Safe. She said he was safe now, and Lord, he wanted to believe her.

When he limped into her kitchen, he glanced around cautiously. Julie stood in front of the open refrigerator, assessing the contents. He couldn't help but stare at her round, perfect derriere under that thin yellow robe.

"Are you wearing panties?" he asked.

"No. Do you want to check?"

His blood pressure zoomed to the stratosphere.

"Are you sure your parents aren't coming home?" He'd absolutely die if they caught him here like this.

"No, they're away all weekend. Mom said they'd be home Monday morning."

Reassured, he sat at her kitchen table and Julie set a cup of coffee in front of him. Then she turned back to the refrigerator and started pulling out ingredients. She set down eggs, cheese, butter, then opened a cabinet and retrieved flour and cinnamon.

"Which do you want?" she asked. "My famous French omelet, or my famous cinnamon waffles?"

Julie, of course, cooked everything from scratch. No frozen toaster waffles or microwave meals ever came from her hands. It was partly her passion for cooking and her skill at it, and partly the way she expressed affection and love.

His stomach spoke to him in a language he hadn't heard in months. Not since before Kaboom. He didn't recognize the sensation at first. What was that?

Hunger. For the first time since Kaboom, he was hungry. He didn't know if it was the release of sex, the reconciliation with

Julie, the sight of her face, eager to create a culinary delight for him, or the result of all three, but his stomach growled and requested to be fed.

Julie was a mind reader, looked at his expression, heard his grumbling belly, and smiled. "OK, both. But you'd better eat this time, Cowboy."

"I promise."

How could it be so erotic to watch a woman retrieve mixing bowls from a cabinet, pull a hand mixer out of a drawer, set packages of flour, sugar, cinnamon and pepper on the counter? He had a sudden mental image of making love to her on a flour-covered kitchen counter that made him gulp and tug his slacks aside to try and hide his sudden erection. He'd even be willing to try it with his prosthesis on.

She picked up an egg, smiled at him, and cracked it on the side of the bowl without taking her eyes from his face, dumping the egg into the bowl without a single shred of eggshell falling in.

God that was sexy. He couldn't help but smile back.

"It's all in the wrist," she said, wiggling her hand at him.

It was a real, genuine smile that came over him. He could feel it. It had been a long time since he had done that, since before Kaboom. So long that the appropriate muscles were surprised at the position he put them in.

But it felt good. He liked it. He might do this again some time.

Julie had a little habit of swaying when she cooked, almost as if she was dancing to some sort of music released by mixing eggs, stirring batter and pouring ingredients into pans. It was far sexier, way more erotic than any exotic dancer he could imagine. The image of sex on the floured counter was enhanced now with a desire to scoop out a bit of the egg mixture she was whisking, paint it on her breast, and lick it off.

"Do you do that at work?" he asked, devastated at the thought of her coworkers in the restaurant kitchen observing her sexy little cooking dance.

"Do what?" she glanced over her shoulder briefly before pouring the omelet mixture into the pan.

"That little dance thing. Moving your hips like that when you cook. It turns me on."

She stopped her preparations for a moment to turn and smile at him. "No, I don't do that at work. Only in my own kitchen when I cook for the man I love."

He felt warmth curl down his spine at her words. Those seductive little culinary movements were for him alone, the man she loved. He wasn't even going to worry about the possibility of his mother being mad at him for missing Mass.

How did he get so lucky?

When she set the dishes on the table and sat down next to him, he easily honored his promise to eat heartily. She even had real, pure, imported from Canada maple syrup to drizzle over the waffles. No artificial grocery store syrup would touch her creations.

He ate everything, both the waffle and the omelet. Every crumb, every drip, every molecule. Along with coffee and orange juice, hand-squeezed. It wasn't only because she was an amazing cook and her food smelled and tasted delicious. It was also because she had cooked it, his Julie, his Viking Princes, the woman he loved. For the first time since Kaboom, he ate an entire meal willingly, without threats from doctors or cajoling from his mother. It was almost with surprise that he found his plate empty, without so much as a shred left over.

Just as he was about to clear his throat and discuss his flour and egg fantasy, a soft ringing sound emitted from Julie's purse, lying on the table near them. She pulled out her cell phone and answered it.

"Oh, hi, Mom."

Oh God. It was her mother on the phone. Surely Mrs. Peterson would murder him if she knew Clay was sitting at her kitchen table after having spent the night here with Julie. And if she knew about the fantasy he'd been having concerning the kitchen counter, the flour and the egg batter, he would be double dead. He slapped his hand over his mouth and prayed she couldn't hear him breathing.

Julie, for her part, seemed unconcerned at the prospect of her mother finding out what had been going on in her home during her parents' absence. She listened to what her mother had to say, then simply said, "Ok, Mom, I'll do that. See you later." Then she set the phone down and smiled at a terror-stricken Clay.

"That was my mom. She said that she and my dad are having a nice time, and she wants me to water her roses before I leave for work. You know how she loves those things."

Clay nodded, hardly daring to remove his hand from his mouth and allow himself to breathe again. "She doesn't know I'm here, does she?"

"Sure she does." That was it. Clay was officially a dead man. "She said to say hello to you and she hopes you're feeling better."

"She *what*?"

With a complete lack of concern about what her mother knew was going on in her house, Julie started rinsing off the bowls she'd used to mix their breakfast ingredients. "She pretty much suggested I have you over, when she and Daddy decided to go to Lake Geneva for the weekend. She said, you'll have a chance to spend some private time with your young man."

"Oh. My. Fucking. God."

Mrs. Peterson not only knew he was here, but also condoned and had practically set up the encounter? His head might just explode with disbelief.

Julie giggled. "Speaking of mothers, you better not let yours hear you talking like that. You know how she hates swear words."

"Let's not talk about our mothers anymore," Clay requested.

"No problem," Julie agreed. "In fact, this cleaning up can wait until later too. Come on, let's make the most of the time we have left today."

She turned off the faucet, turned to him and took his hand. In what seemed like a fraction of a second they were back in her bedroom, laying on her bed. He didn't even remember limping on the way there until his cane made a small clunk sound as it fell against something – the bed frame, the dresser, he wasn't sure what, and he didn't care. Julie was kissing him.

"Clay," she broke away enough to ask, "do you trust me?"

Of course he trusted her.

"Good. Hold still."

He'd do anything she asked him to right about now. But still, he was beyond shocked when she stood up and shifted his legs – both the real one and the prosthesis – over the edge of the bed. "Take off your pants," she requested.

OK. Yeah. He'd be glad to. She was still wearing that silky, sexy yellow robe and he could see down the front of it to the sweet creamy space between her breasts as she knelt in front of him and helped him pull his slacks down.

Wait. She was kneeling on the floor, in front of him, like a Viking goddess, as his slacks were shoved aside. He had died and gone to heaven, skipping Purgatory altogether. "Your underwear too," she ordered.

That was a bit of a problem because it was hard to get them off over the boner he'd sprung. She had to help him. Damn.

"You said you trusted me, right? I won't hurt you."

Hurt him? She could hurt him all right. Hurt him good.

She touched him. *There.* Her slender fingers were around him, and he throbbed under the sensation. Could anything possibly be any hotter?

Yes it could. She smiled at him, then leaned forward.

At the first feathery sensation of her lips on him, his back arched and he came close to exhaling a few more of the expletives his mother disapproved of. This was a completely new, unexpected incandescence.

"God, Julie!" She was killing him, and bringing him back to life at the same time.

She didn't reply because her mouth was full. Full of him, with little Clay. Strike that, big Clay. Big, hard, straining Clay. Was that her *tongue*? It swept over him in lush circles, sending jolts of electric lust throughout his body. He'd never known such a feeling of intoxication.

All sensible thought and reason flew out the window, and all that was left were the sensations, the soft strands of her hair like silk against his thigh. He managed to move one hand to brush her hair aside so he could see. He wanted to remember this experience forever.

She owned him and he was hers to do with as she willed.

He groaned when she began to suck and instinctively pushed in a little deeper. Her mouth was hot and wet and tight and he had to force himself to keep control. But that only lasted so long. Her mouth felt so damn good, and the little sounds she made against him were beyond hot. And she was so damn beautiful, there on her knees, for him.

His hands were in her hair, trying not to pull, until his legs stiffened and a primal groan erupted from his throat. He wanted to prolong it indefinitely, but such a thing wasn't possible. Pleasure of the most erotic kind exploded in him as he poured into her in a hot, pulsing stream.

She swallowed. *Swallowed.*

"Did you like that, Cowboy?"

For a moment he was speechless, trying to think up more glorious words to describe the experience than merely *like*. But even Shakespeare couldn't have described it accurately.

"Um, yeah," he managed to croak out. "Where in all the holy fuck did you learn to do that?"

"I didn't learn it anywhere. Some things are instinctive."

"You didn't have to do that."

"I know. I wanted to."

Maybe he was overthinking things, but he had to ask.

"Julie, last night, was I ..."

"Awesome? Yes you were."

"I was afraid I was too fast." He also hoped he didn't snore, afterward.

"Well, it had been a while. But I was so eager too. It wasn't too fast, wasn't too slow. It was just right. It was the best, Cowboy."

They lay on her bed for a long time, kissing, talking, half drowsing. He nudged aside her silky yellow robe and whispered against her skin, because that was the only way he could do it, confessing all his fears, his despair, the trauma of Kaboom and its aftermath. How amazing that he could hold her, touch her, that she was his woman again, as he'd always hoped she would be.

"I was scared, Julie," he admitted. "I was so scared. I wish you'd been there with me."

"Cowboy, if I'd known, I would have been there. One phone call, and I would have been with you."

"I know. I used to look out the window at the moon sometimes, and imagine you looking at the same moon. But I was so stupid. I should have made that call."

She held him close, stroked his hair, and whispered back that it was all right, that she understood, that they would conquer all his demons together, that those demons weren't nearly as formidable as he'd thought, now that there were two of them together.

Maybe this was all some incredibly realistic dream. If so he didn't want to ever wake up.

He let her take off his prosthesis. He'd almost forgotten he'd had it on during that – he couldn't even think of it as a blow job. Because that was just too crass a term to use for something so incredibly extraordinary. With stomachs full of the awesome breakfast she'd made, they drifted back to sleep for a few minutes, then woke up and made love again. The second time was a slower, sweeter, yet even more erotic, exploratory love-making; not the frantic, haven't done it in a year experience from last night.

With Julie's encouragement, he was even able to be on top, found that the muscles in his residual limb were capable of supporting him, especially when Julie put her hand on the back of it as support. His need for her made him stronger, both physically and emotionally, than he'd felt since before Kaboom. Surprisingly, this time he didn't flinch or stress out over her touching him there.

When he was capable of moving and thinking again, they got dressed and Clay helped Julie clean up the dishes and ingredients of their sumptuous breakfast. He even made sure the toilet seat was down. Obviously, Julie's parents knew he'd been there, but still, he wanted to keep up the pretenses.

In every ointment, there is a fly. He had to do the walk of shame. Or in his case, the limp of shame. When Julie dropped him off at home on her way to work, his parents and Brooke were all sitting in the living room watching the Cubs game on television. Couldn't they have been conveniently out shopping or visiting friends or taking a Sunday drive that afternoon? Couldn't they have gone down to Wrigley Field to watch the game in person? No, all three of them were present and accounted for in their living room, and there was, to his chagrin, no way in the world they could miss seeing Clay coming home at three in the afternoon, unshaven and wearing the same clothes he'd had on yesterday, when Julie had picked him up at eight in the evening.

Maybe if he'd come in through the kitchen door rather than the front door, he might have been able to sneak past them.

Who was he kidding? With his cane and his clomping limp, there was no sneaking anywhere.

Time stood still, as if God had hit the pause button. Embarrassment at being caught coiled around him like a boa constrictor. There were no secrets when both members of a couple lived with their parents.

"Well, good morning, Clay," his dad said. "Or should I say, good afternoon?"

"Father Cross asked how you were this morning," his mother said, but with a smile.

They were all smiling, but it was Brooke, who at the sight of him, had stopped with a potato chip in her hand, halfway to her mouth, whose grin was the widest.

"You look happy," she commented. "I guess all it took to put a smile on your face was for you to get laid."

"Brooke!" both their parents admonished, while Clay's face heated up like a furnace, which only seemed to make Brooke smile more.

"What did Julie's parents think of you spending the night there?" she asked.

"They weren't home," he admitted. He did not, was not going to, let them know about Julie's parents being perfectly aware he'd spent the night with her, or about what had occurred after her mother had called in the morning.

"Convenient!" Brooke crowed. "Just like when we -" She didn't finish her sentence because their mother kicked her ankle.

Clay had to get away. Not for his usual reasons, his discomfort being around people since Kaboom, but because his family's knowing smiles and teasing were embarrassing him to death.

"Um, I'm going to take a nap," he said, inching towards the stairs. "Call me when it's time for dinner, OK?"

"So Julie really wore you out, huh, Clay?"

"Brooke, shut up. Please."

"Yes, Brooke," Mom said. "Clay is an adult and he deserves to have his private life remain private." Yet even believing that hadn't stopped his mother from teasing him about being gone long enough to miss accompanying them to church.

Somehow, getting up the stairs didn't seem quite as much of a chore today as it had been, and his desire to take a nap hadn't merely been an excuse to escape from his family's teasing and knowing looks. Julie really had worn him out.

When his mother called him for dinner that evening, he found himself sitting at the table willingly, eating voluntarily, allowing himself to taste and enjoy the food, and he ate everything on his plate, a fact that did not go unnoticed by his mother.

"It's nice to see you eat again," she said. "I guess we have Julie to thank for that."

"So does that mean you two are going together again?" Brooke asked, but he didn't have an answer for that. He wanted to think that he and Julie were truly together again, that she accepted him even in his damaged condition, but he still couldn't dislodge that small bit of fear that threw a wet blanket onto the situation, despite the wonder and joy of the night they'd spent together. The closeness, the lovemaking, made him want to believe there was hope for the two of them. But what if, despite her claims to the contrary, she still only felt pity towards the cripple?

Chapter Seventeen

The laptop computer he had ordered a few days earlier was delivered. Brooke saw the UPS truck pull up in front of their house, took possession of the box, and brought it up to his room when she saw his name on the delivery label.

"Present for you, Cuckoo!" she said, handing the box to him.

He hesitated a moment to take it from her hands. The portable computer would make it easier for him to complete the digital journal he'd started on his father's computer, but it also brought him an obligation that he wasn't certain he was strong enough to fulfill just yet. Brooke noticed his hesitation and offered, "If you don't want it, I'll take it."

That snapped him out of his funk enough to accept the box and ask Brooke, politely this time and with two sincere uses of that magic word, please, if she wouldn't mind closing his door when she left. Just before she did so she teased, "You want privacy so you can log onto one of *those* websites?"

He showed her innocent eyes. "What do you mean? What are *those* websites?"

She rolled her eyes and shook her head. "Never mind. If you don't know I'm not going to tell you."

She closed his door when she left as he'd requested, but gently this time without slamming it. He opened up the box, pulled out the laptop, and logged onto the Wi-Fi. But he didn't even consider visiting one of *those* websites.

It's just your email, Clay. Just because you haven't looked at it in months doesn't mean it's going to bite you on the ass.

Or at least he hoped not.

When he finally got up the courage to click on the word Inbox, his jaw dropped in shock.

There were over five hundred unread emails. He'd had no idea he was so popular. Even after deleting all the junk mail and ads, there were still several hundred real emails that he'd ignored all these months.

He didn't have the courage to open Julie's emails just yet. He couldn't face reading her words of hurt and confusion after the cruel breakup message he'd sent her.

There were emails from his childhood buddies – the Posse. No wonder they'd been pissed at him, after the way he'd blown them off. Emails from Noah Gadsden and Jonathan Kullander, who'd been in the Humvee with him at the time of Kaboom, and who had survived with all limbs intact. The most recent one from Kullander had been sent a week ago. Frustrated with Clay's lack of response, the last message simply read, "WTF, dude?"

There were emails from the doctors and nurses at Landstuhl who'd treated him while he'd been there. Surely they had better things to do with their time than send emails to Clay. Even the Liaison Non-Commissioned Officer who'd coordinated his care had sent him emails.

There was an email from one person he'd never met in person but whose photo he'd seen. It was almost against his will that he opened the message from Veronica Lopez, the widow of Sergeant Adam Lopez.

"Dear Clay," she wrote. "I know we never had a chance to meet in person, but I feel like I know you. Adam spoke of you often. I appreciate what a good friend you were to him. It means a lot to me to know that he wasn't alone when he died.

"I heard from your platoon mates that you suffered the loss of your leg in the blast, and I am truly sorry for your suffering. I think of you often and I hope you are recovering and able to work towards mobility. I've spoken to Noah Gadsden and Jonathan Kullander and I understand they have recovered from their injuries.

"Though I grieve for Adam tremendously, I am still aware that he was hugely proud of his country and what he was doing to protect it. He was also proud of the men he served with, including yourself. He had hoped to see you step into his position eventually when he moved on. I know that won't happen now, but I am sure you would have continued to be a true asset to the Army if things had happened differently.

"I sincerely hope that you will keep in touch and maybe share some stories about serving with Adam so I can keep his memory alive for our children."

Sergeant Adam Lopez had been the dad to two little kids. The youngest was less than a year old. Lopez hadn't been able to be with his wife when she'd given birth to their second child, and had only been able to see the kid in person once, due to their deployment.

Those kids were going to grow up without a father. And here Clay thought he had problems.

"If you ever get a chance to visit Houston," Veronica Lopez continued, "please stop by. We would love to meet you in person. And Clay, should you ever have the opportunity to get to Virginia, please try to visit his grave at Arlington, and remind Adam that we love him."

By now Clay was so choked up he could barely make out the email address and phone number she'd included at the bottom of her email.

But there was one thing Veronica Lopez was wrong about. Clay had not been with her husband when he'd died. He'd been lying unconscious and in shock, while his sergeant had been bleeding out. How could he ever look the man's widow in the eye?

How could Mrs. Lopez be so damn nice and caring? Her husband was dead and her children were fatherless. Clay remembered when he, and later Brooke, had first started school. Their parents had both taken time off work to walk them to school on each first day right up through middle school, and had proudly taken photos. When they started high school they'd still taken first-day photos, but at their house rather than at the school. What was going to happen to Lopez's kids when they started school? Instead of a dad to hold their hand, all they'd have was a folded flag in a presentation box on a shelf.

Veronica Lopez's letter should have been filled with heartbreak, recriminations and anger, words like, my husband is dead, how dare you live?

Instead she wrote to him with compassion, sympathy and caring, extending invitations to keep in touch and visit, and a wish that Clay might someday visit his former sergeant's grave.

He was humbled by her attitude, and he knew he was going to have to man up and visit Arlington National Cemetery someday.

He sorted the remaining messages alphabetically by sender, but just stared at the list without opening any more. He wasn't sure he had the courage left, especially after reading Mrs. Lopez's letter.

Come on Clay, you are, or were, a soldier in the United States Army, and these are just messages on a computer. They don't have weapons.

But in a way, they did have weapons. Weapons of guilt and fear and his own inadequacy to read them, to face what they had to say, poured over him as if someone was dumping a can of paint over his head. The guilt of having ignored all those well-meaning messages from all those caring people was almost overwhelming. Who was he to deserve that sort of consideration?

Something Nathan Jacoby had said to him sparked in his brain.

"I don't have to give you back your dignity and pride. You never lost them. They're just in the background, waiting for you to acknowledge them."

He wished he could believe that. He wished he had the courage to read more of the long list of emails. But how could he respond to people who had contacted him out of caring, friendship, brotherhood, and in Julie's case, love, when he had been so rude and dismissive and emotionally shut down? How could he expect them to accept an apology?

He had a feeling that if he mentioned his hesitations in this regard to Sergeant Jacoby, his response would be something like, *you'll never know unless you try it.* Jacoby seemed to think it was easy, but Clay wasn't so sure he believed it.

Chapter Eighteen

He couldn't sleep that night. Not even his Vicodin gave him repose, and he was an emotional wreck the next time he saw Jacoby. The sergeant perceived that Clay was on the verge of snapping and rather than talking over coffee, he ordered him into his car for a drive, while Clay looked sightlessly out the passenger window.

Jacoby drove into the forest preserve on Wheeling's eastern edge, into the Dam No. 1 Woods, the deeply wooded area that made one forget they were in a Chicago suburb. Clay was so oblivious, caught up and lost in his own misery, that it didn't even register to him that Jacoby had stopped his car, turned it off and gotten out until he opened Clay's door.

He jumped, startled.

"Hop out," Jacoby invited him, while Clay gave him a dirty look. He limped out, because to hop was above his abilities. "This looks like a good spot." Jacoby indicated the grassy area among the trees.

Bemused and curious as to why Jacoby wanted to come here, and a bit embarrassed at his difficulty navigating the bumpy, grassy field, he followed Jacoby to the center of the small clearing.

"Sit down," Jacoby suggested.

It took a little twisting, but he managed to sit on the grass without falling down.

Surprisingly, Jacoby turned away. "Do what you have to do," he instructed. "You need to let it out or you'll pop like a champagne cork, and not in a good way."

Clay screamed. He shrieked, he yelled, hoping they were deep enough into the woods to not be heard. But maybe he would be heard in Wisconsin. He screamed so hard and so long his throat felt as if he'd swallowed glass.

He screamed his pain, his anguish, frustration and grief, his feelings of uselessness. The heartache, the torment, the terror of the rest of the world erupted out from his belly, his heart, his soul, spewing out to dissipate into the hot, humid air around him. When he simply could not scream anymore, his throat abused into painful friction, he fell to the ground and cried. Worse than when he had cried with Julie, worse than any tears he may have shed as a child. He couldn't believe one set of human sinuses could produce the amount of liquid that flowed from him, so much mucus and general wet, snotty output.

He was panting like a dog at the end, trying to wipe the river of moisture from his face with his hands. He was exhausted, but somehow cleansed.

A flutter of white appeared in his peripheral vision. Jacoby was standing over him with a handkerchief in his hand.

"You look disgusting," he said amiably, as Clay mopped his face and felt embarrassment heat his skin.

"You've been here this whole time?" he asked.

"Of course. Did you think I went home and left you here?"

Clay wouldn't have been surprised if Nathan had done that. "I'm sorry. You must think I'm a total wuss."

Jacoby sat down next to him. Clay still envied the guy's ease of movement as he settled into a cross-legged arrangement beside him. They sat there in silence for a minute, then Jacoby sighed and spoke.

"I don't think you're a wuss. This is all just a part of processing our experiences. It's OK to grieve. Grieving is healthy. Avoiding the guilt and fear and grief is what leads to things like drugs, alcohol and suicide. Those vices only mask the grief. They don't eliminate it."

"How do you know all this?"

"Are you kidding? Do you know how many psych classes I took while getting my teaching degree? I was after all planning on a career dealing with teenagers. You need to be almost as much of a shrink as a teacher.

"When I found myself in the same place, emotionally and physically, as you are now, I sat down in the grass one day and I screamed out all my pain and frustration and hatred. I hated the prospect of living my life like this. And I cried until I was dehydrated. And after it was done, I realized two things."

He was silent long enough that Clay finally asked, "What were they?"

"First, I should have brought a handkerchief. Or a towel. I had no idea so much snot could come out of one person. Second, that I could either sit around feeling like a useless lump of nothing, or I could live a real life with my family. I realized at that moment it was an opportunity for an aliyah."

"A what?"

"It's Hebrew. It means going up. When a Jew goes to a better place, we call it an aliyah. It literally means to ascend. It's usually meant to indicate emigrating to Israel, but it's also used to mean simply going to a better place in general. You can remain an unhappy lump, or you can choose your own personal aliyah."

"Are you trying to convert me, Staff Sergeant?"

"No. Jews don't proselytize. But there's another helpful word, in this case, it's Greek. It's called catharsis. You know what that means?"

"No. I didn't go to college."

"It means cleansing. Emotional cleansing, not like washing dishes. When I sat in the grass and had my screaming crying fit, afterward it was like a catharsis that cleansed me from some of the pain so I could achieve my aliyah."

"Did you do it here?" Clay indicated the grass and trees around them.

"No, in my case it happened at Shalom Memorial Park in Arlington Heights, sitting in front of my father's grave. Fortunately it was a slow day so I didn't embarrass myself too much. The nice thing about screaming and crying in a cemetery is that the dead don't complain, and the living aren't terribly surprised. You know, my dad, may peace be upon him, died of cancer. He had a brain tumor. It was inoperable. It was a horrible, ugly, painful way to go, but he never complained once the whole time. He had to have been suffering, but I never heard one word of complaint or self-pity from his lips. The last thing he said to me, before he slipped into a coma, was what a lucky man he'd been. The man was dying of a fucking brain tumor, and he thought he'd been lucky! I can only hope that when my time comes, I can show a fraction of that courage and grace. Until then, I can only, and I must, honor his memory by living. Not just existing. Living. Five minutes before he died, he was in a coma, and I still heard him murmuring about what a lucky man he'd been."

It was obvious that telling Clay this story was an emotional experience for Sergeant Jacoby. He'd never heard the man use an expletive before. The slight but noticeable catch in Jacoby's voice made Clay consider returning the handkerchief to him, but it was so wet from Clay's use that it would have done no good.

"I realized that if he could endure constant pain, knowing he was going to die, and still manage to be happy, and even grateful, for the time he'd had, how could I be upset by a little thing like an amputated leg? Now I'm not saying your father has to die for you to come to terms with your situation, but I hope you get the idea."

"My dad's pretty healthy."

"Good. I hope he stays that way for a long, long time."

"The way my mom watches what he eats, I'm sure he will," Clay said, thinking about the warning looks Mom shot at Dad over the gravy ladle.

"From your mouth to God's ear," Jacoby intoned, with a reverent glance towards heaven. "Then I put a stone on top of his gravestone, went home, and got on with my life."

"Did you think you had to weigh him down with rocks so he didn't raise up and haunt you?"

Nathan gave him a stink eye. "I'm going to cut you a break because I like you, and assume you asked that because you genuinely wanted to know, and not to be a schmendrick."

Clay had no idea what a schmendrick was, but he was pretty sure it wasn't meant as a compliment. It was nice of Jacoby to cut him a break, though in truth Clay had said what he had purely to be a snot.

"Is that another Hebrew word?"

"No, schmendrick is Yiddish. It's a Jewish tradition to place a stone on top of the grave marker of someone who has been a friend."

"Why a stone? Why not flowers?"

"Flowers die. A stone will not die. It symbolizes the permanence of memory and legacy. And it keeps demons from getting into the grave. It's even better if you can use a stone or pebble that came from a place significant to you or to the deceased."

Jacoby rubbed his head, ruffling black, wavy hair. "You know, one good thing about being out of the Army is being able to grow my hair out enough to not get sunburn on my scalp.

"You're alive, Clay. You can see a sunset. Eat a taco. Well, you can eat a taco. I can't. You can make love to your woman. Be loved. There are so many people who don't have that and they'd be willing to give up their left leg to have it."

"Well, those guys are nuts. Why can't you eat a taco?"

"Are you kidding?" Jacoby rolled his eyes. "Meat and cheese in the same meal? My wife would kill me.

"You have to be grateful to have access to the technology you do." He gave a tap to Clay's leg and the ping of titanium was loud in the still, warm air. "If you had lost your leg a hundred years ago, assuming you didn't die from infections, you'd be stuck with a wooden peg-leg like a pirate."

"Aargh," Clay responded, surprising both himself and Jacoby, who laughed out loud.

"Was that a joke? Finally! I knew you had a sense of humor in there waiting to come out."

Clay couldn't help but smile a little himself in the face of Jacoby's shit-eating grin. Telling Jacoby about his pain was like coming in from the rain, into a shelter. "Yeah, it's my second." His voice trailed off before he added, *since*. But Jacoby homed in on his unspoken reference.

"Since?" He made a motion with his hands, fingers spread wide, indicating an explosion.

Clay nodded. Since Kaboom.

"If that was your second joke, what was the first one?"

Clay looked away and blushed, remembering Julie's fingers on him in bed, while Jacoby demonstrated his near psychic abilities to perceive Clay's thoughts and feelings.

"Oh, ho," he chuckled. "It was while you were with the lovely Julie. Good for you. It's a good thing you came to your senses. She really cares about you. You don't have to tell me about it if it's too intimate."

Although his first post-Kaboom venture into humor had been in bed with Julie, he found it surprisingly easy to talk to his friend Nathan Jacoby. He was someone who could relate to Clay's experience and insecurities in a way a psychiatrist couldn't. He couldn't sit, or lay, on a couch and talk to a shrink, but he could sit on the grass in Dam No. 1 Woods and talk to retired Staff Sergeant Jacoby. He smiled at his memories of being with Julie.

"Julie wanted to give names to my chest hairs and put them on a spreadsheet. The names, not the actual hairs."

Jacoby laughed uproariously and patted the center of his chest. "My wife threatens to take a hedge clipper to me. Maybe down the road, you can get one of those runner's blades. I've seen other amputees use them. It's shaped like a C."

"I doubt that."

"Once I thought I'd never walk normally again. But with practice and encouragement, I've learned to. I know it will seem impossible at first, but like everything else, it will take training and practice to master."

"Highly unlikely," Clay muttered.

"Tell me this, when you first started out as a track runner, were you the fastest guy on your team? Did you win your first race?"

The question brought back memories of his first days of practice on the track team, of the skinny freshman, the shortest runner on the team.

"My first race, I came in dead last."

"But obviously you improved since then. And how did you do that? With practice, training and dedication."

"I've lost," Clay hesitated, because what he'd lost, in addition to his leg, was a lot more difficult to enunciate. "My dignity, self-respect, pride. Worth."

"Healing takes time. Don't expect it in a week or a month or a year. And I'm talking about both the physical and emotional healing. It's not technology that makes you walk and live successfully. It helps, of course, but your heart and will are the important things. The only thing holding you back is yourself."

Clay finally enunciated the question, the despair, that had been fermenting in his soul all these months.

"Why me? Why you? Why Sergeant Lopez? What did we do to deserve this?"

"We didn't do anything to deserve it, because we don't deserve it. As to why it happened to us, to any other person who has gone through this experience, I'm afraid that is a question I don't have an answer to, and I won't pretend that I do. But that doesn't mean we can't learn to live with it and find a way to thrive."

Clay had to say it, had to admit it. If he didn't, he'd pop like a champagne cork, as Jacoby had said.

"It was my fault."

Jacoby glanced at him. "How was it your fault? Did you plant the IED? Did you tell them to drive over it?"

"It was my fault!" He shouted the words this time. Somehow, shouting it out at a desperate volume brought him closer to catharsis, that Greek word Jacoby had told him about. It was even more cathartic than writing the journal had been. He didn't think he had any more tears in him, but somehow, more came.

"I was supposed to be driving that day! Not Sergeant Lopez. Me! If I'd been driving like I was supposed to, he'd still be alive. It's my fault he's dead. I might as well have shot him with my own weapon. I should have been driving that truck. We took turns and that day it was my turn to drive. But Sergeant Lopez was early – he had so much energy, he was always moving. He got in the truck first and said I could drive next time. But there was no next time because he died and it was all my fault for not insisting I drive that day."

"So if you had died that day instead of your sergeant, and one of the others had lost a leg, would that be better? More fair? To have your family grieving your death rather than his, would that have been acceptable?"

Damn Jacoby for being so fucking reasonable.

"Well, no."

"I know it's tempting and easy to say you should have or shouldn't have done this or that, but it's not going to change the reality of here and now."

"It should have been me! Can't you understand that? If I'd been in the driver's seat, Lopez would have lived and I'd ..." He couldn't finish the sentence. "And his wife, his widow, Veronica, you know what she did? She sent me this email, all nice and how she appreciated what a friend I'd been to him. She wants me to come to Houston to visit them and talk to their kids about him. How can I tell those kids I got their father killed?"

"It wasn't your fault."

"Oh yes it was. A friend! She thought I was his friend."

"Were you?"

"Up until the day I got him killed. What kind of friend gets his buddy killed!"

"It wasn't your fault," Jacoby repeated. "You need to let go of that guilt and anger. It doesn't improve anything. It only hurts you and those who love you."

"So I'm supposed to pretend it doesn't matter?"

"No. You don't have to pretend. But while you grieve, you also need to let yourself live."

"Don't you understand? His wife lost her husband because of me. Those two little kids lost their father because of me."

"If you think Sergeant Lopez's death was your fault, you're an idiot, Clay."

That was not the response Clay had expected. He'd expected to hear more gentle platitudes, murmuring at him that it wasn't his fault and he couldn't have changed anything. He'd never expected to be called an idiot. But it was true. Jacoby was right. Clay was an idiot.

"When my wife and I bought our house," Jacoby, weirdly, seemed to be changing the subject. "It was in pretty rough shape. A real fixer-upper. They should have put it on one of those home remodeling shows on TV. We spent months demo-ing, tearing down and rebuilding, sawing, hammering, painting. I went through two sledgehammers and three crowbars. Spent a fortune on drywall and paint and a second refrigerator. My wife said it took months to get the sawdust out of her hair."

"What's your point? Are you asking me to help you fix up your house?"

"If you're offering, I do have a few boards on the back deck that need replacing. But the point I'm getting at is, I developed calluses as a result of that work, calluses that you'd never expect to see on the hands of a history teacher. The reason the body develops calluses is to protect itself. Well, your soul or your psyche or whatever you choose to call it develops calluses too. Emotional calluses to protect you from what hurts you. It's not to make you no longer care, but to help you live without it killing your soul. You need to develop those calluses on your soul as well as on your hands. Let your calluses protect you."

Clay looked at his hands.

"Maybe it happened to you because you're the type of person who's tough enough to handle it," Jacoby said.

Wrong. Clay felt about as tough as a bowl of Jell-O. "I'm not tough or strong. I'll never be strong again. I'm not like you."

"Do you think I was strong at first? I wasn't. I was a whiny limp noodle. But I got strong, because I had to. For my family, for my wife, for myself. You'll get strong too. I can see it. You already have since the day you limped into that coffee shop looking like death on toast. I see a whole new Clay Maslowski today than I did then, and I have confidence you'll allow your natural strength to come to the surface."

"I still limp. And most of the time I do feel like death on toast."

"Both of those will improve with time. Your recovery starts between your ears more than anything, with a mental attitude and toughness."

The shrinks, counselors, chaplains had all tried to help him learn to deal with his new reality, and he had resisted and avoided all their efforts. But this friendship – and yes, it was friendship – had been a completely different experience, one that had helped him immeasurably. If only Jacoby had been at Landstuhl in Germany, he might not have been such a basket case all this time.

Suddenly, without warning, he felt a craving to hear Julie whisper his name in the dark, to feel her slim soft fingers against his temple. She made him forget he was a cripple, an amputee. She just made him feel like a man. Her man, to be precise.

"I've been a shit," he confessed.

"Nobody's perfect. Acknowledging your problem is half the battle in solving it, you know. You're growing as a human, right before my eyes."

Growing as a human? Seriously?

"What Doctor Phil episode did you get that from?"

Jacoby just laughed.

"Tell you what, why don't you come over and have dinner with me and my family tonight?"

"Are you sure your wife won't mind?"

"Nah, she's used to me bringing home strays."

"Wait, why did you need to get a second refrigerator when you fixed up your house?"

"We keep a kosher kitchen," Jacoby said. "Meat and dairy products need to be kept separate. I'll show you. Renee made these cute little labels for the fridges and the drawers and cabinets where we keep dishes and cutlery and pans, so nobody forgets which are for meat products and which are for dairy."

Jacoby offered a hand and Clay took it, allowing himself to be hauled to his feet. It wasn't just the help in getting upright that he had to acknowledge. It was also the emotional assistance. Nathan Jacoby was helping him to his feet in many ways, not just the physical ones.

He sent his mother a quick text while they drove from the forest preserve to the Jacoby home in Palatine, telling her he wouldn't be home for dinner.

It surprised him a bit, but he wasn't dreading this social interaction the way he had been ever since Kaboom.

As soon as they walked in the door of Nathan's home, a little girl whirled into the room in a blur of golden hair and kinetic energy. She shrieked, "Daddy, Daddy, Daaadeee!" as her daddy picked her up and kissed her.

"Does she do that every time you come home?" Clay asked, wondering if perhaps today was a special occasion.

"Yes," Nathan replied. "And I encourage it. I'm stocking up for when she becomes a teenager and hates me."

An adolescent boy was sitting on the couch, his eyes behind nerdy glasses glued to a gaming device, who Clay didn't notice until the kid said, "Don't hate you, Dad."

Jacoby cocked an ear in the direction of his son's voice. "What was that? I didn't hear you."

"Love you, Dad!" He didn't raise his eyes from his game, but his tone indicated this conversation had happened before.

Jacoby flashed a happy grin in Clay's direction. "It's the little things in life that I live for."

"Who's that?" the little girl asked, looking at Clay

"That's my friend Clay,' Jacoby said as he put his daughter down. "This is my youngest, Leah."

Leah walked over and looked up at Clay.

"Do you have a new leg too like my daddy?" she asked.

Wow. Talk about direct. This kid pulled no punches. She reminded him of his cousin Stephanie's foster child. Maybe the two girls could get together for a play date and work on their making Clay uncomfortable skills.

"Leah," Nathan said, "go tell Ariel and Simon to wash their hands and come to the table. You can talk to Clay then."

The girl walked away and tapped her brother on the shoulder to get his attention, because apparently merely speaking to him while he was engrossed in his video game was insufficient.

Nathan smiled at Clay. "Leah tends to be a bit blunt. She gets that from her mother."

"Just from her mother?" Clay responded, and Nathan grinned broadly.

At their dinner table, Mrs. Jacoby insisted that Clay call her Renee. He seriously envied Nathan Jacoby with his lovely family and three cute kids, the older two, Simon and Ariel, with their dad's piercing blue eyes and black hair, and little Leah a blond fairy princess clone of her mother.

"So, Clay," Renee Jacoby asked him, "tell us about yourself. You were in the Army also?"

It was a direct question, requiring a polite, direct answer, but Clay hesitated. How much of his Army experiences were they prepared to hear about at their dinner table?

"Yes, Ma'am," he replied. "I was in the infantry. Stationed at Fort Benning."

Mrs. Jacoby – Renee – smiled and nodded.

"Then, I went to Afghanistan." He was wondering if he could, if he should, mention what had happened in Afghanistan.

Before he could say more, little Leah piped up again. "Do you have a new leg too like my daddy?" she asked, repeating her earlier question.

Clay could only reply, "Um."

Leah was sitting next to him, on his left, and the kid patted him on the leg. On his prosthesis. And somehow, he reacted differently to the touch than he would have previously. He didn't jerk away, didn't demand rudely not to be touched. Had he grown past that neurosis? The girl's earnest, sympathetic face looked up at him.

"It's OK," she said. "You can tell us. It's not like we haven't seen one before."

Stupefied, Clay stared at the kid while she waited expectantly for him to answer her question. Someone snickered softly. It sounded like the other girl, Ariel, but he didn't dare look to see who.

To his right, he heard Nathan murmur, "You're going to have to answer her, Clay. She's not going to give up until you do."

A few months ago, another little girl about the same age as this one had asked him almost the same question. He had refused to answer her and rebuffed her question rudely, and she had called him a meanie. Now, he looked at Jacoby's daughter and felt differently. He was not, *not*, going to be afraid to tell the truth.

"Yes," he said.

"Can I see it?" the girl asked.

"Maybe after dinner," Nathan put in quickly.

Glancing around, Clay could see the entire Jacoby family sitting there smiling at him. Even the boy, despite how he'd pouted at not being allowed to bring his videogame controller to the dinner table. Clay's simple answer seemed to satisfy the little girl and she went back to eating her food.

"See, Clay," Nathan said. "You talked about your leg to someone and it didn't even kill you."

It didn't even kill him. It didn't make him withdraw, get angry, or want to cry. It didn't make him feel like a freak or a cripple or an object of pity. It was an entirely new reality for him and maybe, just maybe, he would accept it eventually. In fact, he found himself, to his wonderment, answering Renee's questions calmly, talking about his enlistment and experiences before Kaboom. It turned out, Nathan had been stationed at Fort Benning also, before the deployment that had ended similarly to Clay's.

After dinner, Nathan took Clay out to his garage, where a punching bag hung.

"Renee gave this to me for my birthday after I lost my leg," he said. "My kids love punching and kicking this thing. Even Simon, when he drags his eyes away from a computer screen. Leah is too little to kick it very well but she's learning to punch. And watch out for Ariel. She may appear to be a quiet little introvert, but do not piss her off. She will kick your head faster than the Karate Kid. She has a right hook that will knock you flat. Renee and I are trying to decide if we should enroll her in karate classes, or kickboxing. Maybe both."

That explained the half dozen pairs of boxing gloves hanging on the wall, including a couple of girly pink ones. Nathan pulled a pair of black Everlasts from a hook and tossed them at Clay, who barely caught them with his free hand.

"Simon!" Nathan called out in the direction of the house. "Come out here and help us with these gloves."

Even though the door from the garage to the house was open, there was no response, and after a minute, Nathan bellowed in a paternal voice that would make a basic training drill instructor sound anemic, "Simon!"

After another minute the boy appeared in the doorway with a petulant, "What?"

"Help us with the gloves." Jacoby nodded at Clay, and the kid came over and took the gloves from Clay's hand and held them up for Clay to slide his hands into.

"Push your hand in firmly," Nathan instructed. "Make sure it's seated tight in the glove."

Of course Clay could only slide in one hand, then he had to transfer his cane to the other hand for the boy to push it on for him, pulling the wrist straps tight before doing the same for his father. A person could put on one boxing glove themselves, but even with both hands available, the second one required assistance.

With the bulky gloves on his hands, it was difficult to hold his cane, especially without being able to feel the handle through the leather.

Please, please don't drop it and have me fall down in front of Jacoby and his son.

"You want to stay out here and punch the bag with us?" Nathan asked the boy. "We can get Ariel to help you with your gloves."

"No thanks, Dad." The kid took off his glasses and used the hem of his worn Chicago Cubs tee shirt to wipe them, then edged towards the door.

"All right," his father acquiesced. "But don't forget it's your turn to take out the garbage."

"But Dad, I'm in the middle of a game. Can't Ariel do it? I'm just about to -"

"Simon! I told you, take out the garbage before video games! I don't care if you're about to level up. Do it now!"

"Fine!" the boy grunted, as he turned away to reluctantly complete his chore.

Just before the pouty kid disappeared back into the house, Jacoby said, "Wait, Simon. Come here a sec."

With rebellion brewing in blue eyes that, behind his glasses were identical to his father's, Simon came back and stood in front of them. Nathan put a gloved hand on his son's shoulder, pulled him close, and kissed his forehead. "I love you, *Bubbeleh.*"

The kid rolled an embarrassed glance at Clay witnessing his father's affections. "OK, Dad!" He squirmed away and disappeared through the door to the house.

"He's a good kid," Nathan said with a sigh. "He's a smart kid. I mean, really really smart. But sometimes I regret getting him that Xbox for his bar mitzvah. Are you into video games, Clay?"

"Not really. My sister likes Minecraft. I don't see the point."

"Let me give you a piece of advice, as a father. Someday when you have kids, tell them you love them every chance you get, even if it embarrasses them."

Kids. Kids with Julie. That was another dream Clay had cherished, then lost when Kaboom had happened.

"Punching this bag is a great stress reliever, as well as a great workout," Nathan said. He gave the bag a few punches that made it obvious where his daughter Ariel had inherited her right hook.

"Have you done this before?"

Clay shook his head.

"Make sure you hit palm down, and with the knuckles flush to the bag, like this. If you bend your hand down you're gonna sprain your wrist." He briefly demonstrated the forbidden bent wrist position before turning his hands into the correct position, and giving the bag a few more punches. How did he manage that, moving his feet in concert with his blows, and not stumbling or falling? Had Clay imagined the fact that Jacoby was also an amputee? "But don't punch the bag," the other man said.

Say what?

"Then why are we standing in front of it with boxing gloves on?" Clay asked with surprise. Nathan touched the surface of the bag. "The target of your punch should be twelve inches past this point. Punch through it, not at it." Nathan positioned himself on the opposite side of the bag, steadying it with his hands.

"Now," he said, "punch me in the gut."

Clay punched the heavy bag, trying to punch through it as instructed, but only with his right hand, because he was precariously holding onto his cane with the other. His technique sucked.

"Again," Nathan barked. "Knuckles flush! I don't want to take you home broken. Your mother might get mad at me and not let you play with me anymore."

What would that matter? He was already broken, and a lot worse than a sprained wrist. After flashing Jacoby a dirty look for his childish attempt at a joke, Clay punched again, remembering to position his knuckles as he'd been shown. Arm muscles that had been ignored for a while perked up and sang, *Oooh, fun!*

"That's better." Somehow, weirdly, Clay felt a bit of pride seep in at hearing the encouragement. He hit the bag again, and again, harder, sending his frustration and grief through the glove and onto the heavy bag. No, through the bag.

"You've got two hands, kid," Nathan observed, interrupting Clay's punching reveries.

Yes, he had two hands, but he needed one to hold his cane. Awkwardly, he tried to transfer it to his right hand to allow him to punch with the left, but boxing gloves were not conducive to the required fine motor movement, and the cane slipped away, clattered on the floor, and Clay found himself slipping, about to fall.

Nathan steadied him with a hand on his arm. "You don't need to balance on the cane all the time. You rely on it too much. It throws you off-center. Using your good leg too much is asking for arthritis in your hip and other wear and tear down the road. If you're going to wear out a leg, let it be the prosthetic one. You're going to have to replace it eventually anyway. Try standing without the cane and use both hands to punch."

The guy was asking the impossible. He might as well try to herd cats.

"I can't," Clay muttered, looking longingly at the cane on the floor.

"I think you can." Nathan encouraged. "Try it. If you fall, get up and try it again. Center your weight in your core. Allow the prosthesis to bear the weight of your left side. That's what it's meant for. Think how proud your lovely Julie would be to see you standing on your own two feet."

"I don't have two feet."

"Yes you do. Sure one of them was provided by the United States Army, but it is still yours. You can stand on it and you should."

Clay hadn't dared to attempt standing without his cane, although he was painfully aware he should have been able to do so by now. But if Julie would be proud of him, shouldn't he at least try it? He looked at Jacoby, and got a nod of encouragement from his mentor. Slowly, Nathan let go of Clay's arm. Clay wobbled, but then recalled those long-ago yoga classes he'd taken back when he'd run track.

Center your weight on your core. The prosthesis is meant to support you.

"Yes!" Nathan said. "See, it's doable."

He was standing on two feet – the one he'd been born with, and the one he'd been forced to accept, without a cane propping him up. For the moment at least.

The heavy bag was in front of him. He stared at it, and it morphed from a hunk of black leather and poly-fiber filling into the shadowy image of a Taliban terrorist who had planted an IED at an Afghan roadside, and who had destroyed his life, and ended the life of his sergeant.

Before he realized it, he was punching that bag as if he'd been reincarnated as Muhammed Ali. He punched it the way he'd screamed and cried sitting on the grass in the forest preserve. All of his pain and doubt, insecurities and anxieties, flew through his hands, through those boxing gloves, and into the heavy bag, until he was again panting, sweaty and drained.

"Excellent!" Nathan crowed. "Your technique is already better. Now try a kick."

A kick? Was the guy joking?

Clay stopped, as his reality came crashing back at him like a locomotive he couldn't step away from. He felt himself teeter precariously as he longed for his cane to keep him upright. But this time, Nathan did not offer a steadying hand, so he was forced to lean and grab awkwardly at the punching bag to keep his feet, as sweat dripped into his eyes.

"No," he said. "I can't do it." Just like he couldn't coach high school runners, couldn't aspire to hope for a real life, couldn't be a real, true man. He tried to pull off a glove with his teeth but it wouldn't budge.

He wasn't ready to socialize with a normal, happy family. If he could only get these stupid gloves off his hands. Maybe he should book an Uber, go home, take a pain pill and try to forget this day.

"Are you just going to give up?" Jacoby demanded. "Crawl back into your bed and pull the covers over your head for the rest of your life like a coward? Or are you going to live? Be a man?"

Be a man? How could he be a man, now? He stared at the punching bag in front of his nose as if it were an enemy, as Jacoby continued to taunt him.

"Do you think I'm not a man? You think it's our limbs that make us men? If you believe that you're an idiot."

Again with the idiot. "It's what's in here." He gave Clay a hard, painful smack in the chest that made him stagger precariously. "You schmendrick."

"Quit calling me that." The blow to his chest seemed to bring his voice back.

"Then quit being one."

"Julie said the same thing."

"She's a really smart young lady. She contacted me after all. Wait, she called you a schmendrick?"

"No, she said it was what was in here that makes someone a man." He raised one glove and touched the spot that Jacoby had smacked. "Ow. I think you bruised me."

"Good. Maybe it will knock some sense into you. Now try a kick."

"I can't do that."

"The word *can't* is not in your vocabulary, Corporal. Didn't they teach you that in Basic Training?'

Clay was tempted to snap that he wasn't in basic training, wasn't even in the Army anymore, but he had a sinking feeling that words to that effect would only earn him another thump on the chest. He was, he suddenly realized, in a different Army now. The Army of living, of accepting, of making a life despite his one-leggedness, and it was just as challenging as the military army had been.

He willed strength into his core and loosened his grip on the heavy bag. There was no way he could get his prosthesis into a kick, so he took a chance balancing on it, and aimed a kick with his right foot at the heavy bag.

And promptly fell back on his butt. Now his ass was bruised as well as his sternum. And his ego.

Jacoby hooked his arms through Clay's from behind and hauled him back up.

"Same thing happened to me the first time I tried it. The first hundred times. You just need to practice."

"And you need to get some mats on this floor if you expect me to practice kicking this thing," he retorted.

Suddenly, Clay realized he had again been standing on his feet without the cane since the moment Jacoby had hauled him off the floor, as well as while he'd been punching the bag before his attempt to kick it. How had he managed that?

"You're right, schmendrick. I think I do need some mats. I'll get some, if you promise to come over and work out regularly. Maybe we can work our way up to going to an actual gym."

"Don't push it, Sergeant."

Jacoby glanced at the sweatpants Clay was wearing in the 90-degree heat. "You do own some shorts, right?"

Of course Clay owned shorts. He had two dresser drawers so full of shorts he could barely close them. Running shorts, cargo shorts, swim trunks. He even had a pair of garish floral print Bermuda shorts that Brooke had dared him to wear in public, on a long-ago family trip to Lake Geneva in Wisconsin. He'd taken her up on her dare, while in turn daring her to admit how nice his legs looked. She'd retorted that his legs would be OK if they weren't so hairy, and he'd zinged back that hairy legs were cute and why did girls have to shave theirs anyway, though secretly he lusted after Julie's smooth gams. Brooke had started to launch into a dissertation on the grossness of body hair until their mother ordered them to stop their bickering.

"You've done really well at this, Clay," Nathan said, while Clay stared at him disbelievingly. He sure had Nathan Jacoby fooled. He didn't think he'd done well at all. He'd whined about his disability and fallen on his ass.

"Let me drive you home, and we'll try this again. Everything improves with practice." Nathan said, as he grabbed the end of the Velcro strap on one boxing glove in his teeth and pulled it away, then held that hand against his chest, using it to hold it still as he pressed the other glove against it and pulled it off. Once he had the first glove off, the second one was easy. He helped Clay undo his gloves, and picked up the cane from the floor, giving it back to Clay before hanging their gloves on their pegs.

"Actually," Nathan said with a twinkly smile, "it is possible to get both gloves on by yourself. I saw a technique in a video on YouTube." He put a finger to his lips in a *don't tell* gesture. "But don't tell Simon about it. Having him come out and help me is one of my little tricks for getting his eyes away from a screen for a few minutes."

"Like having him take out the garbage?"

"No, that he has to do that as a member of this family. The girls have their chores too."

As Nathan drove him home, Clay thought about how things had run at his house since he'd been home. Brooke had her chores, helping with dishes and so on. But since Kaboom, nobody had asked him or assigned him to do anything to contribute to the family's maintenance. Maybe since he'd enlisted in the Army, they had learned to do without him. Maybe they were afraid to, afraid that such a request might inspire an outburst of anger or grief. Maybe they didn't consider him to be a real, contributing member of the family anymore, because of the way he'd retreated into his room and shunned them since Kaboom.

He needed to change that.

Just before he got out of Nathan's van, the older man said, "Just a sec." He fished into his pocket and pulled out a flash drive, handing it to Clay.

"What's this?"

"Remember when I suggested you write a journal?"

Clay nodded. "I've been working on it."

"Well, this is my journal, if you'd care to read it."

Clay nodded and put the flash drive in his pocket, but he didn't read it just yet. The events of today had exhausted him immeasurably and he needed a bit of time before processing more potential trauma.

Chapter Nineteen

When he met up with Nathan Jacoby at Starbucks a few days later, he felt a little more confident.

"What are your goals?" Nathan asked him.

Once, Clay's goals had been to make a life with Julie, have babies, be a man with a purpose and a life. Now, he had no goals. Since Kaboom, he'd considered himself to be only half a man, without much point in anything anymore. He had no real answer to that question, and Nathan perceived his hesitation.

"What would you be doing if you hadn't lost your leg?"

He choked up a little. If he hadn't lost his leg, he'd probably be signing reenlistment papers and planning a wedding with Julie about now. And there was his other ambition, that had exploded into nothing as a result of Kaboom.

"I was going to start Ranger School." A spot in airborne training had been his for the asking, as soon as he'd returned from Afghanistan. He'd already completed all the physical fitness requirements, including the swim evaluation. His commanding officer had requested the required security clearance on his behalf.

But that was all before Kaboom.

Nathan nodded in sympathy. "I was scheduled to start OCS a month after losing my leg."

With a bolt of shock, like a punch to the gut, Clay realized that Jacoby had had his own Kaboom, had experienced an explosive loss of his ambitions as well. He'd been planning to train at officer candidate school and make the jump to becoming an officer, yet now had to live with the realization that he was not going to attain that particular promotion. And yet he was happy and content with what he did still have. The complete opposite of Clay's depressive bitterness.

"Wow. That sucks."

"Sure does," Nathan agreed. "But you can still have goals and plans as a civilian. Have you ever considered welding? The reason I wanted to talk to you specifically today is, that I was just talking to a friend of mine in Virginia this morning. They're building a new aircraft carrier in Newport News, to be named after Ford."

"They're naming a ship after the guy who invented the car?"

"The car was not invented by Henry Ford," the history teacher informed him loftily. "It was invented by a German engineer named Karl Benz. Henry Ford invented the moving assembly line that made it possible to manufacture cars economically so that ordinary people could afford them. The ship is being named for the former President, Gerald R. Ford."

"Oh, him. But I've been medically discharged from the Army. I'm pretty sure the Navy won't want me either."

"Civilian contractors, Clay. They need so many welders to construct that ship, the welding companies are willing to offer paid training, and they are eager to hire veterans such as yourself. They'll even offer on-the-job training to get your certification."

Clay had done a little welding in a high school shop class, and he'd enjoyed it. But that was before Kaboom.

"But will they want a – a guy like me?" A guy like him. A cripple.

"If a guy who lost an arm can play the drums in a professional rock band, what makes you think you can't have a career too?"

Jacoby always seemed to think up questions that Clay couldn't answer.

"Yes, they would want a guy like you. If you could handle moving to Virginia."

"What happens when the ship is completed?"

"There are more planned, enough to keep the construction companies busy for many years. I've heard rumors that the next carrier after the Ford will be named the USS Doris Miller."

Clay looked at Jacoby blankly, and the older man rolled his eyes. "You're just lucky school is out for the summer, or else I'd make you come sit in on one of my classes. Dorie Miller served on the battleship West Virginia during the attack on Pearl Harbor. He was a ship's cook, because back then, the military was still segregated and African-Americans were only assigned to service positions. When his ship was torpedoed by the Japanese, Miller took charge of an anti-aircraft machine gun, even though he had no training on it, and returned fire until he ran out of ammo. Then he helped carry his mortally wounded captain away from the smoke and fire on the ship's bridge. He was the first African-American to be awarded the Navy Cross, and he was killed in action two years later. He more than deserved to have this upcoming ship named after him."

"When I took high school history, Julie was in my class," Clay admitted. "I'm afraid I don't remember a whole lot of what the teacher said."

Nathan chuckled. "Yeah, I've had a few lovebirds in my classes."

"How do you know all this?" Clay asked. "About what ships are going to be built and what kinds of workers they'll need?"

"I keep my ear to the ground. I have contacts. Even in the Navy."

Could he do it? Would he do it? For Julie, yes he could and would. Julie and Jacoby were the only ones who didn't tiptoe around him and his condition.

"I'll think about it," he agreed. "But can I ask you something?"

"Of course, Clay."

"Why are you doing this for me? Spending half your summer vacation trying to get my head screwed on straight?"

Nathan looked serious. "Why? Because once, Clay, I was you."

No, that wasn't possible. Confident, contented Nathan Jacoby was the most together person Clay had ever known. He could never have been the messed-up nothing that was Clayton John Maslowski.

That evening, he sat on his bed with his new laptop, and inserted the flash drive Jacoby had given him into the USB port. A Word document opened. It was titled, "My Journey."

The first line captivated him and he couldn't tear his eyes away. He kept reading it over and over, trying to process the reality encompassed in those five words.

"I was the only survivor.'"

The only survivor. Holy shit. He kept reading.

"We jokingly called ourselves the United Nations squad. I was the token white guy in the group. Royce was a black guy from Mississippi. Liang was Chinese-American from California and Garcia was from Colorado. But regardless of what part of the country they were born in or where their ancestors originated from, they all bled red, and all three of them died that day.

What really sucked was that I somehow remained mostly conscious. I remember the faces of the medics as they loaded me on the stretcher and ripped my pants so they could apply a tourniquet to what was left of my leg, and the looks they gave each other when I insisted they go back and get my guys out of the wreckage. One of them said, "Don't worry, Sergeant. They're being taken care of." I realized later that what they meant was, somebody else would be retrieving their bodies. The medics focus their attention on the living.

I knew my leg was gone immediately. It was obvious, even though the space where it had been a few moments before was in unbelievable pain. I also tried to talk the medics into going back into the wreckage to retrieve it, somehow deluding myself that it could be reattached. I guess they didn't want to lie to me or have to tell me there wasn't enough left to do anything with. They just said, "We're going to give you something for the pain now, Sergeant," and started sticking needles in me.

I didn't cry until Renee arrived at Landstuhl."

What would he have done, Clay wondered, if Julie had arrived at Landstuhl while he was there? Cried for certain, possibly more copiously than he had after he'd arrived home. But would that be a bad thing? There was crying going on all around him there. It was a military hospital treating casualties from all over the Middle East, Europe and Central Asia. He'd seen the family members of other patients during his time there, many times failing to be brave and calm in the presence of their loved one. On more than one occasion he'd observed a mother or father or significant other huddled weeping in a corner. He'd tried to pretend it didn't affect him, that he wasn't envious of those patients who had their families and loved ones there with them, but he'd been deluding himself. In private, in his room in the dark, he had cried and wished for their presence and comfort. Especially Julie's, and he knew that if he'd asked, she would have been there. Maybe his stubborn pride and decision to keep them away, to send Julie that break-up message, had been stupid and misguided.

In amazement, as he read, he saw that Jacoby, cool, calm, accepting Nathan Jacoby, had felt many of the same feelings of helplessness and uselessness that Clay did. The dread of never being a whole person, the hatred towards what he'd experienced. As Clay continued to read, Jacoby wrote about how his wife had encouraged him with her love and support and how he had come to realize he should, to quote Steven King in The Shawshank Redemption, get busy living or get busy dying. Jacoby had chosen to get busy living. Clay blushed, amazed, that Nathan had even written about the first time he and his wife made love after he lost his leg, and how they were sure that was the night they conceived their youngest child. He hadn't included the X, or even R-rated details, fortunately. Clay wasn't sure he'd ever be able to look the man in the eye again if he had. But he'd included enough to show that he had experienced the same insecurities about it that Clay had felt.

Along with the journal, the flash drive also contained several photos, illustrations perhaps, of Nathan Jacoby's journey from patient to happiness. Clay felt a bit voyeuristic, looking at them, but reassured himself they had been included in order to be seen.

The first one showed Jacoby seated in a wheelchair in his living room, wearing shorts with his residual limb clearly showing. He wasn't wearing a prosthesis, and younger versions of his two older children stood on either side of him, as he held a cake with lit candles in his hands. Both Jacoby and the kids were smiling like the happiest people in the world. There was a second photo, apparently taken on the same day, but instead of the kids, his wife, extremely pregnant, stood next to his chair, their smiles just as wide. The birthday cake was still held on his lap, its candles extinguished, and Nathan was leaning his head against his wife's hugely pregnant belly, as if he was listening to a conversation with the unborn occupant. Clay assumed that Mrs. Jacoby had taken one photo and one of the kids had taken the second.

Smiling. The man was smiling, a genuine, happy, contented smile. Not the forced smile of a kid's school photo, but a smile that exuded true happiness. And yet his kids and wife could clearly see him sitting in a wheelchair, with his stump clearly on view.

The next photo also depicted Jacoby wearing shorts, in this case a pair of swim trunks, sitting on the edge of a swimming pool, the same pool Clay had seen at the get-together of Army amputees Jacoby had taken him to, smiling and waving at someone outside the photo. Again his stump was exposed and he didn't seem to care. For a moment Clay thought the guy was wearing a fuzzy black sweater, but quickly realized he was bare-chested. No wonder his wife threatened to take a hedge clipper to him.

The last photo was more formal. Jacoby stood in a black and purple graduation gown, complete with a mortarboard adorned with a gold tassel, holding a diploma. Clay zoomed into the photo so he could read the diploma – a Master's Degree in Education from Northwestern University.

Even though Clay hadn't gone to college himself, he could still read clearly what these photos were saying.

I've accepted the fate I've been dealt. I am not defined by what happened to me, even if it was the worst thing that can happen to a person. I have a family I adore, who love and support me. I'm not ashamed of what I look like, of my leg or my scars. I can and do have an education, a career, a purposeful, fulfilling, meaningful life.

All things Clay hadn't believed about himself.

It was like a slap upside the head. Those were all things he wanted to do, to feel. But was he capable of them?

Chapter Twenty

That night at dinner, he shocked the entire family with his request.

"Dad, does your offer to take the car while you're at work still stand?"

They all kind of looked as if he'd announced an intention to explore Antarctica, but Dad recovered quickly.

"Of course, Clay. Just be ready to leave at seven."

He hadn't been up and dressed as early as seven in the morning since he'd been home. He managed it in the morning, but twitched nervously during the entire short drive to the Wheeling train station.

Was he ready for this? Nathan had offered, back when they'd first met, to help him ease back into driving, but he hadn't taken him up on the offer. It was true that he'd always been a right-foot driver, so maybe having a prosthetic left leg wouldn't be a hindrance. He'd driven his father's car many times in the past, usually a lot faster than Dad would have liked. Still, he hadn't been behind the wheel of a motor vehicle since before Kaboom, and that had been in a Humvee. The last time he'd driven, it had been the exact same Humvee in which Sergeant Lopez had later died.

When they pulled into the train station parking lot, he felt hollow with nervousness. His father, however, was calmly normal as he got out of the car and said, "I'll see you back here at 6:00, OK?"

Clay found himself sitting alone in the passenger's seat of his dad's car, the keys in the ignition, as Dad trustingly walked towards the station and up the steps to the tracks. He had no choice now but to get out of the passenger's seat, pull out his cane, and limp around the car to the driver's seat.

He'd always have to get in a car by sitting on the seat first, then pulling his prothesis in. He'd seen Nathan get in his vehicle the same way, and it didn't seem to bother him, even with his van whose profile was higher than a regular car. Clay sat there for several minutes before turning the key in the ignition, telling himself he could do this. It wasn't a Humvee he was going to drive. It was just his father's black Camry. He wasn't going to be driving on a rutted, dangerous, dusty road where IEDs might lurk. He'd only be traveling on ordinary suburban roadways, roads he'd grown up around, where he'd learned to drive. He'd gotten his driver's license on his sixteenth birthday, for God's sake.

Man up, Clay. You're making this worse than it has to be with your anxieties.

When he finally turned the key, all he heard was the smooth hum of a V6 engine. All he felt was the warmth of summer in the air. No weapons, no terrorists, no blasts happening anywhere. He tested the feel of the gas and brake pedals before putting the car in reverse and backing out of the parking spot. At least his dad hadn't parked in a handicapped spot, even though the placard still hung from the rearview mirror.

It was a good thing he wasn't stopped by the police for any reason. Any officer who might have approached his window would have been utterly shocked. Judging by the way he drove back to his house, the cop would have expected to see a ninety-year-old blind man at the wheel, rather than a young man with perfect vision. He drove like an Auntie Grizelda. He didn't actually have an aunt named Grizelda, but if he did, his driving was like hers would have been. It took him twice as long as it should have to pull back into the safety of his driveway.

He called Nathan only a short while later, hoping he wasn't bothering him too early. It was summer vacation after all, and even a teacher should be allowed to sleep a little later than normal. But Jacoby answered Clay's call on the first ring, sounding bright and chipper.

"Are you busy?" Clay asked. "Can I come over and talk to you?"

"Of course," Jacoby replied. "Come over any time. We'll have the place to ourselves. As soon as the girls get dressed, Renee is taking them shopping for new swimsuits, and Simon stayed overnight at a friend's house last night. Knowing them, they were probably gaming until three a.m. so I don't expect any signs of life from there until at least noon, maybe later. Do you remember how to get here?"

"Are you kidding?" Clay replied. "I have a phone with GPS that would make NASA look primitive. Just text me the address."

This second, slightly longer drive from Clay's house to the Jacoby home was a bit easier, felt more normal, than his first drive earlier in the morning, but he still drove like he deserved the handicapped tag hanging from his father's rearview mirror. The tag was valid for six months. He hoped he wouldn't need to have it renewed.

He hesitated, standing in Nathan's living room, his emotions swirling around in his head and questions, doubt and disbelief pummeling him from all sides. Finally, the sergeant barked at him to sit down, and he did so, but the words he wanted to say still refrained from making themselves heard. Jacoby had to use his sergeant voice to break through.

"Speak, Corporal!"

"Woof," Clay said weakly.

Rather than appreciate Clay's third attempt at humor since Kaboom, Jacoby merely gave him a very sergeant-like look that tolerated no nonsense.

"Where do you get off being so upbeat?" Clay finally demanded. "How can you be happy? You lost a damn leg."

"My leg was the least of what I lost that day. I lost three brothers at the same time."

"But, how do you not just give up and die from the grief?"

"Part of it is gratitude for what I have, what I didn't lose. And part of it is because I owe it to their memories to live. Every time I get a chance to visit Arlington, I put a stone on their headstones, and I tell them they're not forgotten."

"My sergeant was buried at Arlington too. If I get a chance to visit his grave, can I put a stone on his marker? Even if neither of us is Jewish?"

"Of course. If he was your friend, it will mean just as much. You don't even have to wear a yarmulke." Nathan placed a hand on top of his head. "That's a -"

"I know what a yarmulke is," Clay interrupted. "I've worn one. My friend Jeremy is Jewish. I went to his bar mitzvah."

"How did you like it?"

"It was the most fun party I'd ever been to." Nathan grinned at him.

"I've been a shit," Clay confessed.

"Am I supposed to agree with you, or argue the point?" Nathan asked.

"Agree. Definitely agree. But even so, what I came over to discuss was," he hesitated, his self-doubt and insecurities still plaguing him.

Man up, Clay. Level up in your life.

"Would you help me apply for that welding training in Virginia?"

Nathan clapped his shoulder. "Of course! You'll need to apply online. Let me just grab my laptop."

A few minutes later, they were sitting at the same table where Clay had joined them for dinner just a few days ago, and Clay was typing his information into an application for a welding apprenticeship.

"Are you sure they plan to train the people they hire?' he asked anxiously. The procedures described on the contractor's website sounded extremely interesting, but went way beyond the basic welding class he'd taken in high school. Horizontal stringer bead, brazing method, oxyfuel. They sounded fascinating, and yet foreign at the same time.

"Yes, my friend assured me that training was part of the deal, for veterans. Don't worry about it, Clay, I'm sure it will work out for you." Nathan read the hesitation in Clay's eyes. "Yes, even for an amputee. Even for a guy with a limp, who uses a cane, who might still need to keep a pair of crutches at home for when he takes the prosthesis off." At Clay's surprised look, he added, "I still have mine. If I need to get up and pee at night, I don't want to take the time to attach the prosthesis. I've tried hopping, but that makes too much noise and bothers Renee."

"I could never hop on my one leg," Clay said. "I'm sure I'd fall flat on my face and kill myself."

"I tell you what, Clay, I bet you can walk without your cane, or a limp, by this winter. You can do it for me as a Hanukkah gift."

"That's a challenge I'll accept," Clay replied, then looked at his application on the computer screen. All he needed to do was click on the word Submit, and it would be an official done deal. He hesitated a moment, then clicked on it.

"Congratulations!" Nathan said. "Let me know when you hear back. Here, we need to toast this."

He went to the refrigerator and pulled out a bottle. "This is only apple juice," he said, as he poured it into glasses. "It isn't even noon yet, and I know you drove here. Congrats on that too, by the way." Despite it being only apple juice, they clinked the glasses together as if it were champagne.

"*L'chaim*," Nathan said. "To life."

"To life," Clay replied.

To life. He was actually toasting to it, celebrating life. A few months ago he never would have done such a thing, feeling that his life was not worth celebrating, not worth living. His friendship with Nathan Jacoby, and the love he somehow still received from Julie, had changed his mind on that score.

"Do you want to punch that bag a little more?" Nathan asked. "Work on your footwork a little?"

"You mean work on doing a kick without falling on my ass? I'd like to, but I can't stay. I really appreciate your help. I hope you don't think I'm ungrateful, but I need to go talk to Julie right away. If this happens, it's going to affect her too."

"Of course," Nathan assured him. "Go consult with your lovely Julie. I'm glad to hear you say that, considering that when we first met, you said the two of you had broken up."

"I tried to break up with her," Clay admitted. "But she wouldn't let me, and I'm so happy about that. I almost lost her, yet despite what a jerk I was, she's sticking with me."

Nathan smiled, and Clay saw him looking at the gold wedding band on his left hand. "Go, before you make me cry, schmendrick."

He drove to Julie's house, relieved to see her car parked outside. When he knocked on the door, her mother answered.

"May I speak to Julie?" he asked, hesitantly, taking a small protective step backward on the front porch, fully expecting Mrs. Peterson to ream him a new one for his spending the night there with her precious, only daughter. But rather than shrieking *how dare you* and bashing him over the head with a frying pan, Julie's mom smiled broadly, invited him in, and hugged him.

"Clay, it is lovely to see you! How are you doing? I'm so sorry to hear about your injury. Julie says you're recuperating quite well." She glanced at his cane. "Please, sit down. Would you like some coffee?"

"No, thank you." Clay's mind reeled at how downright, maternally sweet Mrs. Peterson was being towards him. If she only knew all of what had transpired here when she and Julie's father had been out of town. "I really just need to see Julie for a minute, if that's OK."

"Of course, dear. I'll get her."

But there was no need for Mrs. Peterson to fetch her daughter, because Julie bustled into the room, dressed for work.

"Cowboy!" Her beautiful face bloomed in a smile, and she kissed him right there in front of her mother, who didn't even faint or get mad.

"I'll let you two talk," Mrs. Peterson said, and tactfully disappeared.

"I have to leave for work real soon," Julie said. "But I'm so happy you stopped over. Kiss me so I'll have something good to think about when Chef is yelling at us to plate up."

He obliged her with the kiss, and it almost made him forget why he'd come to talk to her.

"Did you know that Henry Ford didn't invent the car?" he asked, and she looked surprised.

"Of course I knew that. He invented the moving assembly line. We learned that in high school history class."

"Maybe you learned it. I was too distracted by a beautiful blonde to pay attention."

"That's what you came over to tell me?"

"No, not really. Julie." His serious tone made her stop and look at him. "What do you think of Virginia?"

Her eyebrows came together, thoughtfully, seeming slightly confused at the question. "Virginia? We've been there once. The summer after my freshman year, my brothers had just graduated, and we went on a vacation to Washington D.C. It was very pretty. Why?"

"I just applied for a job there. As a welding apprentice. If I get it, I'll be working on constructing ships in Newport News."

"That's wonderful! Does that mean Navy ships? But what about ..." She glanced down.

"My missing leg and my prosthesis? I'd be working for civilian contractors, and apparently, they seem to think it won't be an issue. But, it is in Virginia. I know you're probably thinking, there are places here in Illinois where I could learn the trade, find work. But the thing that appeals to me about this opportunity in Virginia is, that even though I'm not serving in the Army anymore, I'll still be serving in another way, helping to build our Navy. I'd still be contributing even if it is as a civilian."

"I'm so proud of you," Julie said. "When you first came home you seemed to feel you couldn't contribute at all, and now look at the exciting plans you're making."

"I've only applied. It's not a sure thing yet. But if it happens, if they accept me, I'd have to move out there. It's almost nine hundred miles from here. Would you be willing to be in a long-distance relationship with me?"

Did he dare to believe, to hope, that they were, would be, in a real relationship at all?

"No."

His hopes disintegrated to mush and a knife of sadness pierced his heart, as his soul fell apart, and all the progress he'd made, both physically and emotionally, the reconciliation with Julie, blew apart as if a second Kaboom had happened. His stomach fell to his feet, and he felt as if he just might puke.

You big dummy. Here you thought she still loved you. You thought you had it all figured out. You thought you were safe.

"We were in a long-distance relationship when you were in the Army," Julie said. "It was awful. I mean, I know you were always faithful, and so was I, but the separation was terrible. I tried to tell myself that we weren't the only couple in this situation, that pretty much every other person in the military had to experience the same, but that didn't make it easier. I missed you so much, even though I was so proud of you. I don't think I could go through that again."

Devastation swept his soul, smashing it like waves pounding against rocks in a tsunami.

You. Will. Not. Cry.

"Cowboy, are you alright?" Julie's hands were on his arm. "You've gone as white as a sheet. Here, sit down." She urged him to a seat on the sofa and sat next to him. He was tempted to put his head between his knees as he'd seen done to people about to faint.

"Julie ..." he whispered.

"I know I couldn't be with you when you were in the Army, but I can certainly come with you to Virginia. There is no need for this long-distance relationship nonsense."

Exultation surged through him like a direct injection of caffeine into the bloodstream. "Are you serious?"

She didn't hesitate for an instant. "Of course, my Cowboy. I'd move to Antarctica if it meant being with you."

"Even though it would mean leaving your job here?"

"There are restaurants in Virginia too. Just let me know when, and I'll give my notice and pack my bags."

"Let's not get ahead of ourselves. There's no guarantee right now. And Julie," he took her hand. "None of this would have been possible without you. I know I was mad at you at first for contacting Sergeant Jacoby and telling him about me, but you were right to do it, and I should have appreciated what you were doing for me. Talking to him has helped me get my head screwed back on straight. One of the first things he ever said to me was that his goal was to offer me hope. At first I thought he was full of shit. But he has, and you have too. Thank you for contacting him. I don't know what I've done to deserve it, to deserve you, but I love you."

"I love you too, Cowboy." She put her arms around his neck. And he put one arm around her waist. He did still need the cane now, with Julie close to him, making him feel giddy.

"You know, they gave me a Purple Heart," he said, "but you're the one who deserves a medal."

"You must have been so lonely, alone in that hospital in Germany all that time," she said. "I'm sorry, Cowboy. I'm so sorry you were alone and scared and hurting, and I wasn't there to comfort you. I wish I had known sooner about what happened to you. I would have gone there immediately. One phone call and I would have been with you, you know that, don't you?"

"Yes," he admitted. "If I hadn't been such an idiot I would have told you. I really wish I had made that phone call. I should have allowed my parents and Brooke and you especially to come to the hospital. But I was stupid and scared and weird. I thought I didn't want or need anyone then, but I was wrong. It wasn't your fault, Julie. You have nothing to be sorry for. I was the one who hurt you, by shutting you out, by breaking up with you."

He touched her cheek, her hair. "You're my Viking princess, Julie."

"And you're my Cowboy."

He was just about to kiss her when reality intervened. "Don't you have to go to work?"

"Damn!" she yelped. "Yes, I really do have to leave now. Walk me to my car?" She turned away and called out, "Bye, Mom!", then the two of them walked out to her car. He even gallantly opened her door and she smiled at him as she got in and rolled down her window.

"You've got your chef coat and your apron and everything?" he asked.

"Yes, dear," she replied with a smile.

"And your phone? You've got gas in your car? Are your tires at the right pressure?"

She sat there smiling and nodding at him until he realized he was sounding like a nervous mommy. "I'm being a nag, aren't I?" he asked. "You're perfectly capable of taking care of yourself. You don't need me nagging at you. I'm sorry."

"It's OK," she replied quickly. "I love that you care enough to nag. You know, just because I can take care of myself doesn't mean I don't still need you. What about you, with your dad's car?" She nodded towards the Camry parked in front of her house.

Clay smiled at her. "Yes, I have my phone, the car has gas, and I'm still covered on my parent's insurance. Have a good evening at work. And don't let that security guard get fresh when he walks you to your car after work."

She rolled her eyes. "I don't think that will be a problem. His boyfriend would probably kill him."

"His what? Oh. OK."

Reassured, Clay watched Julie drive away before getting into his dad's car to drive home. Driving was becoming familiar and natural by now. He'd always been a right-foot driver anyway, so having an artificial left foot turned out not to be so much of an issue.

The conversation with Julie had been reassuring. The conversation he was anticipating with his parents at dinner tonight was, however, going to be a bit more difficult.

They all stared at him in stunned surprise.

"Virginia?" His mother said it as if she'd never heard of the place. "But Clay, we just got you back. Aren't there trade schools here in the Chicago area where you could study welding? In fact, I believe there's a technical college over by the airport. One of my clients was talking about her son going there. I'm sure you could find that kind of work here in Illinois."

Although he was getting a lot better at talking about his amputated leg, he still refrained from reminding them of the obvious. He was only there back with them because he'd experienced Kaboom. If that hadn't happened, he'd still be in Afghanistan, or at his home base at Fort Benning, or at Ranger School. His family didn't "get him back". They'd been stuck with him after Kaboom, whether they wanted him or not.

"Mom, didn't you say that Clay was an adult and his life was his own?" Brooke put in. "Or does that only apply to his sex life?"

Clay flushed red at his sister's words, and both their parents admonished simultaneously, "Brooke!" Brooke tried to look abashed and contrite but was unsuccessful, her mouth twitching with suppressed laughter.

"Yes, I realize that, but it's not just about learning the trade and finding a job doing it." Clay leaned forward, eager, for the first time since Kaboom, to explain his feelings. The feeling of enthusiasm coursing through his blood at this opportunity woke him up, broke him out of his cocoon of depression and devastation, as surely as any moth or butterfly undergoing its metamorphosis.

"One of the reasons I joined the Army was because I wanted to be part of something bigger than myself, something where I could contribute, make a difference, and serve our country, to help defend it and keep it strong. If I get this apprenticeship with the welding contractor in Virginia, I'll still be able to do that, as a civilian. I'll be working on the construction of Navy ships, new aircraft carriers that are being built. Sergeant Jacoby says that my veteran status will be an advantage, and my amputee status shouldn't be a hindrance." This was the most he'd spoken out loud to them since Kaboom, and he could see that they were all a bit surprised to hear the enthusiasm in his voice.

"You know, Clay, in all this time, that's the first time you've ever actually talked about your -" his mother hesitated and Clay finished her thought.

"My leg and the fact that I lost it. I know. I hated that it happened. I still hate it, I'll always hate it, but at first I felt ashamed and I felt like I was a hideous freak."

"Clay, you should never feel that way!" his dad said quickly. "You are most definitely neither hideous nor a freak." Mom patted his hand in agreement.

"I'm still not so sure about that, but I'm working on it."

"You can't imagine how amazingly proud we are of you," Dad went on. "If this opportunity in Virginia is the right thing for you, then we'll support you one hundred percent. Right, Gail?" Dad looked at his mom, who nodded, but still looked sad at the prospect of her boy moving across the country.

"Well look at you, being all mature and making plans for the future," Brooke teased, and Clay shot her a look that clearly said, *watch it there, girl!*

Brooke was grinning at him but he could still see a hint of anxiety in her eyes. She was warning him not to bring up the subject of her own possible plans. But as much as she annoyed him with her teasing, he still wouldn't mention to their parents that she was considering enlisting in the Army. His parents had heard enough distressing news tonight at the possibility of him moving away. Spilling the beans about Brooke's possible ambitions would be too much for one day.

Chapter Twenty-One

When Clay woke up in the morning, he felt something, a sentiment he hadn't felt since Kaboom. It was a completely unfamiliar feeling. That was it? It wasn't depression or despair or anger. It wasn't even sadness.

The realization hit him like the proverbial ton of bricks. He was bored. It was unbelievable, but for the first time since he'd woken up in that hospital bed in Germany, he wanted to do something. His parents were at work, and Brooke was apparently sleeping in. After limping down to the kitchen – despite his success in standing without the cane last week in Jacoby's garage, he still wasn't nearly ready to discard it yet – he made a fresh pot of coffee and tried to think of something productive to do. The dishes were clean, because putting them in the dishwasher and then emptying it were Brooke's chores.

He took out the garbage. Maybe it was a small, inconsequential chore to do, but it felt like he had finally done something constructive, something to contribute. As he pushed the kitchen door open with his elbow, because he had the garbage bag in one hand and his cane in the other, he couldn't help but chuckle at the memory of Nathan insisting his son take care of the same chore at their house even if he was involved in a video game. The boy had been about to level up in his game. As for Clay, he needed to level up too. Not in a video game, but in his life.

He looked at the washer and dryer in the laundry room off the kitchen, but didn't dare attempt using them. His mother would probably murder him if he touched the washing machine without her supervision. But maybe after dinner tonight he'd ask her to teach him how to fold towels, and hoped such a request didn't make her faint.

He called Julie. She was breathlessly glad to hear from him.

"Cowboy!" From the tinny tone to her voice, he could tell she was in her car, talking on the Bluetooth speaker. "I'm so happy to hear your voice. I've been thinking about the other night every minute."

She didn't need to specify which other night she was referring to. The night they'd spent together. He had been wondering, ever since then, if his parents or hers would conveniently go out of town again.

"Any chance you're on your way over here?" he asked. His voice was wistful, longing, not even trying to hide from her how much he craved her company. Another level up for him. Somehow he no longer felt the need to push her away.

"I wish. They just called me in to work. One of the lunch chefs was in an accident and broke his leg, and another one called in that his girlfriend just went into premature labor. So we're short two people for a while and they need me to do a double shift for the next few days."

"That's awful!" he exclaimed. "That's going to be a lot of extra work for you. Can you do that, work lunch and dinner on the same day?"

"Sure I can. The overtime will be great. But I'll be thinking about you every minute, you know."

"I love you, Julie." The words were so easy, so natural for him to say. For a long time he'd thought he had no right to say them again, that he should sever their emotional bond, but now, he felt different.

"I love you too, Cowboy. I'll call you later, OK?"

Two days. Only two days after submitting his application for the welding apprenticeship, Clay received an email requesting him to interview via video chat.

It was getting real now. Doubt consumed him, the feeling of inadequacy he'd experienced since Kaboom. What if Jacoby was mistaken? Would he even be considered for this apprenticeship, once they learned about his disability? Could he do the work, with only one real leg? Was Julie really willing to leave her home, her family, her job, to move away with him?

No, he couldn't do it. Maybe he had stood without his cane for a minute or two, maybe he had driven a car, but he was still a cripple who had no place pretending to be a normal person. He would reply to the email saying he had changed his mind and would not be interviewing. After all, he was the guy who fell apart at the sound of a harmless starter gun, who had a psychotic break when an innocent coffee shop employee dropped a coffee pot on the floor. He was the jerk who alienated his friends and relatives with his newly acquired rudeness. He shouldn't be allowed out in civilized society.

He was the man responsible for the death of his sergeant, responsible for making a woman a widow, for causing two innocent children to be fatherless. Jacoby could tell him all day that their switching seats in the truck on the day of Kaboom did not make him responsible for Sergeant Lopez's death, but he still couldn't completely shake off the guilt of it.

Lopez had been one of the best the Army had in its ranks, and yet he had been killed by a projectile so random that if it had flown mere inches in a different direction, would have gone completely unnoticed. The sergeant had been trying to get a specialist with a trained bomb sniffer dog assigned to their squad, but they hadn't gotten one before Kaboom.

And yet, despite his self-doubt, his mental and physical disabilities, his guilt, some people still believed in him. Julie, his parents, Nathan Jacoby, even Brooke seem to find him worthy and capable. Julie, especially, had a way of drawing out the best in him. How disappointed would they all be if he bailed on the opportunity to even interview for the position? Julie would throw up her hands in exasperation and move on to someone who deserved her. Sergeant Jacoby would stop buying him pumpkin spice lattes and having him over to punch the heavy bag, regretting wasting his time with Clay. His parents would be stuck with him whether they liked it or not.

He was being paranoid. His disability status was on the application he'd submitted and if they didn't believe he was capable of undertaking the training and doing the work, they wouldn't have requested an interview. He kept telling himself that until he almost believed it. Julie had faith in him, and so did Nathan Jacoby. They were both smart people and he shouldn't doubt them. His father trusted him with his car. His mother, he suspected, wanted to restrain him, keep him as her little boy a while longer. But he wasn't a little boy. He was a man who should be taking charge of his life, and now he was going to.

But still, he fussed for hours before the appointed time. Where should he do the video chat? Whoever sat at the other end, viewing through their webcam, would see whatever was behind Clay. With his laptop he could go pretty much anywhere, but he wanted privacy.

His bedroom? No, that would look childish, him sitting on his bed with the computer on his lap. His dad's den downstairs had a door that closed, though it rarely was, and while the room was small, it would look more professional to have bookcases and his father's college diploma in his background.

What should he wear? The suit hanging in his closet was the same one he'd worn years ago for his grandfather's funeral, and he was sure it didn't fit anymore.

His Army uniforms? He still had them all, except for the one he'd been wearing the day of Kaboom. That bloody, shredded thing had been cut off him and discarded, except for his body armor, which, being expensive, had been inventoried, checked for quality, and reassigned. Should he wear his dress uniform? His Purple Heart medal? It had been hidden in its box since the day it had been pinned on him at the hospital in Germany.

No, the uniform and the medal would be pretentious. He wasn't an active-duty soldier anymore, and as much as that grieved him, he had to accept the reality of it.

He chose what he thought of as his church clothes. A pair of nice, fresh slacks, free of holes, wrinkles or worn spots. A shirt with a collar and buttons, with a fresh clean tee shirt under it. He could probably borrow a tie from his father, but decided it would be too formal. However, he did swallow his pride enough to ask his mother to iron his shirt. He was afraid he'd ruin it if he tried to do it himself.

He was ready long before the appointed time, sitting in the chair in the small office, the door closed, and a piece of paper with the words Do Not Disturb written on it taped to the outside. It was probably unnecessary, with his parents at work and Brooke in her room playing Minecraft, but he was taking no chances.

The clock ticked. Not audibly, because the digital clock on his phone did not make the ticking noise of an old-fashioned analog clock, but still, in his mind and soul, he still could feel a mental tick, tick as the time for his interview approached. He moved the keyboard of his father's computer aside to make room for his laptop and booted it up. He hadn't been this nervous when he'd signed his Army enlistment papers, or when he'd arrived at Basic Training to be met by a shrieking drill sergeant who at first appeared to hate the guts of each and every one of the recruits in his platoon. He'd thrived in Basic Training, finding a purpose and a focus. Since Kaboom, that purpose and focus had deserted him. Today his hands were damp, his mouth dry, his stomach in knots.

Come on Clay, there's nothing to be nervous about. It's just your life.

The chime of the video chat pinged through the air. He took a deep breath, reminded himself to try to smile, and clicked on Accept Call.

He couldn't eat that night at dinner. He pushed food around his plate the way he'd done when he'd first come home, and his mother noticed.

"Clay, it was so nice to see you get your appetite back. What's wrong tonight? Don't you like it?"

"It's good, Mom." He took a bite of chicken, chewed and swallowed in hopes of avoiding further maternal questions.

"How did your interview go?" Dad asked. The question he'd been dreading. His mother and Brooke both perked up with interest.

"OK, I guess," he muttered, unsuccessfully trying to keep his voice neutral.

"I'm sure you dazzled them," Mom assured him. Of course she'd think that. She was his mother. She was obligated by the code of maternity to believe in him, to think the best of him.

In truth, the interview had gone very well. He'd been outwardly calm and confident, despite his inner turmoil. He'd spoken to two different people, one of them a welding supervisor, the other a lady from the company's human resources department. They had both seemed interested and encouraging, had appreciated his service and sacrifice, and had promised to get back to him soon. But he was still afraid to believe it could really happen.

He'd spent hours after the video interview ended looking up videos online about welding. The physicality of the career was daunting. Walking, bending, crouching, kneeling. He wasn't very good yet at any of those things. Hell, he'd barely mastered the technique of urinating while standing up. How was he going to perform all those tasks with his prosthesis?

Of course, if he put that quandary to Sergeant Jacoby, the answer would most certainly be that if Clay had gone to his physical therapy sessions at the V.A. hospital like he was supposed to, he'd already have learned, or rather relearned, how to do all those formerly simple movements.

Now that he'd found himself able to drive with his prothesis, his dad just assumed Clay would take the car every day. Dad's confidence in his abilities humbled him. As they drove the two miles from their house to the train station the next morning, Dad glanced over at Clay.

"I have a proposal for you," he said. "It would just be temporary. But my admin is going on maternity leave soon, and if you're interested, I could use your help at work. It would give you something to do and you'd earn a little money."

"You want me to be your secretary? Fetch you coffee and type stuff?" Had his mother had given his father permission to make this unconventional job offer? She had been strict about not letting anyone press him about his plans or desires since Kaboom.

"Kendra does not fetch me coffee," his dad protested. "I would never ask her to do that. I'm more likely to fetch coffee for her. But once she starts her maternity leave, I will need someone to help keep the place organized, order supplies, update reports, help me keep the schedules updated. Maybe even visit some of the clients who may be having issues with how their facilities are being maintained. Every so often we get a complaint that someone's floors weren't vacuumed or dusting wasn't finished, and it helps to go and assure the clients that their needs will be taken care of. I know I can get a temp from the agency, but I thought I'd see if you were interested first. We could ride downtown on the train together."

Clay felt his nose wrinkling. It was nice of his dad to offer him work, and he was certainly bored being at home all day, but this was not the type of work he cared to do. Sitting in an office staring at a computer, making sure the supply cabinet had enough pencils and file folders, just wasn't his thing. Give him a power tool, not a keyboard. Give him physical work, preferably outdoors, working with his hands. That was his proclivity. Or at least it had been, before Kaboom.

Then there was getting there. It was more than just a ride downtown on the commuter train. There was the walk once arriving in the Loop. Clay would never be able to keep up with Dad. It would take him forever to limp those six blocks between Union Station and the office building on Randolph Street. His father would be embarrassed at having his colleagues and employees seeing him having to slow his pace to match Clay's, or to have to wait for him to drag himself up the steps of the bus. The last time he'd gone downtown, before Kaboom, he'd had to use his runner's skills while crossing the street to avoid being mowed down by a taxi driver who seemed to think that a yellow traffic light meant, speed up like you're on the last lap of the Indy 500. What if that happened to him now? He'd be dead meat, and so would anyone so foolish as to be matching pace with him.

"Let me think about it, Dad," he said.

Chapter Twenty-Two

When Clay had been deployed to Afghanistan, his squad spent significant time and effort in kicking down doors in Afghan villages. The group of them took turns, just like they did when driving, after getting intel as to the locations of possible tangos. One day it would be Gadsden and Kullander doing the door-kicking, with Clay and Sergeant Lopez covering. The next time, Clay and the Sarge would kick in the door with Gadsden and Kullander covering. Today those two must have been the kickers. Clay knew with certainty that this kicked-in door did not bear the imprint of his boot. He raised his weapon to provide cover against whoever might be inside the building.

But he held no M16A2 assault rifle in his hands, only his cane.

He stopped, blinking. That wasn't the door to an Afghan village hut. His Army buddies weren't with him. That was the kitchen door of his parent's house, bashed in and half off its hinges.

He wasn't in a Humvee, but in his driveway, in Julie's car. He'd told his dad he wouldn't need their car today, since he was going to hang out with Julie until she left for work. As they got out of her car in the driveway, Julie clutched at his arm. "Clay, what happened to your door?"

He stared at the damaged door, the hair on the back of his neck prickling. "It looks like someone tried to break in. Or did break in."

Panic twisted his gut. His parents were both at work, their cars absent from their driveway. He and Julie had just returned from going out to have lunch before she went to work. He'd been nervous at the restaurant, worrying about sudden unexpected or unidentified noises. But Julie's smile had eased his nervousness. Until the moment they arrived at his house to encounter that bashed-in door.

Where was Brooke? Was she home? Was there someone in the house with her, someone who would hurt her? He took a step towards the door, and Julie stepped with him.

"Julie, don't come in here. Go to your car and call the police. Lock the door and stay there until they come. Better yet, drive away."

"No, Clay, I need to stay with you. We need to figure out what happened here."

"There could be a burglar or someone inside. I need you to stay away from the door, call the police, and stay safe. Be sure to tell them that I live here so they'll know I'm supposed to be here. I don't know if Brooke is home or not. She could be in there." Fear chilled his soul at the thought of someone strange, reckless, flagrantly vicious enough to kick in their kitchen door being in a position to hurt or threaten his sister.

Julie continued to hold his arm. "But, Clay -"

"Do it, Julie!" His Army voice came back to him at that moment, putting up with no nonsense. Julie twitched at the command in his tone, an authority she'd never heard from him before.

"OK, Clay," she said, and turned away to do as he'd ordered.

His adrenaline spiked as he approached the broken door and pushed it in, entering the kitchen. He didn't dare call out to Brooke, to see if she was in the house. There was a streak of dirt on the kitchen floor that hadn't been there when he'd left the house this morning, and he followed it across the room to the doorway to the dining room.

The moment he stepped through that doorway, he found himself confronted by a stranger. A stranger holding a gun. The two of them, Clay and the scruffy-looking criminal with a Beretta M9 in his hand, stopped in their tracks, staring at each other in surprise.

Clay had seen weapons pointed at him before. In a dusty, third-world place full of terrorists and warlords, a place lacking in infrastructure and democracy. A place where every day was a danger, every step a risk, where death and injury were everyday occurrences. A place where Kaboom happened. He'd never expected to be looking down the business end of an M9 in his own home.

"What the fuck are you doing in my house?" The question was unnecessary. The burglar, appearing to be surprisingly close to Clay's age, was obviously there to steal something. In that fraction of a second, he tried to mentally categorize the items of value in the Maslowski house that might tempt a thief. Televisions, computers, his sister's Xbox? What jewelry did his mother own and where did she keep it?

Why could not a weapon of his own appear in his hands? An expert marksman such as himself would have this criminal neutralized before he could spit. That is, if he'd had two hands available to hold it. In the Army they'd carried an M16 rifle, a two-handed weapon, with the Beretta at his hip as backup. But today he was armed only with his cane.

"Put 'em up," the burglar demanded, looking as surprised as Clay felt. He almost laughed at the way the guy sounded like a bad imitation of a low-quality Western movie. He raised his right hand a bit, but kept his other on his cane. His heart was pounding and he was certain this wasn't one of those occasions when he'd succeed at standing without the cane. The air was heavy with the smell of desperation and unwashed hair emanating from this person who had dared to invade his home, to damage his door, to threaten Clay and potentially, his sister.

He heard no sound other than his breathing and that of the criminal. Maybe Brooke wasn't home. He prayed that was the case.

The criminal looked familiar, as he gestured towards Clay's left hand, gripping his cane. "That one too," he insisted.

"I can't," Clay said, trying to sound whiny, as a potential solution to this situation began to form in his mind. "I need the cane to stand."

"Oh yeah, you're the local cripple," the other man said, and then Clay recognized him, remembered his name. Kinsella, Joey or Johnny or something like that. He had attended Wheeling High School, a year ahead of Clay. He'd been caught stealing a car and had dropped out before graduation. Apparently his career choices hadn't improved since then.

Even the local criminal network seemed to be aware of Clay's handicapped status. This particular criminal sneered at Clay, apparently recovered from his surprise at their encounter. "I know you. You're that hotshot soldier. I've heard people talking about you. Went to some shithole somewhere. Came back missing some parts. Watcha got under there?" he gestured with the gun, a bit wildly, waving it towards Clay's legs, and Clay pretended to cringe. "A pirate peg-leg?" His guess seemed to amuse him and he giggled at his misguided humor.

"Something like that," Clay muttered, though inside he was silently sneering back, *it's the finest titanium technology money can buy.*

"Where's the jewelry?" the guy asked.

"What jewelry?" He played stupid, trying to look as if he had no idea what jewelry even was.

"There has to be some jewelry in this place. All women have jewelry. Move your crippled ass and show me where it is, before I make you even more crippled." Clay almost hoped that the guy would aim that Beretta at his left leg. It would almost be worth it to see the surprise in his eyes when nothing happened, no bleeding ensued, no falling down. If he was really lucky the bullet might hit titanium and bounce back at the guy.

Wheeling was a small town, and apparently most of its residents had heard about Clay the cripple, Clay the handicapped, including this guy. Who was too stupid to realize that the safety was still engaged on that Beretta, and also too stupid to assure himself of the location of potential valuables to steal. He looked at the criminal's eyes, trying to determine if perhaps the guy was on drugs. Which was ironic really, considering that Clay was the one semi-addicted to Vicodin. His bottle of it was in his room, in the drawer of his bedside table.

"I don't think my mom has much in the way of jewelry," he said. "But there's drugs. I've got Vicodin, you can have that."

The guy's eyes lit up. "I can live with that. Show me."

Shouldn't he be hearing the wail of approaching police sirens by now? Were they not coming? Had Julie called 911?

No, he shouldn't be expecting to hear sirens. The police wouldn't use them on a call like this, to avoid alerting the criminal that they were near. He might expect to hear an errant tire squeal as they arrived, but if it was happening, his hearing loss and the blood pounding in his brain covered the sound.

"It's upstairs, in my room." This was true, but he had no intention of allowing this criminal who dared to violate their home access to the second floor. The guy stepped aside, gesturing with his gun. "Don't try anything funny. I'll be right behind you, cripple."

Clay had no intention of trying anything funny. He intended to try something deadly serious. At the first slight, limping step he made towards the stairway, the burglar tensed, raising the gun. Clay looked down, not meeting the other man's eyes, trying to look submissive. They were only two feet apart.

Clay wasn't afraid. His stomach was in a knot, it was true, but not from fear. It was more the adrenaline rush of impending action, of danger singing in his blood, of a threat to be eliminated.

He lifted his cane, and in a blurred bolt of movement that surprised even him, swatted at the arm holding the Beretta, smacking the wrist with a force guaranteed to leave bruising, and the gun dropped from the man's suddenly numb fingers onto the carpet at his feet. Surprise flared in his eyes, to be replaced by utter shock as the cane whipped out again, this time at his knees, then with whirling arm motions, he fell to the floor in an ungraceful heap, reaching for his dropped gun. A gun he could not touch, because it was already in Clay's hand as he planted his cane back on the floor.

"Now who's a cripple?" Clay looked the criminal in the eye, seeing his eyes widen with a flash of shock combined with fear. "I'll give you some life advice, for when you get out of jail," he said.

The criminal didn't answer. He was too busy staring down the barrel of his own gun.

"Never, ever fuck with the United States Army."

Julie had obeyed him in calling 911. From the kitchen door, he heard an authoritative voice call, "Police!"

"In here!" Clay called out, not taking his eye off his captive. Two police officers were there in a moment, their own weapons drawn. The room crackled with tension.

A minute ago Clay had been looking down the barrel of a Beretta. At this moment he was grateful to now be looking down the barrel of a police officer's Glock. It meant the proper authorities were there to take care of the situation and the now-immobilized criminal.

Even as the first officer ordered, "Drop the gun!", Clay dropped his cane to the floor, ejected the Beretta's magazine into his palm and dangled the pistol from the trigger guard before leaning down and gently placing them on the floor in front of the officer. He straightened and raised his hands, palms out. The criminal still lay stunned on the floor, as the second officer holstered his own weapon and stepped past Clay to apply handcuffs and pat the idiot down.

"I thought he was a cripple," the scruffy, smelly dropout was muttering.

The first officer scooped up the gun and its magazine, and nudged Clay's cane out of his reach.

"I live here," Clay told the officer. "My name is Clay Maslowski. My ID is in my wallet in my left back pocket. I recognize him from high school," he nodded towards the dazed criminal now being pulled to his feet by the other police officer. "He had the Beretta when I entered the house. I was able to get it away from him. You left the safety on, dummy." He addressed the last statement to the criminal being escorted out the same kitchen door he'd recently kicked in. Even that action had been half-assed. If Clay had kicked it in, it would be completely detached. Or at least that was what would have happened before Kaboom.

"Let me see your ID," the officer requested. "Slowly," he added, with his weapon still in his hand, as Clay pulled his wallet from his back pocket, extracted his driver's license, and handed it towards the officer, who checked it out then returned it to Clay.

"Pirate peg-leg my ass!" Clay yelled at the criminal's back just for good measure, as the second officer pulled him out the door and away from the house.

"Calm down, Mr. Maslowski," the first cop instructed, as he holstered his weapon. "Your lady friend is waiting outside and she's pretty upset. You can retrieve your cane if you like." Clay bent down and picked up the cane, realizing suddenly that he'd been standing, even taking a step, bending down without relying on the cane for support. It must have been the adrenaline spike that came with the tenseness of what had just occurred that had given him the ability to do so for a moment, because now he found himself leaning on it heavily, feeling sweat trickle down his spine.

"Is there anyone else in the house?" the cop was asking, and Clay's gut twisted.

"I don't know. I don't know if my sister is home or not." He looked towards the stairs. There had been no sound of voice or movement from that direction. He dared to hope the house was empty. He looked back at the police officer, reading his name tag. "Officer Androssian, I need to check if my sister is here." He started towards the stairs, but the cop waved him back.

"You wait outside. I'll check upstairs."

Clay wanted to disobey, wanted to charge up those stairs yelling Brooke's name, but he obeyed Officer Androssian. As soon as he limped out the back door, Julie ran to him. Two police cars were parked in front of the house, and seeing Clay emerge, another cop went inside to back up Androssian.

"Are you alright?" she gasped. "What happened? I was so scared seeing those policemen going into your house pointing their guns."

"Not guns, Julie. Weapons."

"Whatever! Are you OK?" She was patting him, searching for imaginary injury, and while he enjoyed the attention and affection, it was really unnecessary.

"I'm not hurt," he assured her. The first officer had the criminal, Kinsella, with his belly against the hood of the black and white police car, being more thoroughly searched. "I need to call my parents. I still don't know where Brooke is." He was about to pull his phone out of the pocket of his sweat pants when Officer Androssian walked out of the house, approaching them.

"The house is clear," he said. "There's nobody else inside." Clay sagged with relief. "You need to come down to the station and give a statement," he instructed Clay.

"Do you need me to come now, with you?"

Androssian shook his head. "No, you can come down later. After you get the door repaired or someone here to keep an eye on it." The criminal was now in the police car, and Officer Androssian handed Clay a card. "Normally we advise civilians not to enter a building with a potential intruder, but you apparently seemed to neutralize the situation without injury. Your girlfriend said you were ex-Army when we arrived."

Clay nodded. "Infantry. I just got back from Afghanistan." He tapped his titanium with his cane. "Medical discharge."

Whoa. Had he just voluntarily told someone, a stranger, about his amputated, fake appendage? To quote his friend Nathan Jacoby, doing so hadn't even killed him. Maybe he'd been wrong to shun the world the way he had since Kaboom.

His parents and sister didn't care one single bit that their kitchen door had been damaged, that the floor had been dirtied, that their home had been invaded. They only cared that Clay and Julie were uninjured. His mother gave Clay all sorts of grief for going into the house before the police arrived, then broke down crying on his dad's shoulder.

Clay had been told that his mother had cried over him when she'd heard about his amputation, but seeing her doing it in person was another thing altogether. It was even more disconcerting than seeing tears in his dad's eyes had been, though today Dad was stoic and comforting as he patted his mom's shoulder and told her it was OK.

"I'm sorry, Mom," Clay assured her "Look, I'll fix the door myself right away. I promise." Already he was trying to remember where his toolbox was in the garage. He had one in there somewhere, stocked with tools he'd used to work on his car, to help his dad with repairs around their house, before Kaboom. He hadn't even thought about the thing since he'd returned home, but now he itched to do something physical, something valid, something useful.

Mom transferred her teary face from Dad's shoulder to Clay's. "I don't care about the stupid door! Don't you ever, ever do something like that again!"

"What was I supposed to do?"

"Stay outside with Julie until the police came!"

"But Mom, I thought Brooke might have been in the house."

"I was at the pool with Dana and Marcy," Brooke said.

"I didn't know that!" Clay barked. "I don't keep track of your social calendar."

"You risked your life because you thought I might be in danger? That's so sweet." Brooke kissed his cheek. "You're my hero, Clay."

"If this ever happens again," his dad started to say.

"You are to stay out of it and let the authorities handle it," Mom finished.

"I promise," he assured her, feeling a bit guilty at the lie. He'd do the same again in a heartbeat. "I just had to make sure Brooke wasn't in the house."

Brooke, who though she had looked a bit wide-eyed at the damaged door when arriving home, seemed to view the entire incident as an adventure she was sorry she'd missed. "Tell me again how you knocked the gun out of the guy's hand with your cane," she insisted.

"Like this," he told her, flicking his cane upwards with a ferocious swish that had them all start with surprise. "I hit his wrist. I'm surprised it wasn't broken. The weapon fell out of his hand immediately. It was a Beretta. The same kind we used in the Army." Brooke was watching him, eating up every word with an enthusiasm that Clay hoped his parents didn't notice. "Then I flicked my wrist and swatted his knees." Again he demonstrated the move in the air in front of their sofa. "He whirled his arms like windmills as he fell, and that distracted him enough that I was able to grab the Beretta from the floor even before he hit the carpet. Normally you should be nervous having a gun fall to the floor like that, because there's always a possibility it might go off by accident, but I'd already seen that the safety was still on. Even if he'd shot it, nothing would have happened."

Both his parents cringed with fear at hearing him casually mentioning the possibility of being shot by a gun-toting burglar, and he halted his enthusiastic description of the scene. His mom looked as if she were ready to cry again, and Dad wasn't far behind her.

"Don't worry," he assured them. "I was never in any danger." After all, he'd been in live-fire training, been in the sandbox, been in Kaboom. Other than his worry for Brooke and Julie, today's experience had been child's play for him. He'd even convinced Julie she should go to work that evening.

Clay insisted on sleeping on the couch downstairs that night, because the kitchen door couldn't be locked securely until it was repaired. His dad had offered to stay downstairs, but Clay used his Army voice again to suggest that it would be better if Dad slept in his own bed so that Mom would feel secure, an idea that Mom quickly agreed to. They propped up the damaged door with a chair from the dining room, and taped an old sheet over the exposed opening to keep out mosquitos until the door was repaired.

Though outwardly he was calm, it still clenched at his gut to think of a stranger, a criminal, invading their home and threatening his family. That calm was a result of his army training, coming back to the surface after months of being submerged in the fetid black swamp of his psyche. No matter how jittery you might be inclined to feel, you kept your cool and accomplished the mission. Since Kaboom that insight and determined strength had abandoned him. Was it possible to be returning, growing back like hair after a haircut?

Brooke stayed behind when their parents went upstairs to bed.

"Do you have a gun?" she asked, her eyes gleaming.

Clay set a couch pillow in place. "No," he replied. "But I have a weapon." He brandished his cane.

"You don't have any guns?" She sounded disappointed.

"You don't get to keep them when you leave the Army," he said. His heart still hurt a little at saying the words, *leave the Army* but while it was distressing, somehow, it wasn't quite as traumatic as it had been since Kaboom. Maybe he was starting to feel like a civilian again.

Before Brooke went upstairs to bed, Clay called her back.

"Have you talked to Mom and Dad about what you told me, about the possibility of you enlisting in the Army too?"

Brooke shook her head. "Not yet. I'm kind of scared to. They might try to lock me in a convent or something."

"Do they still lock girls in convents?" The idea of keeping his sister safe in a secure building staffed by ruler-wielding nuns sounded plausible to him. Brooke just shrugged.

"If you're serious about it, you're going to have to tell them about it sometime. You'll be starting your senior year of high school in less than a month. They're going to be wondering what you plan to do after you graduate, unless you plan to just disappear the day after."

"I know," Brooke sighed. "I'll talk to them. But just not yet. They have enough to worry about right now."

She was right. His parents had plenty to worry about without fretting about the possibility of their daughter enlisting in the Army. They had a crippled, depressed son to worry about. And yet, after the events of today, somehow he felt a lot less crippled and much less depressed than he'd been since his arrival home. When Brooke went upstairs, he didn't even ask her to bring him his bottle of Vicodin so he could take one before trying to sleep. The adrenaline still coursed through him at the memory of doing something useful, something physical, something brave.

Once Brooke left to go to her room, he shimmied out of his sweatpants and removed his prosthesis and the shrinker sock to massage the stump. Today's activity had made it ache, but in a good way.

"So that's what it looks like!"

He stiffened at the sound of Brooke's voice, grabbing at the crocheted blanket on the couch to cover himself, and yelped, "What are you doing here?"

"I was thirsty. I wanted some water." But instead of going into the kitchen for water, Brooke sat down next to Clay on the couch. He scooted away from her. God, she'd seen his stump, his scars, his lack of a functioning limb. It could only have been a glance, but that was more than enough.

"Jeez, Clay, you don't need to hide it like it's something to be ashamed of. I didn't mean to sneak up on you, but it should be OK for us to see your leg."

"No, it shouldn't and it isn't." Clay felt himself heat with embarrassment. "It's gross. Go get your water and go to bed."

"I've already seen it now, Cuckoo, despite how hard you've been trying to hide it. It's not gross. How could it be gross? It's you. You may be a cuckoo, but you are not gross. You should let Mom and Dad see it too, so they don't have to imagine what it looks like. You act like it's something disgusting, but it's not. It's just your leg."

"That's just the point. It's not my leg. It's a stump and a prosthesis."

To his horror, Brook bent down and picked up the prosthesis from the floor. "I've been wondering what this looks like too. We all know there's something under your sweatpants but you never let us see it. We're your family, Clay." He knew she was being serious when she called him Clay rather than Cuckoo. "This thing is pretty cool, you know. Whoever invented this technology was really smart." She held up the titanium and polypropylene monstrosity as if it were some new toy. He suddenly had a memory of Nathan Jacoby telling him that his children tried to play with his prosthesis like a toy. He tried to grab it out of his sister's hand's but she turned away and kept inspecting the horrible thing.

"Julie has seen it, hasn't she? When you spent the night with her? You took it off when you got all lovey-dovey, didn't you?"

"Brooke!" He couldn't conjure up any more words than gasping his sister's name. She was just a kid. How dare she refer to the night he'd spent with Julie? She wasn't supposed to understand things like that yet. The idea of locking her up in an old-fashioned convent was sounding better by the minute.

"Think about it. I bet Mom and Dad would feel a lot less bummed about the whole thing if you'd share what you've been through with them, and with me."

Was his sister trying to be an amateur shrink? Or had she been consulting with Nathan Jacoby about what might be best for Clay?

"No, they wouldn't. They'd be grossed out and horrified."

"Was Julie grossed out and horrified?"

No, Julie had not been in the least bit put off by the sight of him. But if he admitted that to his sister, she'd just use it as ammunition in her quest to reveal the thing to them. Despite how his neutralizing of the home invader had exhilarated him, made him feel courageous and viable, he still wasn't quite ready for this next step, both literally and figuratively.

"Look, Brooke, if I promise to think about it will you let up on me?" She looked thoughtful for a moment, then nodded agreeably. "And give that back." He snatched the prosthesis from her hands and thrust it under the blanket he was holding over his lap. "It's not a toy."

"I know," she said, as she headed back to the stairs. "But it's still pretty cool."

Once she left, he shook his head at the notion that she considered his prosthetic monstrosity to be *cool*.

There were levels of bravery. He'd been brave when he'd enlisted, courageous in his deployment. But the courage required to allow, on purpose, his family to view his stump and prosthesis, was a whole other level of bravery that he didn't yet know how to achieve. And yet, Nathan seemed to have no issue with it. His little daughter had said to Clay, "It's not like we haven't seen one before." She just referred to her father's prosthesis as a "new leg" like one might refer to a new car or a new coat, something normal. Why couldn't Clay achieve that level of normality?

He laid down and pulled the crocheted blanket that his mother had made over himself. It took him a while to fall asleep, but once he did, he slept like a baby, no pain medication required.

Both his parents stayed home from work the next day, not only because they were shaken up by the incident, but also to take care of the damaged door. Julie called on her way to work to check up on him, to make sure they were all OK. He wished she didn't have to work such long hours. While his mother dealt with the insurance company, Dad and Brooke went to Home Depot to buy supplies for boarding up the doorway until the door and its frame were replaced.

He stood in the kitchen, leaning against the counter and drinking a cup of coffee, looking at the broken door and listening to his mother on the phone in the other room talking to a claims adjuster about having it replaced. The door itself was most likely beyond repair, and a section of the doorframe had been pulled away from the wall.

He wasn't helpless. The revelation filled his brain and soul like a flower blooming. He could contribute to fixing this situation. He had, after all, successfully disarmed a gun-toting criminal. When he and Julie went to the police station to give their statements about the incident, Officer Androssian had told them that their burglar was looking at three strikes if convicted of this felony.

He should get out his toolbox. It was an old, heavy, metal thing that had belonged to his grandfather. *Babcia* had given it to him after his grandfather's death. Where in the garage it sat now, he didn't know. He hadn't used it or thought about it since before Kaboom. Limping over to the door from the kitchen into the garage to look for it felt like a graduation walk to receive a diploma, even if he did use a cane. He'd graduated from helpless cripple to a person who could do things – defend his home, drive a car, repair a door frame.

The scuffed gray metal box sat on a shelf close to the door, his name written on it with a black marker. He ran a hand over the smooth metal, remembering the pleasure he'd had using those tools, doing physical work, fixing or making something that mattered. It was heavy, but a pleasurable weight. Not so long ago, he'd have said he couldn't so much as carry the thing the few feet back into the kitchen, but today, it wasn't a problem.

He set it on the floor next to the broken door and pulled out a screwdriver. Needing two hands for this task, he leaned his cane against the wall, reminding himself to allow the prosthesis to bear his weight like it was intended to do.

Three hinges attached the kitchen door to its frame, each with eight screws – four screwing the hinge to the door itself, and four adhering it to the doorframe. The bottom hinge had been ripped completely out of the frame by the criminal's kick. The middle one was half askew and the top hinge still clung to its original position. He unscrewed the middle hinge first, muscling the screwdriver past the dented hinge and door-frame, leaving the hinge attached to the door and putting the loose screws in his pocket. Just as he was unscrewing the top hinge, his mother walked into the kitchen.

"Clay, are you sure you should be doing that?" she asked.

"Yes," he told her. "Once I get the door off, I can bang the frame back into place enough that we can nail plywood over the opening until they install a new one. Did they say how long that would take?"

"The insurance company said they'd have someone over this afternoon to look at it, and they'd probably have a repair person out to take care of it in a day or two. But what I meant was, are you sure this isn't too much for you to do right now?"

The second of the four screws popped out of the hinge and landed on the floor with a sharp metallic ping. Even without looking, Clay could see his mother looking at his leg, waiting for him to fall, to be incompetent. While he wasn't yet completely the able-bodied man he used to be, he felt, for the first time since Kaboom, capable of doing something physical.

"I can do this, Mom," he assured her, quickly removing the last two screws and pulling the door away from the frame by the handle. The bent thing fell towards him and he caught it, not even stumbling or falling, but still, his mother was at his side, holding onto the door with him.

He really shouldn't mind her mother-hen treatment. He'd acted like such a helpless cripple since the day he'd arrived home, and his doing so had convinced her it was true. But in reality, he'd realized, he wasn't so helpless, and it felt good to feel that way.

He let his mother keep hands on the bent and dented door until they had it leaning against the wall next to the now-empty frame, but then he turned to her and put a hand on her shoulder.

"Mom, I've got this. It's no big deal. I can handle it."

I can handle it. It was remarkable, the improvement in his attitude since he'd disarmed that burglar. Maybe the guy randomly choosing their house to invade had actually been a good thing, though he certainly wasn't going to say any such thing to his mother. She was upset enough about the incident as it was. Dad had said she'd barely slept last night despite his assurances that it was all OK.

"I just worry, Clay," she said. "I don't want you to fall or hurt yourself or anything."

"Thanks, Mom. I appreciate your concern, but if I fall, I fall. I've learned how to fall the right way, to minimize pain and damage. Then I'll get up. It won't kill me. Just because I have a prosthesis doesn't mean I'm made of glass."

Not too long ago, he had thought he was made of glass, but now he realized differently.

He hammered the dented doorframe back against the wall, not intending it to be perfect, since it would be replaced along with the door itself, while his mother watched and fussed.

"I'm not a child, Mom," he said, painfully aware that his voice did indeed sound a bit childish.

"I know, Clay, but ..."

"Yeah, I know. I lost my leg. But I can still do stuff, Mom."

His mom's eyes misted when he uttered the words *"lost my leg"*. She was probably remembering the broken picture frame and his inability to clean up the broken glass.

That was then, and this was now.

It would be tempting to snap at his mother, *I can do this, quit treating me like a child.* But he had to remind himself that he'd been acting like a child from the moment he'd arrived home. He wasn't going to be that kind of rude, not to his mother who only had his best interests at heart. He just smiled, which brought a confused look to her face because she'd forgotten what his smile looked like.

Further protests about what he was or wasn't capable of doing were mercifully delayed by the arrival of his father and Brooke from the home store, with a piece of plywood to nail over the opening. Both their eyes widened when they saw that Clay had already removed the broken door.

"Thanks, kid, I didn't expect that to get done so quick," Dad said, as he set the plywood against the frame. "Since you got it ready for us, you can hammer the plywood on."

Grinning, Clay leaned down and grabbed his hammer out of the toolbox. "Too easy, Dad," he said, while Brooke handed him a box of nails she'd been carrying in a shopping bag. He pulled three nails out, sticking the ends in this mouth as his father and Brooke leaned the plywood plank against the doorframe, steadying it.

"Lloyd, you should be doing this," Mom fretted. Brooke looked like she had a protest in mind but their dad spoke first.

"It's fine, Gail," he said quickly, just as Clay had told her earlier. "Clay's got it."

Clay proved that he had it by positioning a nail against the plywood and hammering it into the door frame with a few taps. He had so missed this type of activity, working with his hands, doing something useful. How he had wasted these past months laying around feeling sorry for himself! Maybe he still walked with a limp and still needed to use his cane, but he could fix his parents' broken door, and that was a real start to fixing his life. Just to show he could, he positioned the second nail and drove it in with one single, sharp smack of the hammer, while his dad muttered, "Show off."

When he'd first returned from the hospital in Germany, Clay had thought he'd never be able to do even the simplest physical tasks. He'd been an idiot then, as his friend Nathan had realized, and as soon as they were done securing the temporary cover over the doorway, he was going to call Jacoby and

tell him he'd been right, and that he was going to be trying really hard to stop being an idiot.

Chapter Twenty-Three

His parents didn't seem to suspect anything when Clay asked Brooke to go shopping with him, nor when Julie and Nathan both showed up at their house the next evening at his invitation. All of them however were a bit perplexed when, after everyone was seated in the Maslowski living room, Clay handed Nathan a card.

"Open it," he invited.

Nathan opened the envelope and pulled out the card to read it, then laughed like crazy as he showed it to them all. The card read, "Happy Hanukkah."

"You know Hanukkah isn't until December?" he asked with a chuckle. "How did you find a Hanukkah card in August?"

"I got it from my friend Jeremy, or rather, from his mom," Clay said. "She had one left over from last year. Remember you told me I could give you something as a Hannukah gift? Well, you're getting your gift a little early."

Nathan went very silent and just looked at Clay.

Conjuring up a mental image of the guys he'd met at the prosthetic club, the double amputee rising to his feet more easily with two prostheses than Clay had with one, he recalled the things Nathan had taught him – about strength, about ability, about possibility. He remembered his training, his athletics, that long-ago yoga class.

He put his hand on his cane. He could feel his parents, Brooke, Julie and Nathan all looking at him with curiosity. But instead of using the cane to help himself get up from his chair, he set the thing on the floor next to him.

It's now or never.

It wasn't very graceful, but he stood up, pushing himself up with hands on the chair's arms just like a normal person would do.

There was an intake of breath from everyone, but he had eyes only for Julie, sitting across the room. He'd purposely sat in a chair the farthest from her. It was summer, hot enough outside to have the air conditioning on, so the living room was cool, but he still sweated a little. He was going to do the thing he'd once thought he would never do again.

Discipline. Strength. Balance. Channeling them all, he moved his foot – his right foot – just a small step. Instinctively his hand wanted the reassurance of the handle of his cane, but he wasn't going to use it. He just prayed not to fall on his face.

He heard Nathan's voice mutter, "Go ahead, Clay. You can do it."

Surprisingly, his left foot – the titanium one – took a small step also, following the command of the muscles in his stump, as he centered himself on his core and made another step towards Julie, whose face glowed at him with encouragement.

"That's one small step for Clay Maslowski. One giant leap for the Cuckoo." Brooke sneakily picked up Clay's fancy new phone and was taking video of his first unaided steps.

"Sshh," his mother whispered.

It felt like it had taken thirty minutes, but he was most likely standing in front of Julie in only thirty seconds. She looked like she was about to stand up, put out a hand to steady him, but he motioned her to stay in her chair. No Olympic gold medal-winning runner had ever felt as much of a sense of ac-complishment as Clay did at that moment.

He'd been practicing kneeling at church. His mother even complimented him on how good he was getting at it. He was wearing his Army dress uniform, probably for the last time, though he had to pull the belt a notch tighter than he'd worn it before Kaboom. He even pinned on his Purple Heart. Not to show off, however. He had another purpose in mind

"Other than the gifts my kids have made themselves," Nathan said from behind him, "this is the best Hanukkah gift I ever got."

Getting down on his knees was easier than getting up from the chair had been. He let his right leg down first, and the left followed, just as if it were for real.

Of course it was for real. It was real titanium and real polypropylene, but that didn't make it any less his leg. As he'd been told since it was first fitted, with practice he could and did use the limb with everyday, ordinary movements. At first he hadn't believed the people who'd told him that, but now he realized, they were right.

He took Julie's hand in his, as she smiled like a princess.

"Julie." His voice squeaked a little like a thirteen-year-old. He cleared his throat, as they all held their breath in anticipation. "I have something I need to ask you."

"What is it?" Her voice was soft, barely above a whisper.

Anticipation filled the room, silent and yet somehow, deafening. The world held its breath, waiting for him.

"Will you forgive me?"

Everyone in the room gasped a little, and Brooke's voice came through, a bit indignantly.

"That wasn't the question I was expecting him to ask."

"Brooke, hush," his dad admonished.

"When I was in the hospital in Germany, I was an idiot," he admitted. "A first-class jerk. A moron. A schmendrick."

Behind him, he heard Nathan make a small snorting sound, and his mother said, "Sshh!"

"I sent you an email breaking up with you, and I know that must have hurt you, especially since I didn't explain why. I'm so grateful that you didn't accept the breakup, that you insisted on sticking with me, and I need to ask, will you forgive me for doing that?"

"Of course I forgive you!" Julie said quickly.

"Thank you. Also, you brought over that cake you made, and I have to confess I didn't eat any of it. I let my folks and Brooke have it all. I didn't eat any of your cake."

Behind him he heard Nathan mutter, "You didn't eat a cake that she made you? Not cool, dude."

This time both his parents hushed Nathan.

He was beginning to regret doing this in front of them all. Maybe he should have waited until he and Julie were alone. But damn it, he was proud of this small accomplishment, walking a whole six feet without using a cane or crutches or any other assistance, and he'd wanted to show off. Wanted to show the people he cared most about that he could do it, that he'd recovered. Both physically and emotionally.

"That's all right," she assured him quickly. "I'll make you a new cake, just for you to eat."

Brooke laughed suggestively, and Nathan shushed her.

He took Julie's hand, and his breath shook. He could barely refrain from stuttering as he said what he'd been wanting to say practically since the two of them had met.

It was a small question, only four words, but they were the most important, and at the same time the most terrifying four words he had ever uttered.

"Will you marry me?"

She'd say no. As much as she claimed to still love him, as much as she'd agreed to move to Virginia with him, this was expecting her to put her money where her mouth was, and she had every reason in the world to bail. She deserved better than a guy with a screw loose. Or a bunch of screws.

And yet, two days before Kaboom, Sergeant Lopez had caught Clay looking at, or rather mooning over, Julie's photo.

Lopez had given him a comradely smack on the shoulder and asked, "When are you going to propose to her, Maslowski?"

The only thing that had been holding Clay back at that time was that he was waiting for his re-enlistment bonus and combat pay, in order to afford a nicer ring. Of course, that hadn't happened and the ring he had in his pocket was smaller than what he'd liked. Brooke had helped him pick it out and had proclaimed it to be perfect.

"Yes!" she exclaimed, as soon as the words left his lips. "Yes, of course!"

Exultation surged through him.

He dug into his jacket pocket for the ring box he had waiting there. He was surprised nobody had noticed or commented on the small bulge the box made, since one or another of his audience seemed to have a comment on everything. It felt like he had the Rock of Gibraltar poking out of his pocket. The box stuck a little in the pocket, or maybe his hand just went clumsy at the thought of putting this ring on her finger. He held the box up, and opened it.

And found himself looking at the miniature Rock of Gibraltar. Crap, he was holding the box backward. Quickly, he turned it around to face Julie, who now had happy tears in her eyes.

"I think this is the part where you're supposed to put it on her finger," Nathan said, and this time, everyone, including Clay, hissed, "Sshh!"

She was holding out her left hand for him to slide the ring on. Praying it would fit, he removed it from the box.

This was getting real. Once the ring was on her finger, it would be official. They'd be engaged, and committed. She wouldn't be able to snatch her hand back and say, "Nope. I don't think so."

The ring fit perfectly. He took that as a sign that this was meant to be. But he still wished he'd been able to afford a bigger stone.

"Before this happened," he said, glancing down towards his left leg, "I was waiting for my re-enlistment bonus to put the money towards the ring. I wanted to get you a nicer ring, a bigger diamond. Maybe if things work out with the welding job, we can upgrade it later."

She touched the ring possessively, her finger caressing the small round diamond.

"We will not. This ring is perfect."

"I wish it was bigger."

"Don't all men," Brooke quipped, to be quickly hushed by their father.

"Clay, I don't care about the size of the ring," Julie said. "I'd be happy with one of those plastic ring pops if it came from you."

"I hope you don't feel I've wasted my money on this one then."

Julie held out her hand to admire the diamond. "It's the most precious thing I've ever seen."

He was so happy, he almost felt drunk with it. *She'd said yes.* Julie was going to be his wife. They were really, truly adults now. "There's something else I want to give you," he told her.

Brooke made a fake-horrified gasp. "Not in front of the child!" she yelped.

"Should I say it, or do you want to?" his father asked.

"Brooke, stop with the inappropriate comments and stop interrupting your brother," their mother admonished.

He heard Nathan make a small giggling sound behind him as he said, "I like her."

"You hush too," his mother scolded. Clay could just picture Nathan making a zipping motion across his mouth.

Clay put his finger on the Purple Heart medal he'd pinned on the left breast of his uniform jacket. He'd hated that medal at first, due to what had happened to him in order to receive it. He realized now, he should be proud of it, not ashamed. Slowly, he unpinned the ribbon and handed the award to Julie. She held it in her hand, looking at him in puzzlement.

He smiled at her, then closed her fingers over the image of George Washington's profile. "They gave me this medal because I was wounded. But you were wounded too, and that was my fault. I wounded you by not believing in you and sending you that email trying to break it off. I didn't want to break up with you, in fact doing so broke my heart. At the time, I thought it was for the best. I told you that you shouldn't love me, but I was wrong. Knowing that you still love me in spite of the stupid way I acted is what gives my life meaning. I was stupidly wrong, and you were right. You were so much stronger than me and for that, you deserve this medal way more than I do."

Sniff. Everyone was sniffling, even Nathan, and wiping their eyes as if suddenly afflicted with hay fever.

"Jeez," Brooke said, "That was downright poetic."

He was still kneeling on the floor in front of Julie, her sitting on the chair in front of him. She looked at the medal in her hand for a moment, then slid down onto her knees, putting her arms around his neck to kiss him. And kiss him. And kiss him some more.

"Get a room, you two," Brooke said. Clay ignored her, but his parents and Nathan all shushed her on his behalf, though he could hear the laughter in their voices.

One thing saddened him, however. "But I won't be able to dance with you at our wedding." Dancing with Julie at their wedding had been one of his most cherished fantasies. "I don't even have one left foot, let alone two."

"You'd better dance with me," Julie insisted, "or I'm going home with the best man instead."

"Don't worry, Clay," Nathan said. "I'm sure you'll figure it out." This time, nobody shushed him.

"Can we break out the champagne now?" his dad asked.

Brooke immediately put in, "Can I have some?"

"Just this once," their mother agreed. "And just one glass. One small glass."

"Cool!" she said, and he heard his dad and Nathan both chuckle, as he got up from his knees to sit on the sofa, where Julie immediately sat next to him. He would have thought getting up from the kneeling position, especially after being down there for several minutes, would have been a lot more difficult than getting down had been, but with Julie's hands on him, it was easy.

His mother came over and hugged them both. "Congratulations, darling," she said. "I'm so happy for you both." She went into the kitchen to fetch champagne and glasses.

"Let me help," Nathan called after her, then got up and followed her to help carry glasses.

"I don't know if this champagne is kosher," he heard his mom say to Nathan.

"Probably not," Nathan replied. "But don't worry about it. I won't tell if you don't."

When champagne had been distributed and tasted, hugs and kisses and handshakes were given all around to congratulate Clay and Julie's engagement, Clay turned to his dad.

"Dad, if you still need help at work, I'll do it," he said. "But it will only be temporary. I've been offered the job as a welding apprentice at the shipyard in Newport News, and Julie and I are moving to Virginia." He glanced at his new fiancée, who nodded happily.

"So that's what you were talking about on that secret phone call this morning," Brooke said.

Their dad came over and gave Clay a fatherly clap on the shoulder. "Of course, son. I'd be thrilled to have you. Can you start Monday? Kendra, my admin, will be leaving to start her maternity leave soon and she'll want to show you the ropes before she pops."

Brooke gave him another hug. "Do you really have to move to Virginia?" she asked. "I'm going to miss Julie if you leave."

"What am I, chopped liver?" he asked with mock indignation. "Won't you miss me too?"

Brooke looked thoughtful. "Maybe. Oh hell, who am I kidding? Of course I'll miss you."

"Brooke, language!" their mom scolded, as Clay, Julie and Brooke all giggled.

"I have something I need to ask you." Julie turned to Brooke. "Will you be my maid of honor?"

Brooke's reaction was instantaneous and exuberant. She literally jumped up and down, startling Clay so that he almost lost his balance.

"Yes, yes, yes!" Brooke practically screeched. "When can we go dress shopping?"

"Is tomorrow too soon?" Julie asked.

Just before he left to go home, and as he said, tell his family about Clay finally coming to his senses, Nathan drew Clay to the side.

"I'm very proud of you," he said, "And I'm sure your parents are too. You've come a long way since I first met you and it warms my heart to see you and your lovely Julie happy and planning a future together."

Clay gave his mentor a brief hug. "Thanks, Staff Sergeant. I'm not quite sure I believe this is true, that she said yes and everything."

"I know the feeling!" was Nathan's heartfelt reply.

Chapter Twenty-Four

They stepped off the train at Union Station on Monday morning and were immediately thrust into a horde of speed-walking commuters. The place was noisy and crowded with an organized chaos of men and women hurrying to their jobs.

Despite his emotional progress lately, the bustling crowd still intimidated Clay a little. People pushed past him, a couple of them bumping him, throwing a brief, "Sorry" over their shoulders as they hurried away. He clutched his cane and prayed for stability. He'd been doing some walking without it since proposing to Julie, but was glad he'd brought it with him today.

When they emerged from the station's doors onto Canal Street, the bustle of hurrying commuters continued, punctuated by car horns and the squeal of bus brakes, the scents of diesel fuel and coffee, Styrofoam cups clutched in hand as the hurrying speed-walkers emerged from coffee shops and donut shops.

It was at once familiar, and terrifying. He stopped on the sidewalk and his dad stopped next to him.

"You OK, Clay?"

He wanted to be OK. He was almost OK. But not one hundred percent OK.

"Dad, you go ahead. I'll meet you at your office. I remember how to get there."

"Why? Did you want to stop for coffee? We have coffee at the office, you know."

"No, Dad, I'll just slow you down." He glanced towards his cane.

"I don't mind walking slower. I'd rather stay with you. I won't get in trouble if I'm a minute or two late. I am the president of the company after all."

"Yeah, but you might run into people you know."

"Probably. I usually do."

"You won't want to be seen with ... me."

His dad turned to him, and grasped both his upper arms in a firm grip, ignoring the other commuters passing them.

"Of course I'd want to be seen with you, no matter if you're walking slow or fast. And if we run into anybody I know, I will proudly introduce them to my son, the hero."

"I'm not a hero, Dad."

"Yes you are. You are a hero to me, and your mother, and to Brooke. And I imagine, to Julie too. I don't think you understand how incredibly proud we all are of you. Not just because of the way you disarmed that burglar at the house. That was amazingly brave of you even if it did scare the shit out of your mother, and don't you tell her I said that. We are also proud of you, of the man you've become. Not only because of your service and bravery in the Army, but also how you've survived what happened to you, the most horrible thing that could ever happen to a person. I wouldn't have been able to survive it as you have. I would have died from grief. We're damn proud of the way you're triumphing over it. That makes you a hero in our eyes and don't you ever try to convince me otherwise."

Dad looped his arm through Clay's. "We'll walk together. Always together."

It was a surprisingly emotional speech from his father, a usually stoic example of his northern European ancestry. The Polish, much like the Scandinavians, did not emote easily.

And right there, on the sidewalk of South Canal Street in downtown Chicago, Clay's heart healed.

Dad had photos on his desk in his office, similar to those on the piano in their living room. Clay saw images of himself, pre-Kaboom, his sister, his mother, the family together.

"I'm looking forward to putting one of your wedding photos there," Dad said.

Kendra had been his father's administrative assistant for a long time. Clay had met her before, and she'd been very nice to him but had tended to regard him as the boss's little boy. When Dad brought Clay into his office this morning, her eyes widened at the sight of him.

"My, you're all grown up now, aren't you, Clay?" she said with a smile. "Your dad told me you were engaged. Congratulations. Here, sit down and I'll show you the computer programs you'll need to use while I'm gone."

He obediently sat in her office chair as she pointed out programs on her computer. It was a bit unnerving because she was very pregnant and when she leaned over his chair, the roundness of her belly brushed his shoulder. He swore he could feel the kid kick.

"Maybe you should sit, ma'am," he insisted. He'd trained for a lot of different possible scenarios when he'd been in the Army, but delivering a baby in his father's office wasn't one of them.

Kendra laughed. "Am I old enough to be a ma'am? Or is it this?" she patted her expansive frontage. "I know I look like a beached whale, but I assure you, I'm not due for another four weeks."

Still, Clay insisted she return to her desk chair. He suspected she had offered the chair to him in the first place after seeing him with his cane. If his dad had told her about his engagement, she surely had to know about his leg too. But she tactfully ignored that.

"Now, if you need any help with the computer, just call Terrence in I.T. Tell him you're filling in for me, and he'll put you at the front of the line. We have an arrangement."

"An arrangement?" he asked with curiosity.

Kendra chuckled. "My husband was able to score Terrence a couple of VIP tickets to the Star Trek convention last summer, when they were supposedly all sold out. Ever since then he loves us more than his mother, I think. Go over to his office – he has a signed photo of himself with Patrick Stewart that you'd think was the Holy Grail."

"Even I have to invoke Kendra's name when I call Terrence for help," Dad said, placing a cup of coffee on Kendra's desk. "That's for her," he added. "You're on your own, kid."

A few minutes later, Kendra left them to go to the lady's room. Apparently advanced pregnancy caused a woman to need to pee every ten minutes. Clay wandered into his dad's office, and Dad looked up from his desk to smile at him.

"I'm sorry, Dad," he said.

"Sorry for what? Did you put sugar in my coffee?"

"No, Dad. I'm sorry -"

Sorry I blew your world to hell and made you all cry because I went and did a stupid thing like getting my leg blown off.

Those were the words he thought. But he diluted the sentiment by saying, "I'm sorry I was a jerk and a snot to you all when I came home from the hospital. I should have let you guys come to Germany, and I should have gone to Walter Reed for my rehab instead of staying at Landstuhl. But I was too much of a coward to think straight about all this."

To his surprise, his dad immediately got up from his char, crossed to the door, and closed it. Clay stared stupidly at that door. What was that about? He turned a questioning look at his father.

"I thought you might prefer privacy if you were going to cry, Clay."

"No, Dad," he replied. "I'm not going to cry about this anymore. I'm done with crying." His dad's closing his office door for Clay's benefit touched him, almost made him choke up after all, but as promised, he didn't cry. He was past that.

"You are not, nor have you ever been, a coward," his dad assured him. "You were a thousand times braver about this than I ever could have been. I was never brave enough to serve in the military. I only got a business degree. Anyone can do that."

"No, not anyone. I couldn't have." Dad was surely joking. They both knew Clay wasn't the college degree type. But his father's kind words warmed his heart. "Maybe you could point me towards the supply cabinet? And Terrence's office? I think I may need to make friends with him."

He was halfway down the hall, following his father's directions to Terrence's office, when he realized he'd left his cane propped against the side of Kendra's desk.

No point in going back for it; he was already halfway to his destination. For a moment he stumbled, put his hand against the wall to steady himself. A couple of employees in nearby desks glanced up at him briefly but most just went about their work. Fresh energy filled him at the realization that he didn't need it. *He didn't need it.* His two legs could get him where he wanted to go for now.

His two legs. The titanium prosthesis was his leg now, just as much as the other limb made of flesh and bone and muscle. He could center himself and walk. He wasn't a cripple. A feeling of peace settled over him. It was true he still limped, perhaps even more than when he used the cane, but he could still travel down the hall on his own now. A few months ago he would never have thought such a thing to be possible.

When he found the office with a nameplate reading Terrence Carmichael next to the door, he knocked, then peeked into the office to find it empty. Oddly, there was no chair behind the desk in this office. "Terrence?" he called out.

"I'm Terrence," a voice from behind him said. Clay turned around to introduce himself to the all-important IT manager with whom he needed to cultivate a friendship.

And what did he see? A man in his forties, dressed in office casual, curly sandy brown hair, a friendly smile, clean shoes with no scuffs or wear. He had just the beginning of a tiny bald spot forming at the top of his head. Clay could see this immediately because Terrence's head was at about Clay's chest level. He sat in a wheelchair. A *wheelchair*. No wonder his shoes were pristine. They sat on the chair's footrest, never touching the floor.

Clay tried really hard not to stare, knowing how much he hated having people stare at him when made aware of his disability. He looked at the floor, the wall, the space above Terrence's head.

"It's OK," the man said amiably. "I realize I'm in a wheelchair. You can look at me. I'm not Medusa."

Clay looked the guy in the eyes. "Sorry," he muttered.

"Have we met?" Terrence asked.

"I'm Clay Maslowski. I'm going to be filling in for Kendra when she goes on maternity leave."

"I thought you looked familiar! You're Lloyd's son. He shows your pictures all over the office. Come in, let's chat." Terrence smoothly wheeled his chair into the office door and parked at his desk. That explained the lack of a desk chair. He carried his chair with him at all times. "Have a seat," he offered.

As Clay sat in the guest chair across the desk, he noticed the photo Kendra had told him about, Terrence with Patrick Stewart in front of a backdrop depicting the starship Enterprise. Captain Picard's hand rested on Terrence's shoulder, and man oh man, was Terrence smiling. The grin nearly split his face. You'd think he was the happiest guy in the world, and yet he was confined to a wheelchair. Clay at least could walk up-right.

Terrence saw Clay looking at the photo and picked it up to show him a closer view. "Yep, I admit it," he said. "I'm a total Star Trek geek. In fact, I met my wife waiting in line to see The Search for Spock." He patted the right wheel of his chair. "I ran over her foot. Fortunately it didn't break anything, and it was a hell of an icebreaker. Of course, the fact that we were both wearing Starfleet Academy uniforms helped." He returned the photo to its pride of place, setting it carefully in its spot. "So, what can I do for you, Mr. Maslowski?"

"Clay," he said quickly. "Call me Clay. Mr. Maslowski is my dad."

Terrence chuckled. "Even your dad insists we all call him Lloyd. He says Mr. Maslowski is *his* dad."

Terrence seemed friendly, outgoing, a person who enjoyed meeting people and talking freely. It was amazing to Clay that he seemed almost lighthearted in the way he mentioned meeting his future wife when he ran over her foot with his wheel. But based on how Clay felt about discussing his disability or having people notice it, he tried really hard to ignore Terrence's adaptation. He looked anywhere but at the shiny hand rim Terrence used to propel the chair, the pristine shoes on the footrest. Or at least he tried to. He found it impossible not to notice those things.

Maybe that's how people looked at him when he limped, when he used his cane. They didn't mean to pry or stare. But human nature just made it impossible to ignore those types of circumstances.

When Clay had sat in a wheelchair in the hospital, he'd hated having to look up at people who looked like giants when he was down at wheelchair level. And yet, Terrence smiled. Clay found that really weird because it was obvious that he'd noticed Clay's not-so-discreet observation. He didn't try to hide away or refuse to talk about it or get upset at people who noticed his disability.

"OK," Terrence said. "Let's look right at the elephant in the room. Yes, I am in a wheelchair. Yes, the condition is permanent. I'm sure you're curious to know about what happened." He patted a wheel.

Clay did want to know, but felt it would be rude to ask. "You don't have to talk about it if you don't want to."

Terrence however, didn't appear to have any hesitation to tell him. "You want us to be friends, don't you?"

"Well, yeah." Clay knew which side his bread was buttered on. If he was going to work here, even temporarily, it would be to his advantage to be friends with the IT manager.

"Well, then, friends listen when their friends want to talk."

Was this guy for real? Willing, even seeming eager, to talk to someone he'd just met, about what had happened to put him into that rolling chair for the rest of his life? Nathan Jacoby was always trying to get Clay to talk about what had happened to him, and once he did, he had felt so much better, so much closer to healing. Apparently Terrence lived by the same philosophy.

"I was twenty-two," Terrence said. "I'd just graduated from college. I had this beat-up old motorcycle I'd fixed up, and I was getting ready to head for Sturgis. But I never made it out of Cook County. A dog darted out into the road in front of me, I swerved to avoid it, lost control and smashed into a tree. A great big old oak tree. I was really lucky."

"Lucky?" Clay croaked.

"Yes, lucky. If I'd smashed my head the way I smashed my back, I'd have been dead, even though I was wearing a helmet. Now instead of a Harley, I drive an adaptive car with handicapped license plates."

"You can drive?" The surprised words popped out of Clay's mouth before his brain could warn him of their insensitivity.

He'd been hesitant to drive with his one leg, and yet here was this guy able to drive with both legs paralyzed and non-functioning.

"Of course I can drive," Terrence replied with a tiny disbelieving snort. "But if I'd smashed my back a little higher, I'd have lost the use of more than just my legs. I could have ended up a quadriplegic or on a ventilator."

Clay was still trying to wrap his head around the *I was lucky* part. "I was on a ventilator once for a couple of days," he said. "Freaked me out when I woke up with that mask over my face." He'd been even more freaked out a few minutes later. Even now the memory made him shudder. Waking up in panic, pain and confusion with a tube in his throat, unable to speak. The chaplain sitting next to him had held his hand while the breathing tube was removed, leaving his throat raw and aching. *What happened?* were the first words that he was able to rasp out, and the unfortunate chaplain had had the tragic responsibility of telling him why he was there in that bed, in that hospital.

"I'm sure that wasn't fun," Terrence said. "There's nothing fun about being in a hospital. Except maybe for the Jell-O." Terrence looked down at his hands for a moment. "At first, I was damn suicidal. My parents moved me into their house and hid my medications from me, because they thought I'd be tempted to OD on them. And for a while, I considered it, especially when the girl I'd been dating before the accident dumped me.

"At first, I was devastated that she broke up with me because I couldn't walk anymore, but now I look at it as a blessing since I later met the real love of my life. My parents dealt with all the bureaucracy from the accident – the insurance, disposing of my motorcycle. The bike wasn't that badly damaged. It could probably have been fixed. But none of us ever wanted to see it again so they just got rid of it. They even paid off my loan on it. It was a year before I started acting like a human being again. It took a couple more years to pay off the therapist's bills."

"And now you run the IT department," Clay said. "Here."

"Yeah, once I got my head out of my ass and started considering what I could do rather than endlessly obsessing over what I couldn't do anymore."

"How did you do it? I mean, get your head out of your ass?"

"It took a lot of therapy. I got to know my shrinks on a first-name basis. It's funny, but there are people who've actually accused me of faking my paralysis in order to score prime parking spots. I'll tell you something. If God were to come to me and offer, I'll give you the use of your legs back, but in return you'll have to park in the farthest parking spot in every parking lot or garage you enter, including Soldier Field, in all weather conditions, forever, I'd take that deal in a heartbeat. And by the way, my legs are the only things that are paralyzed. Everything else works just as it should, thank you very much. And yes, I've been asked about that too.

"But in some ways, that accident was the best thing to ever happen to me. If I was on my feet, I may never have met my wife. If God were to come to me and offer me the use of my legs back, but on the condition that I lose Eleanor, I'd turn *that* deal down in a nanosecond." A dreamy expression crossed Terrence's face. "I still remember the first thing Eleanor ever said to me. *Watch where you're going with that thing.* By the end of the evening, she was sitting on my lap as we rolled out of the theater together."

"The first thing Julie – my fiancé – told me was how to use a skin treatment to cure my acne," Clay admitted.

"We sure found the romantic ones, didn't we?" Terrence's eyes crinkled with amusement. "But I've learned since this happened, that almost every challenge can be accommodated if not eliminated. Transportation, career, relationships."

What would Clay give up to have his left leg back? The prime parking spots authorized by the handicapped placard in his father's car? In a heartbeat.

Would he give up Julie? Never in a million years. Not even if God threw in a gold Olympic decathlon medal. He'd rather be confined to a wheelchair himself than to lose her. He'd rather give up his other leg.

He'd been really unlucky. But he'd also been lucky, fortunate with what he hadn't lost. He still had Julie. Maybe losing a leg wasn't the worst thing in the world.

And what about Terrence? He'd met his wife after his accident, while already using a wheelchair, but they were apparently happy together.

Terrence's attitude towards his situation humbled Clay. Here he'd thought he and others like him were the most unfortunate people in the world. But to be perfectly honest, if he'd been forced to choose, he'd rather have a prosthesis and a cane than be permanently in a wheelchair like Terrence.

Terrence's chair was different from the wheelchair Clay had been forced to use in the hospital. The back was lower, without handles to push it from behind, as Terrence propelled himself using the rims on the outside of the larger back wheels. Clay still flushed with embarrassment at the memory of that little Red Cross lady pushing him through the Frankfurt airport. Terrence's chair also had a comfy-looking pad on the seat, which made total sense for someone who sat in it permanently.

Suddenly, Clay felt a lot less disabled than he had. Maybe he still limped, but he at least could walk. And here he was meeting another disabled person who appreciated that despite what he'd been through, it could have been worse, and he seemed grateful for what he still had. Both Terrence and Nathan Jacoby had viable, successful careers despite their disabilities.

He made an effort to change the subject to what he'd really come to discuss.

"Kendra said you were her go-to guy for computer issues. I just wanted to meet you since I'll be using her desk for a little while."

"Ah, Kendra. Any friend of hers is a friend of mine. She's the best. And I mean that in a perfectly platonic, fraternal way, mind you. You need any help, you come straight to me. Don't bother with the IT Help Line. Here -" He pulled a business card from the holder on his desk, turned it over and wrote on the back before handing it to Clay. "This is my cell phone number. Call that rather than my office phone, in case I'm rolling around somewhere."

Clay stood up to leave, then turned back to Terrence. If his dad had shown photos of him to his employees, how much of his story had he told them?

"Terrence, did my dad tell you about me?"

"Yes, he said you were in the Army. Then he was away on emergency leave for a few days last winter, and when he got back said you weren't in the Army anymore. I assumed your enlistment was up?"

His dad had taken time off from work planning to fly to Germany to be with him. Instead, Dad had to stay back and grieve because Clay stupidly kept him and everyone else away.

"No, I didn't leave the Army voluntarily. I was medically discharged." He stepped a little closer to Terrence's desk and lowered his voice. "I was in an IED blast and suffered a traumatic amputation of my left leg."

"I thought I noticed a slight limp," Terrence replied, not appearing at all grossed out upon hearing about Clay's amputation.

"Yeah, I left my cane by Kendra's desk."

"It doesn't appear that you really need it," Terrence said.

"Sometimes. Not as much as I thought I did."

"So you have a prosthesis? That is so cool!" Terrence's eyes lit up.

So cool? He thought that Clay having a fake leg was cool? But apparently to someone in his situation, being equipped with something that enabled him to walk would be considerably preferable to the way he lived. And yet he, like Nathan Jacoby, felt lucky that it hadn't been worse, and in Terrence's case, enabled him to meet the woman he loved. Was it possible the two men knew each other? Maybe they were treated by the same psychiatrist.

"Can I ask you something?" Clay said to his new friend. "Do you know a guy named Nathan Jacoby?"

"No," Terrence replied. "I don't. Does he work here?"

"He's a friend of mine. You remind me of him a little."

"Really? In what way?"

"You see the positive side of your situation. He's an amputee like me, but he didn't let it be the end of his life. He's got a career and a great family and he makes the best of it. I had a really bad attitude about my life for a long time after and he helped me get over it."

"He sounds like someone I'd like to meet," Terrence said. "Does he have a prosthesis too?"

"Yes. But when I first met him I didn't realize it, and I was pretty surprised when I found out. He walks just like normal without even a limp."

Too quickly, Clay saw the look of sadness crossing Terrence's face, before he formed it back into his previous calm visage. Now he felt bad. He'd been unconsciously thinking and talking about walking successfully to Terrence, a man who would never walk again.

"I'm sorry," he said quickly. "I didn't mean to bring up any bad memories."

"It's OK," Terrence said quickly. "I admit, I do get a little jealous sometimes. It would be a really hard choice to make – be like me, have all your original equipment but not be able to use it all, or lose a limb and yet have a replacement that allows you to look whole and normal."

Clay didn't answer, but in his heart, he kind of felt that his situation was slightly less sucky than Terrence's. Maybe he'd lost a leg, but it had been replaced by technology created by some really smart medical researchers. He highly doubted there would ever be a way to reconnect Terrence's spinal column to enable him to walk again. Clay had loathed the short time he'd spent in a wheelchair. How horrible must Terrence feel, being in one permanently?

Maybe he was lucky. Weird. Since Kaboom, that word had fled from his vocabulary. But Clay's girlfriend, his fiancé, his Julie, had stuck with him despite his best efforts to sabotage their relationship. He could walk upright, even if it did require the use of a titanium and polypropylene monstrosity. He at least wasn't confined to a wheelchair. He could stand up and look people in the eye, rather than having to look up from chair level. How he'd hated the time he'd spent in a wheelchair in the hospital. Even though he rode in a vehicle with a handicapped placard hanging from the rear-view mirror, at least he didn't have to constantly search for wheelchair ramps. A few months ago, he'd thought himself the most unlucky person ever born. Now, not so much.

Just before he left to go back to his new temporary desk, he said, "Terrence, I'm really glad I met you." Terrence smiled. "And not just in anticipation of needing your help with the computer."

"It's great to have finally met you too," Terrence assured him. "Us special guys can always use all the friends we can get." He briefly patted one of his wheels.

Us special guys. That sure sounded a lot better than *us disabled guys.*

On the train ride home that evening, Clay turned to his father, sitting next to him.

"Dad, I went to see Terrence this morning."

"Good," Dad replied. "He's a person you want to be on good terms with."

"He's in a wheelchair."

Dad's eyes glinted with amusement. "Really? He's worked for us for over ten years. How did that one get by me?"

"You're joking, right, Dad?"

"Of course I am. Does his being in a wheelchair matter?"

"Did you hire him because of it?"

"No, not at all," Dad replied quickly. "In fact, I didn't even know his status until the human resources department recommended him as the best candidate they'd interviewed for that position, and we called him in for another interview."

"He seems pretty cool about it. Doesn't seem to let it get him down that much. He even told me about his accident practically as soon as I met him." Clay looked out the window, considering how closed-off he'd been with people about his own experience.

"I noticed that," Dad said. "He doesn't seem to mind people noticing his wheels or wondering what put him into that chair."

"Unlike me, who had his head up his ass about what happened to me. Maybe I should try to be more like him, and more like Nathan."

"Clay, you don't have to be *like* anyone else. You just have to be you. The person you are is just fine."

"Just with my head out of my ass."

"Well, yeah, there is that," Dad agreed.

Chapter Twenty-Five

He had ignored the calls and emails from his Army buddies since the moment of Kaboom. They had been so close, before Kaboom, living, laughing, crying together. Ready and willing to die for each other if necessary. It was a bond that few civilians could comprehend. But now they were probably so pissed at him they wouldn't want anything more to do with him. If he apologized, would they accept it?

He opened his email and read the messages he'd received from Kullander and Gadsden, starting with the most recent – Kullander's brief but eloquent, "WTF, dude?" and progressing back to messages ranging from sympathy, to confusion, to hurt, to anger from both Kullander and Noah Gadsden. Noah had been Clay's battle buddy in basic training as well as infantry training. The two of them had been practically joined at the hip since day one. Both had applied for RASP, the Ranger Assessment and Selection Program. Gadsden's emails told him that he had been accepted into Ranger School. His most recent message had been sent the day before he left to begin the training, thanking Clay for his help in preparing him for the rigors and challenges of RASP. Clay hoped that Gadsden was succeeding in the endeavor.

That, in itself, he realized, was progress for him. Wondering about his buddies and what they were doing. Since Kaboom, he hadn't cared about them, or at least, he had told himself he hadn't.

Level up in your life. It seemed to be his new mantra. *Send them each an email. The worst they can do is ignore you.* Nathan had told him that there was no reason why his friends would shun him, and so far, the guy had been right about pretty much everything he'd said to Clay since the day they'd met.

How weird was it that sending a couple of emails constituted an act of bravery? He started them each out with an apology and an attempt at an explanation, copied right out of the journal he'd been writing.

I'm sorry I haven't kept in touch. I know I've been an ass. But after Kaboom — he backed up, deleted the word Kaboom — *after the IED blast and I woke up at Landstuhl and realized I'd lost my leg, my head was in a really bad place and I couldn't bear human contact of any kind. I pushed away my family, my friends, even Julie. I'm still kind of messed up, but it's getting better.*

I hope you guys will forgive me. I'd like to know what you are doing now. Are you home from A-stan?

He included his new phone number in the emails, just in case either of them was forgiving enough to want to talk to him.

In the amazing manner of modern technology, he received a response to his email to Jonathan Kullander barely an hour after hitting the Send button, in the form of a phone call.

"He lives!" Kullander crowed as soon as Clay accepted the call and said hello. And within moments, they were friends again. Clay let his friend lead the conversation as he found out that Jonathan was back at Fort Benning, in line to make Sergeant, and happy to be back where he could, as he put it, get a decent steak. Kullander's idea of a "decent" steak was, just knock off the horns and hooves and wipe its ass rare. He expected it to moo when he stuck his fork in it.

Noah Gadsden was deep in Ranger training. "He's kind of off the grid until he graduates and gets his tab," Kullander said.

"But when that happens, I know he's going to want to talk to you."

"I want to talk to him too. I need to apologize for being such a shit."

"We were worried about you, dude. It was beyond horrible seeing them airlifting you and Lopez out of there."

He had assumed that Sergeant Lopez's body would have been taken to the field hospital on the same Lakota with Clay, but hearing it enunciated made it all the more horrible. He tried to subdue the mental image of Sergeant Lopez lying in a body bag on the floor of the helicopter next to him, while the medics worked on Clay.

"I have to admit it, Gadsden and I both cried when they took you away in that Lakota. By the time we got back to the base, you were on your way to Landstuhl."

Was there anyone he knew that hadn't cried over what had happened to him? Had Julie cried when he'd sent her that cruel email, attempting to end their relationship? He didn't want to imagine how she might have felt upon receiving it.

"We wanted to come to Landstuhl with you but we couldn't. Couldn't go to Lopez's funeral either. But we had a memorial at the base."

Clay had seen, had attended, the on-base memorial for fallen soldiers more than once. The commanding officers made it mandatory, though none of them would have failed to participate in any case. Seeing the rifle propped upright inside Lopez's empty boots, the bayonet attached to form a cross, dog tags hung over it with his helmet placed on top, never failed to put lumps in the throats of every soldier. The last roll call, enduring the tragic silence when the deceased's name was called, once, twice, without response, was painful to listen through. Having his buddies come to Landstuhl, for them to see him torn apart and suffering, would have been just as painful.

"Maybe it's best you didn't come to Landstuhl," he told Kullander. "I know you wanted to keep in touch. They told me you and Gadsden had called, but I was in a really bad place. I mean seriously messed up, and not just my leg or my ears or the concussion. I'm talking about, in my head. I was a basket case for a long time and I pretty much pushed everyone away. I even tried to break up with Julie. I was too chicken shit to return your calls, but now I wish I had. I just started looking at my emails a week ago."

"I can't begin to tell you how horrible it was, what happened to you," Kullander confessed. "I guess I'm using the word horrible too much, but that's what it was. God, Maslowski, I mean, yeah, we always know that death and injury are part of the expectation here, but that didn't make it easier. How the fuck are you? Are you home now?"

"Yeah, I'm at my parent's place, for now. I've been learning to walk on the prosthesis. I'm going to start an apprenticeship in Virginia soon. And Kullander – I'm engaged. Julie and I are getting married."

"Congratulations, dude! I knew you two were meant for each other. I take it the breakup didn't stick? And why on earth would you even consider cutting a babe like her loose? Just from the photos you showed us, we all thought you were the luckiest guy in the platoon. And not just because you had the best marksmanship scores and the fastest running time."

"You're right," Clay agreed. "I am lucky to have her. She saw right through my BS when I tried to break it off. I thought she wouldn't want to be stuck with me, like this, but I was wrong. I sure hope you and Gadsden can make it up here for the wedding."

"Short of going UA, we'll be there."

"Kullander," Clay said, letting his voice express his emotion. "I'm sorry. I treated you all like shit and you didn't deserve it."

"Don't worry about it, Maslowski. I can't say that I wouldn't go a little crazy too if I went through something like that."

There was a pause, then Kullander went on. "If I make Sergeant, I'll probably end up back in the sandbox, with a squad of my own. But it won't be the same without you and Gadsden and Lopez in the alpha team."

A moment of silence ensued at the mention of their late sergeant.

"I saw him die, you know." Kullander's voice was soft.

Clay didn't want to hear it. Did. Not. Want. To. But he needed to hear it, if he could somehow tamp down the guilt that threatened to boil over and consume him. He couldn't speak, so Kullander continued.

"When that blast hit, when what was left of the vehicle landed back on the ground, I saw Lopez before I saw you. The Humvee came down on its side, with the left side down. How I ended up with only minor cuts and bruises, I have no idea. I found myself hanging on to the seat and looking down into Lopez's face, six inches from mine."

That made sense. Kullander had been sitting in the front, next to Lopez.

"The fucking hunk of metal was sticking out of his neck and the blood was spurting out around it. I didn't realize how much blood there is in a human body until that day. His eyes were bugged out like a frog and his lips were moving, but I couldn't hear any sound. Don't know if he couldn't make any sound, or if it was because my ears were ringing too hard. I put my hand out to pull out the shrapnel – it was instinctive, you know, you see something stabbing a guy, you think you should pull it out. But Lopez looked at me and I could see him saying, no, don't, but without words. Just from the look in his eyes. He knew that pulling it out would kill him faster. And he went pretty fast even without removing the thing. I could see him trying to form his last words – God, what do you say when you know it's the last thing you'll ever say?"

"Tell my wife I love her." Clay didn't realize he'd spoken until he heard Kullander's intake of breath at the other end of the call.

"Yeah, that's what it was. Even though he couldn't speak, that's what it looked like he was trying to say. Then the lights went out. His eyes were still open but he was gone. Just like that. Still in his seat, covered with blood. I could smell it. Sometimes I still smell it. I couldn't do anything but sit there screaming, *No*, until I heard Gadsden yelling, *shit, shit, shit*! I thought he was hurt too, and he was. The impact threw him clear, but broke his arm. But he wasn't complaining about that, he was trying to get to you, because you'd gotten the worst of it. I heard him scream your name, and heard the guys from bravo team on the comm screaming for air support and the medics. For a second I was paralyzed, couldn't think of what I should do. I could barely see outside the truck, the windows were so covered with the dirt that had been blown around. But Gadsden grabbed the medical kit from the back – thank God it wasn't destroyed in the blast. He yelled, *I can't get the tourniquet on*. Because his arm was broken. So I did it. I knew if I didn't, you'd bleed out too, before the medics got there. I put it on your – um ..."

"You can say it. My stump. Or residual limb if you like."

"Yeah, that. God, Maslowski, I hope I didn't make it worse."

"Fuckadoodle do!" The enhanced expletive spat from Clay's mouth in a burst of emotion. It was a good thing he was sitting in his bedroom with the door closed, out of his mother's hearing.

"What is it?" Kullander gulped. "Maslowski, are you OK?"

"You saved my life. You fucking saved my life. And I never thanked you. God, I feel like the shittiest person ever. Even worse than making my family cry."

"For one thing," Kullander replied reasonably, "I think it would be shitty if your family didn't cry about what happened to you. And for another, you didn't know about what we did at the scene because you were unconscious. At first we thought you were dead. The medevac chopper was there in like, ten minutes. It was well within the golden hour, but it felt like forever. We searched the area for tangos, but they were long gone. They must have set that IED days before."

"What about Gadsden's busted arm?"

"It was his right arm. It's a good thing he's left-handed. He unzipped his jacket and stuck his arm inside to hold it in place until he got back to the field hospital to have it set. Remember how we were joking about the cold, just before it happened? But afterward, I was sweating as if I'd just been dropped into Death Valley in July."

Kullander paused again. "Shit, that was a bad choice of words. But in a way, that was Death Valley. For Lopez at least. Maslowski, how did you know what Lopez's last words were? You were out cold."

"I just know. If it had been me, I'd want my last words to be, tell Julie I love her."

"I feel guilty," Kullander said, his voice almost a whisper.

Guilty? Kullander felt *guilty*? If there was any guilt to be placed, it was Clay's. Didn't Kullander remember that Clay was supposed to be driving the Humvee that day?

"I should have closed Lopez's eyes for him. It wasn't right, for a guy to be dead and have to have his eyes still open. But I chickened out. I couldn't touch him to do it. I couldn't help him, and I couldn't help you."

Clay was beginning to think that maybe Jonathan Kullander had it worse than Clay, at least emotionally. Having been unconscious, he at least hadn't had to see Lopez's eyes, open but dead. If he had been in Kullander's place, would he have had the courage to reach out and close the sergeant's eyes for him?

And yet Kullander seemed to calmly accept the fact that his upcoming promotion to infantry sergeant would in all probability get him deployed right back to the sandbox where the horror had occurred. Was he able to live with the fact, and its potential, because he seemed willing to talk about his experience, unlike Clay, who hadn't?

He'd been so selfish, thinking only about his own trauma and never considering how Kaboom had affected his surviving comrades.

"Have you talked to Gadsden?" Kullander asked. "He's at Ranger training now, at Fort Bliss. He'll probably be going back too, once he gets his tab and transfers to the 75th Ranger Regiment."

"Yeah, I read his emails too, finally. We were supposed to go to RASP together."

He tried to squelch down his jealousy, that his friend Noah Gadsden would be receiving what Clay had also coveted, the Ranger tab. It was a simple cloth patch, yellow and black, bearing just the word Ranger, attached to one's upper shoulder of the left sleeve, but it embodied all that Clay had aspired to. He'd even memorized the Ranger Creed in preparation for the training.

"Yeah, I know. God that fucking sucks." Kullander paused again. "Maslowski, I have to confess something. I cried that day, and I cry about what happened to you and to Lopez on a regular basis. God, I am such a wuss. My enlistment is up in a couple of months and I'm not sure I'm going to re-up, even though I'm up for promotion. I want to re-enlist but I don't know if I have the courage. I'm not afraid of another IED or that I might have to kill someone, or even that I might be killed myself. But I'm not sure I can ever summon up the courage to close the eyes of another dead comrade. The medic who zipped Lopez into the body bag did it. Gadsden didn't even make it onto the chopper to be taken to the field hospital to get his arm fixed. He was so hopped up on battle shock and adrenaline, they almost forgot it was broken. I can't get over feeling I'm not brave enough to serve in the Army, the way I wimp out thinking about that day."

"Don't feel that way, Kullander," Clay assured his friend. "A friend of mine – another amputee, who's super smart about this kind of thing, told me that grieving, crying if you must, is actually healthy and you shouldn't be afraid to do it. If you think you're a coward, you are dead wrong. If I was still there with you, I wouldn't hesitate for a second to have you at my side or to depend on you to have my back."

Wow. This was new. He, Clayton Maslowski, depressed basket case, believing in the advice he'd been given, and passing it on to another person feeling traumatized. Maybe hell really did freeze over after all.

As IEDs went, this one had been pretty inefficient. It exploded off to one side rather than directly under the vehicle, which would have killed them all. Did that make Clay, Jonathan Kullander and Noah Gadsden lucky? The person who planted that IED had been hoping to eliminate at least four American soldiers. Was he disappointed that his error had resulted in only one death, one amputated leg, one broken arm? If Clay's squad had been sent to deliver those medical supplies a week or a day earlier or later, would things have gone down differently? Would the IED have not been planted, or planted elsewhere? What if that anonymous terrorist had been a little smarter and placed his little present where it would have done more damage? There could have been four bodies buried at Arlington rather than just Lopez.

He had to stop this. These were questions with no possible answers, and this endless, useless cycle of coulda, woulda, shoulda, was never going to end well.

"Kullander," he said. "We were actually lucky."

He hesitated, shocked by what he'd just said. He'd never thought, in those dark days after Kaboom, that he would have used the word lucky in the same universe as this situation.

"It could have been worse."

"Worse?" Kullander croaked. "How could it possibly have been worse?"

"If the IED had been positioned more to the center of the road, we'd all be dead. If the tangos had stuck around to see the results, the guys in bravo squad might have been killed too. But we lucked out and got the guy who was at the bottom of his class in terrorist school."

A smart terrorist, one who'd graduated at the top of his class, would have ensured the device was in the center of the road where it would explode directly under the vehicle. That would have killed them all. They should consider themselves fortunate to have experienced the efforts of a less intelligent terrorist whose bomb had been somewhat off-center.

"I guess you can look at it that way," Kullander agreed. "That and the fact that those roads were really just suggestions. It wasn't exactly the 405 in L.A."

Jonathan had grown up in Los Angeles, and he and Clay had had numerous discussions on the subject of whose home town had the worse traffic.

"Maslowski," Kullander said in a low voice, and Clay could hear emotion in the way his friend said his name. "Have you spoken to Sergeant Lopez's widow?"

It was a moment before Clay could answer. "No. Not yet. I haven't gotten up the courage yet. I got an email from her, which I just read this morning. I should email her back, or call her, but ... Shit, I just don't know what to say. How do you tell a woman, 'Sorry I got your husband killed'?"

Kullander's reply was an explosion of surprise. "What the hell are you talking about? You didn't get Sergeant Lopez killed! How can you say that? Or even think it?"

"You know that day was my turn to drive." Clay tried to banish the image of sitting in that Humvee, of a brief glance of the sergeant's profile as he turned his head for a moment to smile at one of their obscene comparisons of the cold weather, the last moment he remembered seeing or hearing before Kaboom.

"So?" Kullander countered. "That doesn't make it your fault, no way, no how. Have you been thinking that all this time? It wasn't your fault, or mine, or Gadsden's, or the sergeant's. It happened, but none of us were to blame."

"What does Gadsden think about it?"

"If he thought you or anyone other than the Taliban were to blame, he would have said so. You know that guy isn't shy with his opinions. When he finishes Ranger School and you can get a chance to talk to him, I'm sure he'll tell you the same thing. Don't beat yourself up over it, Maslowski. You have enough to think about without dealing with some crazy notion like that."

"I'll make you a deal, Kullander," he offered. "I'll try really hard not to blame myself for what happened in the sandbox, if you'll try really hard to believe that you are brave enough to continue in the Army. You know if things had gone down differently, I'd be right there beside you."

"I believe that," Kullander agreed. "And I'll take that bet. Did you say you were moving to Virginia? We have to get together, the three of us, and meet up at Arlington."

He didn't have to say more for Clay to understand what he meant. Now that the three of them were back in CONUS, they should, needed to, visit Arlington National Cemetery to pay their respects at the grave of Sergeant Adam Lopez. It would go a long way in the healing process, for all of them, to place stones on top of his headstone. He'd explain the meaning of it to his friends. And next to those small stones, they would each place a quarter, the symbol of having been with the deceased soldier at the time of his death. It was true Clay had been unconscious, hadn't seen Lopez die or helped to close his sightless eyes, but he'd still been there, and he was going to acknowledge it.

"I'll bring the José Cuervo," Clay said.

"Should I bring shot glasses?" Kullander asked. "Or should we just drink it out of the bottle?"

"Straight out of the bottle," Clay replied. "Remember, Lopez always said, glasses are for wimps."

It was highly likely that the administration of Arlington National Cemetery would frown upon visitors bringing liquor onto the site, but nothing was going to stop Clay and his comrades from toasting the memory of their sergeant with his favorite libation.

Chapter Twenty-Six

There was another stop he needed to make on the Clay Maslowski Apology Tour, and he decided it should happen at the Dam Inn.

He got to the bar early and already had a table, a plate of nachos, a pitcher of beer and four glasses ready before the Posse walked in, choosing the table rather than sitting at the bar so that he could see all three of them together. Surprise and gratitude filled him, that they'd accepted his invitation at all. The last time he'd seen them, he'd cursed at them and driven them away with his rudeness.

They all three looked a bit wary when he waved them over but at least they sat down and accepted the beers he offered.

"Look, guys, I want to apologize to you for how I treated you when I first got home. I've been a shit. A jerk. An ass. A ..."

Ren gave him a quick elbow poke. "Ok, dude, we get it."

"We forgive you," Jeremy said quickly, and Doug nodded his head in agreement.

"I've been talking a lot to this guy, another amputee," Clay told them. "He's been mentoring me through this whole situation. He said if you didn't know what was going on you wouldn't understand it."

All three of them were nodding now. "Makes sense," Doug said. "We didn't know and we didn't understand what was up with you."

"OK," Clay replied. "Here's what's been going on."

He looked at his three friends, who'd been kind and forgiving enough to give him a second chance on their friendship. "I think of it as Kaboom. Because that was the last sound I heard before I woke up in a military hospital in Germany. Our truck hit an IED and my left leg was amputated in the blast, and my Sergeant was killed."

The guys all went a bit pale upon hearing his words. "Shit," Jeremy whispered. "We knew about your leg – your mom told us – but still, hearing you say it ... I can't imagine anything more awful."

He looked at them, these three young men with whom he'd grown up, his best buddies. The Posse. Despite how he'd treated them, they were still his friends.

"I was at Landstuhl – that's the military hospital – for months, recovering, getting fitted for a prosthesis, going through physical therapy to learn to walk on it. But it wasn't only the physical wounds that got me down. I kind of lost my mind for a while there. I thought that I had no reason to live, that I was a freak, that nobody would want to have anything to do with me, because of it. I broke up with Julie and told my family they couldn't come over there to see me. And I ignored everybody else. My Army buddies, you guys, everyone."

"Under the circumstances," Ren said, "I'm not surprised you went a little crazy. But a freak? You? Never."

"Wait," Doug interrupted. "You broke up with Julie? Does that mean she's single?" He looked so hopeful that Clay almost laughed.

"Sorry, dude. We're back together, and I put a ring on it. Watch your mailboxes for wedding invitations."

Doug pouted but sat back and waited for Clay to finish his story.

"It's Julie that I have to thank for getting my head out of my ass about the whole thing. When I got home she declared we were not broken up despite my idiocy, and she put me in touch with another vet who had been through the same thing, and between them, I think I've got my head almost back on straight. I'm sorry I was so rude to you that day at my folk's house."

Ren put a friendly hand on his arm. "We just wanted to be,"

"Friends. I know. And you were. I hope you still are."

"Sure, dude," Doug said. "Takes more than a little thing like an IED to break up The Posse."

"This calls for a toast," Jeremy declared. Clay raised his beer glass, but his friend insisted, "Something more special than just beer." He looked at Clay. "Any suggestions?"

He knew immediately what the perfect toast would be. "José Cuervo."

Jeremy looked a bit confused – none of them were tequila drinkers – but gave Doug a, *come help me* look and the two of them scurried to the bar, returning a minute later with four shots of José, and they each raised one.

"To friendship," Ren said over his glass.

"To The Posse," Doug added.

Jeremy looked into his shot glass for a moment, then glanced up at the three of them, raising the tequila a bit higher. "To our hero, Clay."

Clay smiled, proud that his friends thought of him as a hero, but he had another toast in mind.

"To Sergeant Adam Lopez, may he rest in peace."

They downed the shots, coughing a bit as the agave liquor filled their senses.

"Wow, that was intense," Ren intoned, as they chased the shots with beer.

"I'm sorry," Clay said again. "I've been a schmendrick. I hope you guys forgive me."

Jeremy giggled, the beer and tequila having already gone to his head. "My grandpa used to call me that when I was a kid. I used to think it meant sweet little boy, until I went to Hebrew school to prep for my bar mitzvah, and the rabbi told me it ba-sically meant dumbass."

"He was right," Doug teased, and rather than take offense, Jeremy just nodded.

"You guys probably have questions," Clay said, remember-ing their friendly curiosity at his parents' party the day he'd arrived home. The three of them looked hesitant to talk, re-membering how he'd reacted then.

"It's OK," Clay assured them. "You can ask. And I'll probably tell you. And it won't even kill me. If you want to come over to my folk's house one day, I'll put on some shorts and show you the prosthesis. Just don't try to play with it."

"Dude! We would never." Doug said in a scolding voice. "But there's something else important we need to talk about." He leaned towards Clay. "So, which of us gets to be your best man?"

"Clay! There's someone at the door for you!" Brooke called out to him the next evening.

"Who is it?" he called back from the kitchen.

"God. And his twin brother."

Clay hadn't been aware that God had a twin brother, so of course, he had to go into the living room to check it out.

It wasn't God standing there, but pretty damn close. Julie's two older brothers, the famous Peterson twins, Zach and Kyle, stood there in all their glowing golden glory. Clay felt imminent death approaching. Were the two of them about to destroy him for daring to think he was good enough to marry their precious little sister?

Julie had taught him how to tell the two apart. Kyle was just a tiny bit taller, and he held out a hand in Clay's direction.

"Congratulations!" he said, with a friendly smile on his face. A bit dazed, and grateful to be still alive, Clay accepted the handshake, to be quickly followed by one from Zach. "We just heard about you and Julie getting engaged. We're so happy for you."

They were happy for him? They weren't enraged that their baby sister was going to marry a one-legged cripple?

"Aw, who are we kidding?" Zach said, then the next thing Clay knew, the three of them were in a group hug, his two future brothers-in-law patting his back, and ...

Crying?

If Clay had ever imagined, back in high school, that the legendary Peterson twins would be hugging him, crying at the thought of their sister moving nine hundred miles away to be married to him, and calling him a hero, he would have told himself he was insane. Even if he'd still had both his legs, the Peterson twins would still have intimidated him. He'd expected them to threaten him with fates worse than death if he didn't take good care of their little sister, but surprisingly, they informed him that they had instructed Julie to take good care of Clay.

He had to make sure they understood exactly what kind of brother-in-law they were getting. As they wiped their eyes and smiled happy congratulatory smiles, he invited them to sit down.

"Um," he said, a bit hesitantly, "You guys do know about my, uh, my disability?"

"What disability?" Zach, no, Kyle, asked. "You don't mean your leg, do you?"

"Actually, my lack of a leg."

"You think that's a disability?" Zach sputtered. "You're kidding! That's no disability! I'm sure it's a challenge, but it's no detriment in our eyes. I think something like that makes a guy stronger. Did Julie have an issue with it? She's so happy she's practically glowing in the dark. Our parents are ecstatic too. Jeez, Clay, you're like a hero around here. Everybody thinks so."

Every compliment and encouraging word that came from the twins' mouths tore another brick away from the wall of despair that Clay had built around himself since Kaboom. That wall was crumbling, almost demolished to dust.

Another first for Clay, and he found out, for Julie as well, was an invitation from her boss to have dinner at the Chef's table at her restaurant, even though she had given her notice in preparation for their move to Virginia. He invited them as a goodbye gift, telling them how sorry he was to lose her.

"He never has guests here," Julie said in awe as they sat at the table located, literally, in the restaurant's kitchen. The inner kitchen viewpoint was rather fascinating, as Clay watched food being prepped and plated nearby. But today, rather than Julie in her white coat working, she sat next to him in a pretty blue dress and her engagement ring sparkling on her hand.

Not only did Chef – Julie had told him that the executive chef was addressed that as a title, with a capital C – have them as his guests, he also sat and ate with them, making sure they had the freshest menu choices, had the sommelier suggest the best wines, and praised Julie's culinary skills with enthusiasm. A glowing reference for her to use in securing her next position in Virginia was offered and gratefully accepted. "You'll be running your own kitchen in no time," Chef, whose name was actually Morgan, told her.

Chapter Twenty-Seven

It was a testament to the organizational skills of Julie, her mother, and Clay's mother, that the wedding was planned and executed in less than two months, so that they could make the drive to Virginia before the weather got ugly.

It was a really busy two months for all of them, taking care of everything that needed to be done before getting married and moving to Virginia. Clay had a lot more on his plate than just getting fitted for his tux and choosing gifts for his groomsmen. After much coin tossing, Ren had won the position of his best man, but the other members of the Posse would be standing up with him also.

He worked three days a week for his father, riding downtown on the train together. Kendra left to start her maternity leave and once she was gone, Clay spent a lot of his time filling in for her telling the company's employees things like, "I know that's not how Kendra did it. But Kendra's not here right now, is she?"

As promised, he kept in touch with Kullander and Gadsden, who both requested leave in order to attend Clay and Julie's wedding. Noah called him as soon as he graduated from Ranger School and they shared his sense of pride upon attaining his Ranger tab.

He went to visit his grandmother in the nursing home. She didn't recognize him, though a flicker of memory seemed to shine in her eyes for a brief moment when he called her *Bab-*

cia. She was however thrilled to have a visitor and had been delighted by the candy and flowers he brought her.

He and Nathan met up again with the prosthetic club, and Clay made note of the phone numbers and email addresses of each one of them, with plans to consult them, and his friend Sergeant Jacoby, when he found himself challenged by his situation in the future.

It had been five years since he had been in the high school locker room, but it hadn't changed. The same lockers, showers, tile floors and the lingering, competing scents of sweat and deodorant. Rows of mesh fronted lockers faced benches that had felt the imprint of hundreds of athletic butts, Clay's included. He sat there now, but he was no longer an athlete here. Doors at the end of the room gave access to offices for the coaches, trainers and equipment storage. At the other end were the showers, where Clay and his teammates used to block the floor drains with towels, trying to create steam. But it was the coaches who got steamed when the boys' efforts created floods. It did all seem a bit smaller than he recalled. Or maybe he'd just been smaller back then.

He had to dredge up a lot of interior fortitude to come back here, and to use the room to change from his sweat pants into a pair of running shorts. Coach Swanson and the kids on the track team, including the younger boys who had been witness to his meltdown on the track last spring, were just outside the door to the field house. Coach had brought them in for a "special meeting" when Clay called him and asked to see them all. He knew they were all curious, wondering what was going on, perhaps anticipating another awkward situation like the one back at summer track camp. Nervous sweat trickled down Clay's back. *What do you think you're doing?* he asked himself. *You're about to show your prosthesis, your stump of a leg, to a bunch of high school kids. Are you insane?* So far the only people who had seen his leg were Julie, Brooke and Nathan. Brooke had seen it only because she'd snuck up on him the evening after the break-in at their house, and Nathan only because Clay had gotten brave enough to wear shorts under his sweatpants one time when they were punching the heavy bag in his garage, and he'd only removed his sweatpants then because Nathan's wife and kids hadn't been home, even though they were accustomed to seeing Nathan's prosthesis and residual limb. It was possible his parents might have seen it the night of Independence Day when they and Brooke had peeked in his bedroom door as he lay passed out and semi-conscious, but he couldn't remember if he'd covered himself or not. He'd had a blanket over him in the morning however, so it was possible that someone had come in and covered him up later. He hadn't wanted to ask and none of them had said.

For a moment he was tempted to chicken out of this encounter, but Coach opened the door, poked his head in and asked, "You in there, Clay?"

He was seriously tempted to try to hide somewhere until they all left, but then, how disappointed would Julie and Nathan be in him if he succumbed to cowardice?

"Yeah, I'm here, come on in," he replied, trying to keep his voice from shaking as he stood up.

Coach led the kids in and of course they all stared when they saw Clay standing there in his running shorts, his prosthesis clearly in view. Some of the boys must have guessed or known about Clay's one-legged status, but others looked completely shocked.

A voice in the back muttered, "Oh my fucking god." Another kid elbowed the speaker in the ribs with a scolding, "Dude!" Clay pretended not to hear it.

"Hi guys," he said, with more confidence than he felt. "I asked Coach to have you all come in so I could explain to you about what happened that day at track camp, and why."

"Do you want to sit down?" Coach asked.

"Thanks, Coach, but I think I'll stand for now." A couple of the track team kids sat on the benches but most hung back, almost as if they were afraid of him, probably remembering his demented state the last time they had seen him. Dozens of curious eyes stared at him, at his leg, and he reminded himself what Nathan had told him.

People will stare. It's human nature.

"So," he said, trying to smile, "as you can all see, I have a prosthetic leg. When I was in the Army, I was involved in an IED blast that resulted in the traumatic amputation of my leg, and after a while, I was fitted with this one. Also as a result of that blast, I sometimes have episodes of PTSD. That's post-traumatic stress disorder. It's better now than it used to be, but loud noises, like Coach's starter pistol, sometimes bother me and that's why I had that incident that day."

"I'm sorry about that," Coach said, again. The boys watching him were mostly open-mouthed and a bit shocked. A couple of them flinched a bit when he mentioned the blast.

"It's Ok, Coach," Clay told him, again. He looked back at the track team kids. "I wanted you all to see this so you'd understand exactly what was going on, and I'll be glad to answer any questions you guys might have."

Surprisingly, telling these kids the awful truth about what had happened to him, showing them his prostheses, being the object of their stares and sidelong glances, wasn't quite as traumatic as he'd feared it would be. He reminded himself that Nathan Jacoby did this at the beginning of every school year in his classes, perhaps was even doing it today, and Jacoby was the most together, well-adjusted person Clay knew.

A tentative hand raised at the back of the group – the red-haired Hamilton boy. "Um, Coach," he said hesitantly.

"Call me Clay. He's the Coach." Clay pointed at Coach Swanson. The kid looked at Coach for confirmation, who nodded slightly.

"OK, Clay," the boy said. "How does it work? I'm mean, your leg, that is the ..." He trailed off, blushing at his boldness, being the first one to dare to ask something personal about Clay's leg.

"Here, let me show you." Clay sat on the bench and slipped his fingers under the socket. It took courage for him to take off the prosthesis with all these kids and Coach Swanson watching, and he told himself, if Nathan Jacoby could do this with his students, then Clay could do it too. These boys deserved an explanation and honesty, and Clay needed closure. Nathan Jacoby had taught him that.

Most of the kids gasped a little when he had it detached and held it up. He showed them the socket, the pylon, the foot. He took off the shoe and let them see the artificial semi-toes, maneuvered the artificial knee and ankle joints.

Teenagers, it turned out, were chock full of questions, and once they got started, there was no stopping them.

"Does it feel like your real foot?"

"Some people say it does, but no. I'm always aware of my prosthesis. Even as I've gotten accustomed to it and it starts to feel comfortable, it never feels like my real leg, the leg I lost."

"What happened to your real leg? Where is it? How did you get help when it happened?"

"Did they make you leave the Army? Did you want to stay in?"

"Can you run?"

"Why can't they make it look more like a natural leg?"

"Where do you get it?"

"The Army provided it. They had a prosthetist – that's a person who makes artificial limbs – come in and measure me, my stump, and made me a temporary one and a little later, this one. When it needs to be replaced, the Army will take care of that one too. We, that is, they, take care of their own."

"Do you have to wear it all the time?"

"What about running? Swimming? Driving?"

"Do you have to wear special shoes?"

He answered all the questions as best he could, not sugar-coating it, even when he had to talk about the pain and frustration. Thankfully none of them were bold enough to ask about sex.

"Can I touch it?" someone finally asked.

Clay hesitated a moment, then said, "Sure," and handed the prosthesis to the boy, who for a moment hesitated to take it. But after only a moment the kids were passing it around like a hamster in sixth-grade show and tell. He distinctly heard a couple of kids murmur, "This thing is cool."

Cool. That was a word Clay had never thought would be applied to him or his fake leg.

Just when he thought they'd exhausted their curiosity, the Hamilton boy had one more question.

"Does it hurt?"

Clay found himself laughing, a mirthless snort. Did it hurt? That was the most stupid and yet at the same time, the most honest question he'd ever been asked.

He could say, yes, it hurt. At first, on a scale of one to ten, it had been a twenty. It had come close to making him suicidal. The physical and emotional pain had combined to make him do stupid things he came to regret, like breaking up with Julie, alienating his family, his friends, his army buddies. He could tell them that the levels of pain varied day to day from merely annoying to completely devastating and everything in between. But in this case he settled for a simple, "Yeah, it did and it does."

He had thought, had feared, that this meeting and his revelation and demonstration of his prosthesis and the circumstances of his experience would have ended up with a group of disgusted, turned-off teenagers looking at him like the local neighborhood freak. But to his surprise, he saw none of that. After the initial shock of seeing the prostheses and stump, the boys started to look at him with respect and admiration, and when young Hamilton said, "Wow, Clay, you're a hero," most of the others nodded in agreement.

Coach Swanson put a hand on Clay's shoulder and said, "You did a good, brave thing here today, Clay."

Shortly before the wedding, his dad contacted the temp agency for another admin, to take over now that Clay was about to leave for his new life with Julie in Virginia, as Kendra was still on maternity leave with her new baby. She had sent him a couple of photos of the infant, and he and Julie had purchased a gift for baby Jasmine. He was glad Julie took the lead in the gift purchase, choosing a baby swing and a gift card to be used for diapers. Clay would have been clueless as to what to give them.

Despite school being back in session, Nathan still found time to hang out with Clay. They punched the heavy bag in the Jacoby garage until Clay felt his pre-Kaboom muscle definition returning. Even Nathan's son Simon joined them occasionally, and watching the father and son, who looked so much alike, both with tall, lean physiques, the same black hair and sharp blue eyes, Clay couldn't help but fantasize about having a child of his own with Julie someday.

He also went to visit his grandfather's grave and nearby, the tiny grave of his sister Amelia. He hadn't been there since the day of his grandfather's funeral. He put stones on their grave markers, brushed off the dead leaves and loose grass, and explained what Jacoby had told him about the significance of those small stones. He thought he'd feel silly, sitting on the grass at Memory Gardens, talking to his deceased grandfather and sister, but surprisingly, he just felt peaceful.

"You'd like Julie, *Dziadek*," he said to Grandpa's headstone. "Everybody loves her. Me most of all. I wish you could have met her."

The next day, he met Nathan at Fremd High School after classes finished, and surprised the heck out of his friend by asking to go visit his father's grave.

"You want to see my dad's grave?" Nathan asked incredulously. "A man you never met?"

"Yes," Clay insisted. "Is that so weird?"

"It's very weird," Nathan said, but apparently having become accustomed to Clay's weirdness, obligingly drove him over to Shalom Memorial Park and guided him through the cemetery until they found themselves standing in front of the grave marker of Nathan's father. Clay brought his cane in anticipation of walking over potentially uneven, grassy terrain.

"Here he is," Nathan said, indicating the marble grave marker embedded at their feet. It had a brass plaque attached with a continuous curly design around the edge. Clay read the inscribed words, "Daniel Isaac Jacoby. Beloved husband and father," with a Star of David between the dates of the elder Jacoby's birth and death.

To Nathans' surprise, Clay sat down on the grass in front of the grave marker, as he had when visiting his grandfather's grave just a few miles away. He glanced up at his friend, and waved a dismissive hand at him.

"This is the part where you go away so we can talk about you behind your back."

The look of shock on Nathan Jacoby's face was a thing of beauty. Clay had finally succeeded in stupefying him.

"You're going to sit there and talk to my father's grave marker?" From the look on Nathan's face he obviously believed that Clay had finally lost it.

"Yes, that's exactly what I plan to do. Now shoo."

Muttering something under his breath about insanity, Nathan walked away, and when Clay figured he was out of earshot, turned back to the gravestone.

"Hey there, Mr. Jacoby. May I call you Daniel? I just wanted to tell you what a great guy your son is. If it weren't for him, I'd probably be in a mental hospital or something. He convinced me to stop being an idiot and realize that my life wasn't over, and thanks to him, I'm walking and planning a career and about to marry the woman I love. Maybe you can't hear me, since you're dead and all, but just in case, I thought you should know what a great friend he's been to me. If he gets that kind of attitude from you, then you must have been a pretty great guy too. I just wanted you to know that."

He pulled a pebble out of his pocket. He'd taken it from the flower bed along the front of his family's house. Nathan had told him it would be more significant if the stone came from a place with a special meaning. Placing it on the edge of the plaque, he murmured, "Rest in peace, Daniel. Thank you for creating such a special person."

It was still a bit of a challenge to climb to his feet, but a lot easier than it had been previously, and Nathan returned when he saw Clay get up. Looking down at the grave marker, Nathan asked, just a bit sarcastically, "Did you have a nice talk with him?"

"Yes," Clay replied. "Your dad is a good listener."

Nathan snorted with amusement. "What did you talk about?"

"Oh, that's just between us," Clay teased, just as Nathan had done when he'd first met Clay's parents. He chuckled at Nathan's small annoyed look at being left in the dark, then walked back towards Nathan's van, giving his friend a minute to pay his own respects to his father in privacy.

He was hardly using the cane at all now, only stumbling occasionally, and stood without it at the altar at their wedding. He even danced with Julie at the reception, as she'd insisted. In truth, it was more like moving slightly while holding her in his arms, but at the conclusion, judging by the amount of applause, one might have thought the Rolling Stones had just concluded an encore. Clay was amazed at how proud that made him feel.

They spent their wedding night at the Westin Hotel, but stayed the remaining few days before leaving for Virginia at Julie's parent's house. It made sense, having no stairs there for him to navigate. They didn't go on a honeymoon, at least not yet. Partly due to his starting his training in Newport News, but more so due to their desire to save up their money for a trip to Spain. He wanted to show Julie Barcelona, wanted to use his meager Spanish vocabulary to buy her paella and sangria, to take the public bus to La Sagrada Familia, and the ferry boat to Majorca. He'd heard the beaches on Majorca were beautiful, and when he got there, he just might wear shorts. It would be a sin to wear sweatpants in the warm Spanish sunshine.

You never realize how much crap you own until you start packing up to move. Everything Clay had owned since kindergarten was still in this bedroom. He'd thought a couple of boxes and his big black duffel bag would have taken care of it. How wrong he was.

He was supposed to be clearing the room out, packing what he planned to keep and discarding the rest. Instead, he was sitting on his bed, looking at his and Julie's wedding photos on his phone.

He'd started with three piles – keep, donate, garbage. But a fourth pile created itself and quickly became the largest of them. Undecided.

There were clothes that didn't fit him anymore. They could go into the donate pile. The underwear with holes in it went into the trash pile.

But what was he going to do with his track trophies? He didn't want to look at them for the rest of his life, yet he couldn't bear to just throw them away. Mentally he categorized them into the largest pile – Undecided.

What about his Army things? The uniforms, the tan tee shirts he'd worn under his cammies, his dog tags? Everything he'd had in Afghanistan had been shipped to Landstuhl, then shipped again from Germany to Wheeling. They had even included the single boot whose mate had disintegrated with his left leg. It was all still sitting in boxes in his closet.

He was still sitting there, feeling overwhelmed and pondering the impossibility of it all when his mother came in.

"Do you need help?" she asked, and he nodded.

"Where's your poster?" Mom looked at the spot next to the door where Usain Bolt used to hang.

Clay smiled. "I gave it to Coach Swanson."

"I'm sure he appreciated it. I enjoyed talking to him and his wife at the wedding reception. He told me a couple of things you did in high school that I didn't know about."

"I was just a kid then, Mom."

"And you're a man now, I know." She ruffled his hair affectionately. "But you'll always be my little boy."

"Mom!"

"You'll understand what I'm talking about when you have kids of your own."

"Coach Swanson didn't keep the poster for himself though. He raffled it off. Every kid on the track team bought tickets. Apparently, I'm some sort of hero at Wheeling. They donated all the proceeds to the Wounded Warrior Project."

"How sweet of him. And Clay, you are a hero. To us, you are definitely a hero."

"Thanks, Mom. But what are we going to do with all this stuff?"

They had reserved a moving pod which now sat in Julie's parents' driveway, but it was a small one, and Julie's parents had bequeathed them some family heirloom furniture pieces they'd had in storage. They would go a long way towards furnishing the apartment in Newport News that Julie and Clay had rented online.

"A lot to go through?" his mom guessed and he rolled his eyes in a *you got that right* expression.

"Let's make stacks," she suggested.

"I tried that," he admitted, indicating his pitiful attempt at organization.

"Well, we can start with your clothes." Mom realized she had to take charge of the situation or it would never be accomplished. "You stay there and I'll empty your dresser."

She started to open the top drawer, then hesitated, obviously recalling his reluctance to let her empty his bag when he'd arrived home from Germany.

"Is it OK for me to go in here and take your things out?" she asked.

"Sure, Mom, no problem." To be truthful, he had never had any porn in his possession, and his reluctance to allow his mother access to his things had been misguided and immature. She was, he was certain, a lot more efficient at packing up stuff than he was.

In a brief time of Mom efficiency, they had every stitch of clothing in his dresser marshaled into three piles on his bed. Keep, Donate, Trash. "We'll pack those," she indicated the smallest pile, Keep, "and bag up the others. Do you know where Brooke is? Maybe she can bring a couple of plastic bags up from the kitchen."

Clay nodded towards the wall between his room and Brooke's. "She's making her bed."

"Really? At noon?"

"I told her it was unacceptable and that she had to do it over until it was right. Now she's calling me Drill Sergeant."

Rather than appearing upset at him bossing his sister, Mom just smiled and kissed his cheek. "That's lovely, dear."

Maybe Clay had been brave enough to disarm a twitchy criminal with a Beretta using just his cane. Perhaps he was courageous enough to accept his reality and to live his life to its fullest despite the loss of his leg. But he most definitely was not brave enough to tell his mother that Brooke was considering enlisting in the Army.

Mom stepped over to the closet and pulled out his duffel bag, the one he had refused to let her open when he'd arrived from Landstuhl. It had been stupid of him to think that the packet containing his discharge papers and medical records was something shameful to hide from everyone's view. That bulging envelope of documents now sat on top of the Keep pile.

She opened the bag, spreading the sides out in preparation to receive his clothes.

"What's this?"

He looked up from his seat on the floor to see his mother pulling a blanket out from the bag, a blanket he had left in there since Germany.

Mom sat down on his bed and spread the quilt out over her lap, then looked at Clay with a question in her eye.

"Where did you get this, Clay? This is hand-made, and it's beautiful work."

It was a skillfully crafted quilt, even Clay could tell that, in patriotic colors of red, white and blue, with stars appliqued over it, and he should have appreciated it more.

"They gave it to me in the hospital in Germany."

The memory of waking up after Kaboom with that quilt covering him came up and stung him like a paper cut. It was conflicting. He had appreciated the warmth of the quilt, its fine hand-crafted quality, the concern and caring of the person who had spent hours crafting it and who had purchased the materials at her own expense. He was touched that a stranger would bestow such a precious gift on him, a person they'd never met.

And at the same time, he hated the fact that he fell into the group of people who were given these special quilts. They weren't given to just any soldier. They were made for, and bestowed upon, the wounded. He'd only received it because he'd lost his leg.

It was for this reason he'd left it in the bottom of his bag.

"They're called Quilts of Valor," he told his mother. "Volunteers make them and send them to the hospital, and the chaplains give them to patients. It was covering me when I woke up after," he hesitated. "After Kaboom." He'd arrived at Landstuhl with the remains of his torn and bloody uniform still on him. The quilt replacing those filthy shreds had been warm and personal, something of his alone among the loss and trauma. Even when he was hot or feverish, the quilt had been folded neatly by a nurse or LNCO and placed at the bottom of the bed, close by for his use. The splash of color, that patriotic red, white and blue, had gone a long way towards dimming the antiseptic hospital smell and the sight of endless white walls. He'd pretended to not be impressed with the quilt's warmth and healing properties, but when he was alone and nobody could see him, he wrapped it around himself like a security blanket.

"My mother used to do quilting when I was a girl," his mom said, as she continued to inspect and stroke the quilt. "I used to help her. I could make quilts like this." Mom was running her hands over the quilting, tracing over the sewn-on stars in such a covetous manner that for a moment, Clay was tempted to offer that she keep it.

"Your dad and I felt so helpless since this happened to you. But these quilts – if I can make them for other young men and women who need that comfort – then I won't feel so helpless and unable to help. I'm sure whoever made this one feels that way too."

Clay hadn't thought of it that way. He'd seen the blanket as an advertisement of his disability, rather than as a way for a family member to help people like him.

"Mom, I'm sure if you made a quilt like this, any guy would be honored to get it as a gift. Or any girl."

"Now that you're married and moving away, maybe I'll use this room as a sewing room to make quilts."

"I'd like that, Mom. But I just don't know what to do with some of this stuff." He rolled a helpless glance around the room.

She stood up and picked up one of his running trophies. "These, I'm keeping, if you don't mind."

Yes. That would be perfect. The trophies wouldn't be thrown into the trash, but he wouldn't have to look at them every day and be reminded of his former running abilities. Although he was planning to look into the possibility of getting a runner's prosthesis someday down the road. He watched his mother, gathering up things from the closet and under the bed.

"Mom. I need to tell you something."

She looked at his face and could see that what he needed to tell her was more than just what he planned to do with his childhood stuff and other possessions.

She sat down next to him on the floor, shoving aside a pair of ice skates that were going into the "donate" pile.

"I don't think I'll be needing those," he said, looking down at his hands. His only footwear options now were cross-trainers or shoes with rubber soles.

"Mom, I think..." His jaw worked and his throat tightened with emotion. His mother took hold of his hand.

"Take your time, Clay. I'm not going anywhere."

He smiled at her.

"I think, I'm going to be OK."

OK. It was such a small word. Not even an actual word. Just two letters. But those two letters embodied so much – his healing, his conquest of his insecurities. A sentiment he thought he'd never feel again.

Mom smiled. "I know you are, sweetie. Your friend Nathan was a real help to you, in adjusting to ..."

She didn't finish her sentence but he saw her glance at his leg.

"You can say it, Mom. Adjusting to being an amputee. Yes, he was a big help, but so were you and dad and Brooke. And Julie. That day that he came over here and talked to you and Dad. What did he say to you? Are you ever going to tell me?"

"Nathan said that you were a fine young man with a lot of potential, who just needed a little encouragement to realize it, but that he was, however, a bit concerned about how depressed you were and what a negative attitude you had towards life."

"He was right about the depression and negativity. But I think I've learned to accept some of that. As for the potential, well I guess we'll see about that when I get to Virginia."

"Oh, I already knew you had potential. You always did, Clay. As Nathan said, you just needed a little encouragement to realize it. There was one other thing he told us. He said that if you got upset with us for talking about you behind your back, that it was a good thing. It meant you cared about your life. That was why he asked your dad and me to keep it just between us for the time being."

So that was another of Sergeant Jacoby's little tricks, similar to the things he did to limit the amount of time his son spent playing video games. Do something that would irritate a normal person, and see if he acted normal or uncaring. Clay chuckled to himself. Maybe the guy was wasting his talents as a history teacher.

"You and Dad helped me too," he said, meaning it. "You helped by making me eat dinner with you guys as a family and making me go to Mass and all those normal things. I'm sorry I was a snot about it. And I never thanked you for that welcome home party you had the day I got home."

"You didn't seem too happy about it at the time," she reminded him.

"I know. But I was stupid and I should have appreciated what you were doing."

"No, you weren't stupid, sweetie. You were hurting."

Yes, he'd been hurting. He'd always be hurting, to some degree. But now, he hurt somewhat less. In fact, a lot less.

Apologizing to his childhood friends and reestablishing their friendship had been difficult, but they had worked it out. The same for his comradery with his former army buddies. Fearing the reaction of Julie's brothers to their engagement had been tense. Now he had another difficult obligation to complete, another leveling up in his life.

With his mother's help, everything was packed into boxes or bags, much quicker than he could ever have done it himself. He was stuffing the last of the trash that they'd pulled out from under the bed into a garbage bag when his mom spoke softly.

"Clay." He looked up at her soft tone. She was holding the last item as yet unpacked – his dress uniform, which had hung untouched in his closet since the day he'd proposed to Julie.

Surprisingly, he felt tears gather in his eyes at the sight of it, even now.

"What would you like me to do with this?" Mom asked.

"I'll take care of it," he replied. "Later." He implied with a look that by later, he meant, when she was gone and he could pack it away in private.

When everything else was bagged and packed, his mother took a bag of old clothes that were to be donated downstairs and left him alone in the room. Clay sat back on the denuded bed, staring around at the room that had been his since childhood. His parents had purchased this house and moved in when Clay was two years old. It was the only home he remembered. Once he was gone, this room would be transformed into his mother's sewing room, that closet storing fabric and notions. But for the moment it was still his.

He took the uniform off the hanger carefully, smoothing his hands down the fabric of the sleeves, caressing the corporal's chevrons with reverent fingers. A tear or two managed to escape as he folded it carefully, respectfully, and placed it inside his black duffel bag, sighing back his emotions as he zipped the bag shut. This uniform would never be worn again, but he intended to keep it anyway. He hated the thought of it ending up in some army surplus store.

He was able to carry the duffel down the stairs himself, feeling pride at accomplishing this seemingly small task. His parents and Brooke insisted on carrying everything else down, and he let them, without bitterness. They loaded both Mom's and Dad's cars with the "Keep" boxes to be transported over to the moving pod at Julie's house. The bags with donations were stored in the garage and Clay dragged the trash bags to the curb before returning upstairs to his childhood bedroom. It looked bare and generic now, with only the furniture remaining, empty of all but memories. It warmed his heart to think of this room later being used to create quilts like the one he had packed in that duffle bag with his uniform. As much as his mother yearned to have it, he selfishly decided to keep it for himself, to use for comfort when the depression threatened to consume him.

He sent Julie a text telling her he would be back at her parents' house shortly, then sat on his former bed, now stripped of bedding, with his laptop, reading and rereading the kind email from Veronica Lopez.

Keep in touch, she had asked. Share stories about serving with Adam, she requested. Kullander and Gadsden had not only emailed her, they'd also spoken to her on the phone. Was not Clay just as brave as they had been? Was he not deserving of her forgiveness?

The last difficult email he had sent – to Kullander and Gadsden – had resulted in reconnection and the laying aside of perceived animosities. They didn't blame him for Lopez's death, and neither should he. He could only hope that Mrs. Lopez had been sincere in the amicability expressed in her email.

But as soon as he typed the words, "Dear Mrs. Lopez", he was filled with an unavoidable sense of dread. What would she think once she knew that her husband and Clay had switched seats on the day he'd died? Having that piece of information would surely reverse her friendliness towards him. What if that realization caused her to blame him for her husband's death? How could he ever face her or those two little fatherless children? Being immediately unconscious during Kaboom meant that he hadn't seen Lopez's bloody, mangled body in person, but that didn't stop him from imagining it, especially after hearing Kullander describe his death. He knew how devastated his parents and sister had been when they'd been told of Clay's amputation. How had Mrs. Lopez reacted when told the worse news possible about her husband? Had she shrieked, sobbed, fainted? If she had, it was all Clay's fault.

The doubts paralyzed his fingers on the keyboard.

Man up. Level up. Even if Mrs. Lopez decided to hate and blame him, she was all the way in Houston, and this was just an email. It wasn't even a video chat.

He forced his fingers to type, as slowly as if he had arthritis.

"Dear Mrs. Lopez, I apologize for not responding to your email sooner."

It was almost as cathartic as his journal writing had been, once he started typing. He wrote to his sergeant's widow about what had happened to him in Kaboom, what he knew of Lopez's death, though he did not mention what Kullander had told him about not being able to close the sergeant's eyes. That was Jonathan's story to tell. He emphasized how sorry he was. It was a good thing he was writing this email in his room, in private now that the packing up was done, because he started to cry as he wrote the awful words, "I was supposed to drive that day, not the sergeant, and if he had been sitting in a different seat in that vehicle, he probably would have survived."

He looked at those words a dozen times, wishing they weren't true, tempted to delete them before he hit Send. But he would never be able to release his guilty conscience if he didn't admit the truth to Veronica Lopez, no matter how she might feel when she read them.

He promised to keep in touch with her, if she was still willing to, and asked about her children. After sending the email, he wasn't sure which would be worse, having her reply to him with hatred over his part in her husband's death, or having her write to him about the grief and confusion of her babies over the loss of their father. He was tempted to hope she ignored his communication completely so he wouldn't have to hear about it.

She didn't ignore him. The next day he received another email from her.

"Dear Clay, Thank you so much for your message. I get the feeling from what you wrote that you somehow hold yourself responsible for Adam's death. I hope you do not harbor any feelings of guilt in the circumstances of that day and in the events of what happened. Adam's death, and your wounds, were a horrible, unimaginable tragedy, but you had no way of knowing what was going to happen and if you feel in any way to blame, you shouldn't. You and your comrades should be as proud of yourselves as I am of Adam. Thank you for inquiring about the children. They are too young at this point to understand about their father. Nicky is only ten months old and Leo just turned three. But when they get older I will be certain to tell them about Adam and about the three of you and what good friends you all were. Your courage will be my inspiration for this difficult discussion."

Mrs. Lopez even attached a photograph that her husband had sent to her during their deployment, before Kaboom. It depicted the four of them, standing in front of the tent that was their barracks, smiling, arms slung around each other's shoulders in comradery. Clay remembered how they'd all flexed their muscles and shouted, "Hooah!" as one of their platoon mates had taken the photo.

As he had experienced in his emails and phone call with his buddy Jonathan Kullander, he tried really hard to believe what he was told and to stop blaming himself for Sergeant Lopez's death, and after a while, he almost believed himself.

Chapter Twenty-Eight

"Clay, don't you think it's time for you two to get going?" his mother asked, as they packed the last of their things into Julie's car, parked in his parents' driveway. The plan was for Julie to drive at first, then for Clay to take over as he felt comfortable. He placed his crutches on top of the suitcases laying on the back seat, so he could reach them when he needed to take his prosthesis off. As soon as they got to Virginia, he planned to buy a car for himself.

"Not that we want to get rid of you," Mom added quickly. "But you have a long drive ahead of you."

They'd said their goodbyes to Julie's family last night and surprisingly, both of her brothers had, again, cried as they'd said their farewells. He had never realized how sentimental the two of them were. He resisted his parents' attempt to get rid of them, looking anxiously down the street.

"Not yet," he said.

Finally he spotted a familiar blue minivan pulling up in front of the house, and the entire Jacoby family, Nathan, Renee and the three kids, all poured out to come say goodbye.

His mother, Julie and Renee quickly huddled for a last recipe exchange. The three of them had already become best friends. He heard Renee Jacoby say to his mother, "It was a lovely wedding. Thank you for inviting us."

The Jacoby children and Brooke huddled to discuss their favorite video games, while Clay's dad tucked a package of sandwiches into the last remaining space in the back seat of Julie's car.

Clay took advantage of the opportunity to put a hand on Nathan's arm and draw him away from the rest of the family for a moment.

"Staff Sergeant," he said, a bit formally, then amended himself. "Nathan. I can never repay you for all you've done for me."

Nathan smiled. "Yes you can," he assured Clay. "When you get settled in, find another someone who needs help. Doesn't necessarily have to be Army. There are wounded warriors in all the service branches. Find someone who's lost, like you were, and help them find their way."

"Will I have to be as much of a pain in the ass as you were?"

"Possibly. Probably."

"I may need lessons."

"Well, I am a teacher. Giving lessons is kind of my jam."

"How will I find such a person?"

"In that part of the country, there is a huge military presence. In fact, you'll be just up the road from the Navy, the Marines and the Air Force. There will be plenty of vets you could help. I can give you some names and info and hopefully, another person who's in need of a mentor will have someone in their lives who cares about them as much as she cares about you."

Nathan glanced over towards Julie as Clay said, "They could only be so lucky."

Then his friend put a friendly hand on Clay's shoulder. "Now, you are going to check in with the doctors at Walter Reed when you get there, right? You're doing really good now, but there's still the possibility of infections cropping up in the future and you want to get that treated right away if it happens."

"I promise, Staff Sergeant," Clay agreed. "Besides I'm sure you'll call to remind me every five minutes once I'm out of your sight." He said that with a smile though, not the sarcastic rancor he would have used shortly after Kaboom.

"Smart-ass," Nathan retorted.

"Yeah, I know," Clay replied. "I'm a schmendrick."

They both glanced over to where Julie, Clay's mother, and Nathan's wife were talking. Julie laughed at something his mom said, then glanced briefly at Clay with an amused smile.

"Why do I get the feeling that my mother is telling Julie embarrassing stories about my childhood?"

"Because she probably is," his friend said.

Clay smiled back in Julie's direction and said to Nathan. "I don't deserve her, but, God, I can't live without her."

"I know the feeling," was Nathan's heartfelt reply as he glanced over at his own wife.

"I'll be glad to try to help other wounded vets, Nathan. But I'm pretty sure I'll still need your help."

"I'm always just a phone call away. Come visit and I'll put you to work grading my students' homework."

Clay chuckled. "Can I give them all A's?"

He looked over to where his sister Brooke and Nathan's son Simon were sitting on the porch, close enough that their hips were touching, the two Jacoby girls on the grass nearby. The two of them looked way too cozy for his liking.

"Staff Sergeant," he said stiffly, and at hearing the rank, Nathan looked at him with raised eyebrows. "How old is your boy?"

"He's fourteen. He's a freshman at Hersey High School."

"He doesn't go to Fremd?" Clay asked. The only rival Wheeling High School had worse than Fremd, was Hersey.

Nathan rolled his eyes. "No, I would never torture my kids like that, make them go to the same school where I teach." He followed Clay's gaze over to the youngsters. "How old is your sister?"

"Seventeen. She's a senior at Wheeling."

Surely Jacoby's son Simon and Clay's sister Brooke weren't flirting, but it sure looked like they were trading phone numbers. No, it couldn't be. More likely they were comparing their Minecraft experience points and the merits of survival mode versus creative mode. Brooke had tried to get Clay interested in the game, but he just didn't get it.

"How far will you drive today?" his mother came over and asked.

"It depends on the traffic. If we're lucky, we'll make Pittsburgh before we stop for the night."

"You'll call me when you stop for the night? When you stop for gas? So I know you're OK."

"Mom, we put that app on your phone so you can always see where we are."

"I know, Clay, but I still worry. It's such a long drive. What if you lose your phone, or,"

"Mom! We'll be fine."

Before he could make any further protest at his mother treating him like a child on his way to kindergarten, Nathan reached out and pinched Clay's arm, hard.

"Ow!" he yelped. "What was that for?"

"Let her fuss," Nathan advised. "After all, her first chick is married and about to leave the nest. It's a traumatic moment for a mother. I can only imagine how Renee is going to act when Simon grows up."

"She didn't get like this when I enlisted in the Army and left for basic training."

"I know. But this is different. Cut your mom a break and let her fuss over you. It will make her feel better."

Clay rolled his eyes but abided by Nathan's advice and patiently endured his mother's maternal fussing, promising to alert her every time they stopped for gas or food or to sleep.

All too soon, it was time for Clay and Julie to hit the road. Hugs and promises of phone calls, emails and video chats were exchanged all around. His mother hugged him quickly, fiercely, and for a long time. He'd expected that. He'd expected tears. He expected to hear instructions to do well at his training and at his new job, to treat Julie well, to call often.

She put her lips to his ear. "Clay," she said softly, but with a definite hint of mom-steel in her voice. "I want grandchildren."

"I feel like we're heading to the Emerald City," Julie joked as they pulled away and glanced back at the group waving behind them.

Clay knew he'd never be the same person he'd been before. He'd be lying to himself to think it. But then, nobody ever remained the same person forever, Kaboom or no Kaboom. He had Julie – they were married, with the ceremony being celebrated at St. Joseph's, just as he'd hoped, officiated by Father Cross. He still couldn't quite believe that had happened. He kept rubbing his wedding band between his fingers to verify it was really there. And the most amazing thing was that, despite how selfish and self-centered he'd been, Julie loved him unconditionally and wasn't turned off by his stump or his prosthesis or his perceived disability. She didn't care how many feet he had or how bitter he was about the loss. He'd be honored to spend the rest of his life proving himself worthy of that kind of love.

Everyone had been tiptoeing around him, afraid to hurt his feelings by mentioning his amputation. Pretending that everything was normal. And somehow, that had made it worse. If he'd manned up and let them in, none of that BS need ever happen. Ever since the moment of Kaboom, the word *can't* had dominated his vocabulary, despite what he'd been taught in Basic Training. I can't walk, I can't provide, I can't make love, I can't kick a heavy bag. It was time to eradicate the word *can't* from his vocabulary, from his body, from his soul, as he had been taught in Basic Training, and to replace it with other words, such as can, do, and try.

Although he'd been more of a sprinter, he had participated in a few relay races in his running career, and he realized that his mentor Nathan Jacoby had completed his leg, metaphorically speaking. The baton was now in Clay's hand, and he knew what that meant and what responsibility it gave him. It was up to him to finish the race. The weight of it could crush him, if he let it.

If he let it.

He didn't have to let it. He could accept the reality of being an amputee. He could become stronger. He could be peaceful and happy. He would be, for Julie's sake. She trusted in him, accepted him for what he was, and he prayed he could make her understand how much that meant to him.

Jacoby had been right, life did go on, even if it was irrevocably altered. The Army's basic training had taught him how to be a soldier. But Nathan Jacoby, his family, and his Julie had provided his basic training for Life. He reached over and took Julie's hand.

She glanced at him.

"I love you, my Viking Princess."

"I know."

"You even took my name." That part had surprised him. "That's kind of old-fashioned, but I'm glad."

Julie smiled as she made the turn onto Elmhurst Road. "I just think that when you start a new family, that everyone should have the same name, be it his name, her name or a third name. I think that Julie Maslowski has a really nice ring to it."

"Be prepared to spend the rest of your life spelling it out."

"I won't mind. We should have asked Father Cross to include that in the wedding vows." She lowered her voice a little to imitate the priest. "Do you, Julie Cathleen Peterson, promise to patiently and correctly spell out Maslowski whenever necessary? I do."

Clay smiled, but then his brow furrowed, and Julie noticed. "Are you confused, Cowboy?"

"Yes," he admitted.

"About what?"

"A lot of things. Mainly about why you still love me, now."

"How can I not? I've always loved you. Since we were seventeen. You've always been my man and you always will be. No matter what."

He looked out the window as they drove away from their home town, towards their new life.

"There's one other thing I still can't understand, and I think I'll always wonder. Why did Sergeant Lopez die? Why did he have to?"

Julie thought a moment, then said, "He died so that you and I and our future kids could live." It was a simple explanation, too simple some might say, but in reality, it was enough.

Clay had never seen anything other than love and caring in Julie's eyes for him. And he had almost thrown that all away.

He squeezed her hand for a moment before letting her put it back on the steering wheel, then sat back with a sigh of contentment.

Maybe he didn't have a left leg, but with Julie beside him, he had it all.

Chapter Twenty-Nine

18 MONTHS LATER

Clay recognized the former Marine the moment the door of the coffee shop opened. Even discounting the heavy limp and the cane, the expression on PFC Kent's face was one Clay had once seen in his mirror – pain-filled, both physically and emotionally, with a serious *I don't want to be here* vibe. Not even the fact that this amputee was female, a former Marine, and African-American, could dispel the similarity.

Staff Sergeant Jacoby's words echoed in his brain. "Once, I was you."

He bounced to his feet and strode across the room, offering a hand.

"You must be Jocelyn," he said.

The young woman shrugged indifferently. "If I must," she muttered.

"I'm so glad to meet you," Clay said. "Can I get you an over-priced coffee?"

Jocelyn shrugged. "Whatever."

Clay completely understood the pain she was trying to hide with feigned aloofness. Rather than being offended, he smiled and indicated a seat for her at the nearest table. "I bet you'd like a pumpkin spice latte."

For the briefest of moments, he thought he saw a spark of interest in Jocelyn Kent's eye, quickly extinguished. Had he been that obvious during his first meeting with Nathan Jacoby?

When he returned to the small table with their coffees, the young lady was looking down at her leg with an expression that exuded sadness, but she quickly looked away when he set the cup in front of her and sat down.

"So how are you doing?" he asked. "I spoke to your mother on the phone, and she told me you were having some difficulty adjusting to civilian life as an amputee. I thought maybe we could talk about some of the issues you're experiencing."

It was like déjà vu all over again, except that this time Clay was on the other side of the pumpkin spice latte.

"I know that this is a difficult and stressful adjustment for you," he said, as he watched Jocelyn take a sip of her coffee.

"You think?" She actually said it out loud. When Clay had been in her position, he'd only thought it.

"What I would like to do is to offer you a support mechanism to help smooth out that adjustment."

"You're wasting your time," she retorted. "There's no point."

"I disagree. There's definitely a point. I felt the same way once, when I was in your position."

"You're not in my position. You have no idea what I'm going through."

"I have an exact idea of what you're going through," he assured her. "Look."

He reached down and lifted the leg of his slacks a little, just to reveal a brief glance of his titanium ankle. He didn't want her to think he was just a do-gooder with no common experience. Jocelyn's eyes widened in shock for a moment before she glanced fearfully around the coffee shop, obviously hoping to keep her own prosthesis a secret.

"You?' she spouted incredulously. "You lost a leg? You've got to be kidding me. I saw you walk up to me when I got here. No one-legged person can walk like that."

"I have two legs," Clay replied. "One is just a little newer than the other. So you see, we have a lot in common."

"Are you hitting on me?" she asked him suddenly.

He chuckled. "Absolutely not. See, I'm married." He held up his left hand, showing his wedding ring. "Let me show you a photo of my wife." He picked up his phone and showed her a photo he'd taken of Julie just yesterday, standing in their back yard, smiling and smoothing a hand down the front of her shirt.

"She's pregnant," Jocelyn Kent observed.

"Yep." There was no way he could keep the pride out of his voice. Sure, it was true that millions of men all over the world were fathers but somehow he felt as proud as the first dad-to-be ever. "We just had an ultrasound a few days ago, and they say it's going to be a boy. We're going to name him Nathan."

"That's nice," Jocelyn admitted, but she still looked unhappy. Clay couldn't blame her.

"And here's a photo of our dog." He swiped to the next photo and turned the phone towards her again.

A look of disbelief filled former PFC Kent's face and Clay imagined she was a bit overwhelmed at his insistence on sharing his personal photos. Sarcasm filled her voice.

"So, are you going to show me pictures of your parents and friends and high school classmates next?"

Clay chuckled. "I could if you really wanted to see them, but for now I'd like you to look at the dog."

With a put-upon sigh, she took the phone from his hand and looked more closely at the canine, her expression radiating annoyance.

Good, Clay thought. *Get annoyed. Get pissed even. As long as you feel something other than your own private pain. Right, Nathan?*

A moment later, Jocelyn's expression changed from annoyance to surprise.

"That dog only has three legs."

"His name is Rover," Clay told her. "Julie, my wife, wanted to name him Tripod, but I think Rover is more appropriate. He is a real rover, despite only having three legs when all the other dogs in the neighborhood have four. I wasn't really planning on getting a dog. Between work and fixing up our house and a baby coming, I'd never really considered it. But Julie saw him on Facebook and showed me – this sweet dog that sat in the shelter day after day waiting to be adopted, and everyone just passed him by because he'd had to have his left front leg amputated after being hit by a car. Julie insisted we had to go down there and at least look at him, and I agreed but told her I wasn't planning on actually taking him home.

"But realistically, I was pretty sure he was coming home with us. Julie handed me my car keys while I was still looking at his photo. It was fifty degrees out that day, but I walked into that animal shelter wearing cargo shorts, so that everybody, including that dog, could see I had a prosthetic leg. As you can imagine, it always gets some stares, but I'm used to that. I'm not ashamed to let it be seen, not anymore."

He could see Jocelyn's expression cloud over, and knew she was thinking, *I am never going to let my prosthesis be seen in public.*

"So I found this guy's cage and he was sitting at the back, looking sad. But as soon as he saw me, he perked right up and smiled."

"Dogs can't smile," Jocelyn argued, but Clay just emitted a small snort of disagreement.

"I beg to differ. This guy definitely smiled, and gave a happy bark. I swear, I could tell what he was saying. *I've been waiting for you, Dad!* I knew at that moment that we were meant to be that dog's humans. He left that shelter with us that very day."

The young lady handed him back his phone as he continued. "I can always count on that dog to make me smile. He's like Prozac with paws and a tail."

Jocelyn frowned. "I'm a cat person."

"I'm sure if you call the shelter, they'll keep an eye out for a disabled cat for you to adopt."

She snorted a bit, showing him a *that's ridiculous* expression before looking away. At least she didn't walk out of the place the way Clay had done the first time he'd met up with Nathan Jacoby.

"What about you?' he asked. "Do you have a significant other in your life?"

Jocelyn's face lost its tough *I don't care* façade for a moment, and Clay thought he detected a tiny hint of a tear in her eye. She turned her head away and discreetly wiped her eyes, then turned back to Clay, her tough expression back in place.

"I was engaged," she admitted. "He broke it off after this." She swept a subtle hand towards her slacks, where Clay knew she possessed a technological wonder of titanium and polypropylene. "He said he couldn't marry someone who couldn't keep up with their children. Like, what if we had a kid and they woke up crying in the night? I wouldn't be able to get to it to take care of it until I got this – *thing* – on."

"Sounds like he was looking more for a baby-mama than a wife," Clay observed. "Maybe you're better off without him."

Jocelyn just shrugged indifferently, but Clay was impressed with this young lady. She'd revealed a lot more, and stayed a lot longer, than he had the first time he'd met with Nathan Jacoby. He was going to have to call his friend later and brag about his initial success.

"I keep my crutches handy for when I don't feel like attaching my leg. I hope to be as hands-on a caregiver as my wife when the baby comes."

The girl still looked doubtful.

"Look, Jocelyn," he said. "I know you probably feel that sitting here having coffee with a stranger isn't going to help you any. It's not going to magically make your leg grow back. I'm sure you feel like you just might scream if you have to listen to one more person tell you that your life isn't over, that there were still possibilities for you. But I have gone through what you're experiencing, and I felt the same for a while."

The young woman still looked disbelieving. She had dark skin, dark eyes, and a dark outlook on life that had nothing to do with her DNA. He could see in her face that her soul felt as dark as Clay's had once been.

"Why are you doing this?" she asked.

Clay smiled. "Because, Jocelyn, once, I was you."

THE END

Dear Readers,

While the characters and events of this story are fictional, the Chicago suburb of Wheeling in which it is set is very real, and is the town in which my husband and I grew up, though it has been many years since we've lived there.

Also very real are the two veteran's service organizations mentioned here which help my fictional hero Clay adjust to his life after his Army experiences. If you would like more information on these worthy organizations, please visit:

The Wounded Warrior Project –
www.woundedwarriorproject.org
Quilts of Valor Foundation – www.qovf.org

As always, I honor and thank those whose services and sacrifices continue to defend my freedom.

Writing is more or less a solitary endeavor, with the writer spending multitudinous hours alone with her computer, and, hopefully, her muse. However, despite that solitude, one's project can never come to fruition without the generous assistance of knowledgeable compatriots, and I would like to thank those who have helped me bring Kaboom to life.

Jennifer Sharp – For another awesome cover design

Jessica Cox – For being a sounding board to my hints about this story, and for showing me The Dog

Thomas Hansen, U.S. Army, retired – For generously giving his time and expertise to answer my questions regarding the United States Army. Thank you for your service.

Richard Carlson – For research assistance in police procedures

Anita Weiland – For research assistance regarding Catholicism and the Mass

Roxie Noir – For research assistance regarding Jewish traditions

My beautiful grandchildren - For their brave attempts to explain the intricacies of Minecraft to me. My apologies if I still don't get it.

And above all, my wonderful husband Rick – For not only his continued support and enthusiasm, but also for building me an awesome she-shed, and bringing me tea and cookies when I needed them the most.